TALK TO ME TENDERLY
Tell Me Lies

John Gordon Davis

TALK TO ME TENDERLY
Tell Me Lies

HarperCollins*Publishers*

HarperCollins*Publishers*
77–85 Fulham Palace Road
Hammersmith, London W6 8JB

Published by HarperCollins*Publishers* 1992

1 3 5 7 9 8 6 4 2

Copyright © John Gordon Davis 1992

The Author asserts the moral right to
be identified as the author of this work

A catalogue record for this book
is available from the British Library

ISBN 0 00 223664 8

Set in Linotron Fournier by
Rowland Phototypesetting Ltd
Bury St Edmunds, Suffolk

Printed in Great Britain by
HarperCollinsManufacturing Glasgow

To Harry and June Pearson

'Talk to me tenderly, tell me lies.
I am a woman, and time flies.'

Vivian Yeiser Laramore

I

I

In this land the distances are vast. If you stop your vehicle and listen there is only ringing silence. It is always hot in this part of Queensland, and the rainfall is very spare. Then, almost without warning, the rain can come crashing down for weeks, and the rivers that have been dry for years break their banks, causing devastating floods over hundreds of thousands of square kilometres, and whole villages and towns have to be evacuated. Because of the great distances there are few telephones, so people keep in touch by two-way radio. Outback children have to receive their education from broadcasts and medical attention can only be had through the Flying Doctor Service. The private aeroplane is not a luxury here but a working vehicle. The McKenzies had an aeroplane, but it had not flown for a year because, after several years of very poor rainfall, they could not afford the maintenance to keep it airworthy.

This Monday afternoon, close to sunset, Helen McKenzie was doing her laundry. Her washing-machine had broken down, so she had put a cauldron of water on to the wood-burning stove. She had taken off her jeans and shirt to wash them, and she scrubbed the kitchen floor in her underwear while she waited for the water to heat. She had dispatched Oscar, her dog, outside while she did the job, and had propped the back screen-door ajar with the mop because the damn latch was faulty and often jammed from the inside. The other door, leading into the rest of the house, Helen had bolted closed on the far side, because it too had a faulty latch which allowed Oscar to enter simply by pushing his paw against it.

She had almost finished scrubbing the floor when she heard furious barking outside. Then a big snake, nine feet long, came slithering flat-out into her kitchen, with Oscar in joyful pursuit. She screamed, the back door banged closed as Oscar bounded into the room, and with a terrifying writhing the snake flashed across the floor and disappeared into one of the kitchen cupboards. Helen screamed again as she dashed to the back door, but she slipped on the wet linoleum and sprawled. She scrambled up wild-eyed and flung herself at the door, but the catch was stuck. She shook it desperately; then, in the purest horror, she ran to the kitchen table and hurled herself up on to it.

The long cupboard into which the snake had fled lined the entire wall, from one door to the other. Helen McKenzie crouched in the middle of the table midst the cacophony of Oscar's barking, her heart pounding, eyes wide, desperately searching for the terrible snake amongst the things at the bottom of the dim cupboards. Oscar was charging up and down after the snake as it writhed from one end to the other. Helen shrieked at him to come away but he would have none of that. She could not see the snake, but she knew it was a King Brown, one of the deadliest. Helen crouched on the table shouting at Oscar, her terrified mind fumbling; then she frantically crawled to the end and leapt off to try the back door once more, but Oscar came roaring along the cupboards, slammed into her legs and she sprawled again. She crashed headlong on the linoleum and all she knew was the panicked horror of Oscar furiously scrambling over her. She screamed *'Come away!'* and scrambled up frantically and ran to the back door. She hurled herself against it, wrenching the handle, but still it refused to open. Helen turned and flung herself back up on to the table again, just in time to see Oscar jump out of the dark cupboard with a yelp, the terrible serpent's fangs flashing at his muzzle – then the beast recoiled into the darkness and Oscar lurched backwards into the kitchen, shaking his head.

'Oscar!'

He staggered backwards across the kitchen, yelping, brushing his snout with his paw, then twisting as if trying to find his tail. *'Oscar!'* Helen screamed. The dog crashed over on to his side. *'Oscar!'* Helen heard something fall in the cupboard, she jerked around and saw a long dark slither in the dimness. *'Oscar!'* She scrambled on her hands and knees to the edge of the table, gasping, eyes wide, and down on the floor Oscar tried to clamber back to his feet. He got halfway, then collapsed on to his side. *'Oscar!'* He rolled his eyes at her, and tried to get up, and he crashed again. He lay there, trembling, taking stentorian breaths. Then he spasmed once, his legs went out rigid, jerking, then he suddenly went limp, groaned, and was still.

Helen lay on the table, aghast: then her incredulous face began to crumple.

'Oh Oscar, Oscar, Oscar . . .'

A slithering sound came from the cupboard and she jerked around and stared, heart pounding – but she could not see the dreadful snake. Then she dropped her face in her hands and sobbed.

That is how she was, lying weeping on the table in the dusk, when she heard the motor cycle. She raised her tear-stained face and listened incredulously. Then:

'*Help!*' she wailed.

2

The motor cycle spluttered up the track from the distant farm-gate, its headlight on. It came to a halt opposite the steps leading up to the verandah of the big homestead. The rider climbed off the machine. He was dressed entirely in black leather motor-cyclist's gear. He raised the visor of his black crash-helmet, and looked at the unlit house.

As the house was in darkness he would have gone away, but for the fact that the front door was open. He listened. Silence. Then, uncertainly, he mounted the steps and walked across the verandah to the front door, his steel-tipped boots sounding loud on the wood. He rapped on the frame of the outer screen-door and listened.

Nothing. He knocked again, louder. Still silence. He was about to turn away in discomfort at being on another person's property in the gathering dark, when he heard what sounded like a woman's cry. He listened intently, and the cry came again. He opened the screen-door, leaned into the dark doorway and called tentatively:

'Hullo?'

He heard a muffled, anguished cry: *'The kitchen door . . .'*

The man frowned, then descended the verandah steps. He turned towards the back where he presumed the kitchen would be. 'Hullo . . .?' he called.

He heard another cry as he approached the kitchen door. *'Hullo?'* Then he heard a woman's voice:

'Press the green button inside the door!'

The man walked up to the screen-door uncertainly. It opened satisfactorily. He peered into the darkness.

'There's a green switch just inside!'

He stepped into the dark kitchen and groped for the switch. The door clanged shut behind him as his hand found it. He pressed the switch and somewhere a diesel generator started up, and the kitchen lights came on. He stared.

He saw a dead dog on the floor and a wild woman crouched on the kitchen table in her underwear. She cried: *'There's a snake!'*

The same instant he saw a long writhing streak across the floor. He whirled back to the door, but the handle was jammed. The snake seemed to bounce off the cupboard doors on the opposite wall, then it flashed around and streaked towards him. Helen screamed again and the man gargled in fright and scrambled across the kitchen out of its way. The huge snake hit the closed screen-door, then whirled around and disappeared back into the cupboard with a crashing of fruit jars. The man leapt up on to the table beside Helen.

Helen McKenzie stared at the stranger crouched beside her on the table. He still had on his black crash-helmet, the visor up. He wore gauntlets reaching to his elbows and high black leather boots. His studded leather lumber-jacket was zipped up to a thin, unshaven face, dominated by a beak nose and dark eyes under heavy black eyebrows.

'Who're you?' Helen whispered.

The man saw a worn, frightened, pretty woman, her blonde hair awry, ringlets sticking to her sweaty neck.

'Ben Sunninghill,' he croaked.

Helen's mind was fumbling. 'How're we going to get rid of this snake?'

Mr Sunninghill's brown eyes were wide. He turned and looked fearfully at the dark cupboards, then shook his head. 'I'm from New York,' he said, as if that explained everything. He added: 'I've just come to borrow a spanner.'

'New York?' Helen stared at him a long moment, then she dropped her head and sobbed. 'Oh, thank God, anyway ... Just thank God you're here ...'

They crouched in the centre of the big table. Helen was still weepy about Oscar, but Ben Sunninghill was more composed now. He said hoarsely: 'Where is he now?'

Helen pointed at the open doors of the main cupboards.

'Which end?'

She shook her head. 'They're all inter-connected at floor level. He could be in any of them.'

Ben pointed at the open cupboard on the opposite wall. 'How do you know he's not in there?'

'I don't. But when you came in I think I saw him go there.' She pointed again.

Ben looked very worried. Then he said hopefully:

'Snakes are as frightened of us as we are of them, aren't they?'

'Oh God ... King Browns are very aggressive, particularly when they're frightened.' She looked down at Oscar and her chin began to twitch.

'If we jump off the table together and run for that back door—'

'The bloody catch sticks, there's a real trick to opening it.'

Ben pointed at the other door. 'That one?'

'It's bolted from the other side.'

Ben Sunninghill looked unhappily around the kitchen for weapons. There was a meat-cleaver next to the sink and a broom on the floor. He gingerly reached down, picked it up, and looked at it with misgiving.

'Have you got a gun in the house?'

'Yes, but it's in my bedroom. And it's not a shotgun, it's only a .303. Not much good for a snake.'

Ben took a deep, unhappy breath. 'I've got these boots and gauntlets, and the broom. If I make a dash for the back door and smash it open—'

It was then that he noticed the cauldron of water boiling on the stove. He looked at it, then turned to the cupboard. He considered, then gingerly leant out with the broom and opened it wider. He peered.

Nothing happened. He could see no snake in those shadows. He poked the broom into the clutter at the bottom. Instantly, there was a furious slithering noise and the terrible snake burst out midst a clatter of jars. Helen screeched as the creature flashed across the floor and disappeared into the smaller open cupboard opposite.

Ben stared into the beast's new lair. 'Can you see him?'

Helen peered. 'Oh God, I think so ...'

Ben took a deep breath.

'Right – listen. What I'm going to do is jump across on to the sink, and get that pot of boiling water. I'll bring it back here, and then I'll throw it on to that snake.'

'Oh God ...' Helen whispered.

Ben crouched carefully along the table, to the end. He gauged the distance to the sink. About five feet – easy enough, but could he make it back with a heavy cauldron of boiling water? He began to get to his feet. He straightened up shakily, his arms out to control his balance. Then he launched himself across the gap.

He landed with a crash in the sink. He crouched there for a moment, trembling. He looked back at Helen.

'Before I come back, you must crawl to the far end of the table, to counter-balance me.'

Helen began to edge down the table. Ben looked at the heavy iron cauldron. It had a handle on each side, and it held about two and a half gallons. He got slowly to his feet. Crouching, he reached down to the handles. Even through his leather gauntlets, they were hot.

'Use the oven-mitts!' Helen gasped.

The oven-mitts hung on a peg beside the stove. Ben pulled them on over his gauntlets; then bent forward and began to lift the cauldron. It was astonishingly heavy – and frightening, the boiling water seething in his straining grip. He crouched on the edge of the sink, straining under the treacherous weight. He turned carefully towards the end of the table, looked at Helen and croaked: 'Ready?'

She nodded desperately. Ben leant forward, stretched out a skinny leg, and he went for it, half jumping, half lunging across the gap. He landed on the end of the table, and he howled.

He howled because a pint of boiling water slopped out of the cauldron into his boots. He reeled with shock, Helen shrieked, and for a terrible moment he teetered on the edge of the table, about to crash off and scald himself with boiling water. Then he recovered his balance. He crouched, enduring the agony, eyes closed, still clutching his treacherous burden.

'Are you all right?' Helen gasped.

Ben opened his watering eyes and nodded. He took a deep breath.

'You've got to keep clear of me. You've got to crawl down to this end as I come up to your end. Ready?'

'Yes,' Helen whispered desperately.

He began to make his way unsteadily down the table. They passed each other in the middle. Ben staggered to the end.

He peered into the dark cupboard. And, yes, he could just make out the dreadful beast coiled in there. For a teetering moment he crouched, trying to take aim with his thirty pounds of boiling water, his arm muscles trembling with strain; then he grunted and he hurled the water.

It cascaded into the cupboard with a steaming crash, and all hell broke loose. The snake came bursting out in a great writhing knot, coiling and contorting, a twisting killer three yards long convulsing around the kitchen floor, flashing jaws agape. Helen shrieked and snatched up the broom and swiped down at it with all her might. It skidded across the floor, and she shrieked again and swiped again, and then there was a metallic crash as Ben Sunninghill hurled the empty cauldron. It landed on the beast's head and he leapt off the table, snatched up the meat-cleaver from the sink and ran at the writhing mass. With one furious swipe he chopped the snake in half. No   two sections of it were writhing bloodily all over the floor. Ben raised the cleaver again, aimed wildly for the head, and swiped. He chopped the head clean off, but still the sections writhed all over the floor. Ben Sunninghill frantically chopped and chopped, scuttling around scattering pieces of bloody snake everywhere.

Finally he stopped and stood up, chest heaving. Helen was leaning against the cupboard, her hair a mess, her breasts heaving. She looked at Ben, then she stared at Oscar lying dead. Then her bright eyes filled with tears, her lower lip curled, and she cried: 'Oh Oscar . . .'

She stumbled across the kitchen and fell to her knees beside the dog, gathered him into her arms and hugged him and rocked him.

'Oh Oscar, Oscar . . .' she cried.

3

They sat at the kitchen table, sipping brandy. The mess of snake had been cleared up, the floor mopped, and Helen had put on fresh jeans and shirt. Oscar lay on the verandah, covered in a blanket, awaiting burial in the morning. She was over the immediate grief of it now: the brandy was doing its work and she just felt numb.

'Sorry, what's your surname again?' she said.

'Sunninghill,' Ben said. He had taken off his crash-helmet and gauntlets.

'And how come . . . ? I mean, what brought you here, like a guardian angel?'

Ben smiled. 'I came to borrow a spanner,' he said. 'For my motor-bike. I was having trouble and when I passed your gate, I thought maybe you had the spanner I needed. I did have one, but I lost it somewhere.'

'Spanner,' Helen said. 'Yes, of course, all kinds of spanners in the barn.'

'Thank you.'

'Thank *you*,' she said. 'But can it wait till tomorrow? I mean, it's dark now.'

'Of course.'

'I mean, I've got a bed for you. Plenty of beds here.'

'Well, that's very kind of you,' Ben said uncertainly. 'As long as it's no trouble?'

'No, no, plenty of beds . . .' She rubbed her forehead, then went on: '"Sunninghill"? Never heard that name before.'

Ben smiled. He was a funny-looking fellow with a ferrety sort of face, but when he smiled his cheeks puckered and all his teeth showed in a way that was both mysterious and charming. Mischievous. He was small, only about five foot eight inches in his high-heeled bikers' boots. 'Actually,' he said, 'my real name is Sonnenberg, but my father changed it by deed-poll to Sunninghill. The English translation of Sonnenberg.'

'Oh,' Helen said.

'He wanted to create the impression we weren't Jewish.'

'Oh.'

That smile. 'Trouble is, he looks even more Jewish than I do.'

'Oh.' She was going to say 'Really?' but changed it in her mouth. She added hastily: 'Sunninghill's a nice name. A cheerful name. You look a cheerful type of person.'

'Sure, I'm a laugh a minute. Remember, that was only my first snake, I'll probably improve. Does this happen very often?'

She smiled wanly. 'First time I've seen one in the house. Oscar chased it in.' She dabbed the corner of her eye. 'Seen enough in the bush, though, over the years.'

'How many years have you lived here?'

'Since I got married. Twenty years. Or nineteen.'

'And where's your husband now?'

She waved a hand to the south. 'South Australia. Broken Hill, working on the mines.'

'Oh.' He was about to say 'Why?', then stopped himself. Helen volunteered the reason, as if reading his thoughts:

'The kids' boarding-school fees. With the drought we couldn't make ends meet. So he had to go back to his old job.'

'Oh. How long ago?'

'Two years.' She added: 'He comes home at Christmas, when the kids get their summer holidays.'

'I see. So you run the ranch all by yourself?'

For a moment she wondered what he saw. 'No. We had to get rid of our foreman last year when we sold most of the cattle, but we've still got one Abbo stockman and his wife. They live about five miles away. So you really were a guardian angel, showing up like that, otherwise I'd have stayed on this table all night.' She smiled wanly. 'So, what brings you to Australia on a motorbike?'

'Just seeing the world. I saw on your gate the farm's called Whoop-Whoop. Does that mean anything special?'

'The real name is Edenvale Station, because we've got a few wells that are usually quite good, but because it's so remote we've nick-named it Whoop-Whoop. That's a mythical Australian place. It means to Hell and gone. In the middle of nowhere.'

'Beyond the black stump?'

'Right.' She poured more brandy into his glass. She didn't feel so shaky any more. Just grief for Oscar. *Oh Oscar* . . . 'So, Mr Sunninghill, from New York. What do you do in New York?'

'Used to do. Jeweller.'

'Oh?'

'Well, a gemologist. Buying and selling stones, setting them, creating jewellery pieces.'

'"Used to"? Have you quit?'

'Sure have.'

'Why? Don't you like it?'

He said: 'I like jewels. They're beautiful. And I like making pieces of jewellery, that's artistic. But buying and selling? The hassle? The cut-throat competition? And spending the rest of my life in that little shop? In New *York*?' He shook his head. 'There's more to life than that. There's a whole beautiful world out there.'

She looked at him enviously. 'So you've sold up entirely?'

'Not mine to sell. Family business. But my father's cut me out entirely for leaving him in the lurch.' He smiled then clasped his breast: 'How can you do this to your Papa, my boy, my life? And you a gemologist – three years your Mama and I starved to send you to Technical School and now all you want is a Harley-Davidson to kill yourself with already, this is *gratitude*?' He smiled. 'He forgets I've worked for him since I was sixteen.'

Helen held out her hand, to show him her engagement ring, then slipped it off her finger. The diamond in the centre was missing. 'It fell out somewhere,' she said. 'How much would it cost to replace?'

Ben examined it. The bed for the gem was substantial.

'About a thousand dollars,' he said regretfully. 'Counting cutting, and so forth.'

Helen sighed. 'Forget it . . .' She looked at the empty ring sadly, then put it back on her finger. She went on: 'So – how long have you been in Australia, Ben?'

'A couple of months. Landed in Perth. Covered the west coast, then crossed the Nullarbor Plain. Adelaide, Melbourne, Sydney, et cetera. Then up here into Queensland.'

'Landed in Perth? Where from?'

'Africa. Came across on a freighter, with my bike.'

'Africa?' Helen sounded envious. 'Where were you in Africa?'

'I sailed from South Africa, but I was all over the place. Crossed from Gibraltar into Morocco, then made my way down along the western bulge to Nigeria, Ghana, et cetera. To the Congo. Got on a steamer up the Congo River into Zaire and crossed over to Uganda and Kenya. Then down through Tanzania and Zambia and Zimbabwe, et cetera, into South Africa.'

Helen smiled. '"Et cetera", huh? And, before Africa?'

'Well,' Ben said, 'I went round South America, then crossed to the Far East. Japan, Hong Kong, then got a freighter to Thailand. Did a side trip by air to the Philippines and Indonesia, then rode the bike over to India.' He smiled. 'Decided against trying to ride across the Middle East – not the healthiest place for a Jew. So from Bombay I got a freighter through Suez to Greece.' He shrugged. 'Went around Europe for a while, then crossed over into north Africa.'

Helen was fascinated. '*Wow*. How wonderful! And where're you going from here?'

'Brisbane. Then up through northern Queensland to Darwin, see that Northern Territory.'

'And from there?'

'Back down to Perth. And then back to South Africa. I want to make a base there, then go off and do my thing.'

Helen echoed: '*South* Africa again? Why there?'

'Great country.' Ben shrugged.

'But what about the politics?'

Ben shrugged again. 'Great things are happening.'

Helen snorted. 'Is there going to be democracy?'

'That's what the negotiations are all about.'

'What's there to negotiate?' Helen demanded. 'Why not good old-fashioned democracy? Is there going to be One Man One Vote or not?'

'I believe so, but they'll work it out to suit the local conditions.'

'You mean the *white* man's conditions?'

Ben shook his head. But he didn't want to argue about it – people who hadn't been to Africa just didn't understand. 'However, the reason I'm going back there is not for the politics, interesting though that is, but because of the animals.'

Helen was disarmed. 'The wildlife?'

Ben sat back. 'Oh, the wildlife out there is wonderful. And it's being butchered out of existence. Not in South Africa, but in the rest of the continent.' He shook his head. 'There're only three black rhino left in the whole of Kenya, d'you know that? In ten years the only wild animals left north of the Zambesi will be in isolated pockets, unless a great deal more is done. And that's what I'm going to do. I'm going to join the guys who're trying to do something about it.'

'Like who?'

Ben said: 'I'm a life-member of Greenpeace and the World Wide Fund for Nature. But there're various outfits you can join who believe in fighting fire with fire, and they're the guys I want to team up with. As a foot-soldier.'

Helen frowned at him. 'Foot-soldier? And what does a foot-soldier do? Shoot people?'

Ben smiled. 'There're more ways of killing a cat than stuffing its throat with butter. Like destroying their infrastructure. Destroying their camps, their weapons, their snares, their vehicles. Their routes. Their products. Raiding the warehouses of their middlemen down on the coast in Mombasa and Dar es Salaam and Zanzibar and Maputo – generally knocking the living shit out of them.' (Helen blinked – she didn't like that familiarity.) Ben shrugged. 'But if it comes to shooting the poachers themselves, why not? Those bastards shoot game rangers all the time in Africa.'

Helen sat back. And folded her arms. She didn't know what to make of Mr Ben Sunninghill, jeweller, from New York. On his motorbike. *Foot*-soldier? 'Have you ever had any military training?'

'Sure, I was in the National Guard. That's the States' militia. Volunteer basis.'

She thought, Volunteer, huh? 'Did you enjoy that?'

'Sure. Most of the time. And nice to get away from the shop.'

'And they trained you in . . . weapons and all that?'

'Yeah. I was in the infantry.' He smiled. 'Never killed anybody though. I was too young for Vietnam.'

She said. 'What're you – about thirty-five?'

He took her aback by saying: 'Right, and you? Forty-ish?'

'You might have been gallant and said thirty-nine-ish!'

Ben gave that smile. 'But forty is a beautiful age for a woman.'

Helen managed to return his smile, though she somehow didn't like the comment. 'Well, I'm forty-two, actually. That is hardly a beautiful age for *this* woman.'

'But you *are* beautiful.'

Helen certainly didn't like that forwardness. Oh no, she thought – not one of those, and him a guest in my house for the night! She sat up and said brightly:

'Well, we better have something to eat, it's getting late.'

Ben said earnestly: 'Don't worry about me, I had supper just before finding your gate.'

That was fine with Helen. 'Some coffee, then?'

'No, it'll keep me awake.'

Well, that gave her an opening. 'Yes, you must be tired. I'll show you to your room. I'll put you in the foreman's cottage, it's empty. It's just half a mile over there.' She pointed.

Ben said: 'I don't mind sleeping outside in my sleeping-bag, in fact I like it. Pity to use your sheets.'

'I wouldn't dream of it. You deserve a nice soft bed after all the way you've come.' She stood up.

Oh dear, Ben thought. He looked up at her. He said:

'I hope I haven't offended you – I mean by saying you're beautiful. Please don't think I'm . . . that I had an ulterior motive.'

Helen was further taken aback. 'Of course not,' she said self-consciously. 'Well, I'll go in the Land Rover, you follow on your bike.'

Ben stood up. 'No need to show me the way, just point me in the direction and I'll find it. There can't be many cottages round here.'

'Of course I will. I'll just get some sheets.'

'I'll use the nice soft bed but I'll sleep in my sleeping-bag. I insist on not using up your sheets – you said your washing-machine's broken.'

Helen hesitated. 'But . . . it seems so inhospitable.' Then she added: 'And please don't think I'm inhospitable in putting you in the cottage. But it wouldn't be . . . *proper* for you to sleep in the house with my husband away.'

'I understand perfectly,' Ben said earnestly. He added with a grin: 'What would all the neighbours say?'

4

It was a beautiful morning. The sky was magnificently blue, the early sun cast long shadows through the trees, and the world was old and young at the same time. And on this glorious morning Helen McKenzie had to bury Oscar.

At nine o'clock she drove to the cottage to fetch Ben Sunninghill for breakfast. She found him outside, wearing shorts and singlet, his motorbike engine in pieces. He stood up when he saw her vehicle approaching. His skinny chest was covered in curly black hair, and he was only about five foot five in his bare feet.

'G'day. Breakfast time,' Helen said through the window. 'Then I'll show you our collection of spanners.'

He smiled. 'I've already found the spanners – went for an early walk and found the barn unlocked, hope that's okay.'

Again she was a little surprised by his forwardness. 'Sure.' She nodded at his motor cycle. 'How're you doing?'

'Fine. Say, that's a nice little airplane you got in that barn.'

'Would be, if it worked.'

'What's wrong with it?'

'Starter set-up, Clyde says. Clyde's my husband. We've got to get spare parts.'

'Has the engine been stationary for very long?'

'No, I turn it over once a fortnight to keep it loose.'

'Ah. Can you fly?'

'Sure, when I have to.'

'I've got a licence.' He said it proudly. 'Went down to Florida one winter and took a crash course. Don't you enjoy it?'

'Don't like heights, and all that radio stuff about winds and weather. But you really need a plane out here. Do you – like flying?'

'After sex and sailing, it's what I like best.'

She didn't like that – 'after sex'. Far too familiar. 'So, you're a sailor too?'

'An intrepid one. Want me to look at the airplane's starter motor?'

It sounded a pushy offer, as if he were looking for an excuse to stay longer. 'Reckon you could fix it, huh? Like you intrepidly kill snakes?'

'I'm scared of snakes. But I can fix most anything. Does that old VW van in the barn work?'

'Doubt it, we haven't started it in a year and it's as old as the hills. My father gave it to me when the kids were little so they could sleep in it when we went on holidays. Why, want to buy it? Swap it for your bike, maybe?'

Ben smiled. 'No thanks. But I'll have a look at it for you, if you like.'

That disarming smile of his. No, she decided, he hadn't meant to be pushy. 'Thanks anyway, but better let sleeping dogs lie. What's wrong with your bike?'

'Just a split head-gasket. That's the thing—'

'Sure, I know what a head-gasket is, helped Clyde put in new ones often enough in twenty-some years. Cuss, cuss, cuss.'

'Nineteen,' he smiled. 'See, I remembered.'

Again, somehow she didn't like that. Almost suggestive. 'Okay,' she said: 'I've put everything on the table, just help yourself. Bacon and steak's in the fridge.'

He walked towards his shirt. He was even smaller than she'd thought. His legs were wiry and his back was hairy too. 'Aren't you having breakfast?' he asked.

'No, I had mine hours ago, I've got to go'n fetch Billy to dig Oscar's grave. Billy's our stockman. If he hasn't gone walkabout.'

'Walkabout, huh? Look, I'll dig Oscar's grave.' He pulled on his shirt.

'Thanks, but I want that grave good and deep so the dingoes don't dig him up, and believe me that ground's stony – Billy's got nothing much to do anyway.'

'Do you want me to come with you to fetch Billy?'

She sighed inwardly. 'If you like.'

Her tone made him look at her more closely. Her face was strained, as if she had done some crying in the night. He knew she didn't feel up to being sociable. 'Look,' he said, 'I have my own breakfast right here; you go'n see to Billy.'

'Come *on*,' she said, 'it's all waiting.'

*   *   *

24

He fried some eggs and bacon in her kitchen. He wasn't hungry, but he was sure she would worry about being inhospitable if she saw he hadn't eaten anything when she came back. She was a sensitive one, all right. He washed his plates, then went out on to the verandah.

Oscar lay under the blanket, and on the blanket was a flower.

'Oh, dear . . .'

He pulled the blanket back a little. There lay Oscar's old-young Boxer head, his worried frown stiff, his tongue clenched between his sharp young teeth.

He returned to the kitchen. He went to the washing-machine, crouched and examined it; then he pulled it away from the wall.

Some time later he heard the Land Rover return; its door slammed and Helen strode into the kitchen. She found Ben sitting on the floor, the washing-machine's innards surrounding him.

'Hi,' he said.

She was surprised. 'What are you doing?'

'Here's part of your problem.' He held up the filter. It was clogged with fluff and small gravel chips. 'You also had a loose connection. And,' he plucked up something from the floor and held it up to her, 'your engagement ring's diamond.'

Her face lit up. 'Oh, my God! *Thank* you!'

'Takes a jeweller to find a jewel. Obviously fell out of your ring when you were loading the machine. I'll stick it back in for you properly.'

'Oh, thank you! Wow, a thousand dollars saved!'

He nodded in the direction of the verandah. 'Can I help? With Oscar?'

Her cheerfulness at making a thousand dollars faded. 'No, thanks anyway.'

She took a determined breath, turned and left the kitchen. He thought, Poor lady . . .

He checked through the rest of the washing-machine's parts. They looked okay, so he reassembled it. He hooked it up to the tap and filled it. He went to the wall and pressed the green button, and heard the distant *doem, doem, doem* as the generator started up. When he switched on the washing-machine, it burst into shuddering life. He turned it off and pressed the red button on the wall to stop the generator. The sound died away, and from outside he heard the distant clank of a pickaxe.

He went out the back door, into the sunshine. He walked towards the corner of the verandah. He stopped.

A hundred yards away, beyond the patchy lawn, her back towards him, Helen was swinging a pickaxe. She wrestled it out of the stony ground, then swung it up above her head, and swiped down again. Ben looked around for the Aborigine, but there was nobody else in sight. He hurried across the lawn. 'Hey . . .'

She did not hear him coming. She swung the pick up again, and swiped it down with a grunt. Her face was flushed, hair had broken loose from its bun and tendrils stuck to her neck. She was wearing a hat with corks dangling from the brim to keep the flies off her face.

'Hey – where's this Billy?' Ben said.

Helen swung the pick over her head furiously. 'Drunk!' She grimaced and swiped into the ground, with a spurt of sparks. Ben reached down and took hold of the shaft.

'Drunk? Let me do this.'

'Blind, rotten, stinking drunk! And his wife. No, this is not fair on you!'

'Perfectly fair.' He took the pick from her firmly. She stepped aside angrily, panting, and he lined himself up at the hole. 'Does he do this often?'

'Whenever they get the chance to go into Burraville and buy the stuff! Today it's metho.' She sat down in a furious heap.

Ben lifted the pick. 'Metho?'

'Methylated spirits, the stinking blue stuff you put in Primus stoves. Didn't know he had any, the crafty bastard! I confiscated the bottle.'

Ben swung the pick down with a clanging crunch. God, it *was* hard ground. He wrenched it out and swung again. Three swings and he was panting.

'Well, he'll be sober tomorrow.'

'If they don't go walkabout.'

'Do they do that often?'

She snorted. 'Abbos? Don't get me wrong, they're sweet people and they're good stockmen. But walkabout . . . ?' Ben began taking off his shirt. 'The flies will make you put that on again. Come on, let me take over.'

'No.' He slung his shirt on the ground and hefted the pick again.

He was skinny, but his shoulders, arms and gut were muscular. He doesn't weigh more than a hundred and thirty pounds, she thought, less than me. And half my size. He swiped the pick down again and grunted: 'How long do these people disappear for?'

'A month? Three? For ever? They come back and they can't understand why they haven't got a job.'

He wrestled the pick out of the ground, threw it down and snatched up his shirt again. 'Goddam flies. And how many times has Billy gone walkabout?'

'Three or four – I've forgotten. The whole family just disappears. Last time they came back without the kids – they were almost grown up. Let me get you a cork hat.'

'I'm okay.' He waved flies off his face and lifted the pick again. 'What do you do when they go walkabout?'

'Do it myself,' she said grimly, 'unless another Abbo happens along. Fortunately there's not much to do, with most of the stock sold.' She heaved herself up. 'I'm going to fetch you a hat. Then I'll take over for a while . . .'

The grave was dug. Ben was exhausted, though Helen had dug the greater part of it. She was worn out too, flushed and sweating. 'Like a pig. Bloody Abbos!' She threw down the pick.

'Shall I fetch Oscar?' Ben asked.

'No, I'll do it.' She turned abruptly and walked grimly back towards the house.

Ben followed her. He mounted the wooden steps to the verandah behind her. She walked up to Oscar, and stared down at the blanketed mound. Then she suddenly brought her hands to her face and burst into sobs.

Ben looked at her uncomfortably. Then he put his arm around her shoulders. She was half a head taller than him. She sobbed and sobbed into her hands. *'Oh Oscar . . .'*

Ben squeezed her once. Then he got down on to one knee to pick up the body.

'No,' she sniffed. 'Thank you, but I want to do it.' He stood up and she turned, eyes wet. 'Please go inside and let me do this.'

'He'll be heavy.'

Helen closed her eyes in exasperation. 'Please . . .'

Ben went into the house, walked down the passage and turned right into the living-room.

It had a miscellany of worn furniture, none of it matching. A carpet of rosebud persuasion, a lounge suite with zebra stripes, pale pink walls. Ceramic ducks, a gleaming artist's impression of Jesus Christ, prints of Scottish lochs. Assorted ferns and bookshelves, an old record-player, a big television set. An array of family and school photographs in frames. An elaborate two-way radio.

He ran his eye over the photographs. He picked up one frame, then another, and studied them for a minute. Then he turned and looked out of the window.

Helen was staggering across the dried-up lawn towards the grave, Oscar in her arms. The blanket trailed over the ground on either side, threatening to tangle with her feet, and Oscar's rigid legs poked up on both sides of her head. She struggled to the edge of the grave. Then she slumped down on to her knees, and carefully lowered Oscar to the ground.

Ben watched her from the back. First she appeared to pray, the corks dangling around her bowed head. For some minutes she held her face, and he saw her shoulders jerk a little. Then she got to her feet and began to inter Oscar.

She hefted him up and struggled forward, legs astride over the grave. She bent, and lowered him to the hole. But, evidently, she ran into difficulties; she crouched, her blue-jeaned buttocks up, head and Oscar down. The dog's rigid legs made him too wide for the grave. It was impossible to bury him lying on his side.

Helen remained still, wrestling with this problem; then she edged backwards and laid Oscar down on the ground again. She got his fore and hind paws in each hand, heaved him up, staggered over the grave again, and lowered him on to his spine.

From the living-room, it appeared to Ben to be the only solution. He could see Oscar's paws sticking up, but they were below ground level. But Helen did not seem satisfied. She stood there, looking down at Oscar's undignified posture; then she put both knuckles to her eyes between her dangling corks for an exasperated moment. Then she grabbed the legs again and heaved him up out of the grave.

She struggled backwards, put him down, and he collapsed stiffly on to his side. She crouched and got her hands under his chest and heaved him up on to his feet. With a hand on each side of his ribcage, she manoeuvred him back over the grave. She lowered him.

Oscar stood in his grave, his head twelve inches below ground level. Helen cautiously let him go, and put both knuckles to her eyes again. For a minute she stood motionless, evidently praying again. Then she scrambled backwards hurriedly, snatched up the spade and began to shovel the stony earth over him.

Ben turned from the window and went down the passage to the kitchen. He felt as if he had been eavesdropping. He went into the pantry and found the brandy bottle and two glasses.

*   *   *

Five minutes later Helen came in, sweating, her hands earthy. Ben was sitting on the kitchen table. She looked at him, her eyes brimming, then she blurted:

'I had to bury him standing up . . .' Her lower lip trembled. *'But I prefer it like that! He was such a stand-up dog!'*

She burst into tears. Ben's heart went out to her and he slid off the table. He put both arms around her. 'There, there . . .' She dropped her forehead on to his shoulder, and sobbed and sobbed.

Ben held her gently. 'There, there . . .' She leant against him, arms hanging, crying her grief out. 'There, there . . .' he murmured again: and, oh, the wonderful female feeling of her in his arms, her sweaty warmth, the earthy smell of her. And with all his compassionate heart he ached to clutch her tight against him. Her sobs stopped suddenly. With a tearful sigh she moved to turn out of his arms, but he held on to her.

For a moment neither of them breathed. They stood against each other, pressed close. And for a wild moment he thought she was going to put her arms around him. Then she turned firmly and he dropped his arms.

She walked towards the sink. She spun the tap, cupped her hands and splashed water up on to her face vigorously.

Ben stood there, wanting to apologize – but for what? He had done nothing that couldn't have an innocent interpretation. And it almost *was* innocent. He said:

'Can I pour you a drink?'

She reached for a kitchen towel and thrust it to her dripping face. 'No, thanks,' she said into the towel.

He wasn't sure if she was annoyed. 'You deserve it, you've had a harrowing time.'

'Yes.' She tossed the towel on to the sink; she stood looking at it. Then: 'Yes, dammit – I will have a drink.'

He poured some brandy into a glass. He held it out to her. She accepted it without looking at him.

'Thanks.' She took a swallow, and shuddered at the burn. 'Oh boy,' she said, eyes closed.

He pulled out a kitchen chair. 'Sit down.'

She turned and slumped down on to it. He sat down in the other chair, across the table from her. She stared across the room at nothing.

He said tentatively: 'Well, I've fixed the washing-machine – it works fine.'

'Oh. Oh, thanks very much, that's wonderful.' She gave him a bleak, mechanical smile.

'You must remember to clean out the filter basket every now and again.'

She nodded. 'Okay. I usually do. But thank you.'

5

She offered to make him some lunch, but he would not hear of it.

'You've had a rough day, and I've got plenty of food in my saddle-bags – can I make you something?'

She said: 'No, I think I'll have a little lie-down. I hardly slept last night.'

'Sure, you do that. I'd take you to lunch in town, if there was a town. I'll finish slapping my bike back together. Then this afternoon I'll be on my way.'

'Oh. Okay.' Then she added: 'How long will it take to fix your bike?'

'A couple of hours. But I won't leave until you've finished your rest. Give me a shout when you're up.'

'Okay.'

He walked back to the cottage, feeling he'd smoothed over that momentary lapse when she was in his arms. Her annoyance that he'd held on to her – if annoyance it was – seemed to have dissipated after the brandy.

He finished repairing his motor cycle, climbed astride it and kicked the starter. It roared sweetly to life.

He looked even smaller on the big, sleek black machine, barefoot and without his lumber-jacket and crash-helmet. He revved the engine up in neutral, feeling the pleasure of the power beneath him, its eagerness to surge forward and go go go, take him anywhere he wanted. *Anywhere in the world.* And he was glad all over again with what he was doing. How could you put a price on this feeling? *Go anywhere in the world. Whenever you like.* He closed the machine down affectionately.

He opened his saddle-bags, took out his camping stove, a packet of rice, a can of bully beef, a little pot, and carried them all into the cottage kitchen. He put water and rice in the pot, cranked up the stove, put the pot on top, and sat down to wait.

Man, he was tired from the digging; he'd thought his shoulders and arms were tough after holding down that motorbike for three years, but that pickaxe in Aussie terra very firma was something else.

God, he felt sorry for her about the dog ... He closed his eyes. But instead of Oscar, he saw again those long, plump, bare legs beside him on the kitchen table, her dimpled bottom barely covered by her knickers.

He ate a bellyful of rice and bully beef, then collapsed on the bed.

He lay there, thinking of the way she had felt in his arms. Had she been annoyed? No, he was almost sure not. In fact he was almost sure that for an instant she had almost responded – then she had backed off, as if she'd been surprised at herself.

He stared at the ceiling, trying to remember and interpret every moment; then he smirked mirthlessly: it was just his wishful thinking, imagining she had wanted to respond. That was Ben Sunninghill hoping his luck had changed, stumbling across a lonely woman in the middle of the Australian Outback. No, she hadn't wanted to respond, she was just taken by surprise ...

He sighed, closed his eyes and resolved to put it out of his mind. Too bad. And he wasn't going to have a chance to find out for sure, leaving this afternoon; he'd never get another natural opportunity of taking her in his arms.

Too, too bad ...

Ben awoke an hour later feeling refreshed, though his shoulders were stiff. It was half past three. The ringing silence of the Outback. He creaked off the bed, went out on to the porch and listened.

Not a sound of life. Helen had been resting for almost three hours. He hoped she was sleeping, not lying there red-eyed.

He washed his dishes, packed his saddle-bags and straightened up the bedroom. He found a broom and gave the place a quick sweep, and scoured the sink and the bathroom. Then he put on his black leather breeches and boots.

It was after four o'clock when he was ready to leave. He took his box of jeweller's tools from his saddle-bag and started walking to the main house to see if Helen was up: he didn't take the motorbike in case she was still asleep.

The kitchen was empty. Silence. He went quietly to the inner door and carefully opened it.

Helen gasped and jumped backwards. She had been about to open the door from the other side. She was wearing only her panties, and

Ben glimpsed two large breasts before her hands shot up to cover them. He slammed the door. 'I'm terribly sorry,' he called. 'I was coming to find out if there was any sign of life.'

Helen was dashing back down the passage to her bedroom. 'I was just coming to put the kettle on!'

'Shall I do it?' he called.

'Yes.'

He went to the sink and filled the kettle. God, he hoped she hadn't misinterpreted *that* incident, thinking he was tiptoeing through the house to get between the sheets with her! Your actual Ben Sunninghill may have been fool enough to think earlier that his luck might have changed, but he wouldn't be so crass as to try *that* – God . . . He turned and walked out into the yard, as if to disassociate himself from her nakedness until the kettle boiled.

Five minutes later she came into the kitchen, dressed in jeans and a shirt. She had put on some lipstick and run a comb through her hair, but wisps hung untidily.

'I'm very sorry,' Ben said sincerely.

'That's okay,' she said briskly. 'Nothing you haven't seen before.' Her face was strained.

'A handsome brute like me,' he agreed, then regretted the words at once, and added hastily: 'Did you get some sleep?'

'No,' she sighed tensely. 'I couldn't stop thinking about Oscar. But I'm all right. Tea or coffee?'

'Coffee, please. Well,' he went on brightly, to put her mind at rest, if that's what it needed, 'I'm all packed and ready to leave. Just give me your ring and I'll put the diamond in.'

'Oh . . . Thank you.' She slid the ring off her finger and took the diamond from her pocket.

Ben sat down at the table, opened his toolbox, and selected a small pair of pliers. He picked up the diamond and carefully slotted it into its bed.

'Or would you prefer a beer?' Helen said.

'Coffee's fine.'

'Well, dammit, I'm going to have a beer!' She went to the pantry, opened the refrigerator and came back with two cans. 'Four-X.' She ripped open a can and passed it to him, then sat down.

'Thanks.' He lifted the beer and took four long swallows. As he began to clamp the diamond into its bed, he asked: 'Can you get another dog easily? A puppy?'

'Oh,' she said, 'I don't want another one. Not yet. Jack Goodwin –

33

he owns the hotel in Burraville – his Boxer bitch has a litter of puppies, but I couldn't face taking one yet. It wouldn't seem . . . right.'

'*Tempus luctus?*' he murmured as he worked. 'Well, I think—'

She demanded: 'How do you know Roman law?'

He was equally surprised. 'How do you know *tempus luctus* is a Roman law maxim?'

'I did two years of it at Uni. *Tempus luctus* was a period of mourning, during which a widow was not allowed to remarry.'

Ben grinned. 'Yes, but I think it had something to do with paternity, didn't it – being able to establish who was the father of any child born within a certain time of the first husband's death?' He smiled. 'So it doesn't apply to your case. I think you should get another puppy as soon as possible.' He gave the ring a final tweak, and handed it to her. 'Here, that won't fall out again.'

'Oh, *thank* you . . .' She slipped it back on her finger. She admired it. 'Great. You're really being a great help around the McKenzie household.' She admired the ring again. 'So, how does a gemologist know so much Roman law?'

Ben took a swig of beer. 'I don't. I just bought a book on it once. Bedside reading.'

'Good God – Justinian's Twelve Tables for bedside reading?'

He smiled. 'Did you get a degree in law?'

'No.' She sighed. 'I didn't get a damn degree in anything. Got married instead, in my third year.'

'Pregnant?'

She gave him an amused look that was not a smile. 'You're rather blunt, aren't you? No, I can't blame my stupidity on the slings and arrows of outrageous Mother Nature. I was simply in love.'

'Was?' Immediately he wished he hadn't said that.

Her reply was a touch pointed: 'I still am.'

Ben took another swig of beer. 'Then it wasn't stupid.'

She looked at him, then sighed. 'Oh, of course it was. I should have finished my degree first. I could have had that achievement to . . . to my name. To be proud of.'

Ben said: 'Aren't you proud now? You've raised a good family.' He waved a hand. 'You run this station.' He added: 'You're a fine woman. A good woman.'

She shot him a look. 'Thanks. Oh, of course I'm proud of my family. And of Clyde. I simply mean I could have had both. All that, *and* a degree, if I'd been patient. And maybe . . . travelled a bit.'

'Enriched your life first?'

She lifted the can to her mouth and swallowed. Then sighed.

'Exactly. I intended to see the world after I got my degree. Like you're doing. I don't mean on a Harley-Davidson, but what kids did in those days – hitch-hike around Europe, knock around on student railpasses. Maybe buy a camper. Work in London a few months.' She sighed again. 'It broke my parents' hearts.'

'That you didn't travel?'

'No, they're old-fashioned about travel – Australia has everything, why waste money on travel? No, that I didn't finish my degree. They thought I was going to be the one to break out of the farming mould and have a sophisticated life as a schoolteacher or doctor's wife in Sydney or' – she waved a hand – 'even the glittering lights of Bundaburg itself.' She snorted softly. 'They're sheep farmers near there. That's how I met Clyde. Anyway, they had to save hard to put me through Uni, and I threw it all away.' She added, in self-defence: 'Though I did help by working at night as a waitress and so forth.'

'Which university?'

'Brisbane.'

'Did you enjoy it?' He upended the beer can and emptied it.

She sighed. 'Beaut. Have another one?' She got up before he answered and fetched two more cans. 'Left over from Clyde's last visit. Or would you prefer brandy?'

'No, it's good beer. Why do they call it Four-X?'

'Because Queenslanders can't spell beer.'

He threw back his head and laughed.

She smiled: 'Old joke.'

'Good joke.' He took a grinning swallow. 'So? Your parents didn't approve of Clyde?'

She took a big sip and shook her head.

'No, they thought Clyde was beaut. Even though he's a Catholic. He was a sheep-shearer. You know, in this country sheep-shearers are highly skilled itinerant workers. And well paid. And he's a very solid bloke, Clyde. Nice-looking, good manners, hard-working. He'd also worked on the mines and been a shift-boss at only twenty-six. That mightn't sound like much, but believe me, underground is very responsible work. Anyway, he was buying this station on a mortgage, that's the only reason he was sheep-shearing, to make extra seasonal money.' She sat back. 'No, my parents had nothing against Clyde – my mother even flirted with him! Not seriously, of course, she just thought what a nice man, and Dad thought he was a great guy. But in their view I was destined for greater things than the Outback. They begged me to at least finish my degree first.' She sighed again. '*But*, we were madly in love. *And* he was about to disappear into the Outback again and he was afraid that in another year I'd meet somebody else. "All those smart guys at Uni," he said. And I was scared he'd meet some other lusty wench. Et cetera, et cetera.'

Ben smiled. 'How old is he?'

'Seven years older than me. Forty-nine.'

'So you got married and came straight to this station?'

'Yes. Dad shouted us a week's honeymoon on Lord Howe Island first as a wedding present. That's beautiful. Wonderful reefs . . .' She grinned mirthlessly: 'The furthest overseas I've ever been.'

'That was nice of him.'

'Very. Oh, my parents are lovely people. Dear, *dear* people.'

'Do you get to see them much?'

She twirled her beer can. 'Only very occasionally. Two years ago was the last time. They're over a thousand miles away, and you know what the roads are like out here.' She got up. 'I'm going to have a brandy. And you?'

He looked at his watch. 'Not if I'm riding. I'll have another beer in a minute, if you've got one.'

She hesitated a moment; then she said: '*Must* you leave today? It'll be sunset soon.'

Ben was taken by surprise. He was delighted to stay another night. And, who knows . . . ? But he put on a show of indecision.

'No, I shouldn't. I don't want to impose—'

'You're not imposing. The cottage is empty. And I'm enjoying talking. It's a nice change for me to have company.'

He smiled: 'Instead of talking to . . .' – he was about to say 'Oscar', then managed to change it – 'the wall?'

She smiled bleakly. 'Oscar, you mean. Oh . . .' She slumped her shoulders. 'Oh, I'd give my front teeth to have that doggie back. However . . .' She forced a bright smile. 'So you'll stay another night?' She added hastily: 'In the cottage.'

'Of course. I mean of course I'll sleep in the cottage. If that's okay, I'd love to – thank you.'

'Thank *you*, for all your help. *Good* . . . So, you'll have a brandy?'

'Sure,' he grinned. 'What the hell!'

'What the hell!' she agreed. She disappeared back into the pantry and returned with the bottle and two glasses. 'Water?'

'Straight. What the hell.'

'What the hell. Aussies make good brandy.' She sat and sloshed the liquor into the glasses. He noticed she suddenly appeared a little tipsy, as if she had dropped her guard.

'And good wine,' he said.

'*And* wine.'

'I've got a couple of bottles of Shiraz in my saddle-bags I can fetch.'

'Keep it for the road. Where're you heading tomorrow?'

He took a sip. 'East. Brisbane. Then Townsville, Cairns, then across to Darwin. I'll have to look at the map.'

'Oh, Brisbane . . .' She sat back with a sad smile. 'Those were happy days.' She sighed nostalgically, and took a big sip of brandy.

He did the same. He was glad she was relaxing after the trauma of burying her dog – and optimistic about the evening ahead? 'So,' he said, 'you regret . . .' He changed it. 'I mean, but surely you don't regret getting married?'

She snorted softly. 'No,' she said, 'how can you regret all that? Your husband? Your children?' She waved a hand vaguely. 'Even this lonely life. This is my *home*. It would be . . . un*natural* to regret that. Like Lady Macbeth saying "Unsex me here". She shook her head. 'No, of course I don't regret any of those actual things – I just wish I had *got* my degree, *done* my travelling . . . en*riched* my life first.' She shrugged. 'For just a couple of years, *then* done what I did. With Clyde.'

She looked at Ben, as if about to continue, but didn't. 'But?' he said.

She hesitated. 'But nothing.'

'You were about to say "but".' He smiled that smile.

'Was I?' She smiled back at him, self-consciously. 'Yes, I was.' She breathed deeply. 'What I mean is this: *But* the kids have all left the nest now. One by one they had to go off to boarding-school in Rockhampton, when the School of the Air wasn't enough for them anymore.'

'"School of the Year"?'

'*Air.* The radio. The government broadcasts lessons for Outback kids. At regimented hours the kids sit at their desks and tune into the government's education programmes, just as if they were at school. Very good it is, too. And my kids were very conscientious. I *made* them conscientious. And I helped them, and the older ones helped the younger ones, et cetera, and it's all pretty effective. But,' she shrugged, 'you reach a point where that's not enough. They need the society and competition of other kids – and sport, and the *esprit de corps* of normal schooling. So . . .' She sighed. 'One by one, off to boarding-school they had to go. Until even little Cathy went, year before last.'

'How old is she?'

'Eleven, now.'

'And the eldest?'

'Tim. Seventeen.' She smiled wanly. 'We kind of had them bang, bang, bang. Went to bed too early, I guess. There was no television out here in those days.'

He grinned. 'And . . . ?'

'And what?'

'You started off by admitting the "But".'

She smiled. 'Well, so, the kids are all doing fine at school. Good at games, good at their lessons. They come home once a year, Christmas holidays, for six weeks. The other holidays they go to my parents.' She shook her head. 'And when they come home, they're full of what it's like in Rockhampton, what fun it all is, and after a couple of weeks they can't wait to get back there. Their mates and all. And Tim thinks he's in love with the head girl – he's head prefect this year – and Wendy's got a crush on some young giant in the footie team, and there's no social life for them here, and so on. And Jacqueline's mad about tennis. Even Cathy complains that there're no newspapers – she wants to be a *fashion* reporter, would you believe? Age eleven! And they all want to go and disport themselves on the beaches and ride on those surfboards.' She raised her eyes in despair. 'And the *bosoms* on my girls . . . ? Even little Cathy is busy hatching two beauts.'

Ben smiled, and couldn't help glancing at mother's endowments. 'And . . . ?'

Helen took a sip of brandy. She gave an appreciative shudder.

'And, well, now Clyde has had to go back to the mines to pay for this little lot. With the droughts, and all. And, in fact, he's okay, too. He's got a nice bachelor bungalow, good tucker, good pay – thank God. He's very generous, sends me enough money and all that – he's even got a laundry and a cleaning lady. And he deserves it. But the point is . . .' She paused, then took a deep breath. 'The point is, none of them *need* me anymore.' She shook her head at him. 'They're all okay. Well provided-for. As I am. But the point is, what about *me*?' She looked at him. 'What is *my* purpose now?'

He ventured: 'You're *here*. They *know* you're here to come home to. Mum.' He smiled. 'The rock in their lives. And, you're looking after the station. The cattle.'

She snorted. 'Oh, the station . . . Do you know how many cattle we've got out there now? Sixty-five only. And a hundred and fifty or so sheep, until the lambing begins. We sold off the rest last year when they still had some meat on them. And even they don't need me – they've got Billy.'

'When he isn't drunk or on walkabout.'

'But that's one of the reasons he's so hopeless – there're so few animals. Nothing. We haven't even got a drinking-water crisis because there're three windmills still producing and fifteen acres of lucern under irrigation to feed the animals if the drought continues.' She shook her head. 'The station doesn't need *me*. The home doesn't need *me*. So . . . ?' She looked at him. 'Everybody's okay. But what have I got?' He started to speak but she continued, in exasperation: 'Oh, I don't mean, what have I *got*. I've got a perfectly good home and a loyal husband and enough money to get by. We're hard-up, but we're not broke. What I mean is – what is my *usefulness* now? What am I doing with my precious one-and-only *life*? With my perfectly good *head*? With my *hopes*? With the . . . remnants of my *youthfulness*, my energy and . . . *creativity*? With my *life*?'

Ben looked at her sympathetically. It was getting dark. He got up, went to the back door and pressed the green button. There was a distant *doem doem doem* as the generator started up. The kitchen light loomed on.

'Thanks,' she said, without looking up.

He sat down again. 'What do you *want* to do with it? Your life.'

She snorted softly, put both elbows on the table and rested her chin in her palms. 'I don't know.'

He said: 'Leave? Go and do the things you wanted to do when you'd finished your degree?'

She pressed her fingertips to her eyelids. 'Oh, how can I do *that*?'

'Easy. Just pack a bag and do it. Even if it's just for a year or two.' He added: 'You could crank up that VW van.'

She lowered her hands. 'Just take off on a holiday? Clyde would have a fit! Him working so hard to provide for the family and me just taking off, spending the money?'

'You need only spend the money he sends you anyway for your own maintenance. As you say, the ranch doesn't need you – why should Clyde be a dog in the manger over your time? Your life? Have you any money saved? Of your own, I mean.'

She made a wry face. 'A couple of thousand dollars, maybe, in the post office.'

'You could get a job somewhere.'

'Doing what? The only thing I'm trained for is damn housework. Though I did do a short course at Uni in shorthand and typing, but I've forgotten it all.'

'You'd pick it up again quickly. You'd be able to get a job in an office somewhere, an intelligent woman like you.'

She looked at him, then sighed.

'Oh, I'd love to do it. But Clyde would never allow it.'

Ben frowned. 'You don't need his permission. As you say, it's your precious, one-and-only life, to do with what you want. If you want to keep Clyde happy, forget it. But if you want to have a couple of years enriching your life, do it, even without his permission if necessary. But then there would be a price.'

She rested her face in her hands again. 'And that is?'

'Depends. You may never be the same again – you mightn't want to come back. Or Clyde might not want you back. In both cases the price would be called Sadness. Even Grief. And there's another one, unless you've got enough money – it's called Hardship. And another, called Loneliness. Enriching your life can be the loneliest business in the world.'

She looked at him through her parted fingers.

'What are you saying to me, Ben?'

He smiled. 'I'm just being realistic. You said you wanted to do more with the precious remnants of your life. You said you were helpless to do so. I'm just trying to show you that you're not helpless, but there's probably a cost. So, you must weigh the cost and decide what's worth what, and try to be satisfied with your decision.'

She gave a big sigh.

'Oh how I envy you.' She sat there, her face in her hands. 'Oh . . . I'm drunk.' She sat up and lowered her hands. 'Brandy and beer will do it to me every time. I had a couple of brandies before you came in, to try to sleep.'

He shrugged. 'So, get drunk.'

'I'm supposed to be the hostess.'

'So, I'll get drunk with you.'

She looked at him; her eyes were a little puffy. 'Why?'

He smiled at her. Why had she said why, like that? Because she suspected he wanted to get her drunk so he could have another grab of her? Perish the thought! That sweet possibility hadn't entirely escaped him, but even sex-starved Ben Sunninghill wasn't a cad, was he? His reply was almost truthful:

'Why not? We're enjoying ourselves. They're our lives, they'll be our hangovers. You're answerable only to yourself.'

'What does that mean?'

Oh, dear. Tramsmash Sunninghill. So she really did think he might be after her drunken body. 'Only what it says. You've had a tough day. You want to get drunk, do so. Nobody's here to criticize you.' (He wished he hadn't said that, too.)

She snorted wearily, apparently satisfied.

'No . . . I won't get drunk. Or drunker. I'll go'n sleep now, if you'll excuse me.'

'Of course.' He was very disappointed that the party was over almost before it had begun. 'But let me make you something to eat, you haven't eaten all day.'

'I'm not hungry. I had a big sandwich this afternoon, with the brandies. I should offer to make you something but I'm suddenly too drunk to try. I'm a piss-poor hostess, aren't I?'

'You're a lovely hostess. And I've plenty to eat, in my saddle-bags.'

'I'm sure you have, Mr Adventurous Sunninghill. You're self-sufficient. Answerable only to yourself.' She looked at him, then repeated wearily: 'Oh, how I envy you.'

He smiled. What to say? She held up a finger. 'There's one thing I'd like you to do before you go to bed. Please wait right here until I'm in my bedroom. Then press the red button and shut the generator down.'

'Sure.'

'Otherwise,' she said, 'what always happens is I've got to press the red button myself, then dash through to my bedroom in the dark. Which gives me the willies.'

'You could have a candle ready,' he said. 'Or a flashlight.'

'Yes, but I never do have a candle ready, do I? And besides, candle-light is spooky when you're walking alone through a big empty house, isn't it? I kind of prefer to run, then lock myself in the bedroom.'

He frowned. 'Do you really lock yourself in your bedroom every night?' (Oh God, that sounded a terrible question.)

'Absolutely.'

'But why?'

She grinned. 'To keep the spooks out.'

'Really?'

'No, not really. I know there're no such things as spooks. I've told all my children that ad nauseam, so it must be true because mummies don't tell fibs, do they? *Mummies*,' she went on, 'are absolutely pillars of truth and common sense, aren't they? Mummies are *rocks*. Veritable lighthouses in stormy seas. Absolute *bricks*, aren't they? And mummies know *best*. Know *every*thing. Mummies aren't scared of spooks, are they?'

41

'Aren't they?' Ben grinned.

'Absolutely not. Mummies are *absolutely* not scared of the dark. Even in big, empty houses slap-bang in the middle of the Outback. What spooks could there *possibly* be out here in Whoop-Whoop?' She elaborated. 'That means in the middle of nowhere. Whoop-Whoop is a remote, mythical Australian place—'

'I know,' he grinned. 'You told me.'

'Indeed,' she said, warming to her theme, 'what ghost would *want* to infest such an outlandish neck of the woods?' She narrowed her eyes: '*Only a real mean, nasty, sneaky son-of-a-bitch?* A veritable *pain-in-the-arse* of a spook!'

'Indeed.' Ben's grin widened.

'Anyway, will you be so kind as to stand by that switch? And I'll run. When I get to my bedroom, I'll light my candle, then shout. Then you hit the red button. Okay?'

'Okay.'

'Right. Goodnight.' She stood up, unsteadily. He stood up too. She grinned at him, then she kissed her fingertip and put it on his cheek.

That was his moment, to step towards her and take her in his arms unsuspectingly. They were less than two feet apart and it seemed he could almost feel the warmth of her body. But he hesitated, and the moment was past.

'Night.' She twiddled her fingers and turned to the passage door.

2

6

Helen was woken at sunrise, with a hangover, by the sound of his motor cycle. She frowned into her pillow. The noise increased, passing the side of the house. Then it began to diminish, heading towards the gate. She lay a moment, frowning; then got out of bed and shuffled to the window, holding her head.

Ben was riding down the track towards the gate, wearing crash-helmet, gauntlets, the works.

Helen stared. She was amazed. *Without even saying goodbye?* He hadn't said goodbye last night, had he? Her memory was a bit blurred around the edges, but she was sure he hadn't said goodbye! She stared at him angrily, her hungover heart sinking.

'Well, I'll be damned . . .'

She glowered at the empty track, then tottered back to the bed and collapsed on to it. She pulled the covers up to her chin. She lay glaring at the ceiling.

'Well, I'll be damned . . .'

She was indignant. And her spirits were sinking. Oh God, the loneliness again. The emptiness of the Outback. It had been nice yesterday, knowing there was somebody around. *Nice?* Knowing she had to bury Oscar? Oh God, Oscar. She closed her eyes. *I mean, it was good knowing there would be somebody to talk to afterwards.* And she hadn't made the most of it. She hadn't *talked* enough – she had gone to bed like a delicate bloom when she could have stayed up and *talked*, talked out her grief for Oscar. He was such a sensible bloke, Ben Whatever-hisnamewas. Sunninghill. A goddam hippy, but sensible and cheerful, and she had wasted the opportunity for a bit of human company!

The story of my life . . .

And she was *hurt*. Couldn't he have hung about long enough this morning to say goodbye? Thank you, perhaps? Good luck? But no – the story of my life again. Just like the kids – he doesn't need my help anymore. My usefulness is over – he's got his spanner, fixed his bloody bike, had a couple of nights in a decent bed, a nice hot shower – which he doubtless needed – and now he's on his bike again. Without so much as a cheerio . . .

Then she thought: Maybe he left a note on the kitchen table?

She began to scramble out of bed to check; then she restrained herself angrily.

A note – so what? Is a note good enough for a guest to leave his hostess? Is that how to treat people?

But maybe the note said he was just test-riding his bike after its repairs? *I'll be back in an hour*?

Again she began to get out of bed, then she stopped herself once more.

What's this? she demanded. Why this frantic curiosity to see if that little hippy left a bloody note? Frantic *anxiety* . . . This *hope*. You're *hoping* that he hasn't left. God, this is pathetic. You're pathetic, Helen McKenzie! You're turning into a dotty middle-aged woman desperate not to be slighted by a little New York hippy on a Harley-Davidson! *This* is what you've become!

She closed her eyes and lay there, her head hurting.

But isn't it *normal*? Normal just to . . . hope for some enjoyable conversation? Shouldn't everybody have the right to wake up expecting at least some human company?

She threw back the covers and swung out of bed. She unlocked the bedroom door, dashed on tiptoe down the passage to the kitchen door, slid back the bolt and hurried in.

There was no note on the table.

She stood there, naked, eyes darting over the surface as if she could will a note into existence.

Her shoulders slumped and she felt like bursting into tears. She put her hand to her throbbing brow.

Pathetic, McKenzie.

She took a deep breath. And, oh, her head . . .

Well, to hell with it, she was going to chase this hangover away with a beer! She'd never done this before, but what the *hell*! Clyde thought nothing of treating a hangover with a beer at sunrise, so why shouldn't she? He was a responsible man and if it wasn't degenerate when he did it, why should it be for her? Besides, she *felt* like being degenerate.

She fetched a can from the refrigerator. She poured it into a glass and took three big swallows. It went down into her system like a

46

balm. She immediately began to feel better. With a grim sigh, she slumped down at the kitchen table.

Not only pathetic, but *boring* – that's what she was! That's why that little jerk had left without even a see-yer ... Boring, and so insignificant that it didn't matter if he was rude to her. A has-been Outback wife who's so boring he'd wanted to leave yesterday afternoon – she had encouraged him to stay and then got so drunk that he thought it was best if he just folded his tent and pissed off in the dawn to avoid another encounter, another *boring* entreaty for him to stay yet one more *boring* day ...

Boring boring boring and useless – that's what she'd become! *Because she hadn't used her head for years. She wasn't even physically attractive anymore!*

What's that got to do with it? she demanded. That's how boring you've got, you mix things up, muddle arguments, bring in irrelevancies! What's your fat body got to do with this? With that little hippy on his 1000cc Thunderbird or whatever it's called? God knows – and this is the absolute honest-to-God dinkum truth – God *knows* she hadn't the slightest physical interest in him. He was so ... *little*. Besides, she'd never been unfaithful to Clyde in her life – *and* she'd had a few opportunities – possibly more than most wives out in the boondocks – and it honestly hadn't crossed her mind to be so with little Ben Hippy Sunninghill. He had made a few remarks that could have been interpreted as a come-on, and there was that moment he tried to hold her – but she'd frozen him right out! And he'd backed right off, hadn't he? So maybe they weren't come-ons. So what's your dis*gust*ing body got to do with this?

But, anyway, it's true. Look at you!

She looked down at her naked legs.

Look at those cellulite-dimpled thighs, your tummy sticking out. Your *stretch*-marked tummy. Look at your floppy boobs ...

Helen sat up straight, pulled her stomach in, crossed her legs and stuck her chest out a little. She looked down again.

Now *that* is how she used to look all the time. That's how she *should* look, and could again if she wasn't such a boring mindless slob!

She got up impatiently, fetched another can of beer, ripped off the top and took two big swallows.

Oh, she was impatient with herself ... She strode from the kitchen into the hall, and glared at herself in the full-length mirror, her can of Four-X in her hand.

What a slob! She pulled her shoulders back, tummy in. Stick your tits out! There . . .

She looked at herself. Not bad – for forty-two. And four kids. Okay, she was about ten pounds overweight, but then she always was a big girl – 'well-nourished', as Clyde said (he'd got that out of some book and loved to raise a laugh with it). She would have preferred 'Rubenesque', or better still, 'statuesque'. But dear old Mother Nature never meant her to be *slim*, and certainly not flat-chested – she was intended for breeding, that had been clear at Cathy's age. (As it was clear about Cathy: but at least she wouldn't be stuck in the Outback – she'd probably end up editing some glossy fashion magazine.) *But, my word, she needed to lose those ten pounds . . .*

'Don't I, Oscar?'

She froze, staring at herself. *Oscar?*

She closed her eyes. *'Oh God, my Oscar . . .'* And she gave a deep sigh, and turned and walked slowly back to the kitchen. She sat down heavily at the table, leant on both elbows and dropped her head into her hands.

She sat there, nursing her light, unreal head, trying fiercely not to think about Oscar. Then she snapped herself up straight, stood up grimly, went to the sink and tipped away the rest of her beer.

'Out, out, damned spot! Damned cellulite!'

She turned and strode back to her bedroom.

She had a shower, and washed her hair. She pulled on a fresh shirt and jeans, combed back her wet hair and tied it in a ponytail; she even put on some lipstick. Then she stomped through the house, out the back door, to the Land Rover. She started the engine, rammed the gear lever, and roared off up the track towards Billy's hut.

To see if he had sobered up. To give him a few instructions. To bring some order to this neck of the woods!

7

It was eleven o'clock when she came grinding back down the track towards the house. She slammed to a stop in the yard, scattering chickens and ducks. She scrambled out, slammed the door, and strode for the kitchen. She was going to radio Clyde right now – haul him up from underground if necessary – and tell him about Billy! She flung back the screen-door and burst into the kitchen, then came to a halt, staring.

Ben Sunninghill was sitting at the kitchen table, grinning that wide, impish grin, with a six-pack of beer beside him, one opened. A big coil of electric cable and two new doorlocks lay beside the beer. And on his knees, with a ribbon round its neck, was a Boxer puppy.

Helen stared at them. At the puppy, at Ben, back at the puppy. Then her eyes began to moisten. 'Oh *Ben* . . .' she cried. She dashed to the table, dropped on to her haunches, grabbed the puppy.

She held it up to her grinning face, shining-eyed. The puppy blinked at her inquisitively, unalarmed. 'Oh Ben! And a Boxer! Where did you get him?' She pulled it to her neck joyfully.

Ben smiled. 'Burraville Hotel. Jack Goodwin. You told me his bitch had a litter.'

'Oh, he's *gorgeous*!' She clasped the little animal to her joyfully. 'But I must pay for him! I bet that Jack Goodwin didn't give him away!'

Ben smiled. 'No, my shout. He didn't cost much, not with your actual Ben Sunninghill of the New York diamond market doing the bargaining. He's not pure-bred, his mother went to a picnic – even Jack Goodwin finally admitted that under my ruthless cross-examination. His father was a dingo.'

'A *dingo*!' Helen held up the grunting puppy and waggled it. 'I don't believe it!'

'But that's what I told Jack Goodwin. Nearly threw me out. Said at worst it was Mrs Johnson's Labrador, Fred.'

'Oh, Fred's a beautiful dog!'

'Don't bank on Fred. I went over to the schoolhouse to check him out. Black as the ace of spades, Fred is, and this guy' – he indicated the puppy – 'is nearly all brown. I saw half a dozen likely candidates for fatherhood as I left town.' He added: 'He's not a very likeable man, Jack, is he?'

'Jack? No. Has he got a name, this little feller?'

'Jack called him Biggles, because of that white mark round his neck, like a scarf. Think he was trying to impress me with how well-read he was.'

'Biggles?' She looked at the grunting face doubtfully.

'I thought of Hogan. After Crocodile Dundee, because he came at me with those sharp little teeth—'

'I know what we'll call him – *Dundee*!'

'Dundee? Yeah, that's better.'

'Dundee!' She jumped up, held the unworried puppy aloft and waltzed around with him. 'Oh, you're much more beautiful than Paul Hogan, even when he's scrubbed up!' She turned to Ben, eyes shining. 'Oh, *thank* you, Ben . . .' She crossed the kitchen impetuously, flung an arm around his narrow shoulders and planted a kiss on his bristly cheeks. 'Thank you.' She stood back, beaming at him, her eyes moist.

Ben grinned up at her happily. 'I'm glad. Enjoy.' Then he glanced at his wrist-watch, banged his hands on his knees and stood up. 'Well, I thought I'd fix those doorlocks and put an extension on to that generator switch for you, then I'd better be on my way.'

Helen stared at him, clutching the puppy. 'Oh, you can't leave *today*, Ben!'

Ben grinned at her. He could see she'd had a drink already and that was fine with him, he'd had a couple of beers himself in Burraville and felt in the mood for a few more. He didn't want to leave today either. And who knew what might happen? 'But I hate to impose,' he said. 'I really should leave—'

'Oh, not *today*! And you're not imposing! You can't leave the day you thrust a new puppy into my arms! We've got to . . . *celebrate*! Welcome him!' She shook her head: 'Let's have a nice lunch! I haven't cooked you anything yet! You probably think all I do is drink!'

'Isn't it?' he grinned.

'No!' she laughed. 'You beast! No, no, no, I'll have you know I'm a pillar of Australian society! I'm the lady they all talk about in reverent whispers in Burraville! I'm the After-lady in the Before and After advertisements! Have another beer?' She sparkled at him, clutching her puppy: 'I will if you will...'

Dundee was waddling around the kitchen, sniffing here, sniffing there, occasionally squatting. Helen pulled some paper off the kitchen roll and dropped it on a puddle.

'I'll start teaching him tomorrow,' she said cheerfully.

'But,' Ben said, 'I wouldn't have left without saying goodbye and thank you. What kind of hippy do you take me for?'

'I know that now. But I didn't this morning with a king-size hangover and a terrible case of the blues. And you're *not* a hippy.'

He gave that smile. 'Aren't I? What's a hippy? Some guy who doesn't give a shit about making money and just takes off?'

'On a 1000cc Thunderbird!'

'Harley-Davidson. Anyway, that makes me a hippy in the eyes of most Australians I've met. Or a wandering Jew, which is worse.' He added: 'Without the commercial instinct anymore.'

Helen had moved on to the wine which Ben had produced from his saddle-bags. She held up her glass: 'Here's to the wandering Jewish hippy on his 1000cc Harley-Thunderbird then!' She took a big sip. 'Did you ever have it? The commercial instinct, I mean.'

'You can't spend your life in the diamond trade and not have it, baby.' (She wished he wouldn't call her 'baby'.) 'You can't spend your life amongst Jews – even if your name's Sunninghill – and not have it. Cash-flow,' he rubbed his fingers together, 'that's what business life's about. But,' he shrugged, 'no more, for Mrs Sonnenberg's little boy.'

She said enviously: 'But you've got enough cash-flow to say to hell with it.'

'Enough? Yes, if I take it easy on the fleshpots.'

'And when it starts running low?'

'I'll work somewhere for a bit. I've got my jeweller's tools with me; jewellers can always get a job. Anyway, what I'm going to do soon is buy a small yacht – you can always make a bit of money with a boat.'

'A yacht?' she echoed, almost indignantly. 'I thought you were going back to Africa to do your foot-soldiering for the animals?'

'I am. But when I get back to Africa I'll need a home of some kind. So instead of paying rent I'll buy a yacht and that'll be my base – a mobile one. Between stints in the bush I'll sail it here and there. In fact, when I get back to Perth I'll buy a boat there, if I find one at the right price, stick my motorbike on the stern and sail back to Africa.'

Helen didn't know how much of this to believe – it all sounded too romantically macho for a little New York jeweller. 'Single-handed?'

Ben shrugged. 'I'll try to find somebody who wants to come along for the ride. But, if not – sure, single-handed.'

She looked at him, trying to imagine him doing it. The wind in his hair, his beak-nose to the flying spray. 'So you really are an intrepid sailor?'

'It's not such a big deal, crossing oceans. There're no rocks out there, are there? The danger for a boat is when you get near the real-estate. It's like flying an airplane – the higher you are, the more air you have beneath you, the safer you are.'

Helen wasn't so sure he had a licence to fly a plane either. But it was fun to talk. 'What about the big waves?'

'Well,' Ben admitted, 'I haven't crossed an ocean on a small boat yet. But there's probably more danger from big trucks when riding a motorbike. However, I've done a lot of sailing round New York. I know the winds – what to do with them, how to harness them.' He smiled. 'Maybe my Jewishness – getting something for nothing. The wind, the elements, they're free – and non-polluting. It's very satisfying working with the sea. So clean. So . . . harmonious with Nature.' He shrugged. 'Sure, I can cross an ocean.'

Helen sighed. She believed him. 'And how much will such a boat cost?'

'Maybe forty thousand bucks. Depending on where you buy it, its condition and so forth. But I can fix just about anything.'

She believed it. His self-confidence was infectious. 'And you can always make money out of a boat, huh?'

'Well, you don't pay rent, for a start. And if I run low on money I'll look for yachtsmen who want their boats fixed up. Ten bucks an hour.' He shrugged. 'Easy, I've tried it. Walk along any marina and holler "Who wants jobs done?" Plenty of work. Anyway, I don't need much. A bag of rice goes a long way, and the seas are full of fish.'

Oh, she envied him his freedom from worries. That reminded her of Billy. 'I must radio Clyde at lunchtime about Billy. The bastard's still drunk. Drunker. His wife too and you know what they've done? Torn the bloody door off the hut and used it for firewood!' She waved a hand. 'Plenty of wood out there. But no – the door.'

'Really?' He added: 'And what will Clyde do about it, two thousand miles away?'

She glanced at him and sighed.

'Nothing, I guess. He'll tell me to get on with it.'

'And do what?'

She nodded wearily. 'What indeed? Give him a bollocking when he sobers up. What else? I can't fire him – I'd just have to look for another Abbo stockman. The devil I know is better than the one I don't.'

'So you're radioing Clyde for his sympathy?'

Helen raised her eyebrows wanly. 'Guess so.'

Ben sat back and shrugged. 'Sure. Why not? That's what marriage is all about. And you deserve sympathy.'

She glanced at him. Was that sincere? She decided it was.

'No, you're right – I won't call him. I called him only last week, and it's quite a performance to get hold of him. I've got to radio the mine captain's office and get them to tell Clyde to stand by the radio at a certain hour, then call back.'

'Does Clyde ever call you?'

'Occasionally. But it's a favour really, to use the mine captain's office – he doesn't like asking too often. And it's not very satisfactory – you can't get too personal on the air, can you? Anybody can listen in if they find your frequency. He won't discuss money, for example – he doesn't like the neighbours to know we're hard-up. Though it's obvious – why else is he on the mines? And,' she smirked, 'he can never bring himself to tell me he loves me.'

Ben raised his eyebrows.

'Well, as long as he tells you in private . . .' He paused, then: 'Does he?'

For a moment she wondered about that question's possible direction. 'Of course he does.'

'Enough?'

She was taken aback by his persistence. No matter how grateful she was for his help and company, she didn't like that. She frowned. 'Yes. Why?'

He disarmed her with his impish smile. 'Because I'm told it's very important. And I've heard that Aussie men are often a bit too macho to show much affection. I've heard that the definition of an Aussie male's foreplay is' – he put on a creditable Australian accent – '"You awake, luv?" Heard that in a New York bar, from an Aussie girl.'

She smiled. 'Yes, that's an old one. And I believe it's mostly true, unfortunately.'

'But not in Clyde's case?'

She resented that. Too familiar. 'No!'

Ben sat back. 'Sorry.' He smiled self-effacingly: 'Too familiar.'

Again she was disarmed, and surprised at his perceptiveness. Word for word!

'It's all right.' She took a sip of wine. 'But what do you mean you're "told" demonstration of affection is important? Don't you *know*?'

Ben grinned honestly. (No harm in honesty when you've got little else to offer.) 'Well, look at me, I'm not likely to have had much experience in that area, am I? Let alone success.'

Helen was disarmed further, because it seemed so plausible. 'Oh Ben . . . But you're a lovely bloke . . .'

He grinned. 'That's what I tell all the girls – all the time. But nobody seems to believe me.' He added sadly: 'Except my mother.'

'I don't believe it!'

'See? It works.'

'What?'

'I've got your sympathy. Your disavowal of my physical limitations. But, unfortunately, that's all I get.' He took a sip of wine. 'Oh, I've got lots of women *friends*. I get along famously with women as a gender. But unfortunately sympathy only works that far.'

Again she wondered whether he was trying to steer the conversation in a certain direction, despite his expression. 'You've never been married?'

'Married? I've never had a woman I didn't pay for.'

That took her aback. That was astonishing self-effacement. 'Whores, you mean?'

Ben sighed cheerfully. 'But even that's not on these days, with Aids.' He grinned at her. 'Don't worry, I've been tested and I'm a Lloyds A1 insurance prospect.'

She blinked. *Why should she worry?* She began to change the subject, and Ben groaned: 'Oh, my big mouth . . .' He looked at her apologetically. 'Sorry – again. Why should you worry? But that was just a figure of speech. Believe *me* . . .' he put his hand on his breast solemnly and said, not entirely truthfully, 'I have enough bitter experience of life not to be so presumptuous as to think I could talk you into the sack.'

Helen stared at him a moment. Then she dropped her head and giggled. 'Oh, you're funny.'

Ben nodded wearily. 'Funny ha-ha or funny peculiar?'

'Both!'

'I knew it,' Ben sighed, 'I knew I couldn't just be funny ha-ha.'

'I mean unusual—'

'Almost rare,' Ben solemnly agreed. 'My mother thinks I'm an endangered species. *She* thinks I'm *beautiful*.'

Helen threw back her head and laughed. It all seemed terribly funny. *Little Ben Sunninghill* ... 'But you are, Ben! I mean, you've got the loveliest smile. It makes you ... shine. And it's so ... *laughy*.'

'Got to have a sense of humour with a face like this,' Ben agreed. 'What about the nose? I could have it straightened, but not shortened, regrettably. Because, like most people, I do need the actual nostrils at the tip.'

Helen snorted into her wine glass. 'And you've got the loveliest eyes, Ben! I mean, they're so naughty. And kind.' She smothered her mirth, her eyes moist, and waved at little Dundee. 'Like getting me him.'

Ben smiled. 'I'm glad.'

Helen wiped the corners of her eyes. 'And,' she said brightly, 'you've got all your hair!'

'All over,' Ben agreed.

'It shows virility!'

'I tell the girls that, but I'm just told I'm a fire-hazard.'

She laughed at him: 'Oh, *Ben* ...'

He smiled, then picked up the new doorlocks and the coil of electrical cable. 'Well, I'll fix the locks and extend that generator switch to your bedroom. To outwit the spooks.'

Helen brought her mind to this change of subject.

'Oh, that's very kind of you, but Clyde said it's best where it is.'

Ben said: 'You're the one who lives here all alone each night with the spooks, not Clyde. It's just a simple override switch, so you can shut down the generator from your bedroom when you go to bed. Clyde will still be able to start it and stop it from the kitchen.'

'Really?' she said. 'Why didn't he know that?'

'Maybe Clyde's not a smart-ass like me.'

Ben changed the locks while Helen got her laundry together. Then she fed Dundee while Ben started work on the switch. The puppy wolfed down his food. 'Like he's never had meat before!' she called happily from the yard.

'Probably hasn't, living with Jack Goodwin.'

'Oh, he's gorgeous!'

'Jack or Dundee?'

'Dundee! Oh, Jack's a real miser. And a terrible gossip. "Radio-Jack", we call him – tell him anything and it's all over the Outback by nightfall. *Who's a beautiful boy, then?*'

'Me. Ask my mother.'

'Oh, you ass!' She came back into the kitchen, holding a glass of wine. 'Oh, dear ... I'm having a lovely day. Now then – got any laundry you want done? *Smart*-ass.' She burst into giggles.

Ben picked his wine glass up from the floor and took a sip. 'No, thank you, only dirty people need machines to do their laundry. I did mine by hand this morning.'

'Well, it can't be very dry. Where is it? In a plastic bag in your saddle-bag?'

'Right.'

'Right, and where is it?'

'Just behind the saddle.'

'I mean the bike, you fool. Even I can figure out where the saddle-bag is once I find the bike. But I didn't see it when I came back from Billy's.'

'Outside your front door. Black, you can't miss it, the only black 1000cc Harley-Davidson there.'

'Oh, you ass!' She marched to the front of the house. She ferreted through his saddle-bag and found the wet clothes. She took them to the line in the yard, and hung them up. Socks, underpants, vests, shirts. Then she took one shirt down again and returned to the kitchen.

'Well, this garment needs strong machinery.' She stuffed it into the washing-machine with her own laundry.

'Thank you. But you can't start up the generator to do the washing while I'm working on these wires.' He added: 'You *could*, but you'd have to bury me soon afterwards.'

'Standing up beside Oscar?'

'So the grave would have to be a bit deeper, and that ground's hard. Not *that* much deeper,' he admitted reasonably.

She prepared lunch while he led the cable along the kitchen walls and down the passage, tacking it to the skirting board. He bored a small hole in the doorframe and fed the wire through into her bedroom.

It was not very feminine; it seemed a worn, hard-up sort of room. On the far bedside table was a framed photograph of a man, doubtless Clyde: Ben peered across at it, but couldn't make out much. On the dressing-table near the door was a photograph; four children. Taken recently, Ben thought. The boy, Tim, looked about sixteen: he was a strapping, good-looking lad; short hair, a generous open face, white even teeth – he was going to be what Americans call a 'hunk'. The three girls were all pretty, with neatly combed blonde shoulder-length hair and generous mouths like their mother; the little one, Cathy, was going to be a beauty. Ben glanced around the room. The double-bed was neatly made. The rugs on the floor were patchy. The wardrobe door was open, he could see dresses hanging, the shelves jumbled with underwear. Below lay a muddle of high-heeled shoes, several mauve pairs among them. So she likes mauve? It would suit her, too – her blue jeans suited her, with her blue eyes and blonde hair. One pair looked very sexy, with thin leather straps that she would wind around and tie above her ankles. He felt a desire to tiptoe across and pick them up. He could imagine them on her. Her toenails painted red? Oh dear, dear ... The dressing-table was old and chipped. The little jars and bottles of lotions and creams and perfume had a frugal, husbanded air. He felt sure most of them were almost empty, kept for the last smear or drop. Between the dressing-table and the wardrobe was the bathroom. He glanced towards the kitchen, hesitated, then went to the door and looked inside. Untiled walls, an old tub with claw-and-ball feet, the enamel worn away near the plug. An overhead shower with a dull plastic curtain. A toilet. A bidet, obviously recently installed because the cement around its base looked newish. Some towels, a big, damp bathmat, a broken laundry basket. And, on the floor beside the basket, a pair of panties. They lay there with an air of abandonment, as if she had just stepped out of them.

Ben Sunninghill looked at them. They were red, and lacy. And see-through, and brief. He had an almost irresistible desire to tiptoe inside and pick them up. To feel them between his fingers, to hold them to his face ...

'Gotcha!'

He jerked around. Helen was in the bedroom doorway, smiling, Dundee in her arms. 'Lunch is ready when you are!'

Ben recovered himself, and said easily: 'I was considering the best place for this override switch. Here by the bathroom door, which is easy for me, or by your bedside? That way is easy for you, but I've got to lead the cable right around the room.'

Helen considered the problem tipsily. 'Bedside makes sense, provided you've got enough cable. Then I haven't got to get out of bed in all my nakedness when I've finished reading, hit the switch, dash back, trip over the rug, bark my shins, cuss, scramble up in the dark, feel for the bed, et cetera.'

Ben grinned. 'Right.' He added: 'You're a funny lady.'

'Funny ha-ha or funny peculiar?'

'Both. But delightfully so.'

'I knew it. Now I'm not only bushwhacked, I'm peculiar!' She entered the room. 'Trouble is, if it's on my side of the bed, that means Clyde's got to get up – when he's at home – if he reads later than me, and switch the damn thing off. That'll irritate him.'

'Look, who's this switch for? And how often is Clyde home?'

She pondered a moment. 'True. To hell with Clyde?'

'Absolutely.'

'Okay, on my side of the bed, please.' Then she happened to glance into the bathroom and see the panties. She went in, scooped them up and stuffed them into the laundry basket. On her way back she closed the wardrobe door. 'Lunch is ready!' she repeated. 'Finish the switch afterwards.'

She had gone to some trouble over lunch. Ben fetched another bottle of wine from his saddle-bag. But he ate very little. 'I had two meat pies in Burraville just before I left,' he explained.

'That's not very good for you – have some more salad, grown with my own fair hands!' She was thoroughly enjoying herself.

'Yes, I saw your vegetable garden. Very impressive.'

'We're lucky to have enough water for it – it's a good well. And we swim in the holding reservoir.'

Ben imagined her in a swimsuit. He suggested: 'Shall we do that, after we've finished work?'

'*Why* not?'

Great things can happen in a swimming pool after a long boozy lunch. Ben couldn't wait. At the very least, the prospect of being semi-naked with her in the common caress of cool water was wildly erotic. He said, for something to say:

'So Clyde's a Catholic? And Catholics were bad news in Australia?'

'Oh, in those days, yes. Australia was very provincial when I was a kid, stuck out on the end of the world, and the majority of us are Protestants. Catholics were regarded as blighted with misinformation. Wops were Catholics – Italian immigrants who ran milk bars. As a girl I felt sorry for Catholics. And *marry* one? Never! It's different now, of course.'

'And Jews? How were they regarded?'

Helen hesitated. 'Well ... Jews have always had a hard time, haven't they? I guess Australia Fair was no exception.'

'Go on,' he smiled: 'say it. Regarded as furtive. Devious. Clannish. Money-grubbing. And too successful.' He added, regretfully: 'Present company excepted.'

She felt uncomfortable with this subject. 'Well, maybe when I was a girl, but it's quite different now, of course.'

'Is it? Jack Goodwin evidently doesn't think so. And that was before I started bargaining.'

'Forget Jack Goodwin.' Then she decided to be bold on this touchy point. 'But why is it that Jews are so successful?'

He grinned. 'Because they're superior.'

'Seriously.'

'Seriously. Because we believe we're the Chosen Race. Says so in black and white in the Bible. We're different from other people, we're privileged. So, as the Chosen Race, we have to work hard to justify it, and help each other, to maintain our position. We've got an Us-against-Them clannishness. So, we're rather disliked. And we're generally physically conspicuous, identifiable as Jews; an obvious target for prejudice.'

'Well, *I'm* not anti-Semitic.'

'No ... But do you want your daughter to marry one?'

She was taken aback by the bluntness of the question, even though feeling so jolly.

'I couldn't care less, provided he's a good husband!' But then she added: 'Well, I suppose every mother hopes her daughter will marry into her own culture. Religion ...' She faltered, then went on a trifle hastily: 'But do *you* believe yours is the Chosen Race?'

He sloshed more wine into their glasses. 'Yep. Learned it at my mother's knee. And I've only got to look around at all my successful Jewish brethren.' He grinned. 'Heard a joke in the Burraville pub this morning. I suspect it was told for my benefit. Anyway, what did the Australian Prime Minister say in his telegram to Golda Meir congratulating her on winning the Six Day War? "Now that you've got Sinai, can we please have Surfers' Paradise back?"'

Helen laughed. She'd heard it, but it was funny again coming from a Jew.

'No, it wasn't said for your benefit!' She took a sip of wine, then asked: 'Did Jack Goodwin know you were buying the puppy for me?'

'Yes. Why? He asked me what I wanted a puppy for, on a motorbike. I told him about Oscar.'

Helen puckered one corner of her mouth. 'Hmm. Did the other blokes in the pub know Dundee was for me?'

Ben shrugged. 'Sure. Why?'

Helen sighed, but said cheerfully: 'No, it's okay. But it'll be all over the Outback on the bush telegraph.' She shrugged. 'So what, I'll say you're my cousin from New York!'

'Your cousin? With *this* nose?' Ben sat back. 'I see. It's a matter of "What'll the neighbours think?"'

'To hell with them!'

'But would Clyde be annoyed?'

She frowned. 'No, Clyde knows I would never be ... silly.'

Silly? That was a dampener. He wished he hadn't mentioned Clyde – Clyde wasn't a subject to bring up when nursing ambitions about that swim with his wife. But all he could do was make light of it. 'To have an affair with me would be *silly?*' Then he added: 'You're right, of course. So – to hell with the neighbours; I'll be gone tomorrow, anyway.'

'Oh Ben, you shouldn't talk yourself down so! You're not so ...' She paused, wishing she hadn't started the sentence that way.

Ben wished she hadn't started it that way too. '... Totally unattractive?' He smiled.

She tried to avoid grinning, and tried to speak earnestly: 'You know what I mean ... You've a very attractive personality, Ben ...' (Oh Gawd, why'd she put it like that?) She waved a hand and blundered on: 'You're *charming*. Amusing. Witty. And I'm delighted to have your company ...' She trailed off, then ended brightly: 'And beauty is only skin-deep!' *Oh, God, why had she said that?*

Ben smiled wanly. 'But ugliness goes right to the bone?' His optimism about that swim was going right out the window. He stood up, embarrassed. 'Well, I'll finish rigging that switch—'

'Oh *Ben*,' she cried, 'you're *not* ugly! Finish your wine! Let's have another bottle ...'

He grinned. 'Sure, bring it to the bedroom and talk to me while I finish that switch.'

8

She sat cross-legged on the bed with Dundee, sipping wine, aglow with wine, thoroughly enjoying herself. 'I wasn't sure whether I wanted to be a lawyer or a teacher. So I took a general arts degree – or started it – majoring in English Literature, but I squeezed in two years of Roman Law, to get credits in case I went on to do an LL.B.'

Ben was crouched at her bedside table, under Clyde's photograph, rigging the cable along the skirting board. He indicated the picture. 'Is that Clyde?'

'Yes.'

'May I?' He picked it up. Clyde smiled self-consciously at him, a burly, nice-looking, no-nonsense balding man, uncomfortable in a suit and tie for the occasion. 'Looks a nice guy.'

'He is. Very.'

'Wouldn't want to get on the wrong side of him, though.'

'No. But he's a softie, really.'

Ben replaced the frame on the table and resumed work. 'I took a degree in English Literature,' he said.

She blinked. 'I thought you did whatchacallit – gemology?'

'I did. But a few years later I decided to do English Lit on the side. University of New York, night classes.'

Helen sighed. 'Oh, wow. Good on yer. Wish I could do that. Did you think you wanted to teach English?'

Ben tapped a tack into position. 'No, just for interest. Had a vague idea I'd try writing one day, or try to get into publishing. But, bought a motorbike instead.'

'But a degree like that's never wasted! Oh Ben, why do you say you're not a success? I so envy you your life.'

Ben worked with the wires. 'Yes, I suppose I'm a success in that I'm doing what most people fail to do, namely savour the world. Or I'm trying to. And I'm *learning*, the while.'

'Becoming *wise*,' she said with glowing solemnity. 'That's what I'd love to do – become wise. . . . And I've got all the time in the world to try to achieve it, by reading. And I *do* read. But there's a hell of a lot more to wisdom than book-learning.'

'Indeed.'

She waved an expansive hand. 'It's out there. Beyond the blue horizon. Where you're going back to. Or *forward* to. Always forward, that's the trick!' She sighed, staring across the room. 'That's why I thought I might be a lawyer. The daily human drama of the courtroom, seeing human nature at work. Arguing a case.' She frowned tipsily. 'The beauty of words. Of persuasion. Of logic. By the time a lawyer's my age he must have seen it all.' She sighed again. 'I used to spend hours in the gallery of the Brisbane courts.'

'And why did you consider being a teacher?'

'Again, the words. The beauty of the English language, and the satisfaction of using it to guide the young.'

He began work on the switch. He said: 'Have you tried writing? With all this time on your hands?'

'Have *you* ever tried?'

He said: 'No, but I'll write a book one day. Even if it's never published, I'll have done it.' He smiled. 'But I wrote a poem once.' He sat back on his haunches, put one hand on his heart and pointed his screwdriver at the ceiling.

'The moon shines up there like a cuspidor,
Doris, oh Doris, what are we waiting for . . . ?'

There was a pause, then Helen threw back her head and burst into laughter. *'That's hilarious!'*

Ben grinned, and resumed work. 'That's what Doris thought. She couldn't get over the cuspidor, didn't think it romantic at all. She was a dancer – the longest legs you ever saw, and I was bursting to get her into bed. That's pretty optimistic when you're five-foot-five. Still, I gave her a good laugh.'

Helen giggled. 'If I'd been Doris I'd have fallen for that one!'

Ben felt a flicker of hope. 'Better be careful, I might think my luck's changed and re-write it.'

Helen tried to stop giggling. 'But have you *seriously* tried to write, Ben?'

The flicker faltered. Nothing like a hasty change of a subject like this to falter flickers.

'I've made lots of notes every day. One day I'll get my arse to an anchor for a few months and start it.'

'And what will it be about?'

He was screwing the override switch into the wall. 'Hemingway said you should only write about what you know. So my book will be about this little New York Jewish jeweller, oversexed and underloved, who chucks it all up in disgust and goes off to savour life as best he can.'

She grinned. 'Oh, Ben . . .' She was about to query the underloved playfully, but thought better of it. 'Will it include this visit to the Outback?'

'Oh yes.' He paused and took a sip of wine. 'You'll be in it.'

She fluttered her eyelids tizzily. '*Really?* Dull old me?' Then she narrowed her eyes theatrically. 'What will it say about me, Smart-ass?'

Ben twisted his screwdriver, considering.

'I assure you, Helen, that you're not dull. You're a very interesting woman.'

'"Interesting"? You make me sound like a "case"! What kind of case of most interesting woman am I? A case of rather interesting bushwhacked *mindlessness?*'

He grinned at the wall. 'You're highly intelligent, Helen. And . . . appealing.' He was going to say desirable, but changed it in his mouth.

'Intelligent? I ain't said anything intelligent yet. But I'm a humdinger when I get going. Ask Oscar, bless his soul . . .' She sighed, then added glumly: 'I haven't done anything intelligent for twenty years.'

He had wasted the opening. 'You've raised a lovely family.'

'Any dumb blonde can do that. I mean *intelligent.*' She banged her brow. 'Something that requires the ability to grasp new concepts and apply them. De*velop* them. *Create* with them . . .'

He tightened the last screw, and stood up.

'There. We'll test it later.' He turned to her. And this was the moment to make his pass at her: they were in the bedroom, and about to leave it. He felt just bold enough, with all the booze inside him. He was about to sit down on the bed beside her – and he lost his nerve. He said instead:

'You're right, of course, we could all do so much more with our brains. Have *you* ever thought of writing?'

'What's there for *me* to write about?'

The moment was definitely past, and he felt a kind of relief that he hadn't made a premature blunder.

'Write about you. Like Hemingway said. You're what you know

best. Write about being a woman. Your kind of woman, in your situation. It's something that most women will understand and empathize with.'

'Empathize with? How many women live in the Outback?'

It would have been absolutely natural to sit down on the bed beside her. But again he lacked the nerve. He said:

'The Outback is only an extreme example of the condition in which many women – if not most women – find themselves in suburbia. All over the western world.' He waved a finger. 'They start a career. Then they get married and raise a family and the career is sacrificed to the drudgery of housework. The struggle to make ends meet. Meanwhile, the husband's career goes on. He has the stimulus, the companionship, the promotions, the job-satisfaction. Finally the kids grow up and leave home. What's Mum got left? Even her housewife's job is virtually taken away. What does she *do*?'

Helen was staring up at him. *'Right!'* she said emphatically, and took an aggressive swig of wine.

Her emphasis surprised even the optimist in him. Surely this was the moment to sit down beside her? He did so, three feet away, and marshalled his thoughts rapidly.

'But you must write it as a story, Helen. Not as a poor-me autobiography. You must create verbal pictures the reader can see and feel. With a plot which makes the reader want to know what happens next, how the heroine handles this problem. *Then* . . .' He raised his thick eyebrows. 'Then you've created a worthwhile work of art, baby.'

Helen was hanging on wisdom. That familiar *baby* didn't offend her this time. 'And?' she demanded. 'What *does* our heroine do?'

Oh, indeed, what does she do? He said, cautiously: 'Depends on who she is. You know yourself properly – I don't.' He decided to say it: 'Maybe she has an affair? Many women do.'

'But,' she protested, 'I could never do that, that wouldn't be me! I'm supposed to write about *me* . . .'

Ben Sunninghill gave an inward sigh. Had he blown it? Hope winced and subsided into its shell. He tried to make himself sound academic:

'But maybe your heroine does. Half the ladies bored out of their minds in suburbia would, and the other half would understand, even applaud.'

'But an affair doesn't solve her basic problem!'

Oh well . . . 'That's your task, as the story-teller – to show us what it does or doesn't solve.' He sighed and abandoned the subject of adultery. 'Or maybe she takes a job – any job, because she's too old now to resume her career. Or' – he shrugged – 'maybe she leaves. To go off and do her own thing, whatever that is.'

She said emphatically: 'But she loves her husband! And her family!'

Oh dear. Hope curled up in its shell. 'Ah, that's the tricky part. One of the most difficult parts. Remember what I said about the price? The heartache? The loneliness? The financial hardship?' He shrugged. 'It's your job as story-teller to make all this real for the reader.'

Helen looked at him unsteadily. 'But what makes her leave her family? Her loved ones?'

Ben said: 'But they've already left her, haven't they?'

'Yes, but only . . . physically. Geographically. They're still a *family.*'

Ben shook his head. 'Yes and no. That's the whole point. The family goes on, sure, but it ain't what it used to be. The story is how the heroine who's left behind handles that problem. Look at your friends and ask yourself what you think *their* problem is. The details of it. And look at yourself.' (It was on the tip of her tongue to protest that she didn't *have* a problem.) Ben pointed at the photograph of Clyde, and for the moment he was entirely altruistic: 'Ask yourself how your life with Clyde has changed – for better or worse – and why. Is there the same excitement of facing the future together? Obviously not, now *is* the future. What's the difference between that excitement of yester-year, those hopes, and the reality of now? How much disappointment is there?' He looked at her earnestly. 'What do you talk about these days? The same things you talked about twenty years ago when you were fresh from university and he was a horny young sheep-shearer desperate to carry you off to his mortgaged station?' He shook his head. 'No, of course not – you've said all that: but have you . . . *supp*lemented your conversations – together – so that you've still got things to talk about, to interest each other in? If not, why not? For example, do you both read good books, or only one of you? Do you even share the same interests now – or is it really only the common interest of survival?' Helen was hanging on his words. 'Yes, you love him, but not in the way you did when you first married him, when you were so crazy about him that you quit university. What does he mean to you *now*, Helen, twenty years on? And why? And is it enough, in all the circumstances, that you – or your heroine – must pay for it with the precious remnants of her youthfulness?' He looked at her, and his altruism faltered. 'What's her sex-life like? Ask yourself what yours is like.' Helen blinked. 'Is it what it used to be twenty years ago, when you couldn't get enough of each other? Of course not, nobody can keep up that enthusiasm. No, it's changed, but to what?'

Helen blinked again. 'Once a week, when he's home – once a fortnight? Once a month? Why so seldom? Is it because you're ageing? No. Is it because *he*'s ageing? No, he'd do three times a night with a new chick. So?' He tapped his head. 'So it's up here.' He leant out and tapped her head. 'But *what*'s up here? Or in your heroine's head? And what does she want to do about it, and how? *That's* what the story-teller's got to fascinate the reader with.'

Helen was following this intently.

'But what *makes* her leave?' she demanded. 'What's the catalyst? The final thing?'

Ben ached to lean forward and tilt her mouth to his. Instead he took the bottle from her and poured more wine into their glasses. He said quietly:

'That's the question, isn't it? That's what the story's about. What makes her, after all these years, finally find the courage to quit. To act, upon her convictions? *That* . . .' he nodded at her, 'is what women will sit on the edge of their chairs to find out. And if you succeed in making them understand that – empathize with *that* – you've been successful.' He looked at her earnestly; and oh, he was within a whis-ker of leaning out to touch her; then his nerve failed him and he just gave his wide impish smile: 'Make it this little New York Jewish jeweller who rocks up on his Harley-Davidson.' He grinned, then stood up and jerked his head. 'Come on – let's crank up the generator to test this switch, then go'n have that swim.'

9

The switch worked like a charm. Helen was delighted; now she could go to bed without running through the dark house pursued by spooks.

'Now you can start the washing-machine,' Ben said. She hit the button with a flourish. The machine burst into shuddering life. *'Eureka!'* she cried. Dundee began to make another puddle. 'You and I are going to have a little *talk* tomorrow, Dundee!'

Ben smiled. 'Well, I'll ride back to the cottage and put on my swimming trunks. Meet you at the reservoir?'

'Haveanotherdrinkfirst! Did you get all that? I'm having a lovely day! First a washing-machine again, then Dundee, then a thousand bucks' worth of diamond, now no more goddam spooks hard on my heels!' She leant boozily towards him. 'Do you think I'm childish, believing in spooks?'

It would have been so natural to lean forward too, and put his mouth on hers. 'No.' Ben grinned.

'I don't *believe* in spooks. I just *suspect* there are some!'

'I believe in ghosts.'

'Do you? A big brave man like you? Maybe I'm not such a bimbo!'

Ben smiled. 'I also don't like the dark in big empty houses. That's natural. Man has been afraid of the dark ever since the cave. And if you believe in God, and a spiritual life after death, what's so improbable about there being a few maladjusted spirits knocking around?'

'Right!' Helen cried. She stuck out her hand. 'Shake on that! You're not *Christian* if you don't believe in spooks!'

It was another moment when he could have enfolded her. 'Or Jewish.'

'Or Jewish,' she assented reasonably. 'So are we two reasonable people going to have another drink?'

'Sure – but up at the reservoir while we're having our swim. To freshen up.'

'Brilliant! To sober up! I'm almost as bad as Billy.' She leaned breathily towards him again. 'Ben, will you do one more small thing for me tomorrow?'

Oh, he would do all kinds of things for her tomorrow. Including crawl on his hands and knees over broken glass. 'If I can.'

'You can! Oh, you *can*. Because you're a *man*.' She held up a finger. 'Tomorrow, when Billy's sobered up – and me, hopefully – tomorrow will you accompany me to his hut to kick his Aboriginal arse? Figuratively, I mean. But help me to give him a bollocking. I mean, *I'll* do the bollocking, but I'd appreciate your moral support. So he doesn't think I'm a helpless female on my own with whom he can be cavalier over his putative duties.'

He grinned. 'You're not a helpless female.'

'Oh, I know that! Boy, do I know that! Dumb, maybe, *stultified* maybe, believe in ghosts definitely, but helpless I am not!' She looked at him cheerfully. 'But will you come with me tomorrow to Billy's?'

'Certainly.'

'Thank you. So let's have a drink to that! To our united front against Billy the Blackamoor. He of the sooty breast. That's Shakespeare.'

'Othello.' Ben grinned. 'But let's have that swim first.' He could hardly wait. 'Go'n put on a swimsuit, I'll meet you at the reservoir in five minutes.'

'You're quite right! Sober up – that's me every time!' She frowned happily, then pronounced: 'Ben, if I appear a bit pissed, it's not an optical illusion, it's just because I'm having such a good time! All that heady stuff you gave me about that crash-hot number-one sheer-genius bestseller I'm going to start writing tomorrow – it's been very stimulating! Gone to my head like wine. Yes, I shall meet you at the reservoir! In my itsy-bitsy teeny-weeny yellow polka-dot bikini! Pronto!'

Ben rode back to the cottage, not knowing what to think. He had lived long enough to know that he certainly couldn't be confident about his chances with the gorgeous Helen McKenzie, even though drunk and all by herself in the middle of the Outback, but he was tipsy enough and certainly horny enough to be optimistic as hell all over again. He unpacked, pulled on his swimming trunks, then got out another bottle of Shiraz, a corkscrew, two glasses from the kitchen, and set off jauntily, barefoot and tingling with anticipation.

He arrived at the big circular reservoir beside the windmill behind the eucalyptus grove. Helen was not there yet. He climbed the steps to the rim. The interior had been painted blue. There was hardly any sediment on the bottom. It was a perfectly good spot for seduction! He opened the wine and sat down on the concrete steps to wait for her, looking impatiently towards the house. It was just visible through the trees.

He wondered what she looked like in her itsy-bitsy bikini, and he wanted her so much he didn't care what she looked like. She had lovely big tits, that much he had seen – a real Earthmother type. Her stomach was probably a bit fat, and doubtless stretch-marked, but so what? Her thighs? Oh, he longed to see her thighs again . . .

The flies spoilt his anticipation. He stood up, waving them aside, looked back towards the house, then turned and plunged into the pool, to get away from them.

The surface was lukewarm, but deeper the water was cool, a delightful, sensuous balm. He swam underwater to the opposite side, then back again. He did the diameter four times underwater, to contain his impatience, then burst the surface. He gripped the rim, tossed back his hair, and looked over the top.

Helen was still not in sight. He looked at his watch, sighed and subsided back into the water, wallowing impatiently.

It was over twenty minutes since he'd left her. He muttered aloud: 'Remember the story of your life, Sunninghill, my boy, my life . . .'

He wallowed some more, trying not to feel unduly expectant. And he really did feel sorry for her, all alone in the Outback. It was a hell of a life for a woman . . .

It would do her the world of good to be laid . . . ?

He snorted at himself: there you go again, Sunninghill! He submerged his head in an attempt to dampen his expectations.

But, by God, if ever you've had a chance it's this one . . .

He plunged his head underwater again and swam hard to the steps. He reached for his wine glass and looked again towards the house. Not yet . . . He subsided back into the water, sipping.

After another five agonized minutes he just knew she wasn't coming – she had thought better of it. *So much for thinking your luck had changed, you fool. You asshole . . .*

He banged his glass on the rim, heaved himself up. He descended the concrete steps, grabbed his towel, picked up the glasses, corkscrew and wine bottle, and set off down the path to the main house.

The kitchen was empty, and the whole place had an abandoned air. 'Helen?' he called.

No response was the stern reply. He put the wine on the table, walked to the open door and peered down the passage. He listened. Not a sound. Then Dundee came waddling through from her bedroom.

'Helen? You all right?'

No reply. He hesitated, then walked down the passage and knocked on the half-open door. 'Anybody home?'

Silence. He cautiously stuck his head inside.

Helen's jeans and shirt were slung on the floor, and one shoe lay on the bed. An empty brandy glass stood on the dressing-table.

'Helen?'

He took a step inside, then went towards the bathroom. He peered through the open door. He saw Helen's bare foot.

'You all right, Helen?'

Silence. He hesitated, then took another step and peeped inside.

She was sitting on the toilet. She was slumped sideways, against the wall, eyes closed, her legs stretched out. She was naked but for a bunch of swimsuit around her knees. She was fast, fast asleep.

Ben stared at her. In a confusion of surprise, lust and disappointment. Then, with difficulty, he pulled himself together, and he was about to leave hastily, as was the correct thing to do – then he stopped, heart knocking, and allowed himself another look.

Oh . . . Yes, there were stretchmarks on her tummy, and her posture did not show her breasts to best advantage – they lolled down her chest. And her thighs were flattened by the lavatory seat. *But, oh, she was all woman* . . . And, oh, he felt a yearning in his hands to touch her, to feel her womanness, to seize her, to devour her.

Ben Sunninghill tore his eyes off her, and turned back. He stood just outside the bathroom, a little shakily. He closed his eyes, trying to think.

Well, this was the end of this little party. And, he was bitterly disappointed. *Bitterly* – and he was annoyed with himself for getting his stupid hopes up. *But at least she hadn't decided against having a swim with him. She had only fallen by the wayside* . . .

He took a deep breath, to smother the image of her defenceless nakedness, and tried to consider what to do.

Well, she should be woken up, surely, and either go to bed and sleep it off or rejoin the party – though there was little hope of that.

He sighed, then walked out into the passage. He filled his lungs and bellowed:

'HELEN! WAKE UP!'

He listened, his heart thumping. His voice seemed to echo over the Outback. But there was no response.

'HELEN! WAKE UP! FIRE! FLOOD! EARTHQUAKE!'

Nothing.

'RAPE! PILLAGE! PESTILENCE!'

Nothing.

'SNAKES!'

Still nothing.

'*SPOOKS!*' he bellowed.

He slumped his shoulders, and leant against the wall. *Forget it.* He grimly retraced his steps to the kitchen.

The hell of it was, it was all such an anticlimax, such a waste. Of a nice day, a promising day. An *opportunity* . . . And he really did enjoy talking to her – she was so appreciative. And so lonely . . .

Like me.

He stood in the empty kitchen, feeling sorry for himself. He sighed with frustration, poured a glass of wine and sat down at the table.

Dundee appeared, sniffing at his toes. 'Hullo, Dundee, where's Mommy?' Well, he might as well go to bed himself – but perhaps he should leave a note for her to wake him if and when she roused herself.

Then a thought occurred to him: She might topple off the toilet, and bash her head . . .

He sat there, considering the possibility and what could be done about it.

Stop looking for excuses to handle her womanflesh, pal!

But it was true – she *could* fall off and injure herself. And that would be terrible.

Bullshit. She'd bounce.

Yeah, but if she doesn't? It could be very serious. How do you call the Flying Doctor?

Well, all right, he said to himself reasonably, so you should put her to bed, shouldn't you?

Ben Sunninghill sat, considering this, trying not to be excited at the prospect. Trying to feel chivalrous. And he was right, dammit – she *could* topple off that john and crack her head. So there was only one sensible thing to do . . .

He got up, and walked back to the bathroom. He stood looking at her.

No, she was not truly beautiful, but to Ben Sunninghill she was. Maybe it was because he had had a lot to drink – but no, he wasn't that drunk. To Ben she seemed the loveliest woman in the world, and possibly the nicest. She was so sweet and defenceless sitting there.

He took a deep breath and tried to thrust carnal thoughts from his mind. He picked up her limp wrist and shook it.

'Helen? Come on, pal. Bedtime.'

Helen gave a groan, then slowly toppled forward. Her head slid across the wall in an arc. Ben dropped to his haunches in front of her, his arms out. She slumped to a stop against his narrow shoulder.

He held her, his hands on her bare back. And, oh, the feel of her soft smooth flesh, her breasts brushing his bare chest. He closed his eyes, overcome by the soft female feel of her, the woman smell of her. Her hair against his cheek, her breathing against his neck. The defencelessness of her. And, for an instant, it almost felt like love.

He took a deep, shaky breath, opened his eyes, and considered the problem of moving her.

She was too heavy for him to pick up in a fireman's lift. So? Drag her? He looked down at the bathmat. If he could get her on to that, he could drag her.

He reached out and pulled it nearer. Then he swivelled on his haunches and eased her weight forward, trying to turn her at the same time. She groaned, and slid slowly off the toilet, on to her knees. He knelt beside her, holding her tight, terrified of dropping her; then he shuffled backwards, grunting, and tried to control her dead-weight descent on to the mat.

She landed on her side with an alarming thump, but showed no sign of waking. Ben got to his feet, crouched and heaved her over on to her back.

She lay there, deep in drunken sleep, her legs half apart, her swim-suit stretched between her knees, her arms out as if in surrender.

He looked yearningly at her nakedness. Then he gently moved her arms to her sides. He put her legs together. Oh, the lovely feel of them. He looked down at her again, at her pretty face in drunken repose, her full lips a little parted, her breasts lolling; then, trying to ignore her nakedness, he gripped the corners of the mat and began to drag her.

He manoeuvred backwards across the bathroom. Helen did not murmur. He had difficulty steering her through the doorway – her hip caught. He dragged her on down the side of the double-bed, shoving the other mats aside with his feet. He dragged her past the foot of the bed, up along the other side. He stopped and looked down at her. 'Out to the wide, wide world . . .' he whispered tenderly. He turned to the bed and pulled back the covers.

Then he hesitated – no way could he hoist her up there without giving himself a hernia. How? Legs first? Head first? All together and break his back? And he certainly didn't want her to wake up and find herself naked in his arms en route to bed. In fact, having done his Good Samaritan number he should now make himself scarce; just put a pillow under her pretty head, throw a blanket over her and get out. He took one more look at her, and was reaching for a pillow when another thought occurred to him: he'd better get that swimsuit into a more decent position, because when she woke up and found herself neatly at her bedside she might think *he'd* pulled it down . . .

He got down on one knee, gripped the swimsuit in trembling fingers. He gently manoeuvred it up her soft thighs.

Then came the obstacle of her hips and buttocks – and there, *there,* was her pubic triangle.

Ben Sunninghill crouched over Helen McKenzie, his smouldering face eighteen inches above her, and with all his heart and loins he wanted to bend lower and lower, and then fiercely kiss her soft curly sweetness. For an agonized moment he hovered poised above her – then he screwed his hungry eyes closed, and hastily wrestled the swimsuit upwards. And Helen said:

'. . . we'll merry-merry be . . .'

Ben froze, his heart pounding. She was half-smiling; he crouched there, waiting to make sure she was asleep, then feverishly dragged the swimsuit up over her belly. Was that as far as he dared go? *Yes.* He got up, grabbed the sheet and blanket off the bed and hastily spread them over her. He grabbed a pillow, got a hand under her silky head, gently lifted it. He shoved the pillow underneath.

He crouched over her, his breath trembly, looking down at her.

Oh, it was such a woman's face . . . it wasn't beautiful in the classic sense, but beautiful it was, in the woman sense. And now that her nakedness was past, he felt only a throbbing tenderness. Of course he had lusted after that body under the blanket, but right now, looking down on that lovely, rather worn, half-smiling face, it was *tenderness* that he felt. And with all his heart he yearned to press his lips to hers.

But he did not. He forced himself to his feet. *Make yourself scarce, Sunninghill . . .* He looked down at her and whispered:

'. . . we'll merry-merry be, tomorrow we'll be so-ber . . .'

He left, closing the bedroom door behind him.

And, oh boy, tomorrow we *were* sober. 'Are we *not?*' she inquired huskily of her dressing-table mirror. 'Is that really us, Helen? Or Granny come to give us a nasty surprise?'

She turned for the bathroom, holding her head. Then the fact registered that her swimsuit was hanging from her midriff.

She stared down at herself, trying to think, her heart sinking; then she closed her eyes. 'Oh, *God* . . .'

She hurried to the bathroom, fumbled on the shower taps. She got under the hot water. Then she remembered Dundee.

'*Dundee!*' she shrieked. 'Where are you? Oh God!'

She washed her hair frantically, trying to wash out her conscience. She burst out of the shower, slung a big towel around her chest and hurried through to the kitchen. 'Dundee?' she croaked. There was no Dundee. But on the table she saw a note. She snatched it up. It read: *I've got Dundee.*

She closed her eyes. 'Thank God . . .'

She turned and slowly retraced her wet footprints to the bedroom, trying to remember what had happened. She brushed her teeth vigorously, her head hurting, and dressed, feeling terrible. She put on some make-up with exaggerated care. 'Patch up the wounds . . .' It seemed like the first time she'd worn cosmetics in a month. 'It *is* a month . . .' The last time she'd been to Burraville. Back in the kitchen she made a cup of strong black coffee, sat down and forced herself to eat a slice of bread and honey. It was hard work.

They'd been going to have a swim – she remembered that far. There had been a lot of heady crap about how she was going to write a book. Or was that the day before yesterday? She remembered deciding to have a brandy, taking it through to the bedroom to drink whilst she changed into her swimsuit. Then, *kerpow* – blank.

She gave a deep, hungover sigh. Then? Well, then, obviously, Ben had put her to bed on the floor. With only half her swimsuit on. How had that happened? Oh God – what else had he seen? What had he *done?* And what would Clyde say if he knew? Oh God again . . .

Helen took a grim, uptight breath. Well, well, lady, better pull yourself together! You don't go getting pissed half naked with strange men, no matter how lonely you are! So, take hold. You've been pissed for two days! Thank God he's leaving today . . .

And there's no need to look to him for moral support when giving Billy a bollocking. Fight your own battles!

Helen tossed back her coffee resolutely, banged down the mug and strode out into the backyard. The sunlight hurt. She strode for the Land Rover, got in, slammed the door and started the vehicle. *Get this Billy business over with, then retrieve Dundee from Ben and say goodbye. Goodbye, Ben Sunninghill, thanks for putting me to bed – and keep your mouth shut . . .*

She roared out of the yard on to the rough track to Billy's shack, bouncing and grinding, slamming the gears. She was glad to be doing something active whilst she nursed her guilty conscience and tried not to think. About her drunkenness, about what Ben Sunninghill had seen . . . *Oh, dear God, had she been snoring? Was her mouth open? Oh dear. And, oh, Clyde McKenzie I love you . . .*

Twenty minutes later she arrived at Billy's hut. And as she pulled up in a cloud of dust she just knew that goddam Billy and his wife had gone walkabout! She skidded to a stop and flung open the door.

There wasn't a sign of life, except the horse in the paddock near the windmill. The cooking fire was dead, the broken-up door was scattered about. Helen strode to the hut and peered inside angrily; their blankets were gone, and an empty bottle lay on the floor. *'Billy!'* A hundred yards away was the shed for the lucern and the runabout utility truck. She strode over to it. She peered inside. 'Billy?!' No damn Billy asleep in the hay. Nor in the truck.

She rubbed her aching eyes. She walked back to the Land Rover and slumped against it.

God, God, God. Now this . . .

Then she heard Ben's motor cycle. She looked up, her face grim, in no mood for Mr Sunninghill.

Ben came riding along the track, wearing only a shirt and shorts. He turned into the clearing round the hut and came rumbling up beside her. He cut the engine as he glanced around.

'So, walkabout, is it?'

Helen glared as if it were all his fault. 'Yes.'

75

He put his hands on his narrow hips. 'So, what's to be done?'

Helen closed her eyes in exasperation. 'Where's Dundee?'

'In the empty chicken run. So what do we do about Billy?'

We? She sighed furiously. 'How did you know I was here?'

'Heard your Land Rover, realized what had happened. Followed your dust.'

'Realized *what* had happened?'

Ben smiled. 'That for some reason you'd decided to handle Billy by yourself. Yesterday you asked me to give you moral support. But I thought I'd better come, in case you needed me.'

'And why do I want to handle Billy by myself?' she demanded.

He smiled that smile. He knew what she was worried about but his conscience was clear. If only by a whisker. 'Because you're feeling fragile – and you're worried about what may have happened last night. So you want to distance yourself from me.' He raised a palm. 'But please don't worry, because nothing happened.' He added: 'And I have to leave today, anyway.'

She was glad to hear that. She said grimly: 'What *did* happen last night, Ben?'

Ben said cheerfully: 'When you didn't show up at the reservoir I went to see if you were all right. I found you in the bathroom, passed out. Tried to wake you, failed, so I tried to put you to bed. Couldn't, so made you comfortable on the floor.'

Helen looked at him narrowly. 'Why didn't you just leave me to sleep it off in the bathroom?'

'Because you might have fallen and injured yourself. You were asleep on the john.'

Helen stared at him, then closed her eyes.

'The *toilet* . . .' she groaned. '*Oh*, how ladylike . . .'

'Actually,' he smiled, 'you looked rather cute.'

'Cute?' She flashed him a look. 'Oh, how undignified . . .'

'I mean . . .' he smiled, 'defenceless.'

'I'll say I was defenceless. What was I wearing?'

'Your swimsuit.'

'All of it?'

Ben sighed. 'No, well, it was around your thighs. But I pulled it up as far as I could.'

Helen winced. 'Oh, Clyde would love this.' She looked at him. 'You didn't . . . ?' She stopped in embarrassment.

Ben had had enough of being a misunderstood Good Samaritan. 'No, Helen,' he said, 'I didn't. Your swimsuit was around your knees, and I pulled it up as far as I could.' He gave her a glare. 'What kind of a jerk do you take me for?'

She closed her eyes again. 'Oh boy ... Thanks,' she said, less than graciously. Then she added grudgingly: 'No, Ben, I didn't think you'd done anything ungentlemanly.'

'Then why did you say it?'

'I *didn't* say it.' Then, more reasonably: 'But I admit it crossed my mind. Unworthy thought.' She sighed again, still angry with herself. 'I was just imagining what Clyde would think if he knew.'

'Well, he's not going to know, is he?'

She snorted bleakly. 'I may feel I have to confess it.'

Ben was astonished. '*Confess* it? Why?' He waved a bemused hand. 'Confess *what?* What did you do? Have you done him any harm? Have I?' He sighed, then shook his head at her. 'It'll only provoke suspicion. And discord. "What the eye does not see the heart does not grieve for". Look, Helen ...' He was almost at a loss where to begin with this delicate female conscience. 'Look, you were having a fun day for a change, as you're fully entitled to do. So, you got a bit drunk because you were letting your hair down for once. So what? You're your own person. Enjoy what happened. Look back on it with pleasure – or at least amusement. You didn't do anything wrong, Helen, even if you did fall asleep on the john with your swimsuit half on and had to be put to bed.' He glared into her embarrassed, hungover eyes. Then he held a finger out at her nose and said: '*And*, you're going to write that book, baby.'

Helen looked at him, finding some consolation for her remorse but in no mood for flights of fancy about becoming an authoress. Ben let it go. He said, businesslike: 'Okay, so what do we have to do now Billy's gone awol?'

We? She wasn't sure about that. 'I've got to find another jackaroo.'

'And how long will that take?'

She snorted wearily. 'Days? Weeks? I'll have to go and look for one in Burraville.'

'And how urgent is it to get one?'

She sighed angrily. 'Very. The windmills have to be serviced. Should have been done when Billy started his bender. The lucern was supposed to be irrigated day before yesterday, and another section must be cut before it goes to seed. And every few days a feed-drop's got to be driven to the sheep and cattle.'

'Well,' Ben said decisively, 'let's get that lucern irrigated fast. Then the windmills greased, that sounds important. Then do a feed-drop to the livestock.'

Helen hesitated. She said: 'You told me you wanted to leave today.' She was going to say 'intended to', but that sounded too much as if she wanted him gone. Which she did.

'I intended to, but I can't leave you with all this work; I'll leave tomorrow. Or tonight, if you like, but not till we've straightened this crisis out.'

She said with unjustified exasperation: 'Ben, it's not if I *like* . . .'

Ben grinned. 'It's what Clyde would like if he knew?' He jerked his head. 'Come on, lady, to work.'

'But you don't know anything about windmills and lucern.'

'Do you?'

'Of course!'

'Then show me. I'm pretty bright.'

It was hard, hard work with a hangover. The sun beating down. And the flies.

The big lucern field was surrounded by a high diamond-mesh fence to keep the kangaroos out. It was on a slope, so the water could be gravity-fed down from the windmill's reservoir. Getting the water to the field was easy enough, but the trick was distributing it economically. It had to be led through a series of furrows that turned to deep mud, and earth-locks had to be hastily built with hoes and then opened again to channel the water evenly. They had to run in mud, pursuing rushing water, to open locks and make new ones. Helen's heart was pounding in time with her head; her hair hung in her eyes, mud streaked her forearms. 'Do you do this often?' Ben yelled from across the field.

'Not if I can help it!'

It took three hours to irrigate the dry section of field. They plodded back to the windmill and washed off the mud. Helen shut the valve and they sat down wearily, their backs against the reservoir wall. She said, eyes closed:

'It's about these little men with hobnailed boots running around inside my head.'

'Have they got little green tunics and little red caps with pointy tops?'

'How did you know?'

'There's one sitting on your shoulder, having a rest.'

Helen grinned bleakly and flicked his leg. 'You're an ass. How come *you* haven't got a hangover, Mr Sunninghill?'

'I have. But I didn't have as much brandy as you. I'm only amongst the walking wounded.' He banged his hands on his knees and stood up creakily. 'Okay, show me how to service this windmill.'

But first they spent another two exhausting hours on their haunches, cutting lucern with sickles.

'Isn't there a better way of doing this?'

'Well, the tractor's got a mechanical scythe. But Clyde won't let Billy touch it.'

'So all this is always cut by hand?'

'Except when Clyde's here. Billy hasn't got much else to do.'

They lugged it out of the field in great armfuls and spread it to dry outside the feed-shed. 'How much more do you want cut?'

She pointed, sweating. 'This whole section's got to be done in the next few days, before it turns to seed. I'll have to get a jackaroo fast.'

'Well, tomorrow we better keep cutting.'

Then they packed dry lucern from the shed into the utility truck, drove over to the north-western cattle enclosure, and loaded the feed-rack next to the drinking trough. They took another load down to the south-west enclosure, to the sheep.

'Billy could drive, could he?' Ben asked.

'Yes.'

They finished offloading the lucern. Ben blew out his cheeks and said:

'Right. Show me how to service these windmills. And then, Madam, we are going to have that swim.'

'Right,' she said.

The sun was getting low when they set off for the main house from servicing the second windmill, exhausted. Ben arrived well ahead of her on his motor cycle. His hopes were high again, about the swim. *'Right,'* she had said -- she had obviously worked off her guilty conscience. *Good.* He considered riding to the cottage to fetch beer to jolly the party along, but decided not to give her a chance to change her mind in case she got to the reservoir before he returned. He rode straight there, stripped and plunged in.

The cool bite of the water on his hot, fly-harassed skin was delightful. He swam across slowly under water, then back again. He burst up through the surface, gripped the rim and looked up the track for Helen. Her Land Rover was coming through the trees.

His hopes were up again, but there was no sense in alarming her. He swam to the steps, grabbed his underpants, pulled them on underwater, then folded his arms on the rim and waited for her to arrive.

She drove out of the trees, and slowed when she saw his dripping face above the reservoir. She pulled up.

'So?' Was she blushing? 'Nice swim?'

He grinned airily. 'I've been thinking about this all day.'

She heard herself say: 'So have I.' But she began to put the vehicle into gear. He called:

'Aren't you coming in?'

Hesitation crossed her face, then decision. 'No, I'll go'n see to Dundee, poor little bugger's been in the chicken run all day.'

Ben was taken aback. And hurt. And bitterly disappointed. But he smiled at her, his frustrated heart sinking. *Smile, smile,* Sunninghill – so what else is new? – if that's how exquisite your conscience is, madam, that you can't even swim with me, far be it from me to nurse further pathetic amorous aspirations! He swung himself up on to the rim. 'I'll go'n see to Dundee, you take a swim while you're still hot. It's delicious.' He descended the steps and pulled on his shorts. He walked towards his motor cycle, a man without a carnal thought in his head, slung his leg over the saddle with a cheery smile and kicked the starter. He jerked his head at the pool and called above the noise:

'Go on! Do it naked, it's delightful. Meet you in the kitchen for a beer in half an hour, if you like.'

She was taken aback by the abruptness of all this. 'If I *like . . .*?' But apparently he did not hear her. He waved cheerfully and rumbled away.

Helen watched him go, with a frown. What the hell was that all about? Was he in a huff because she didn't intend to tear off her clothes and hurl herself with gay abandon into the reservoir with him?

She watched him disappear in the direction of the cottage. Then she sighed. Now she was worried she'd hurt his feelings; after all, he was her guest. He had been a great help, and he hadn't done anything untoward . . . But for God's sake, he was being rather precious! Wasn't it understandable, how she felt after last night?

She rammed the Land Rover into gear. Hot and sweaty, and with another anxiety now about hurting Ben Sunninghill's feelings. Then she looked at the reservoir.

It was true, she was had been thinking about it all day. And she was bloody exhausted and fly-bothered, and still very, very fragile. And alone now . . .

Helen pulled the stop button with grim resolution, climbed out of the vehicle and walked to the concrete steps. She looked towards the cottage; Ben was nowhere to be seen. She took off her shirt. She unbuckled her jeans, pulled them down over her hips, then sat on the steps and wrestled them over her thighs. So *fat* . . . She stood up again in her underwear, looked again towards the cottage; then she ran up the steps, to the rim. She was about to plunge – then she stopped.

'Do it naked,' he had said.

And yes – why not? It would be lovely to dive in stark naked. That wonderful feeling of the water absolutely all over her . . . and she was all alone, wasn't she? Helen hesitated one more moment, then reached back and unclipped her bra. She put her thumbs into the top of her panties, and wriggled them halfway down her thighs – then she stopped again.

What would Clyde think, her swimming naked, with a man around? Even in her underwear . . .

She crouched on the rim of the reservoir, her thumbs in the elastic, assailed by her hungover conscience again; then she sighed and pulled the panties up. She snatched up her bra, scooped it on, twisted her arms behind her back and clipped it together.

She hurried down the steps and dressed quickly. She walked soberly to the Land Rover.

She drove to the house, and had a chaste shower.

It was a hotter evening than usual. Ben showed up at the kitchen door on foot, carrying Dundee and a six-pack of cold beer which he'd bought in Burraville. Helen's hair still hung in damp tresses. She had not put on any make-up.

'Hi, Ben.'

'Dundee needs reassuring that he's not a chicken.' He was in something of a feisty mood, but trying not to show it.

'Oh, Dundee, you're not a chicken!' She took him in both hands and rubbed his grunting face against hers. Then: 'I'll make us some supper,' she said brightly to Ben.

He surprised her by saying: 'Not for me, thanks, Helen, I'm for a very early night and I've already had supper.' He ripped the top off a can for her.

'Eaten already? But I was going—'

'I was starved after that work and I'm full now, thanks all the same.'

For a moment Helen was annoyed. Suddenly she'd had enough of all this, exhausted and hungover and conscience-stricken as she was.

Enough of her guilt, enough of this delicate bloom who'd landed in her life. 'Ben, is it because I didn't swim with you?' She wanted to say 'In which case to hell with you', but she changed it, trying not to sound crisp: 'I hope I didn't hurt your feelings.'

'Not at all . . .' (He wanted to say 'I'm used to that sort of thing.') 'Good God, I understand perfectly, Helen.'

Helen looked at him. 'What do you understand perfectly, Ben?'

He disarmed her by saying: 'About last night. About Clyde. You're alone and I'm a stranger. Et cetera, et cetera. Now, come on, relax and drink this, you've had a tough day.' He held out the can of beer.

Helen looked at it with misgiving, and puckered one corner of her wide mouth. She was torn between being a hostess, patching up Ben's feelings, and her bruised modesty. 'Ben, I wasn't going to drink tonight.'

'Beer, Helen,' he said. 'It's medicine. Hair of the dog. You deserve it.' He opened another can for himself, sat down and up-ended it to his unshaven mouth.

Helen slowly sank to a chair, Dundee clasped to her bosom. She felt silly and unreasonable. She didn't touch the can. 'I'd absolutely love to have a beer, Ben, but I swore I wasn't going to drink tonight.'

Ben looked at her, then leant forward and frowned. 'Good God, what kind of a child are you?'

Helen bridled. 'Child?'

Ben sat back. He said: 'And why? Because you're trying to salve your conscience about being put to bed last night half-naked by a stranger. Because you're remorseful and worried about what Big Daddy would think. So you want to be good, to make amends. And that's why you didn't want to swim with me this afternoon – you wanted to somehow distance yourself from the *temptations* of my magnificent body.' He suppressed a smile. 'And being good now means not having a medicinal and sociable beer even though you've worked your guts out today doing a man's job in the Outback.'

She was piqued by his choice of words, and his tone. Big Daddy? She lifted the can and took three long swallows, her eyes on his; she replaced the can with a slight bang.

'Now, didn't you deserve that?'

Helen looked at him, thinking, What nonsense all this is – yesterday morning I was angry because I thought he'd left! So just *enjoy* . . . 'But do you promise we won't get drunk again tonight?'

Ben leant forward again. 'For God's sake, Helen,' he said quietly, 'you don't need my promise to ensure you don't get drunk. Or Clyde's permission to do so. You're your own woman! It's *your* life, to make of it what you will.' He paused, then shook his head at her. 'You're the only one who's responsible for whatever you want, for what you do with your life.'

Helen sat back, sullenly embarrassed. Then he put her further off balance by demanding quietly: 'Why *didn't* you want to swim with me after that hard day's work, Helen?' She blinked. Before she could think of a face-saving answer he continued: 'Did you swim after I left?'

She hesitated. 'No,' she admitted.

Ben nodded. 'No. Why not? Did you think I might sneak up on the reservoir and make a grab at you?'

'Of *course* not . . .' It was almost the truth.

He said: 'In fact you could see I wasn't anywhere around. You knew I was at the cottage. So it was for Clyde's sake that you refrained from swimming, even though for your own sake you wanted to do so. So you were submitting yourself to Clyde's will, *in absentia*, even though he wouldn't know anything about it. And you thus denied yourself a simple, harmless pleasure.' He smiled grimly. 'That was an irrational decision, but it made you feel virtuous – right? You felt you were being good?'

'Anything wrong in feeling good?'

'No. Do what makes you feel good. But you must understand why you're doing it, understand the illogical basis of the feeling. As long as you recognize that, you're doing okay. Enjoy the feeling – but understand it.' He added: 'Especially for that book of yours.'

She was on her mettle now. 'I believe I do understand that, Ben. But why are you saying all this? You're being rather aggressive.'

He sat back. Yes, beneath his smile he was feeling a bit aggressive. Hurt. His company had been shunned; he had been under some kind of suspicion. (What a towering injustice!) He looked at her solemnly and said: 'Only because I like you, Helen.'

And it was the truth – *like*. If he had said, 'Because I want you', it would have been more true. If he had said, 'Because I love you' it would have been arrant nonsense, because he had lived long enough to know something about love. But right that red hot moment, looking at her, it would have felt true, like it would have been last night when he was pulling her swimsuit up her silken thighs.

'Of course,' she said, 'I know you like me as a friend, or you wouldn't have been slogging your guts out today to help me. As I like you – as a friend. Or I'd have politely encouraged you down the road to Brisbane day before yesterday, hangover and all.' She looked at him archly. 'I mean, what's the purpose of all this advice, Ben?'

'I've no ulterior motive, Helen.' (That was almost true now.) 'The purpose—'

'Is that you feel sorry for me,' she said accusingly. 'You feel sorry for my shitty life, alone in the Outback.' Ben started to speak but she continued resolutely: 'Well, it's not such a shitty life, Ben. In fact, all up, compared to millions of women, it's a pretty damn good life! I've got a decent loyal husband who's working hard to provide, and four lovely kids at a good school. I've got two loyal parents, a solid roof over my head and enough money to maintain myself. There's a Land Rover that works, a two-way radio, a television, a horse, sixty-five cattle, a hundred and fifty sheep, forty-two thousand acres, three bore-holes and twelve ducks, chickens and geese. And now, Dundee – thanks to you.' She added: 'And a washing-machine. And a thousand-buck diamond ring.' She looked at him challengingly, and folded her arms. 'God, what more can a girl want?'

Ben was sitting forward, his smiling eyes on hers. He admired her pluck, and he didn't want to undermine it. More than he had admired anybody in his life? Possibly not, but at that moment it felt like it. He did not like saying it, it was almost heartless, but it was true and the subject had been opened. 'Less self-sacrifice.'

She looked at him grimly. 'That's putting it very, very strongly.'

He sat back. 'You've often thought it yourself, Helen,' he said quietly. 'You just don't like me saying it.' He shrugged solemnly. 'The children have gone, one by one; Clyde has gone. So even this ranch is almost gone, a shadow of its former self – an Aborigine jackaroo could run it single-handed. But *you* haven't gone away like the rest of your family to do what you want to do – what you need to do, for your soul. No, you've stayed on, alone, to keep the fiction of a home going, for their sakes.' He raised his eyebrows at her. 'So you're sacrificing the remnants of your precious life for them. Those were *your* words: "remnants of my precious life".'

'The *fiction* of a home?' she said archly. 'But you forget, I love my children. And my husband.'

'Ah,' Ben sighed. 'So you're enjoying being self-sacrificial? Denying yourself the things you want?'

'Of course I'm not enjoying being alone!'

'Alone and doing nothing stimulating, self-enhancing?'

'Of course I'm not enjoying it, I've said that!'

'So why do you do it?' He smiled.

She folded her arms more firmly. 'Because it's my duty. As a mother and a wife.'

Ben shook his head. 'You're not mothering them anymore – the school does that. And you're not able to be wifely to your husband, either.' He took a long swig of beer, looking at her. 'And you won't stop loving any of them if you stop being self-sacrificial – in fact you'll probably love them more. You could get a job in Broken Hill, for Christ's sake, and be with Clyde until he can afford to quit and come home. Or in Rockhampton, and be near the kids. Or you could go back to university and finish your degree.' He shook his head again. 'You could be a mother and wife *and* a fulfilled person.'

She looked at him for a long moment. '*Or*,' she glared, 'if I slept with you.'

For an instant Ben's pulse tripped; but there'd certainly been no invitation in that challenge. He felt a blush rising, then a surge of indignation. The sheer, towering injustice of it! Good God, here he was genuinely trying to help her! 'Good *God*,' he said, 'is that what you're thinking I'm up to?'

She looked at him; then closed her eyes. 'No . . .' she muttered.

'Trying to get into your *pants*?' He seethed with unrighteous indignation. 'By telling you what I think about your patently hard life alone in the Outback when you could be with your husband in Broken Hill or near your children or back at university employing your excellent brain – did I or did I not say all that?'

She held her head. 'You did. I'm sorry—'

'Have we or have we not been talking over the last few days about how you envy my freedom, about the book you could write—'

'Oh Ben, I'm *sorry*.'

He glared at her remorseful, averted brow. Then he had to suppress a grin. 'So why did you say it?'

She moaned. 'Oh, perish the thought! It's just that . . .' She sighed heavily, then muttered: 'Well, you're a man, whom I know almost nothing about, and here I am, a woman all alone in the middle of nowhere and you're telling me all these things—'

'In the hopes that I can fuck you? Well, if it's of any interest to you, of course I want to fuck you, Helen.' He glared at her. 'So would any man, unless he was a pansy! I'd love to fuck you black and blue! That's life. But' – he shook his head at her almost truthfully – 'that wasn't why I said what I did. I really like you, Helen – if not I'd have sidled off down the track, day before yesterday. But I've stuck around because I enjoy your company; I want your friendship.' He shook his head at her again, and this was almost the truth: 'Believe me – just look at me and believe me, Helen – I haven't had that much success with women to imagine that I can turn up in the middle of Australia to borrow a spanner and be so lucky as to get laid with Helen McKenzie on the strength of a little philosophical honey-talk about what a shit life she's leading!'

She'd had her head averted through all this, but now she turned to him and said soberly:

'I said I'm sorry, Ben. Forgive a bushwhacked Aussie woman her unworthy thoughts. And I accept they *were* unworthy, you've impressed that upon me successfully.' Then she glared at him. 'But why were you being so goddam melodramatic? Rubbing it in about how I'm wasting my life?' She appealed: 'What are you trying to *do* to me?'

Ben looked at her. He felt sorry for her, but he was right, and he was going to finish it now. 'Melodramatic?' He raised his eyebrows, then stood up. 'I'll show you melodrama, Helen. Wait here.'

He left the kitchen and went to the living-room. He switched on the light, went to the framed photographs on the shelf. He selected three and returned with them. He said:

'I'm not being entirely original, now. I saw this done in a movie called *Dead Poets Society*. But it's very apt.' He put the first photograph on the table in front of her. It showed eleven schoolgirls in swimsuits, posing formally. He said:

'Your mother's school swimming team, right? Taken in the early post-war years. And that' – he pointed – 'is your mother.'

She was surprised. 'That's right. How did you know?'

'Not by any name printed below,' he said significantly, 'because I don't know your mother's maiden name, do I? But I know her by her face, Helen, I recognize her. Because she looks so like you.'

'Oh.'

'Pretty girl, isn't she, here?'

'Yes. Yes, she was very pretty.'

'Like her daughter.' He ran his fingers along the photograph. 'And look at all those other good-looking, healthy girls. Look at their fresh, young faces, their bright smiles, their fine, strong, young bodies.' He turned to her. 'Yes?'

Helen looked up at him. 'So?'

'And now look at this.' He laid down the second photograph. 'This is *your* school swimming team. Taken about twenty years later. And this' – he pointed to a girl – 'is you.'

She glanced down. 'Yes. So?'

He said quietly: 'Look at you all . . . what fine examples of Australian girlhood. Bursting with health and energy, your whole wonderful lives ahead of you.' He paused, then indicated the first photograph. 'Now look at your mother's team again.' His finger moved across it. 'See any difference between the girls in your mother's team, and those in yours, apart from hairstyles?'

She looked with some care. 'No.'

'No. Now look at this.' He put down the third picture.

It showed an elderly woman standing beside a beach-chair, smiling at the camera. She had sparse grey hair and wore spectacles. Her flattened breasts were hardly visible in her swimsuit, her back stooped a little and the skin on her arms was wrinkled.

'A recent picture of your mother? A candid-camera shot.'

'Yes.'

'She looks a sweet old lady.'

'She is.'

Ben said quietly: 'She's going to die soon.'

Helen blinked at him, shocked by his brutality. Then she bridled: 'Do you *mind* . . .'

He said: 'No, I don't mind shocking you. Because that girl *there*' – he put a finger on the young Helen in the second photograph – 'will soon become this old lady *here*.' He touched the last photograph. He looked down at her. 'Far, *far* faster than you think, Helen.'

Helen looked up at him grimly. He held her eye, then continued:

'In fact, do you know where half of these pretty girls in your mother's team photograph are now?' He ran his finger slowly over their young, rounded limbs. 'In the cemetery, Helen. Involuntarily going through the long and disgusting process of putrefaction and decomposition.'

He picked up his beer and drank the rest of it, looking down his bristly cheeks at her. He returned the can to the table.

And with all his heart he yearned to lean down and kiss her shocked eyes, her wide, soft mouth, and tell her he thought she was terrific, that he'd give his right arm to make love to her.

'Goodnight, Helen,' he said.

II

It had taken her a long time to get to sleep after that, and she woke up at sunrise embarrassed at having accused him of trying to seduce her. Oh God, that had been immature – so *crass* ... She was startled out of her remorse by the sound of an engine. For a moment she thought it was his motor cycle, that he was taking off in high dudgeon, but then she identified it as the tractor. She lay there for a moment, astonished. Then she scrambled out of bed, slung on a dressing-gown and ran to the kitchen and out the back door.

She saw the tractor and trailer disappearing up the track into the bush, driven by Ben. *'Hey!'* she hollered. But he did not hear her.

She hurried back to her bedroom. Agitated and annoyed. He *knew* Clyde was touchy about the tractor! Okay, he was determined to help her, but this really was an impertinence! She pulled on clothes and rushed back to the kitchen. She had made sandwiches for today after Ben's dramatic exit last night – she snatched them up. She did not delay to make coffee for the thermos flasks – she filled them with cold water from the refrigerator and dashed out to the Land Rover.

She caught up with him within two miles. He was riding along jauntily, apparently enjoying himself hugely, singing, waving his arm to the early-morning sun. He could not hear her above the tractor's noise. Helen smiled, despite herself: *Cocky little bugger* ... She hooted imperiously but he still did not hear, his head thrown back as he sang. She swung out into the bush to overtake him.

She roared up alongside, her hand on the horn. Ben turned to her, bouncing along, apparently quite unsurprised at her arrival: he put his hand on his heart, his face soulful, his mouth working in song. She grinned and hollered: *'Stop, you bastard!'*

He gave her a cheery wink and came to a rumbling stop. She slammed to a halt beside him. Ben swung out of the iron saddle and sauntered over to her window.

88

'Morning, officer, my licence is in my other trousers.'

She had to work at it to keep a straight face. 'Ben, what are you doing?'

'I was singing "Oh, what a beautiful morning!", officer. Which it is.' He waved his hand at the horizon. 'If there was any corn it would doubtless be as high as an elephant's eye.'

'*What*,' she grinned, 'are you doing with that tractor?'

Ben raised a finger. 'Ah, the tractor ... Well, as you know, it's a useful item of agricultural machinery. I was going to use it to reap lucern.' He put his hand on his heart earnestly. 'I swear to God I wasn't taking it to the Burraville Annual Tractor Race.'

She was not smiling now. 'Ben, you know Clyde doesn't like anybody but him using the tractor!'

Ben frowned anxiously. 'Big Clyde?' He peered worriedly into the back of the Land Rover. Then up at the sky. 'Arriving by parachute, is he?'

She didn't smile. 'We don't know how to use it properly, and those scythes are dangerous.'

'I found out how to work it. Even Billy could work it. What *is* dangerous are those sickles we used yesterday – *very* dangerous to one's sense of humour.'

She kept a straight face. 'Okay, but we should take it back right now.'

Ben made big eyes. '"Should"?' Then he leant against the door. 'Helen,' he sighed. 'If, as mistress of this farm, you instruct me to return it to the barn forthwith because you're worried we will damage it through our inexperience, I will do so. I will think you're quite wrong because I know I can work the machine in all its applications because I've read the handbook I found in the toolbox, and I've tried it. I will also think you're crazy to waste time and break your back – and mine – and to frazzle your temper – and mine – by insisting that we cut the wretched lucern by hand like yesterday. Nonetheless, I will respect your decision because it comes from *you* – not from the absent, oblivious Clyde. I will even admire your courage, for it is rather embarrassing to have to give an order which throws cold water on my enthusiasm to help you. *But* ...' He held up a finger and looked at her soulfully. 'If you are giving the order, which is obviously of questionable merit – if not a classic case of insisting on doing things the hard way – just because Big Clyde wouldn't like you using his precious tractor and would rather you sacrificed your back and your temper, I intend to argue with you. Repeating the tedious things I said

89

last night.' He smiled at her brightly, then frowned. 'For God's sake, woman, you're doing a man's job!'

Helen looked at him steadily, her lips pursed. Then she had to suppress a smile. She jerked her head.

'Okay, let's get it over with.'

He flicked his finger to his forehead. 'Yes, *ma'am*.' He started back to the tractor.

'Ben,' she called.

He turned. Helen hesitated; then she said, uncomfortably:

'I'm sorry about last night. For saying . . . for suggesting that you might be trying to . . . sleep with me.'

Ben looked at her serious, embarrassed face, taken aback for a moment. Then, he wanted both to laugh and tell her he loved her.

'That's quite all right, Helen. I'm glad it's out in the open.'

He gave her his impish smile, turned, mounted the tractor. He put it into gear with a flourish, gave her a wave and rumbled off.

Helen sat, staring after him. What did that mean – 'Glad it's out in the open'?

It was almost fun. Ben drove slowly down the field of lucern, clearly enjoying himself, the scythe chomping through the stalks. Helen followed behind with the pitchfork, tossing the stuff up into the trailer. When they came to the end of the first row, Ben manoeuvred the wheels into the next irrigation furrows, put the machine into neutral and swung down out of the saddle. 'Okay, now you drive.' He said it like a kid sharing his toys.

'I'm not tired.' She smiled, like an adult.

'*You* drive,' Ben insisted. 'You've got to learn for next time – and I'd like to develop my shoulders.'

'I'd rather you did it, you've got the hang of it.'

'You're the boss,' he shrugged.

When they approached the end of the second row, Helen was struggling to keep up, her face flushed and her shoulders aching. Ben kept an eye on her, but he did not decrease speed to accommodate her. As he turned the tractor around for the third assault, Helen panted: 'Okay, I'll drive.'

'Good. Pole-vault up here on your pitchfork and I'll show you round the levers.'

It was noon when they finished. The trailer had been piled high several times, and they had exchanged jobs frequently. Helen slumped over the steering wheel, weary but flushed with success. 'Bloody good! Now we've got to spread this stuff out and dry it.'

'Can't we please let the sun dry it?'

She threw back her head and laughed.

After that they went to service the last windmill, miles further out. It was mid-afternoon when they finished. They drove back to Billy's hut.

'What about the horse?' asked Ben.

Helen slowed the Land Rover. 'I think he's all right for another day,' she decided. 'He's got feed and water; I'll fetch him tomorrow.'

'Tomorrow you've got to go to Burraville to find another stockman. Leave the tractor here – we've got to come back in a day or two to turn the lucern over. You drive the Land Rover and I'll ride the horse home.'

'Can you ride?'

'Sure.'

The next trick was catching the horse. He cantered skittishly round the paddock, dodging them, eyeing them as they closed in, then darting away again. After ten minutes of this he surrendered, like a martyr. Ben fetched the gear from the feed-shed and they saddled him. They led him outside the paddock. Helen held the bridle and Ben began to mount, grinning with anticipation.

'It's usual to mount from the left side,' Helen pointed out.

Ben held up a finger. 'Ah. Just testing. Good that you noticed.'

He walked around to the other side, gripped the reins and saddle, lifted his right foot into the stirrup and sprang, swinging his left leg up. Helen guffawed. Ben landed astride the saddle, facing the animal's tail. He contemplated it. Then turned to her. 'Notice my deliberate error?'

She was laughing. 'Ben, I hope you're clowning!'

He frowned down at her imperiously. 'Of course I'm clowning, woman! You don't seriously imagine this is how we ride horses in New York? Is this how John Wayne would ride a horse if he had a choice? Jesse James? Captain Mark Phillips?'

She grinned. 'Ben, I think you'd better get down.'

'Certainly not.' He kicked his feet out of the twisted stirrups, and scrambled up on to his knees in the saddle. The horse jerked its ears back restively.

'Ben!' Helen gasped.

Ben clambered to his feet on the saddle. He stood up straight. He turned around precariously, and faced her, grinning.

'Get down, Ben!'

Ben put his hands on his hips and looked at the horizon. 'Saw something like this in that movie, *Dead Poets Society*. You've no idea how different the world looks from up here.'

'Ben . . .'

'In the movie the teacher makes all those stuffy American kids stand up on their desks during their poetry class, to see how different the world looks when you climb above it. He was right – great stuff. It makes everything down there where you are look less important. More easily surmountable. It gives you a different perspective on life.'

'Will you for God's sake get down!'

Ben surveyed the world, arms akimbo. 'You must try it. It makes you feel that if you can stand up on a horse fearlessly you can get on top of just about anything. It makes you feel different from other people. More gutsy, less serious. And, of course, it's *feelings* that count in this life.'

'Less serious, my foot! This horse can throw you very seriously at any moment!'

He looked down at her witheringly. 'That's the point, woman. There's *risk* – but come up and look at the rewards! We take our little lives down there so seriously.' He sprang down off the horse, landed lightly and took the bridle. 'Try it.'

She grinned. 'Thank God . . . I'll take your word for it.'

'Ah, but you probably won't. That's the pity.' He held up a finger at her. 'It's feelings that count, Helen. Those intangible, unseeable emotions that medical science cannot put under a microscope or treat with medicines. We know so little about feelings and yet they rule our entire lives. We thrash around in ignorance. Yet with a feeling of self-confidence you can do just about anything. With a *lack* of self-confidence, just about nothing.'

'So, I should stand up on a horse to get self-confidence?'

'To see the world better. Absolutely.' He walked around the horse to the left stirrup, put his left foot into it and heaved himself up into the saddle. 'See you at home. *Hey-ho, Silver!*'

She jumped aside and the horse sprang forward. It went bounding off straight into a gallop, heading down the track for home.

Helen stared after them, horrified. Ben was hunched forward, clutching the animal's mane, his legs flapping wildly. Then he raised an arm and hollered: *Ya-hoo!*

'*Your knees,*' she bellowed, '*grip with your knees!*'

But he could not hear. He disappeared, pounding down the track, waving one arm joyfully and clinging for dear life with the other.

The cocky little bugger can't ride at all!

She ran for the Land Rover and scrambled in.

12

The horse galloped all the way, hooves thundering, dust rising, the bush flashing past, and Ben clinging. It pulled up to a clattering halt in the yard, in a lather of sweat. Helen was a few hundred yards behind. Ben slumped in the saddle, panting, his legs trembling, a grin all over his exhausted face.

'Are you *crazy?*' Helen shouted. But she was grinning too, mighty relieved it was over.

'Oh . . .' Ben panted. 'Oh, what a thrill! Always wanted to ride a horse.'

'But you told me you could ride, you stupid bastard!'

'And *didn't* I ride? Oh, that was lovely.'

'But you could have killed yourself!'

'But I didn't, did I? What's his name?'

'Fury. Or you could have broken your back!'

'Never came close to falling off after the first two minutes. Got the hang of it. Fury, huh?' He patted the sweating horse.

'I was behind you all the way, buster, and it didn't look as if you got much of a hang! You've got to grip with your *knees.*'

'Found that out.'

Helen shook her head at him. 'That was silly, Ben. What would you have done with a broken leg?'

'But I did it, didn't I – I rode a horse, flat out.' He kicked his feet out of the stirrups, slithered to the ground, and lurched. 'Or maybe I did break a leg? Boy, that beats motorbikes for fun.' He clung to the bridle shakily.

Helen climbed out of the Land Rover. 'I'd better give you some lessons before you try that again. I'll put him away; he wants his wheaties, that's why he bolted all the way.'

'But I wasn't trying to slow him down. I felt confident going flat out – I enjoyed it. Let me give him his wheaties, I'd like that. Then let's have a swim . . . ?'

He stabled Fury in the barn and gave him more corn than she'd told him to do. 'To beef you up, boy.' Then he hurried back to the cottage for his swimming trunks. He returned to the reservoir carrying a six-pack of cold beer.

Helen hadn't arrived yet. He plunged in, rejoicing in the coolness after his hot, hard day. He swam a few widths underwater, then gushed up at the steps, and reached out for a can of beer. He ripped the top off, swallowed thirstily. He sighed with pleasure, then subsided back into the water, swigging from the can, pleasurably anticipating her arrival.

Anticipating, yes – but tonight Ben Sunninghill was relaxed. Oh, he was looking forward to seeing her semi-naked in her swimsuit, of course – but after last night's little scene he had got a few things in perspective. Now that she had blurted out her suspicion of his motives for talking to her as he had, he had made up his mind to put all that nonsense – that *sex* nonsense – that self-inflicted *tension* – right out of his mind. As God was his witness he had meant every word for her own good, because he *liked* her, because he felt sorry for her. (Well, God also knew about the other thoughts which had crossed his mind, but that wasn't really why he'd said what he had.) Anyway, last night he'd realized the embarrassing light he was putting himself in, he'd seen the error of his ways and he'd decided to cut through all that crap, all that amorous nonsense. That *immature* nonsense – for God's sake, she was a married woman, doing a bloody good job running her difficult life, but she was vulnerable to his worldly-wise ideas and envious of his life-style, wanting all the things she'd missed. And he was her guest, in a position of trust, so he had no right to destabilize her with exhortations to do her thing. And even less right – *much* less right – to entertain romantic notions about her.

All this Ben Sunninghill had figured out last night, and he'd felt much better this morning, and he had had a bloody good day as a consequence. He'd really helped her today, and he now considered himself relaxed about his brief relationship with Helen McKenzie as he wallowed in the reservoir drinking beer, impatiently waiting for her to show up. Oh, true, he was still looking forward to satisfying his male curiosity about her body in a swimsuit, but now that he had got his act together he could relax and enjoy this unexpected Outback adventure with this delightful lady. That's what bumming around the world was all about, the nice people you met in outlandish places . . .

His beer can was almost empty. He looked at his wrist-watch: it was forty-five minutes since he had left her outside the barn. And he sighed.

She wasn't coming. Again...

No, his heart did not sink because he still nursed lascivious ambitions about Helen McKenzie despite his newfound serenity – he was just very disappointed. Annoyed, even, that she had once again backed off from having a harmless swim with him, after saying she would; that she had obviously found something sinister in his suggestion, suspected he had an ulterior motive. He was rejected again, under suspicion. And, by God, he'd had enough of this foolishness, hers as well as his own! He was going to go down to her house as if nothing had happened, as if he found no significance in the fact that she hadn't shown up, and he'd make it abundantly clear by deed and demeanour that he entertained no improper aspirations whatsoever.

He heaved himself up out of the reservoir. He dried off roughly, then pulled on his shirt. He picked up the beers and set off down the path to the main house, combing his hair, whistling tunelessly.

It was dusk. The generator was thumping and all the lights in the house were burning. She was not in the kitchen. He went to the other door. 'Hullo?' he called airily into the passage.

He listened. He heard garbled speech, and realized it was the bush radio. Then he heard Helen say:

'Hi everybody, this is Helen McKenzie. Listen, my Billy's gone goddam walkabout, does anyone know of a good Abbo who's looking for a job? Over.'

There was crackling, then a male voice said:

'Billy? I thought his name was Hymie.'

Ben felt his pulse falter. There seemed to be a shocked pause in the air, then an atmospheric tinkle of nervous laughter. Ben sighed wearily. He tiptoed down the passage and stopped near the living-room door. He heard a female voice say: 'Well, I don't know of anybody, Helen. Over.'

Helen said tersely: 'Very funny, Jack Goodwin. Over.' There was silence for a moment, then Helen said: 'Was that you, Jack? Over!'

No response – it seemed as if the whole Outback waited, listening. Helen snorted: 'Coward!' Then she went on: 'Well, if anybody knows of a jackaroo, please let me know urgently. Over.'

'We'll put the word out, Helen,' another female voice said. 'Over.'

'So sorry to hear about Oscar, Helen dear,' another woman said. 'He was such a beaut doggie. Over.'

'Thank you, Edna,' Helen said. 'But I've got another pup now, also a Boxer, but his mother went to a picnic. He's called Dundee, after Paul Hogan. Over.'

'That's a *beaut* name, Helen! Over.'

'His mother,' Jack Goodwin said, 'did *not* go to a picnic, he's a damn pure Boxer! Over!'

'So it was you, Jack, you coward! Over!'

'I never said a word,' Jack giggled. 'Whoever it was, wasn't me. Over, over, over.'

'What do you want us to bring next Thursday, Helen?' a woman said hastily. 'The usual? Over.'

There was a pause before Helen said: 'Oh, anything, Jenny, please. Okay folks, I'm signing off now, g'night. Over and out.'

Ben retreated to the kitchen. He sat down and opened a can of beer. Oh dear . . . But at least the radio was a possible explanation for her not showing up for the swim.

Helen came in looking tense. 'Hi.' She gave him a mechanical smile.

'Hi.' He opened a can for her. 'The bush radio?'

She snorted softly. 'Yes, the so-called Galah Hour.' She sighed angrily and sat down. 'A service run by the Flying Doctor, so us lonesome Outbackers can yack to each other.' She added grimly: 'The galah is a very noisy Australian parrot. Sounds like a goddam gossip.'

Ben smiled. 'I didn't mean to eavesdrop but I heard the crack about Hymie.'

She shot him an agonized look. 'Oh, I'm sorry. What a crass remark. I hope it didn't hurt you.'

'Hurt *me?* Hell, I'm used to it. It's *you* I'm worried about. The innuendo is that you've got yourself a boyfriend.'

She gave an angry sigh. She ignored the beer, went into the pantry, came back with a wine bottle and filled a glass.

'Oh, that Jack Goodwin's a slimy bastard.'

'A *Jewish* boyfriend, at that.'

She snorted. 'Does that make any difference?'

'I assure you it can make all the world of difference in most WASP countries like Australia. *White Anglo-Saxon Protestant* countries. An ordinary boyfriend might be understandable, even applauded by some as romantic – but a Jewish one?' He added, with a smile: 'A dark, sinister, scheming Jew with Satanic adulterous joy in his eyes?'

She smirked mirthlessly. 'It doesn't mean that.'

97

'You mean not as *bad* as that?' He decided this was the opportunity to make clear his harmless intentions. 'And,' he said, 'what will Clyde feel?'

'I thought I wasn't to worry about Clyde?'

'Not when it comes to things like tractors and swimming. But I never said you mustn't consider Clyde, his feelings. You don't want to hurt his pride. And certainly not lose his trust.'

'Oh, Clyde trusts me ... He knows I wouldn't take a boyfriend. He'll believe me when I explain it, that you were just a friend.' She smiled at him wanly. 'A good friend.'

Well, that was a dampener to any lurking remnants of romantic notions. But he was touched by her sincerity. To make light of it he sighed: 'The story of my life ...'

She was astonished to feel the beginnings of a blush. She went on quickly: 'No, I can handle Clyde. It's me, personally, now it's on the air. It'll be the talk of the Outback.'

'Exactly.' Ben shook his head. 'But you must be like me, Helen – sticks and stones may break my bones but words cannot hurt me. I understand your concern for your reputation in a small community like this, but you must rise above worry. Have an inner strength. A sense of humour.'

'Yeah?' She smiled bleakly.

'Yeah. And so what, I'll be gone as soon as we've found you another stockman.' He looked at her questioningly. 'Unless you feel you want me to go now, in view of the gossip?'

'Oh, Ben, I don't want you to go,' she said anxiously. 'I haven't had such a good time in years.' She smiled earnestly. 'Such a stimulating time.'

His eyes burnt for a moment. Okay, he decided, he'd made his good intentions clear enough. 'Well,' he said, 'tomorrow we'll go to Burraville to look for a jackaroo and the guys in town will see how unlikely a lover I am.' He changed the subject: 'What happens next Thursday, heard that mentioned on the radio?'

'Oh,' she said, 'the Flying Doctor comes here, to our landing strip – it's my turn to be hostess. People come from miles around to have their grievous ailments treated, and the healthy ones come for the ride. It's a bit of a party.'

'The Flying Doctor? Gee, I'd like to see that, your actual Aussie Flying Doctor ...' Then he added: 'And the rest of your neighbourhood would be able to see that Helen McKenzie couldn't possibly have lost her marbles over a five-foot-five-inch New York jeweller.'

Helen grinned wanly. 'Oh, *Ben* . . .'

He slapped his hands together. 'And now go'n put on your swimsuit, the water's great!'

He waited in the kitchen for her to change. And now, dammit, despite what he'd resolved, he was again full of anticipation of seeing her in that swimsuit, seeing her body – Goddammit, he was almost optimistic again about the possibilities inherent in the dark intimacy of the pool. *You're pathetic, Sunninghill – there you go again.* He tried to push it out of his mind.

A few minutes later Helen appeared in the doorway, fully clothed. Her face was solemn. She announced:

'Ben, I don't want to swim.'

Ben was taken aback once more. Had she said it almost as an accusation? Okay, madam . . . For an instant he was annoyed at her tone, embarrassed, and disappointed yet again. But he smiled brightly.

'Sure, Helen.' He was about to say 'Clyde, huh?' but stopped.

She said, with a hint of sullenness: 'Please understand it's got nothing to do with you – nothing to do with what I said last night.' (Ben knew it had everything to do with him and what she'd said last night.) 'It's just . . . that damn crack of Jack Goodwin's.'

Ben sighed inwardly. 'I understand perfectly.' He did, and more. To ease her embarrassment, he added: 'And I agree.'

She looked at him. 'You don't.'

'I do! So, you go'n have your shower and I'll do something about supper. How about a barbecue? It's a heavenly night.'

She was in no mood for a jolly barbecue either, thanks to that crack on the radio. She reappeared in fresh jeans and shirt, without make-up, her hair wet. (Ben wished she wouldn't wear damn jeans all the time.) She sat silently at the folding table, staring into the flames, Dundee in her lap, a can of beer in her hand, while Ben did the cooking, trying to sound cheerful. He glanced at her impatiently. 'To hell with 'em, Helen.'

'Yes . . .' She took a swig of beer. 'Abso-bloody-lutely.'

'If you like I won't come to town with you tomorrow.'

Silence. Then: 'And what'll you do?'

Oh, so she was going to accept that suggestion? That really made him feel dandy. 'I'll go'n cut some more lucern, I enjoy that tractor.' He shrugged. 'You can tell them I've already left, nobody'd be the wiser.'

Helen stared into the fire. '*Or*,' she said to the flames, 'I could tell them to mind their own bloody business.'

Ben raised his eyebrows, unsure what she was thinking. 'Indeed. Though you don't want to lose friends. Just make a joke of it. "Ha-ha-ha, yeah, yeah, yeah . . ." Tell 'em what a funny little fella I was. Joke at my expense, if you like.'

She glanced at him. Was he hurt? She smiled wearily.

'Ben, you're not a "funny little fella".' Then she dropped her head and half-giggled, despite herself. 'Though you should have seen yourself on that horse! I was having hysterics all the way home, even though I was terrified!'

Ben hoped she was cheering up. 'I thought I cut rather a dashing figure!' He went on more soberly: 'I don't mind you making a joke at my expense tomorrow, Helen. It's your reputation you want to save, not mine. Tell 'em about the snake, both of us marooned up on the table, terrified, that's pure comedy – in hindsight.'

She smiled mirthlessly. 'Me in my knickers.' It almost sounded like remorse again.

He glanced at her. 'I'd leave that detail out.'

There was a moment of silence.

'No,' she said grimly, 'you're coming to town with me. I've got nothing to hide.'

Ben didn't know whether or not to be pleased with the way she'd put that. 'That's the attitude.'

She was silent again, glaring at the fire. 'And,' she said wearily, 'you may enjoy it. Tomorrow's Saturday and a lot of farmers come to town to buy gear and have a bit of a booze-up – it'll show you a bit more of the Outback life. For that book of yours.'

He was touched that she was considering him. In an attempt to animate her he said: 'And what about that book of *yours*?'

The attempt failed. She groaned, took a swig of beer, banged the can down, picked up a wineglass and sloshed it full. 'Oh, I'll never write a bloody book.'

He prodded the chops for a moment.

'You need to stand up on that horse, Helen.'

She stared into the fire. 'I haven't got the guts to face failure, Ben.'

'Ah, yes, nobody likes failure. But at least you will have had the guts to try, and that's an achievement. As long as you finish the book, and don't give up halfway. Once you've stood up on the horse, you mustn't forget what you saw.'

She snorted at the fire. 'And if those horizons are unattainable?'

'Then at least you've tried – almost got there. You'll be wiser.'

'And even more frustrated.'

'Creativity is the product of frustration.'

'So try, try again, huh?'

'If your frustration is that strong. If not, accept defeat. That's wisdom. But at least you'll have seen the horizon.'

She snorted again, staring at the fire.

'The trouble is I don't feel *wise* enough to write. Not what I want to write. Oh,' she elaborated impatiently, 'I realize I should write about what I *know*, and I know all about Outback life, motherhood, wifehood, et cetera. But there's so much more about woman's life that I don't know, being stuck out here. What the modern woman is thinking, feeling, demanding.'

Ben turned the chops. 'You could research. There're umpteen magazines that'll give you insight into the modern woman.'

'But who says those writers have got it right? Just because it's printed in *Cosmo* and *Woman's Weekly*.' She shook her head, very dissatisfied. 'I don't trust all that glib stuff about how us ladies are entitled to multiple orgasms. "The Whole Truth About Bosoms". And "Can Love Survive the En-suite Toilet?".' She snorted.

He grinned. 'Sounds good stuff to me.'

'I mean,' Helen sighed impatiently, 'I feel I need to see it all for myself before I start writing, form my own judgements – acquire my *own* wisdom. Otherwise I'll write something half-baked.'

Ben raised his eyebrows, and for a moment old hope stirred. Then he stamped on it. He turned the chops again and said nothing.

'Well?' Helen demanded.

Ben hesitated. 'Good.' He said.

'What does that mean?' she demanded.

He said: 'It means it's probably good that you want to do it. But in the first instance you should write about what you already know, surely? And you know plenty.'

'"Probably" good that I "want" to do it?'

'Because there'll be a price to pay which may be too high. And if you don't do it, it's not good that you want to do it, because you'll be dissatisfied with your lot.'

She studied him in the flickering firelight. 'What are you trying to say to me, Ben?'

He sighed. 'I've said it. And these chops are done.'

'*Oh . . .*' she seethed.

He didn't know what was coming. He dished out the food. She ate in moody silence for a minute. Then she said truculently:

'What were you really saying to me last night in that melodramatic speech about my mother's classmates mouldering in their graves?' She waved her fork impatiently. 'Oh, I know you were saying life is so short. Tempus fugit. But because tempus fugits you want me to—' She changed it: 'I should seize time by the forelock and do my own thing?'

'No,' he said carefully, 'I don't have the right to say you should do anything that may be at odds with your other responsibilities. I just wanted you to realize that you do have the option to do anything you want.' He added: 'And, yes, that tempus fugit.'

'Why do you want me to realize that?'

Was he under suspicion of seduction again?

'Because I thought you didn't really understand it. And because I like you.'

'And because you think I have a lousy life in the Outback.'

Now he felt responsible for making her dissatisfied with her lot. 'Personally,' he said, 'I like it out here. I'm having a great time playing farmers.' He shrugged. 'But that's because I'm a cityboy – the Outback is an exciting change.' He paused and tried to weigh his words. 'But for what my opinion is worth, I think your circumstances are ... unworthy of you.' He made quotation marks with his fingers. 'Your brain. Your ... *soul*. No, not "unworthy" – you just deserve more. But not because you're living in the Outback. I'd think the same if you were in the suburbs of Sydney, alone, the kids flown from the nest, your husband working far away for the foreseeable future, your whole purpose and meaningfulness as a wife and mother taken away from you.' He ended: 'That's all I think.'

'But it's worse because it's the Outback? And wanting to write?'

'You've got plenty of time to write in the Outback, Helen. But my sympathy's got nothing to do with writing.'

She pressed on relentlessly: 'But if you were me you'd do your own thing, even if only for a while – go'n get a job and save up for a trip overseas, maybe, and ... well, *do* something.'

'But I'm not you,' he replied pointedly. 'I'm not a mother and a wife, I don't love the people you love, I can only imagine it. Vividly. So I can't say.'

Helen banged her knife and fork together and sat back. 'I'm not hungry,' she declared angrily.

Ben said nothing. He picked up a chop and sank his teeth into it.

She glared, then complained: 'The other night you spoke with such ... *authority*, such assurance. Now, you're qualifying it. Because you don't want to be responsible for influencing me!'

'Quite right,' he said quietly. 'Because you, and only you, must be your own person and make the decision.'

She pounced. 'So you're saying a decision *should* be made. That's the logical deduction from what you said!' She waved a hand. '"Then do it," you said the other night, with the authority of a man of the world who's seen and done it all!'

'I only said that because you said you wanted to do what I'm doing.'

'I never said *I* wanted to. I said I envied you.'

Ben sighed. 'Doesn't envy imply a want? No, not necessarily, I suppose.' He shrugged. 'For example, a man, a husband, may *want* another woman, yet he *doesn't* want her because he fears the remorse he'll feel for being unfaithful to his wife.'

For an instant she wondered whether he was trying to steer the conversation in that direction again – then decided he wasn't.

'That's a perfect example! In other words, I want to do my own thing, but I *don't* want to do it because that'll upset my family.'

Ben put his knife and fork together. 'Maybe.'

'Maybe? *Maybe?* Oh, we are being cautious tonight, aren't we?' She glared at him. 'I'm trying to figure something out, Ben! And you're not being very helpful! Because you want this' – she thumped her breast – 'delicate bloom to flower by itself! So you don't carry any horticultural responsibility!'

Ben looked across the table into her shining eyes, and at that moment he wanted her more than he had ever wanted the many, many unattainable women in his life. *Horticultural responsibility?* She really should write. He had to work at it to keep his face straight. 'Right,' he murmured.

'Why're you trying so hard to keep a straight face?'

He wanted both to laugh and sob out what it felt like.

'Because I want to treat this moment with the solemnity it deserves.'

'What is this moment that deserves such solemnity, then? The moment that my bird-brain finally arrives at the shatteringly logical conclusion that I *don't* really want to go and do my own thing? I'm like the randy husband in your brilliant example!'

Ben wanted to burst out laughing and take her in his arms and hug her. 'Yes,' he said.

She glared at him, then tossed her head and glowered at the fire. 'Oh,' she said witheringly to the flames, 'what a piss-poor, pusillanimous, gutless reason that is! Because in effect my family has already deserted me. Not wilfully, of course, not cruelly or disrespectfully – they've gone because they had to. But in effect it's the same. I'm left high and dry, like so many women my age. *Use*less. Hardly women anymore, wasting the remnants of their precious lives on ... what?' She twitched her shoulders. 'Memories? Bygone glories of full womanhood? In a sort of restless lethargy, a wastefulness. Because we haven't got the guts to do what we want to?'

Ben watched her. Hope flickered again.

She demanded sullenly: 'Am I right?' He averted his eyes. '*Well?*'

Ben still didn't respond. He stared at the fire, trying to deal with his conscience for opening a can of worms for her. Helen grabbed her wine and quaffed it, banged down the glass and refilled it. 'Well, Mister New Yorker who did have the guts. Mister Snake-killer. Mister Stand-on-Horse. Mister Give-it-a-gallop?'

Ben slowly turned his head towards her, hope simpering. She looked at him angrily, then cried: 'Oh, you make me sick, trying to avoid responsibility for this delicate witless bloom!'

'You're not witless, I assure you.'

Helen looked away in disgust. 'Ah! What crap!' Then she turned on him again. 'Not witless? Then why didn't I swim with you this evening?'

Ben stared back at her, half a smile fixed on his face, his heart suddenly pulsing with anticipation.

Helen glared at him, then whispered witheringly: 'Not because I didn't want to, Ben! Good Lord, I'd been working my guts out, all day I'd been thinking about that plunge into the reservoir. And are we not two adults, capable of swimming together without becoming so maddened with lust that we hurl ourselves headlong into the abyss of sins of the flesh?'

Ben's heart seemed to turn over, and for a confused moment he wondered if she was trying to tell him something. Then she subsided with sullen exasperation. 'Oh, I'm exaggerating, of course. What I mean is, after Jack Goodwin's crass remark I denied myself a well-deserved swim because I was pathetically – *girl*ishly, even – trying somehow to be *good*. For Clyde. For the Outback. God, how pathetic can you get!' Ben started to say something placatory, but Helen seethed bitterly: 'Oh, I so badly want to use my brain. I'd give my eye-teeth to finish my degree at least. Go back to Uni and at least do that much.'

Ben sighed. Yes, yes, of course she should ... But he really wanted to get back to the subject of that reservoir, and sins of the flesh. He trampled that underfoot and tried to be constructive.

'Could Clyde afford that? To send you back to university?'

'Of course not. So I'd have to get a job in the evenings, waitress or something.'

'Would that pay enough?'

She shot him a resentful look. 'I don't know, do I? I haven't been in the job-force for twenty years.' She muttered: 'Get two goddam jobs, if necessary.'

'Night work can be tough at your age,' Ben murmured.

She turned to him. 'Thanks, pal. You're really being a great help. Great encouragement.' She added: 'And I can get a better job during the summer vacations.'

Ben lowered his eyes, then ventured: 'But your children come home for the summer vacations, you wouldn't see them if you were working.'

She looked at him. 'You're throwing an awful lot of cold water tonight, Ben,' she said dangerously.

'I don't mean to, I'm just—'

'You just don't think I should go back to finish my stupid degree! You think I'm too old, too soft, you think it's unrealistic, pathetic even, for a woman of my age to be grubbing for money as a silly student again!'

'I haven't said that.'

'Then what are you saying? What *do* you advise, sir? Should I go back to Uni or not?'

Ben raised his eyebrows and shifted on his chair. 'What about accommodation at university?'

'I'd have to find student digs, like everybody else! A room in a private house maybe, or a flat with some other girls. Maybe I'll be able to afford my own little flat after I've got a job, even if it's just one room. Maybe I could even take Dundee...'

Ben sighed inwardly. She was imagining it all, her heart almost set on it, and he felt responsible. 'But sharing digs with a bunch of young girls again, stumbling over their boyfriends in the mornings, competing for the bathroom—'

'Oh, you're being so encouraging!' She crossed her arms angrily and glared at the fire. 'It would only be for a year if I work hard, and if they grant me all my old credits. Two at the most.' She turned to him. 'So, friend? Am I being pathetic, or is finishing my degree commendable, admirable, *ennobling*, even? What's your *advice*?'

Ben looked into the fire, weighing his response carefully.

'Talk to me!' Helen cried.

Ben murmured:

'"Talk to me tenderly, tell me lies.
I am a woman, and time flies"?'

She glared at him. Then:

'Wow, that's loaded. Did you write that?'

He shook his head at the fire. 'No, it takes a woman to write that. I forget who she was.'

Helen said: 'Damn right I'm a woman and time flies. Yes, talk to me tenderly, Ben – but *don't* tell me lies!'

Ben sighed again. 'It very much depends, Helen.'

'On what?! On how much guts I've got? To live like a teenager again, which is all rather undignified. Grow up, Helen McKenzie, act your age, grow old gracefully?' She snatched up her glass, drained it and splashed it full again. Then she stood up and glared down at him. 'Ben, I was asking for your advice ... your help with something I consider important, and all you do is throw cold water and answer with the voice of the oracle and shirk responsibility for all that heady stuff you've been giving me about being my own woman and doing my own thing! Well, goodnight, pardner, I'm tired of this bullshit – particularly my own!' She turned and walked out of the firelight towards the kitchen door, carrying her glass.

Ben was startled by her dramatic exit. 'Helen?' he called. 'It's certainly not pathetic. Come back and talk it through!'

She did not look around. 'Forget it, I'm over my starry-eyed enthusiasm!' She shot an arm aloft and cried: '*Gaudeamus igitur, juvenes dum sumus!* I'm over that undergraduate Student Prince crap already!' She stopped and turned. 'Just don't *you*' – she jabbed a finger – 'tell *me*' – she jabbed her breast – 'to stand up on a goddam horse!'

13

She fetched him at the cottage early the next morning. Ben was sitting at the kitchen table writing up his notebook when she appeared, shamefaced, in the doorway.

'Sorry about storming off last night. It was childish.'

Ben stood up, smiling. He started to deny it but she interrupted him. 'Don't say it wasn't, don't say anything, let me wallow in remorse in peace. You were only trying to be practical, I know, for my own good. And I was churlish, and I'm sorry. You were right. Now – are you ready to go?'

'Yes. But I want to talk more about this university business some time, Helen, I didn't mean to discourage—'

'Please.' She held up a hand. 'Not now. Let's go.'

He hesitated. 'Are you sure you want me to come to town with you?'

'Yes, dammit. There you go again, confusing me. Yes, to hell with them. I've got nothing to hide.'

He went to the refrigerator, put a few beers in a plastic bag and followed her outside. She was wearing espadrilles, a blue skirt and a pretty blouse, a wide-brimmed straw hat that would have passed muster at a garden party. It was the first time he had seen her in a skirt, let alone dressed-up. She looked very attractive indeed.

'You look great.'

'All a hundred years old.' She got in behind the wheel.

They drove in silence, grinding down the long farm track. They crossed the causeway over the dry riverbed, over the ridge of hills beyond, then swung on to the dirt road towards Burraville. Ben let her have her space for a while, then he said:

'You've got nothing to apologize for, Helen. Friends can unload their minds to each other – that's what friendship's for.'

She shot him a bleak smile. 'Thanks, Ben.'

Silence again. Ben waited a few minutes, then asked:

'Did you reach any conclusions after you went to bed?'

'Yes, I did, but I don't feel like talking about it now.'

'Okay. Fine.'

They drove in uneasy silence. Then Helen said bitterly: 'Yes, I reached a very sagacious, mature conclusion.'

'And that is?'

She glared at the road. 'That I'm my own person, indeed I am. And that person is an Aussie country matron, a dull stick-in-the-mud who'll never get off her fat arse and seize time by the forelock even though she'd be justified in doing so – because she's too frightened. Too much of a coward to go back to Uni, even to look for a job, let alone take off and see the world for a bit. And she *prefers* to be a coward, nice and safe – that's what I concluded. So I'll proceed slowly to my disgusting putrefaction of the grave gracefully – or with as much grace as such a self-confessed coward can muster. Okay?'

Ben succeeded in keeping a straight face. 'Okay?' Helen repeated.

'Okay.' He smiled.

She stared angrily ahead, then turned on him abruptly. 'What d'you mean it's okay? It's pathetic!'

He grinned. 'Not entirely. You had the courage to reach that conclusion.'

'All by my little fat self? Yeah, that's beaut. So I can congratulate myself on that. Now I can relax. What're you grinning about?'

'I was about to opine that you're neither dull nor fat.'

'Not *fat*? Now I can't believe anything you say!' She smiled bleakly. 'Please, I don't want to talk about it now. I don't want to confuse my self-effacement. Let me simmer.'

They drove in silence again, bouncing over the corrugated road, sending up a pall of dust. Finally Ben ferreted into the plastic bag, pulled out a can of cold beer, ripped it open and offered it to her.

'No, too early for me,' she said. 'You go ahead. Oh, okay, just a sip.' She accepted the can and took two swallows. 'Ah, good stuff.'

She had left a red mark on the tin. Ben lifted it to his mouth, and for an instant he could both smell and taste her lipstick. It seemed a delightful moment of intimacy. He put the can down on the seat between them. Helen drove in silence for another half-minute, then turned to him with a small smile.

'Sorry about being cranky, Ben.'

'That's okay, I understand.' He took another swig and changed the subject: 'So, how do we go about finding a stockman in town?'

'Ask around. At the pub, the store, the tea-room, the police station. And there's a shanty-village on the edge of town, though they're mostly deadbeats on the bottle.' She grinned wanly. 'Like me?'

'Where do they get the money for it?' He smiled at the 'like me'.

'Government pays them.'

'Unemployment benefits?'

She changed gears. 'Unem*ployable* benefits. No, that's not quite true – we've got a guilty conscience for pinching their land, as well we should have. Now there're so few of them compared to us, we can afford to compensate them. In fact we go overboard – Government even pays their taxi-fares from the pub in certain circumstances, would you believe?'

'Really?'

She shrugged. 'And why not, I suppose – what's cab-fare to the corrupt politicians who're busy milking every project they can.'

He was glad she was talking again. 'There's a lot of corruption in Australia?'

'Oh boy . . .' Helen took a small sip of beer and resolved to cheer up. 'Not *all* politicians, of course, not all cops, not all trade-unionists. But you should hear Clyde on the subject. So, the Abbo, who's pretty ill-equipped for this big wide world, deserves a small piece of the pie, as it was his land in the first place. Did you know that in Tasmania we actually exterminated them?'

This was news. Australia was the flavour of the month in America, and nobody had told him this. 'No, I didn't know that.'

She took another swig, on her hobby horse now. 'You Yanks did a pretty good job on wiping out the Red Indian, but, boy, we simple Aussies outdid you. In Tasmania we actually had an official Abbo *drive*. Everybody was organized to string out across the island and beat the bushes and drive the poor bastards to the beach at the end. It took seven weeks and they didn't catch one! But they got them in dribs and drabs over the years and stuck 'em all on Flinders Island in the Bass Strait, where they pined away and just died out. And all this was organized by a certain *evangelist* called George Augustus Robinson, who held the glowing title "Protector of the Aborigines".' She snorted. 'When there were only about forty left they let them return to Tasmania and live in a slum called Oyster Cove. The last one died in 1876, a pathetic old woman called Truganini – and they even dug up her skeleton and put it on show in a Tasmanian museum.' She sighed. 'You won't read any of this in our school history books – at least not in my day – but it's true. So why shouldn't the government give them a few handouts?'

The opinions she had expressed of Billy's boozing and walkabouts had not prepared him for this generosity of mind. 'So you're a liberal, Helen?'

'A liberal or a *Liberal?* A Liberal with a capital L, I am not. A Liberal in this country is a misnomer for a Conservative. A Labourite is a capitalistic Socialist, whatever that means. Ask our former Prime Minister Bob Hawke and his trade unions, but I'm not sure he knew either, judging by the mess he made of our economy – ten years ago we had the fourth highest per capita income in the world and now we rank *sixteenth*, do you know that? And our foreign debt has quadrupled, thanks to the government spending as if money grows on trees. And mortgage rates are sky-high.' She sighed. 'Anyway, a liberal, with a small l, I am. I believe in our responsibility to help the underdog.'

'And Clyde – is he liberal too?'

'*Clyde?* Clyde's so conservative he thinks John Major and George Bush are dangerous left-wingers.' Ben grinned and Helen smiled wryly. 'No, he just believes in the Protestant work ethic. A man's entitlement to keep his rewards and not have it thrown away on taxes to keep corrupt trade-unionists in clover, and jobs for the boys. He's very anti-communist, Clyde. He's delighted about the collapse of all these regimes in Eastern Europe, and he's very opposed to the way we "lavished" aid on all those African countries – "corrupt Marxist dictatorships", he calls them.'

'And you, what do you think about all that?'

She pursed her lips. 'I think the rich nations have a moral obligation to help the poor nations. I believe in striving for international social justice. A fair division of the world's goods, the underdog having a fair share of the economic pie. I'm a Christian-Socialist, not a Marxist, Ben.' She added: 'Though I admit I was a bit of a Marxist at Uni.'

'Are you religious?'

She sighed at the road. 'Not really. Well, fairly, I suppose. I believe in God, anyway.'

'And Clyde?'

'Oh, he's a Christian too, in his bloody-minded way, though he hasn't been to a church since we got married.'

'Clyde's bloody-minded?'

She smiled. 'No, he's just . . . no-nonsense. Calls a spade a bloody shovel. But underneath his brusque exterior he's got a heart of gold, has my Clyde.'

My Clyde ... That put a damper on any embers of hope. And the man sounded a trifle daunting, especially when you're shacked up on his station at his wife's invitation while the big man himself is shifting tons of rock underground, doubtless with ease.

'And what about the taxes,' Ben asked, 'to pay for the *lazy* underdog who doesn't want to work?'

'Lazy? How about under-privileged, under-educated? Under-motivated, because he comes from a poor background? Without hope? I think people who pass sweeping judgements about the under-privileged are prejudiced, like Clyde, who says that African politicians just feather their own nests.' She raised a finger and intoned: '"Spare the rod and spoil the child."' She glanced at him. 'You've been to Africa, what do you think?'

Ben said: 'Oh, I'm a liberal too, in a conservative sort of way. But I also believe that sparing the rod spoils the child. Meaning Africa's been spoilt – absolutely ruined in fact – by us lavishing aid on them for thirty years without disciplining them – without supervising where the money's spent. So, most of it's gone into feathering the nests of African politicians, as Clyde says, because that's the African way.'

'*What*'s the African way?' she demanded.

'The king owns everything,' he explained. 'The king may listen to advice but he does not tolerate opposition, anybody who wants his job. The king giveth and the king taketh away. Including foreign aid.'

'*Oh* ...' Helen groaned. She simply did not believe it. Doubtless some black politicians were corrupt but the African mess, if such it was, was the result of exploitation by whites. She didn't feel up to an argument – she'd heard it all before from Clyde – but she couldn't resist saying: 'But *South* Africa is just great, of course?'

'No.' Ben smiled. 'They've got plenty of long-term economic problems too. And, ironically, this is because they also followed the African Way in many respects. Like the black dictators, the white man was also a dictator and used his power to spend most of the nation's wealth on himself – schools, housing, agriculture, amenities, industrial training, et cetera. So, they're going to reap the wages of their sins with a vast under-privileged majority, clamouring for their share. But they're trying hard to make amends.'

Helen was not convinced of the white man's eagerness to make amends, but she was somewhat mollified by his inculpation of them. She took a swig of beer. 'And what d'you think of Nelson Mandela?'

'A man of great courage. Very admirable.'

'I think he's one of the greatest men of our age.'

'Possibly, in terms of integrity,' Ben agreed. 'But as a politician he's still talking the dead Latin of Marxism – nationalization of industries and so forth, which is hardly greatness. It's . . . a pity.' He was going to say 'dumb', but changed it. 'It's the African way, all over again.' He decided to get off this touchy subject – she'd loosened up enough. 'Helen, I know you don't want to talk about it now but I just want to say this: it is commendable that you want to go back to university. And courageous. I'm sorry I appeared to throw cold water last night. I was only trying to point out the down-side.'

Helen stared through the windscreen, aware that he was deliberately changing the subject; but she didn't mind. She smiled wanly, and put her hand on his knee.

'Thanks, Ben. And I'm sorry I was such a pain, flouncing off like that. But I was exhausted, and Jack Goodwin had upset me.' It was the first time she had touched him. For a moment her hand lingered there, then she flicked his knee with her knuckles and declared: 'You're right – and I *can* do it . . .' She sighed. 'Oh, it's so good to talk, isn't it? I really miss not having anybody to discuss things with.' She turned to him. 'I've so enjoyed having you around, Ben.'

'It's great being here.' He went on brightly: 'So, first stop the police station to ask about jackaroos in Shanty-town? Then the pub? Then?'

'Well, I always meet the girls for tea in the Niagara Milk Bar – one of them may know of a jackaroo.'

'For *tea?*'

'Oh yes, my dear, the Aussie male doesn't like sheilas in his watering-holes. Perish the thought, he's not a *sissy*. Anyway, I want you to meet the girls.'

'Show me off, huh?'

She knocked his knee admonishingly. 'You mustn't talk yourself down so, Ben!'

'The pot,' Ben said solemnly, 'calling the kettle black?'

14

Burraville consists of one old hotel, a few shops of general dealer persuasion, the Niagara Milk Bar & Grill, a small Farmers' Co-operative, a first aid clinic attached to the post office (which also had a room for the circuit magistrate's court), a police station, a small school with hostel next to the house of Mavis Johnson, the teacher, a railway siding with some sheds, a filling station which also did a useful line in agricultural machinery, maybe sixty houses scattered down a miscellany of gravelled roads, a brown football field beside a cricket pitch which together served as a horse-race track. And that's about it. For other requirements – such as a chemist – you had to drive about a hundred and fifty miles further south to Charleville. Only about two hundred people lived permanently in Burraville, Helen told Ben. 'Whites, I mean. But there's a floating population of Abbos, who mainly live over there.' She pointed at some huts set amongst blue-gum trees beyond the railway line.

She stopped the Land Rover outside the police station, a small red-brick building, with a house attached. There was a pole with a limp flag, a patchy garden, and a police vehicle parked in the short drive. Ben followed her up the gravel path, through a screen-door into the charge office.

It was empty. Beyond the counter were two desks and an open door heading into the house. 'Hullo?' Helen called.

'Just a mo,' a woman's voice responded.

She emerged shortly afterwards, in a housecoat and curlers. 'Oh hi, Helen,' Anne Keenan said. Her eyes slid to Ben.

'Hi, Anne. Is Vincent here?'

'Just a mo.' Anne looked at Ben, tore her eyes off him and disappeared back into the house. *'Vince, it's Helen McKenzie!'*

There was the sound of a chair scraping, then heavy footsteps, and Vince Keenan appeared in his shirt-sleeves, wiping his mouth with a paper napkin. He was a lean, tough-looking man in his mid-forties, with short greying hair and blue eyes. He glanced at Ben expressionlessly, then turned to Helen. 'Yes, Mrs McKenzie?'

Helen was taken aback by the formality. 'Vince, this is Ben Sunninghill, from New York. He's helping me out on the station for a few days.'

Ben said cheerfully: 'How d'you do?'

'G'day,' Vince said, without looking at him. He waited.

Helen said: 'Vince, I'm wondering if you know of any good Abbo jackaroo who's looking for a job. Billy's gone walkabout.'

Vince appeared unsurprised. 'Clyde know?'

'No. I haven't called him yet.'

Vince looked at her steadily. 'Reckon Clyde should know; he won't want you having just any old riff-raff, all alone out there.'

Ben thought he caught a message. So did Helen.

'That's why I came to see you first, Vince. Reckoned you'd know who's riff-raff and who's not in Shanty-town.'

Vince didn't take his eyes off her. 'Yeah, heard you lost your jackie.'

Helen waited. Then: 'Well, can you help me, Vince?'

He looked at her unwaveringly. 'Reckon I'd like Clyde to know about this. Suppose I recommend some jackie and he rapes you or something? Or steals. If Clyde knew he'd probably come home and handle this problem himself.'

'Clyde's working, Vince – *I've* got to handle it.'

'More's the pity, don't hold with women bein' alone in the Outback.' He paused. 'Okay, I'll keep my eyes open but they're all up their gum-trees over in Shanty-town.'

Helen pursed her lips to control her anger at his tone. 'If you find someone, will you call me during the Galah Hour?'

'Okay. Though this is a police station, not an employment agency.'

Helen was absolutely taken aback. At a loss for a retort. Then she said stiffly: 'Thank you very much, Sergeant Keenan. Good*bye*.'

She made for the door. Ben frowned in surprise, nodded to the policeman and turned. Vince did not even glance at him. Helen reached the screen-door.

'Helen?' Vince said.

She stopped and looked back.

'I shouldn't have said that. I want you to have a good stockman as soon as possible.'

'Thanks, Vince,' she said tersely.

She strode through the door and down the path to the Land Rover.

She climbed in, slammed the door and started the engine. Ben got in beside her.

'Boy!' she exploded. 'Did you get all that?'

Ben sat back. 'Sure did.'

'Oh . . .' she fumed, 'God spare me from small-town gossip!' She let out the clutch and roared off.

'Maybe I shouldn't go into the bar with you?' Ben suggested.

'Bullshit! You're my friend, I'm not ashamed of you. We've got nothing to hide.' Then she slowed and clutched his knee. 'Oh Ben, I'm so sorry, he was so rude! But it's nothing against you personally, he just imagines he's being loyal to Clyde.'

Ben sighed. 'I wouldn't be so sure about the "nothing personal". I'm a Jew.'

'*Bullshit*, Ben,' she wailed. 'It's just that Clyde's so well-liked.'

The Burraville Hotel is an old Victorian building on one of the few corners of Main Road. It has white walls, black doors, a red corrugated-iron roof with twirly eaves supported by ornate iron pillars. A cement verandah runs along the front but the floors inside are creaky old pine. It was half past ten when Helen and Ben arrived. Only one vehicle was parked outside.

'The men are still about their business,' Helen said. She sighed grimly. 'So, we'll have to speak to Jack Bloody Goodwin himself.'

'Let's come back later. Rather than upset yourself with the dreaded Jack.'

'Oh bugger Jack Goodwin! Sticks and stones may break my bones.'

'Okay, that's right . . .' Ben murmured.

They entered the foyer. There was a smell of distant cooking. On the left was a dining-room, and to the right a door led into the bar. Ben looked in; it was empty. There was a dartboard, beer posters on the walls. Helen banged the bell on the shabby reception desk.

A silhouette appeared down the hall from the direction of the yard. Jack Goodwin materialized, big and sweaty and shirt-sleeved.

He beamed. 'Oh, Helen . . .' Then he saw Ben, and gave an unctuous smile. 'And Mister . . . ?'

'Sunninghill, Jack,' Helen said sharply. 'You remember Ben, he bought my puppy from you.'

Jack Goodwin raised a finger. 'Of *course* I remember.' He smiled at Ben again. 'What a bargain he got! Is the dog all right? If it's sick, raffle it quickly, you can always give the winner back his dollar, aha-ha-ha!'

'Dundee's fine.' Helen smiled frostily. 'Jack, as you know I'm looking for a good Abbo jackaroo. Would you mention it around the bar when the boys show up? I'd be so grateful. I'll call back later and see if you've got any information?'

'*Cer*tainly,' Jack said. 'I'll also mention it in the Abbo bar, if there's any sober enough to understand, let alone remember. Not,' he turned to Ben, 'that there's anything racist about *me*.' He grinned and looked back to Helen. 'What time will you be back? Lunch time? Will you be staying for lunch?' He added hopefully: 'Rack of lamb, Saturday Special.'

'I don't think so.'

'Yes,' Ben said brightly, 'sounds good.'

'Oh it *is* good,' Jack said. 'I'll see you get a nice table, Mr Sunningberg.'

'Sunninghill,' Helen said.

'Sunningberg's fine.' Ben grinned.

They walked back to the Land Rover in silence, and got in.

'Oh, that smarmy, publican bugger,' Helen seethed. 'Radio Jack – it'll be all over the Outback that Helen McKenzie was taken to lunch by Ben Sunninghill.'

'Sunning*berg*,' Ben corrected her, grinning.

'Now, *he* was being racist,' Helen seethed. She started the vehicle.

Ben smiled cheerfully. 'Oh, so what? We're all racists to some extent – I'm not too wild about JAPs either. I mean Jewish American Princesses.' He tried to cheer her up: 'You know a JAP's favourite love-making position? Facing Bloomingdale's . . . That's a swish New York department store—'

'I've heard of Bloomingdale's, Ben, even in the Outback – read about it in *Cosmo*, so it must be for real. But that's funny.'

'Well,' Ben said, 'we needn't go for lunch at the hotel if you think it's best.'

'Bull*shit*,' she cried. 'Who's Jack to spoil our day? I haven't been out to lunch for a hundred years . . .'

The Niagara Milk Bar & Grill had large glass windows with lace curtains below a big red Coca-Cola sign. Writing on the panes announced an irresistible line in hamburgers, pies, hot-dogs and other delicacies, supported by vivid illustrations. Last week's newspapers occupied a rack outside the door and immediately inside was a shiny chrome counter with red vinyl pedestal stools. A mirror decorated with palm trees and beaches lined the wall behind the bar. There was a stall of fading fruit, a sweet counter holding everything from chewing-gum to Red Tulip chocolates. Beyond, through a beaded curtain, intended both for decoration and to confuse the flies, was the grill-room. Through this curtain came Stavros Popodopolous, the proprietor, beaming behind his walrus moustache, thrilled to the back teeth with his Saturday. 'Mrs McKenzie, beaut to see you!'

'Hullo, Stavros. This is my friend, Ben Sunninghill.'

'Welcome . . .' Stavros grasped Ben's hand in both of his.

'Helen!' a woman cried from the grill-room. Through the curtain Ben saw half a dozen ladies sitting at two tables pushed together. Beyond, several other tables were occupied.

'The girls,' Helen whispered to Ben. 'Just be yourself.' She swept through the curtain.

Ben followed her, the plastic beads trailing over his ears and shoulders. A silence had fallen and smiles were frozen on the women's faces. Helen said brightly:

'Everybody, this is Ben Sunninghill, who all the excitement's about . . .'

There was a ripple of nervous laughter. Ben stepped forward, blushing, the last of the bead curtain falling from him.

'Ladies . . . In the flesh. And, as you see, there ain't much to be excited about.'

There was another ripple of laughter. Smiles frozen in place. Then Edna Parker gushed: 'G'day, Ben! Welcome to the Outback, sport, sit down!'

There was a matronly giggle of agreement all round, and half a dozen ladies shuffled their chairs to make space. 'Thank you . . .' Ben reached for two chairs from an adjacent table. 'Thank you,' Helen said, as he held hers for her. They sat.

'Well!' Six pairs of smiling eyes were fixed on Ben. 'Well,' Edna gushed again, 'what'll it be? Tea or coffee? Or Stavros does a beaut line in milkshakes, don't you, Stavros?'

'Very beaut.' Stavros beamed, hovering, hands clasped.

'Passionfruit milkshake for me, Stavros,' said Helen. 'To hell with the waistline.'

More ladylike laughter. 'Do you have beer?' Ben asked Stavros.

'Ah, no alcohol.' Stavros clasped his hairy hands together regretfully.

'Yeah, you can get a beer,' Molly Wright said. 'This is a BYO.'

'Yeah,' Edna agreed, 'a Bring-Your-Own, but you've got to have something to eat, this is the grill-room, see – then you're entitled to fetch a beer or whatever you like! Stavros, bring this gentleman a hamburger. Or maybe you'd like to see the menu?'

'A hamburger's fine.' Ben turned to Stavros. 'Rare, please.' He added: 'But not unusual.'

'Sir?' Stavros smiled uncertainly.

Helen began: 'He means—'

'Rare but not unusual!' Edna guffawed. 'That's *beaut*! Get it, girls: *rare* usually *means* unusual!'

Everyone laughed heartily. 'What's an unusual hamburger like?' Jenny Wilcox asked, grinning shyly.

'Well,' Ben said, 'it could have a little grass hut on it, with maybe a little man in a beach-chair beside it—'

There were shrieks of laughter.

When the noise subsided Ben smiled. 'Okay, so I'll go'n buy some beer. Who else would like one?' He looked around at the grinning faces.

'Yeah,' Molly said, 'I'll join you, I've had something to eat.'

'Have you ever! Does a lammington qualify?'

'Maybe a *whole* lammington does – *aha-ha-ha!*'

'Or wine?' Ben asked.

'Yeah,' said Helen, 'I'll have a glass of wine – I'll qualify by sharing your hamburger.'

'Let's *all* share his hamburger,' Edna guffawed.

'Stavros,' Molly Wright called through the curtain, 'another hamburger, but cut it into six to save our waistlines!'

'*Rare*,' Freda Morris shouted to Stavros, 'but not unusual, *aha-ha-ha!*'

Ben stood up, grinning. 'Where's the liquor store?'

'At the back of the hotel,' Helen pointed, 'next to the Paradise Bar for the Abbos.'

As Ben disappeared through the milk bar there was an exchange of giggly glances round the table. 'Well?' Helen smiled. 'Isn't he sweet?'

'He's *darling* . . .' Edna whispered.

'And as you see,' Helen said, 'quite harmless.'

'Oh absolutely,' Molly giggled, 'but so *beaut* . . .'

'I'm not so sure about the harmless,' Edna snickered. 'I think he's kind of cute!'

'Oh Edna!'

'To tell the truth,' Freda giggled, 'I think he's kind of sexy! Even if he is very Jewish.'

'Oh *Freda!*'

'In a revolting sort of a way, of course – but, *yeah*! And *funny* . . .'

Helen dropped her head and giggled. Then she looked up, her eyes wet. 'Can't you see it – this hamburger arriving with the little grass hut in the middle and the little man in the beach-chair?'

They roared with laughter. *Stavros twinkle-toeing in with it like a ballet dancer . . .*'

Gales of laughter.

'With his violin . . .'

Screams of laughter. 'Oh . . .' Helen dabbed at her laughing eyes. 'Oh, he's very amusing . . .' Then she struck a dramatic pose and recited:

> 'The moon shines up there like a cuspidor,
> Doris, oh Doris, what are we waiting for . . . ?'

She looked at them, then guffawed: 'He wrote that to a girl he was in love with!'

More screams of laughter. *'Like a cuspidor!'* Molly screamed.

The laughter died down and Helen continued: 'And do you know what a JAP's – that's a Jewish American Princess – d'you know what a JAP's favourite love-making position is? *Facing Bloomingdale's . . .*'

Shrieks of laughter. Then: 'What's Bloomingdale's?' Jenny asked.

'Oh Jenny!'

When the laughter died down Molly giggled. 'But *how* exactly did you come to *meet* him?'

Helen grinned at them, her eyes wet.

'Well, you see, there I was, all alone, scrubbing the *floor*, when this snake comes *bursting* into my kitchen . . .' She burst into giggles again.

Freda slapped the table. 'Tell me *more*! Sounds like something out of Genesis, Chapter *One*!'

Howls of laughter.

'And there I was, on the kitchen table . . .' Helen dropped her face into her hands and guffawed: 'in my *knickers* . . .'

'Oooooh . . .'

Ben drove the Land Rover down to the hotel, feeling good. He'd enjoyed meeting those women – he liked Aussies, and how nice to live in a country with so much space yet where everybody knew everybody, not like New York. He turned around the back of the hotel, into the yard.

He tried the door with the sign 'Bottle Store', but it was locked, so he went to the entrance of the Paradise Bar next door. It was bleak and dirty. A dozen Aborigines lounged around. An unshaven, elderly white man in a singlet was behind the counter.

'Excuse me,' Ben inquired, 'are you in charge of the bottle store?'

The man said: 'He'll be back in five minutes.'

'Oh. Can you open up and serve me?'

'Sorry.'

'Oh. Okay. Well...' Ben walked up to the counter. He had seen a few Aborigines in his time in Australia but he was fascinated yet again by their brows, their heavy skull-structure. The place smelt of sweat. The Aborigines eyed him blankly. 'I'll have a beer while I wait, please.'

'There's a proper bar round the front. This is for Abbos.'

'Oh,' Ben said. Then he asked: 'Is it actually illegal for me to have a drink in here?'

The man eyed him. 'Reckon it ain't. If you can stand the smell. I'm used to it.'

'Then I'll have a Four-X, please.'

The barman didn't move. 'It lowers the tone,' he said.

Ben wondered if he'd heard right. 'Lowers the *tone*?'

'Of the white man. To drink in here.'

Ben smiled. 'I see. Well, I'll take the chance.'

The barman said flatly: 'Round the corner, on Main Road.'

Ben leant on the counter. 'Look, is this a licensed establishment?'

The man looked at him sullenly. 'Reckon it is.'

'Licensed to sell malts and spiritous liquors to the public? Well, I'm a member of the public.' He smiled.

The barman gave him a look, then reached under the counter, produced a can of beer. He slid it across to him.

'Thank you.' Ben handed over the cash. He was going to ask for a glass, then thought better of it – when in Rome. He tore the top off the can, took a swallow. Then he said conversationally: 'You see, it's interesting for me to have a drink in here. I come from America—'

'I know you come from America.'

'Oh. Anyway, we don't see Australian Aborigines there.'

'See plenty of drunken coons, though, don'cha?'

Ben wondered if the Abbos understood. He shuffled. 'Well...'

'But they ain't so primitive? So pre-historic?'

Ben wished he hadn't started this conversation. He took a swig of beer and didn't answer.

The barman scrutinized him. 'You the jeweller bloke from New York?'

Ben smiled. 'Maybe I am. How many jewellers you got in Bur-raville?'

'None'

'Then I'm your man.' Ben grinned.

'Staying at Clyde McKenzie's?' It wasn't really a question.

Ben sighed. 'Yes. Well, I'm passing through.'

'Just passing through Burraville, the asshole of the world?'

Ben had heard that joke, but he wasn't sure whether the barman meant it that way. 'I think Burraville's nice. He added in the vernacular. 'Beaut.'

The barman said: 'That what's holdin' you up?'

Ben took a deep breath. Now he was in no doubt.

'No, I'll be on my way soon.'

'Hope Helen McKenzie finds a jackaroo soon.'

Ben looked at him. And smiled. What the hell. He lifted his can, drained it and put it down firmly. 'See you.'

'G'bye,' the barman said.

Ben walked outside grimly

The bottle store was open now. He bought a case of beer, a case of assorted wine and two bottles of cognac.

He headed back for the friendly Niagara Milk Bar & Grill. He left half the booze in the Land Rover to take to Whoop-Whoop, took the rest inside and joined the ladies.

15

History is divided on what happened thereafter. Eye-witnesses differed, hearsay further confounded the facts, by radio-waves and direct word of mouth.

What is clear is that Sonnenberg, or Sunningberg, or Hummingbird, or Cohen, returns to the Niagara Milk Bar & Grill, laden with booze, to squeals of wonder and applause from the enthralled women. Women, that is to say, or it came to be said, in his personal thrall, squealing not at the sight of so much strong drink – for Aussie women can handle that, having seen plenty of same – but because he was supposed to be so bloody funny. Meaning *amusing*, not just funny-*looking*. Even Stavros Popodopolous, that shining example of a New Australian, who tried so hard despite his unfortunate origins to adapt – even Stavros' eyes boggled more than usual at the sight of so much booze in a BYO for only two hamburgers; because lammingtons, being a cake, don't count, strictly speaking. (Sergeant Vince Keenan confirms this interpretation of the law.) All this is testified to by Burt Wilcox, Steve Browning and Kevin Sinclair who were talking business in the far corner when Sunningbloom makes his dramatic entrance. Stavros protests at this cornucopia of alcohol and begs the assembly to order at least *one* hotdog each, to keep him within his BYO licence. Not content with this suggestion, Sunningstein, *grandiloquently* – Mavis Johnson, the schoolmistress's word – grandiloquently orders an *unusual* hamburger for everyone, 'on him'. (And as you know Stavros' hotdogs are quite enough, what with a bun and side salad.) (Especially after lammingtons.) The enthralled women protest at this expense, but Sunningberg insists and, of course, Stavros is delighted, and so the *orgy* takes off . . . Well all right, not exactly an orgy, but they were all laughing their heads off at Hummingberg's jokes about the Japs' favourite love-making positions and other dirty stories, Burt Wilcox says – and they were all getting so pissed that Burt finally comes over and insists on taking Jenny away to the hotel to sober up – whereupon Edna calls him a silly old *fart*! Nothing so terrible in that because Burt *is* a silly old fart, but the point is Edna and Mike Parker were supposed to be having lunch at the hotel with Jenny and Burt Wilcox, and now Burt storms off dragging Jenny down to the hotel, finds Mike, and tells him that Edna's getting pissed up at the milk bar, and Burt says anyway he refuses to have lunch with Edna because she called him a silly old fart in public! So Mike goes storming up to the Niagara to give Edna a piece of his mind, and finds *Stavros* pissed too, and the ladies all huddled around Sunningstein screaming with laughter, and now Edna gives *Mike* a piece of *her* mind and calls *him* a silly old fart too, and she refuses to have lunch at 'that crumby hotel' – and *Helen* then says to tell Radio-Jack to stick *her* unusual lamb chops up his jumper, and then *Stavros* – who should have been keeping order – comes veritably – (Mavis Johnson says) – veritably *waltzing* out the kitchen clutching a toy violin and gleefully offers Mike a hamburger with a figurine of a *naked* woman on it! And the girls *kill* themselves laughing, and Mike goes storming off! Then Sunningbloom makes matters worse by running down the street after Mike, to apologize, he says, and Mike tells him to you-know-what off! And Sunningbloom decides to make himself scarce, or maybe he just wants a joy-ride, because he takes Helen's Land Rover, as if he owns it, and drives to *Shanty*-town! Helen says he went to look for a stockman but he was drinking in the Abbo bar earlier, eyeing the Marys, the barman says – he didn't want to drink in the other bar, oh no. Anyway, while he's away the *orgy* carries on in the Niagara, and now they're drinking *brandy* milkshakes! Anyway, when that bottle's finished and the boy-friend still hasn't returned, they all decide to go down to the hotel to look for him – and they're going to 'take over' the men's bar, can you imagine! They go marching down the street singing 'She'll Be Coming Round the Mountain' and 'California Here We Come', both at the same time, and they *burst* into the bar and announce they're taking it over! *Well!* Actually, some of the blokes thought it was a bit of a joke, but most of them were pissed off, and then Radio-Jack comes in *highly* pissed off about the commotion and about his wasted lamb chops – *and* they'd reserved a table – and what's this rubbish about his lamb chops being unusual? Jack's lamb chops are *excellent*! – and Edna calls *him* a silly old fart! Jack *orders* them out of the pub, and then Edna *defiantly* starts doing a Knees-up Mother Brown, showing her knickers, and then Helen joins in, and then *all* the girls do, all showing their knickers! – and Jack hollers to them to get out, and then Helen shouts she can *lick* any man in the house, and Fred Morecomb shouts *'Yes, please'* – and at that moment Mike Parker bursts into the bar from the dining-room to drag Edna away, and he shouts at Helen: *'I thought that was reserved for Cohen!'* – and then Helen whirls around in mid-knees-up, and she *slaps* Mike in the face! And at that very moment the boyfriend, who's caused all the trouble, walks into the bar . . .

There was a shocked silence. Mike Parker clutched his stinging face, eyes wide. Helen said furiously:

'Say that again, Mike Parker . . .'

More silence. Then Parker began to open his mouth, and Edna hissed at him: 'Say it, and the next one's in the balls, you big oaf!'

Mike Parker took a deep, angry breath. Then he turned to Ben slowly, narrowed his eyes and said venomously:

'I'll say this loud and clear . . . Clyde McKenzie's my friend, and I don't like anybody screwing around getting his wife pissed – *and* my wife – let alone some hippy Cohen on a motorbike—'

There was a flashing crack of Helen's hand again, and Mike Parker staggered, shocked. Then Edna was kicking his shins, and then Radio-Jack was rushing from behind the bar – and Ben lunged at Helen and grabbed her arm as she was about to hit Parker again.

He yanked her backwards; there was another panting, stunned silence. Then Helen hissed:

'His name is Sunninghill, Mike Parker, and he's not—'

'Shuttup!' Ben shouted.

Silence again. Everybody staring. Then Ben firmly led Helen backwards towards the door. She was flushed and glaring.

Ben smiled, and raised his free hand.

'Peace, ladies and gentlemen,' he said. 'Go in peace . . . And you'll be pleased to hear I think I've found Helen a stockman.'

16

It was an unrepentant Helen who let herself be driven back to Whoop-Whoop. 'I'm not drunk!' 'Fine, but I'll drive anyway.' The new jacka-roo, whose name was Green, plus his wife and child were sitting on the open back of the Land Rover with their belongings. Helen took an angry swig of wine from a bottle.

'You told me I should be my own person!'

'But not like that,' Ben said grimly.

'Well, I'm *glad* I slapped him. No regrets!' She glared through the windscreen. 'And I didn't need you to tell me to be my own person before hitting him!'

Ben sighed, and decided not to comment.

'I hit him because I've *always* been my own person! And because he goddamn deserved it, the full-time *shit*. "I thought *licking* was reserved for Cohen" ... Oh, of all the *school*-boy, *locker*-room repartee!'

'But hitting him reduced you to his level.'

'Not in Australia it doesn't, mate.'

'Maybe, but in *real* terms.'

'You don't think Australia is *real*? I tell you, what you saw in Burraville are *my* real terms, what *I* live with.'

'But in terms of being a dignified adult. In sophisticated ... Chris-tian terms. You're worth more than that.'

'In *Christian* terms? Are you a closet goy?' Then she giggled and put her hand on his knee. *'Oh, I'm sorry, Ben ...'*

Ben smiled. 'That's actually funny.'

Her laugh faded, and she sighed angrily. 'Oh, I must apologize for what Mike Parker said. Believe me, anti-Semitism is not typical of Australians. Maybe years ago when I was a girl, but not today, Ben, honest.'

'Sure,' Ben said. 'You needn't apologize.'

'But it must upset you when people call you a . . . Cohen?'

'It *hurts* me, because it implies that people don't welcome me, but it doesn't up*set* me,' he said. He added: 'Because I'm a mature, dignified adult.'

'Almost a Christian even?' she asked with a grin.

'Almost,' he agreed.

She sighed. 'Oh Ben, you were so funny today.'

'Thanks.'

'I mean so *amusing, witty*. The girls absolutely *adored* you, you had them eating out of your hand!'

'It was a fun lunch, wasn't it?'

'It was a riot! And Stavros getting pissed – and his unna-*usual* hamburgers!' She slumped back giggling. 'You must have told him how to make them unusual?'

'Yeah, I snuck into the kitchen. Had a bit of difficulty explaining the joke because Stavros don't spikada English too good but once he caught on he thought it was a riot too.'

Helen was convulsed. *'And the little grass hut?'*

'I made it out of paper while Stavros went reeling upstairs to raid his daughter's toybox. I don't know where he got the figurine of the naked girl from.'

Helen dabbed her eyes. 'Oh, Ben, you were such a success. Such a breath of fresh air.' She turned to him. 'I was very proud of you. I mean, that you were my friend, that *I'd* found you.'

'Thanks.' Ben smiled.

'And,' she said 'the girls thought you were *sexy*.'

Ben sighed elaborately. 'But I thought they were quite sane.'

'They did, really! Even Jenny – the shy one, remember?'

'Because I made them laugh,' Ben sighed.

'Yes – because you made them *laugh*. An entertaining person gets to be kind of sexy, you know – it's *personality* that counts with women!'

'Careful, don't get my hopes up.'

'Ben, be *serious* – the girls all thought you were terrific.'

'But not their menfolk.'

Helen sat back, angry again. 'Oh, that Burt Wilcox is a little prick. And Mike Parker is a full-time shit to say what he did! I had no idea he was anti-Semitic. And he's probably not really.'

'They're probably both good, solid Aussies, they just didn't like Clyde McKenzie's wife's lover around.'

'Bullshit! They know I wouldn't take a lover.'

'Not if I know human nature.'

Helen sat forward earnestly. 'Ben, they just didn't like some . . . stranger charming their wives.'

'And getting them pissed.'

'We got ourselves pissed. Because we were enjoying ourselves with you. Without *them*. *That's* what they didn't like.'

'Some little *Jewish* stranger,' Ben said. 'On a motorbike.'

Helen sat back. 'Oh, will you please, please, please stop flagellating yourself with your precious Jewishness? I told you we're not anti-Semitic.'

Ben glanced at her. 'Maybe you're right. Anyway, we've got a stockman. So I can leave tomorrow, and it'll all blow over.'

Helen blinked. She stared through the windscreen at the road. Then she said: 'Ben?'

He waited. Helen took a deep breath and turned to him:

'Ben, *please* don't leave tomorrow. Unless you want to. But *I* want you to stay for a while . . .' She looked at him earnestly, then waved a hand at the back. 'And not just to help me settle in the new Abbo. I mean, I'd *like* you to stay for a bit and . . . maybe write your book. Or just enjoy the Outback, learn about it. Learn to ride the horse properly. And – well, maybe, I'll start writing my book too!'

Ben turned and looked at her. And he felt his heart quicken.

'But what would Clyde think about that? And Burraville?'

'Oh bugger Burraville! Clyde will understand when I explain it to him, he's a beaut bloke . . .'

3

17

But Helen McKenzie did not have a chance to explain it to Clyde – to 'seek his permission', as Ben put it. She tried to call him on the radio that evening when they got back to Whoop-Whoop, against Ben's advice – 'Helen, you're a bit drunk and you're still inflamed with the passions of Burraville' – but there was no response from the mine office because it was Saturday night. She tried again the following day, feeling rather fragile and a lot less sure of herself; again there was no response, which wasn't surprising because it was Sunday, though the mine often worked shifts on weekends. Ben, to give her privacy, and a chance to reconsider the whole thing, spent the day with the new jackaroo, showing him the job; when he went over to the main house at suppertime he found a note saying she'd gone to bed early, and any optimism rekindled by her invitation to stay evaporated. He spent most of Monday out with the jackaroo again; Helen finally got through to the mine on the radio and asked the secretary to tell Clyde to call her urgently when he came off shift. Clyde did not call back, but that wasn't surprising either because it could take a day or more for a message to reach him. Nor did he call on Tuesday. What was surprising was that Clyde McKenzie showed up, in person, late that afternoon, to find out what his wife was up to.

He had driven all the way from Broken Hill in two days, departing on Sunday, after receiving a telephone call from Burraville. He was dog-tired when he pulled into town, having slept only a few hours beside the road. He had a coffee with Radio-Jack whilst he got the story. It was five o'clock when he arrived at the station, with a face like thunder.

Helen was alone in the house, about to do the laundry, again in her underwear because she had thrown her jeans and blouse into the washing-machine, along with Ben's gear; she did not hear the car arrive because of the generator. Clyde pulled open the kitchen's screen-door, and Helen gasped and turned, her hands covering her breasts. Clyde filled the doorway in silhouette, staring at his nigh-naked wife.

'What's this?' he said quietly.

'Clyde!' Helen cried, astonished. She stared, then her face broke into a smile, and she rushed across the kitchen and flung her arms around him. *'Oh darling . . .'*

Clyde stood like a rock. 'Where is he?' he said softly.

Helen leant back, looking up, still holding him. 'Who?' She grinned nervously. 'Ben?'

'How many guys you got here? Yeah, Ben Sunningberg.'

'Sunning*hill*,' Helen laughed shakily. 'Oh, darling, he's in his cottage, I think, writing—'

'*His* cottage?'

She still held him, smiling up at him. 'The foreman's cottage, Clyde. That's where he's staying. He's writing. And *I'm* writing a book, too, now! Oh Clyde, how lovely to *see* you – what's the matter?'

Clyde looked down at her.

'You know very well what's the matter, girlie.' He did not move. 'What's all this about you having this hippy on the station?' He jerked his head down at her. 'And you in your underwear.'

She blinked, then cried: 'Darling, I'm doing the laundry!' She turned and pointed at the shuddering machine. 'My jeans are in it!'

'I thought it was broken?'

'Yes, but Ben fixed it. And I've torn your jeans off you before to throw into the machine!'

'And this Ben's jeans – are they in there too?'

Helen stared up at him, then said: 'Well, yes, they are, Clyde. So what?'

'And Ben's swinging around the gum-trees writing his book in his underpants?'

Helen stared up at him, astonished at all this – then she had to suppress a smile at the image.

'No, I don't believe so, Clyde. I believe he's at his cottage writing in a fairly conventional manner.'

'So you're writing a book, too, are you?'

Helen closed her eyes in embarrassment. 'Well,' she said, 'I'm *trying* . . .'

'And this Ben's helping you?'

'Oh Clyde! I only started it yesterday. But yes, he is helping me. But he's not sitting beside me telling me what to write.'

Clyde looked down at her grimly. He said. 'And what's this about the drunken orgy at the Niagara Milk Bar, girlie?'

Helen stared at him, her arms still around his waist.

'Oh boy . . .' she whispered.

'An' you flashing your knickers all over the hotel?'

Helen closed her eyes. 'Oh boy . . .' She dropped her arms and turned away.

Clyde remained still. 'And *him*,' he jerked his head in the direction of the cottage, 'gettin' you girls all pissed an' drunk an' disorderly over his dirty jokes about Chinese love-making positions?' Helen's brow crinkled incredulously. Clyde went on: 'And him ordering Stavros to make pornographic hamburgers with copulating dolls on them—'

'Oh *boy*!' Helen dropped her hands to her knees and laughed at her bare feet.

'*And*,' Clyde said, 'you hitting Mike Parker in the bar – unprovoked.'

Helen raised her head. 'Un*provoked*?' she cried. Then she straightened and took an exasperated breath. She pointed angrily in the direction of Burraville. 'That bastard – your friend Mike – was not only a rude *shit* to me but he suggested that I'm . . .' She groped for words, and her eyes moistened, and filled; then she blundered to him and grabbed his hands. 'Oh *Clyde* . . . *Darling* – please sit down and let me explain all this bullshit.'

Clyde stood in the doorway like a colossus. 'And what's this about him going over your head – and mine – and hiring and firing jackaroos as if he owns the joint?'

Helen stared. 'Oh *Clyde*!' She jerked his hands and appealed up at him, almost laughing: '*Please* sit down and have a beer and listen to the *truth* . . .'

Clyde McKenzie was a solidly built man, with a balding head and a rather truculent face. He did not smile easily, and he spoke quietly and soberly – and he was nobody's fool. He sat there stolidly, his eyes never leaving his wife's, scarcely speaking except to clarify small points. When she had finished, her eyes full of tears, of indignation and anguish, he asked his questions. He asked them almost expressionlessly and almost as skilfully as a lawyer, having had two days to think them through. An hour later he was satisfied that she was telling the truth. But he was far, far from happy.

'You shouldn't have hit him, girl.'

'All right,' Helen sighed. 'I *know* . . . All right.'

'I won't tell you to apologize to him. Mike's a good bloke, but he was an asshole to say that. I also resent what he said, but he was provoked by Edna getting pissed and missing lunch and all. But you shouldn't have hit him. You're a lady.'

'I *know*...'

'But so were *you* an asshole, getting pissed and taking over the men's bar and saying you could lick any man in the house.'

'Yes, yes,' Helen groaned.

'And showing your knickers doing that stupid dance. You're my *wife*, girl.'

'Oh *Clyde*...'

'And I don't like the impression that this Ben's running the station, like he's ... me. This is *my* territory, girl.'

'Oh Clyde, he's *not*,' she protested. 'He's a little New York jeweller who knows *nothing* about farming. He was only trying to help. And he *was* very helpful when Billy went walkabout—'

'I told you nobody but me drives that tractor.'

'But we couldn't have cut all that lucern otherwise.'

Clyde took a deep breath. 'Okay, I suppose you had to.'

'And he wasn't "taking over" when he went to Shanty-town and found the new jackaroo! He knew I wouldn't get around to it, in the circumstances. And he didn't *hire* him, he brought him back to town for my approval.'

Clyde sighed. Then asked flatly: 'And how's he turning out? The new jackie, I mean.'

'Okay. Early days yet; a bit inexperienced but okay, Ben says.'

'*Ben* says? Haven't *you* been up to check on him?'

Helen blinked. 'He only started two days ago, Clyde. Ben showed him the ropes and checked every day, I believe.'

'You believe?'

'I'm sure he did, Clyde! I haven't seen Ben today yet.' (She was glad she could honestly say that.) 'But I heard him return on his motorbike about an hour ago.'

'Shouldn't you have taken time off from writing your book and gone to check on the Abbo yourself, girlie?'

Helen looked at him. 'Yes, maybe you're right, Clyde. But I was trying to call you. To ... tell you about Ben staying here.' She was going to say 'to ask your permission', but changed her mind.

'And how come this Ben knows so much about the station? Did he go up with you to check on Billy?'

Helen frowned. 'Yes, Clyde, he did. But Billy had gone walkabout.'

'Why did he go with you?'

'*Why?* Because I needed him. Billy was on the bottle! And Ben was interested.'

'In you?'

She cried: 'Interested in helping! In the Outback! And, yes, he is interested in me, Clyde – but *not* in the way you and Mike Parker seem to think!' She glared at him. 'He's a very nice, harmless guy.'

'I don't think what Mike Parker thinks, girl. I think I know you better. I'm asking what this *Ben* thinks.'

Helen closed her eyes. 'He's interested in me as a *friend*, darling.'

Clyde nodded slowly, nod, nod. 'Not because you're a good-looking woman alone?'

'No! In me as a person. He's a *good* friend, the only one I've got out here.'

'You knew what it was going to be like when you married me.'

She was taken aback by this. 'Of course I did. And I'm not complaining now. But you've had to go away – that wasn't on the cards when I married you. And so I'm very glad to have such nice company for a few days. Even if you were *here*, I'd be glad. And so would you be, once you'd met him. Look, I wish you'd go over to the cottage and see for yourself what a funny little fella he is, you'd see how nothing like *that*'s going on—'

'Yeah, I heard he's a little runt.'

Helen blinked. But didn't argue.

'But even little runts like to screw,' Clyde continued. Then he sighed. 'Oh, girl, I'm not saying anything's going on. But what's in *his* mind, and what's *he* going to do about it?'

'Oh, Clyde, *nothing* but friendship – please go'n meet him and see.'

'Of course I'm going to meet him, girl. You bet I am. And how's he helping with this book?'

She slumped, and sighed. 'Clyde, I told you, I only began it yesterday. He came over yesterday evening and read what I've done. That's all.'

Clyde nodded again. 'Does he eat here?'

'Usually,' she admitted wearily. 'But only the evening meal. And he's paying his way, he's given me money to cover his share of tucker and booze.'

'And what does he say about this book of yours?'

She said wearily: 'Well, I've only done two chapters.'

'And?'

She winced. 'And he thinks it . . . shows promise.' She smiled wanly. 'Talent.'

'"Promise"? And what does he know about writing books?'

She sighed. 'Maybe nothing.'

'Maybe? He's a jeweller, ain't he?'

'Yes. But he's well-read, and he's got a degree in literature. He's writing a journal about his experiences. And sometimes he writes poetry.'

'Poetry? Yeah. And what poems does he write?'

'Oh Clyde, does it matter? I've only read one. It was a lament for—'

'What's a bleedin' lament?'

'A sort of . . . cry. It was a long poem about the ecological mess the world's in. About the wildlife and so on being exterminated by Man. He's a very *feeling* sort of person, Clyde, sensitive . . .'

Clyde wanted to say that the man might soon have a very sensitive arse. 'An' what's this poem he wrote about you? The one about the spittoon?'

Helen frowned at him, quite nonplussed. 'Come again?'

Clyde said: '"The moon shines up there like a spittoon".'

Helen stared at her husband for a second; then her hands shot to her mouth and she burst into shrieks of laughter.

'Like a *cuspidor*!' she hooted. ' "*Doris, Oh Doris, what are we waiting for?*" ' She dropped her hands and grinned at him, eyes moist. 'Oh Clyde, it's just a joke-poem he wrote about a New York dancing girl called *Doris*.'

Clyde said: 'I heard it as *"Helen, oh Helen, I'm such a baboon".*'

Her hands shot back to her face and she wanted to shriek with laughter again. 'Oh Clyde – that's just malicious gossip . . .' She grinned at him, eyes wet. 'Darling, can't you see what happens? He tells it to the girls at lunch and it gets back to the bar, and one of those oafs knows what a cuspidor is!' She giggled. 'Spit*toon* . . . ?'

'A cuspidor's a spittoon?' Clyde said.

'*Yes.*'

'Well, not very nice, is it?'

'No! It's not meant to be! That's the joke!'

Clyde looked at her, a smile twitching his lips for an instant. 'I mean it's not very nice having poetry like that about your wife spreading round town, is it? Even if he did write it about some sheila called Doris.'

Helen just managed to keep a straight face. 'No. It's not. You're damn right.'

Clyde took a deep breath. 'And how long's he think he's staying, this' – he jerked his head – 'Ben Sunning ... what?'

'Sunninghill.'

'Never heard of it. How long's he think he's staying?'

'He'll leave today, gracefully, if you tell him to, or make him feel unwelcome.'

'Welcome? Damn right he's not welcome. But *you* don't want him to leave, do you?'

Helen looked her husband in the eye.

'No, Clyde, I don't. I'm enjoying his company ... having him here. But I don't want to upset you, so it's your decision.'

'Damn right it's my decision.' He studied her. 'And what's your book about, girl?'

She hesitated – this was going to be difficult. 'It's about ... a woman.'

'You?'

She sighed. 'Yes, I guess so. Partly.'

'What about you?'

'Oh *Clyde* ...' she appealed.

He demanded quietly: 'What's wrong with you? What's wrong with your life that you want to write about it?'

'Oh Clyde, nothing's wrong—'

'Has he' – Clyde jerked his head at the cottage again – 'been stuffing your head about what a piss-poor life you have?'

No ...' she groaned.

Clyde was unconvinced. 'I hear he's a trouble-maker.'

'What *rubbish*!'

'Mavis Johnson says he's a Rasputin character.'

Helen was amazed. Rasputin? 'Mavis Johnson's never clapped eyes on Ben,' she protested. 'That school-marm! Only that stupid bitch would know about Rasputin in Burraville! D'you know who Rasputin was?'

'Yeah, a communist trouble-maker, Jack says. Even the Russkies had enough of him.'

Helen stared at him, then she dropped her head and giggled. 'Oh Clyde, I love you ...' Then she looked up at him again with wet eyes. 'Darling, Rasputin was years before communism took over in Russia. He was an evil character in the Tsar's court who gained tremendous hypnotic influence—'

'That's him,' Clyde said. 'That sounds like your Mr Sunningberg.' But he had to suppress a smile.

Helen cried: 'Ben is the *kindest, gentlest*—'

'Sure,' Clyde cut her short. 'Can I read it? Your book?'

Helen was surprised. 'Of course. But why?'

'To find out if it's got "promise".'

'Oh boy . . .' Helen squirmed inside again. 'Sure. It's not very good. And only two chapters.'

'And "talent". Maybe I'm not as good at books as Mr Wonderberg but, like a baboon, I know what I like.'

She turned to him, anguished. 'Oh *Clyde* . . .'

He took a deep breath and said quietly: 'How would you like it if you went away and came home to find a sheila living in the cottage? A sheila off a motorbike. An' she got me pissed in town last weekend. An' she's helping me write my book . . . An' I tell *you* how wonderful she is, how she's such a shit-hot poetess?'

Helen looked at him, sighed and nodded. 'I see . . . Yes, of course. In fact, I did think of that myself. That's why I was trying to call you.'

Clyde looked at her hard; then he stood up. 'Well, I'm goin' to look at him myself.'

She said anxiously: 'Good, darling. Do you want me to come?'

'No. I'll make my own judgements, girlie. Without any female bullshit.'

Helen sat back. 'Okay. Good, Clyde. My conscience is clear.'

Clyde looked down at her. 'But how clear is *his* conscience?' He thought for a moment, then said expressionlessly: 'I don't mind you writing a book, girl. You need something to do.'

For a moment she was angry. *You don't mind . . . ?* Then her eyes moistened and she smiled wanly because she knew he meant it well.

Clyde walked the eight hundred yards to the foreman's cottage. He stopped outside and grimly studied the big motorcycle, his big hands hanging at his side. Then he turned and mounted the steps to the porch with heavy tread. He pulled back the screen-door without knocking and walked in.

The small living-room was empty. A few books lay around. He went through to the kitchen. Ben was sitting at the table, surrounded by notebooks. He looked up, astonished. Clyde stood solidly in the doorway, his broad face impassive.

'G'day. Name's Clyde McKenzie . . .'

Ben felt his face go white. Then he stood up, assumed his most charming smile, and thrust out his hand.

'Clyde, how nice to meet you! And thank you so much!'

Clyde did not extend his hand. He said flatly:

'The moon shines up there like a cuspidor.'

Ben stared at him, his mind fumbling. Then he understood, and he wiped the smile off his face. He said:

'Doris, oh Doris, what are we waiting for?'

The words hung. Clyde studied him expressionlessly. Then:

'And who's this Doris?'

Ben said, straightfaced: 'A New York dancing girl.'

18

Two hours later Clyde walked back into the kitchen of the main house, still grim but smelling of beer. The supper Helen had frantically prepared was spoiling on the stove. She turned to him, her eyes nervous, then hurried across, put her arms round him and kissed his cheek and squeezed him. He did not respond. She stood back and looked up at him questioningly. Clyde walked stolidly into the pantry, and poured a glass of brandy. He brought it back and sat down at the table.

Helen slowly sat down opposite him and smiled, waiting. Clyde pursed his lips. He said:

'Well, I'm satisfied nothing's going on, girl.'

Helen felt limp with relief, but tried not to show it.

'I knew it anyway,' Clyde went on. 'I know you, girl.'

She closed her eyes. 'Thank you.'

Clyde took a sip of brandy. 'But I still don't like it. Any more than you would, if it was a sheila.'

Helen frowned. 'But if she was a fat, funny sheila?' she appealed.

'Fat, funny sheilas still fuck.' He looked at her, grimly. 'Which is much, much better than jerking off. In fact they probably fuck more enthusiastically than the pretty ones.' He added: 'Believe me.'

Helen's eyes widened. 'I thought you said *you* believed *me*?'

He smiled at her mirthlessly. 'I do.'

She blinked, then cried: 'Thanks a million! And what do you mean "believe *you*"? What do *you* know about fat enthusiastic sheilas?'

He smiled widely for the first time since his arrival. But it was a hard smile. 'Maybe plenty. I wasn't born yesterday.' Helen stared at him. He held her eye, inscrutably, then he said: 'See?'

'See what?'

'The little green man. You're jealous. Well, that's something like I feel, girlie. Except, Mr Gumboil Wonderhill is *here*. To be seen, heard

140

about. And you' – he jabbed his finger – 'can't see the fat sheila who gives these marvellous sexual performances. In fact you don't even believe she exists. And you're still a bit jealous, aren't you?'

She looked at him, and her eyes moistened.

'Yes,' she admitted softly. 'I'm sorry . . .'

'But,' he said, his eyes fixed on hers, 'but still you don't really panic about her. Why? Because women don't really mind about fat ugly sheilas, especially if they're to hell and gone in Broken Hill. They're no real threat, they're just another form of jerk-off. And so that's almost okay – as long as you don't actually *know* about it. Right? Isn't that how women think?'

She frowned at him. 'No.'

He smiled thinly at her. 'But anyway, men are different. Men don't think that what the eye doesn't see the heart doesn't grieve for, girl.'

He had always called her 'girl' and she didn't mind – indeed she liked it, it made her feel protected, but today, and in this context, she didn't like it. She said: 'Okay, so men and women may be different in that respect. But *I* would grieve, Clyde.'

Clyde studied her, then slumped his tired shoulders. 'Well, let's eat.'

Helen had to control her tension. 'But . . . ?'

Clyde smiled thinly at her. 'I've got a week's leave, another three days here. But,' he ended grudgingly, 'I think he's all right.' He added: 'Probably. Just.' He added, further, for good measure: 'We'll see.'

She made an effort to conceal her pleasure: 'Good, Clyde. I told you he's okay.' She was going to say bonzer, but changed it. 'So, let's eat, shall we?'

Clyde looked at her.

'I just said that.'

19

It was touch-and-go whether Ben Sunninghill stayed.

Of course, he did not show up at the main house for supper that night, nor did he go over the following morning to see if there was anything Helen needed him to do. Not only had Clyde left him with the distinct impression that he could handle things very nicely by himself, he presumed that they would kind of stay in bed a little longer than usual. He shut his mind to that image. Indeed, he even managed to hope that Helen made such a good job of it that Clyde was entirely convinced. But, wasn't the man already convinced? If he wasn't, yours truly Benjamin Sunninghill should take a powder immediately. But sure to God Clyde McKenzie didn't look the type to tolerate doubts. And the man had even, eventually, begun to untense a little – he had even finally accepted a beer – and although his eyes had never lost their penetrating steadiness he did almost smile once or twice during the two hours in which he had relentlessly gone over the details of Ben's story, comparing his answers with Helen's evidence. He had apparently satisfied himself of the facts, because he had finally stood up and said:

'I'll be getting on home, then.'

Ben had risen also. 'Well, I'll be getting on the road, too, I'll call over in the morning to say goodbye.'

'No rush.'

And Clyde had walked out as abruptly as he had entered, leaving Ben staring after him. In a quandary. *No rush?* What did that mean? Stay? Or, 'no rush as long as you're gone by sunset'?

It was the question of face that decided Ben not to leave the next morning, a question of appearances – of dignity, Clyde's as much as his own. If he left so soon, it would seem that Clyde had sent him packing because he had good cause to be jealous, which made Clyde appear a cuckold. Which made Ben appear to have a guilty conscience.

That was okay with Ben Sunninghill, but it would all reflect very badly on Helen. It was really for Helen's sake, and Clyde's, that Ben decided to stay another day.

And again it was for the sake of appearances that he went over to the house at sunset the next day. He was, after all, a guest, if an unwelcome one, and guests are expected to show up. He took the motor cycle: without transport they might feel obliged to invite him to supper, a proposal for which he had no relish. He dismounted outside the kitchen door and knocked. Clyde called gruffly:

'Who're you kidding, Ben? Come in.'

Ben opened the screen-door uncertainly. Clyde was sitting at the table in a singlet, a can of beer in his hand. Helen stuck her head out of the pantry. 'Hi, Ben,' she said brightly.

'Good evening.' Ben smiled. 'Kidding about what?' he asked Clyde.

'By knocking.'

'We were about to call you for supper,' Helen said.

'Oh, thanks, but I've had my supper, I've just come—'

'Like what?' Clyde said. He had not moved an inch.

'Oh, I've got all kinds of hard rations in my saddle-bags: rice, bully-beef—'

'Not enough,' Clyde said flatly. 'Helen's cooking some steaks.' He added: 'Rare, but not unusual.'

Helen laughed nervously from the pantry: 'Joke, Ben.'

'No joke,' Clyde said flatly, 'I want mine to have Bob Hawke's head on it. That would be funny as hell. Or Paul Keating's will do. You can have Mr Kinnock's, whether you like it or not. Whose head d'you want, Helen?'

'Mavis Johnson's,' Helen called through.

'Yeah,' Clyde said, 'another trouble-maker. Like Bob Hawke and that other red-ragger, Rasputin. I tell you, one day even the KGB's going to poison that bastard. What do you say?' He looked at Ben.

Ben wasn't sure whether the man was drunk. 'Maybe.' He grinned.

'But,' Clyde said, 'I bet you that bastard's so tough he's somehow going to crawl away full of arsenic, take a couple of Alka Seltzer and live to trouble-make another day.'

Helen was poised at the refrigerator. 'Clyde, please . . .'

He ignored her. 'So Mr Yeltsin – who's the first decent Russian we've seen since Attila the Hun – who was a Russian, you know, in terms of modern geography – even Mr Yeltsin is going to try to shoot this Rasputin bugger. But d'you know what's going to happen? That bugger's going to somehow crawl away from the palace full of bullets and live to trouble-make yet another day.'

Ben wore a puzzled smile. 'Rasputin? We are talking about the same Rasputin . . . ?'

'Certainly we are. Or maybe there're two. How many Rasputins are there?'

Helen came out of the pantry. 'Clyde!' she said. *Please . . .*'

And then Ben understood. He stared a moment at Clyde; then suddenly it all seemed quite funny. The man was a hell of a lot brighter than he'd thought. He smiled politely. 'Clyde – and Helen – I won't stay for supper. I've just popped over to thank you for everything and to tell you that I'll be off first thing in the morning.'

Clyde was insistent: 'You're staying for a nice, unusual steak.'

Ben turned to Helen. Her face was a mask. 'Please – I've eaten already, I couldn't enjoy it.'

Clyde said tersely: 'Sit down an' have a goddam beer, Ben.'

'Yes, do,' Helen gushed.

Of course, he had to accept. 'Okay, thanks. But I won't stay long, got to get going early.'

With relief Helen turned back to the refrigerator and snapped the cap off a beer can. 'Here you are!' Ben sat down.

'How early you getting going?' Clyde said.

'Sunrise.'

'An' where you heading?'

'To Brisbane. Then up north. Then Darwin.'

'Just sleeping rough all the way?'

'Well,' Ben smiled: 'not so rough. I've got a good sleeping-bag and a good little rubber mattress, all the gear. Sometimes I sleep in motels, I'm not broke.'

'I don't give a damn whether you're broke or not, Ben. Though it might be kind of nicer if you were.'

There was an astonished silence. Then Helen cried: 'Clyde!'

Again Clyde ignored her and continued quietly: 'You're not leaving tomorrow morning, Ben.' He let that announcement hang. 'Maybe tomorrow night, but not tomorrow morning.' There was another silence. 'Because tomorrow the Flying Doctor's coming, Ben.'

Ben looked at him, frowning. Then comprehension dawned. Clyde went on: 'An' all the folks from miles around are coming here, Ben, to see the doctor and have a little party. It's a big deal, a big social event for Helen, and everybody. And *you*, Ben, are going to be here

. . . Isn't that what you're here for? To experience Australia? Wouldn't the Flying Doctor be good for your book?'

Helen had a half-smile frozen on her face, Ben the same.

Clyde continued relentlessly: 'I want you to see that. The Outback folk flocking to see their famous Flying Doctor. And I want all those folk to see *you*, Ben.'

Ben's face tensed, his mouth half smiling but his eyes not. He was prepared to accept jokes about his appearance but not insults. Helen stared at her husband aghast. Clyde continued quietly:

'I want them to *meet* you, Ben, and I want you to be charming, to entertain them, Ben. To make them laugh.' He paused, his eyes fixed. 'And they're going to see that you and I are the greatest of *friends*, Ben. Aren't they?'

Ben stared at him. Now he understood. 'Okay, Clyde,' he said quietly.

'*Won't* they?' Clyde insisted flatly.

Ben nodded. 'Sure.'

Clyde looked at him fixedly. 'You're my welcome *guest*, Ben. Is that understood?' He paused. 'Any questions?'

Ben held his eye.

'Yes,' he said brightly. 'Is the Flying Doctor any good at nose-jobs?'

Clyde's fist clenched; then he controlled himself. He heaved himself up. He glared down at Ben, then turned and walked heavily out of the kitchen.

Ben closed his eyes for a second. Then he stood up too.

'Goodnight,' he said to Helen. 'From me and my big mouth.'

Helen whispered: 'Yeah, I think it better be goodnight . . .'

20

Ben was up before dawn; he cleaned the cottage and packed his saddle-bags, so he would be ready to leave the moment the last of the Flying Doctor's patients departed.

At sunrise Clyde arrived at the cottage. He knocked once on the living-room door and walked through to the kitchen. Ben was sitting at the table with his notebooks as before. Clyde stood in the doorway and said:

'I apologize.'

Ben was taken by surprise. He stood up slowly, with an uncertain smile. 'That's okay . . .'

'Helen says I was real mean last night, and she's right. But I was a bit drunk and I was feeling cranky, because of those stupid rumours.'

Ben nodded. 'I understand.'

'I know they're stupid – because I know Helen. And now I've met you. But you know how you feel when you hear rumours.'

'Sure.' Ben added, flustered: 'Won't you sit down?'

Clyde soldiered on: 'So I'd be glad if you stayed today and showed the folks that the rumours are rubbish.' He looked at him. 'Just be . . . nice and normal. Will you? Even though I was cranky last night?' He added: 'Please.'

Ben felt for the man.

'Sure. I'll be glad to.'

Clyde hesitated. 'Okay; thanks.' He turned to go. 'See you at the house at about ten-thirty.'

Ben said: 'Clyde?' Clyde stopped and turned. 'I just want to thank you for having me here. I've had a great time.'

'You're welcome,' Clyde said. He walked out heavily.

At about ten o'clock the folks started arriving.

They came from a radius of hundreds of miles to consult the Flying

Doctor, and to see Ben Sunninghill. Burraville had its own medical service, a doctor who came from Charleville once a fortnight, but nonetheless a few came from there too. They travelled by car and aircraft, whole families and hired help, the women bearing cake-tins and sandwiches and crockery. Helen had set up tables on the verandah and the kitchen was full of chatter. They all knew each other. Clyde McKenzie had never seen such a crowd at his house on Flying Doctor day. He stood at the top of the verandah steps making a patient-list, greeting each new arrival with a dour smile. Less than half of them wanted to see the doctor – they wanted to see Ben Sunninghill. (Affairs were not unheard-of in the Outback – *but Helen McKenzie and a hippy New York jeweller . . . ?*) There were vehicles parked all around the house and eleven aeroplanes on the airstrip when the Flying Doctor's aircraft appeared.

Clyde drove out to meet it. He was surprised to find Ben there, astride his motorbike.

'Hi,' Ben smiled. 'I just wanted to see him come in – never seen a Flying Doctor before.'

'You've never seen anything like what's waiting for you at the house, either.'

Ben sighed. 'Oh boy.'

'Yeah,' Clyde said dourly. 'Oh boy.'

The aircraft turned, lined up with the strip. It came in lower, droning louder and louder. Its wheels hit the earth with a puff of dust, and it came careening towards them. It reached the end of the strip, slowing; then it turned around, spluttering, and parked near the treeline. Clyde put his car into gear. He looked hard at Ben.

'I'm relyin' on you. Make 'em laugh.'

'I can't turn it on and off like a tap.'

Clyde said: 'Heard you can. And remember, you and me are the greatest of friends. Right?'

'Right,' Ben agreed. Then he couldn't resist saying: '*Aren't* we?' He grinned bleakly.

The corners of Clyde's mouth twitched. Then he revved the engine and drove off towards the plane.

Ben watched from a distance. The aircraft's door opened and folding steps came down. Clyde pulled up alongside and got out of the car. The pilot descended first, then the doctor, a young man, followed by a middle-aged nurse. Clyde shook hands all round, led them to his car, and they drove off across the strip in the direction of the house.

Ben waited two minutes, then he sighed and kicked his cycle into life. He wasn't looking forward to this.

Outback history is again in disagreement on the events of that morning. But what is more or less established is the following:

Clyde arrives at the front of the house, where there is the usual welcome for the doctor, though everybody is really just dying for the jeweller to arrive, to see what all the fuss is about, to see how Helen behaves and particularly how Clyde reacts. Of course, Helen is as usual being the perfect lady – well, as usual until last weekend in *Burraville* – and she's just managed to 'mention' to a few of the girls in the kitchen how 'lovely' it is to have Clyde home 'so unexpectedly' and how everything is 'so harmonious' and 'how much Clyde likes Sunningstein', even though he wasn't very amused at first about her getting '*so* pissed' last Saturday, though now he 'saw the funny side of it'. And there's old Clyde, having a hard time cracking a smile, though of course nobody says anything to *him* about it. The doctor arrives, gulps a cup of tea, and goes straight into the living-room to start his clinic, and the tea-party begins in earnest, everybody *agog* waiting for the jeweller to show up. And then round the corner he comes, on that evil-looking motorbike of his. He gets off, he walks towards the verandah steps – and, my dear, you could hear a *pin* drop – and he mounts the steps with a kind of nervous smile – as well he might – and everybody's staring – then Clyde sort of croaks:

'Ben! Come and meet my neighbours!'

As if he wasn't coming anyway, and he almost *throws* an arm around the guy's shoulder and then makes the farce *worse* by trying to introduce him to everybody! Well, I suppose everybody was kind of silent and staring, so Clyde has to do *some*thing. But, of course, Clyde – you know how *stodgy* he is – a beaut bloke but he is a bit stodgy – though not humourless, mind you – anyway Clyde *stammers* around and fumbles and forgets half our names, and there's the jeweller making matters worse by solemnly walking around trying to shake everybody's hand, with Clyde sort of blushing and stammering and forgetting behind him! And then they mercifully get to the end of this *charade* – because nobody, my dear, has the sense to start talking again and break the tension – you could have cut it with a *knife* – finally they get to the end of these so-called introductions, and it looks as if mercifully the conversation is going to pick up again, but then *Helen* walks out of the house on to the verandah with a teapot, and instead of just bustling about as if nothing *anguished* was happening she stops dead in her tracks, and she blushes beetroot red as if she's just been caught *in flagrante delicto* – that's what Mavis Johnson said, it means 'on the job' – no, of course Mavis wasn't there, she lives in Burraville – anyway Helen blushes and sort of gasps:

'There you are . . . !'

Clyde and the jeweller turn and they're both blushing, and there's a nervous titter followed by a deafening silence, and this little guy is looking absolutely *pathetic* beside great big Clyde, almost like Beauty and the Beast, or Laurel and Hardy. Then Sunningstein mercifully breaks this *preg*nant silence – yes figurative, my dear, we *hope* – but suddenly he claps his hands together and rubs them very macho-like and says:

'Well, is he ready then? For my nose-job?'

And, my dear! You'd have though he'd said the funniest thing! It was the Flying Doctor's pilot who started it – he didn't know the *dramatic* background. First there was this kind of stunned silence, then suddenly the pilot – not our normal pilot, but a stand-in – he sort of *laughs* into his cup and then sprays tea everywhere, and guffaws, and then suddenly *everybody* is guffawing, and then somebody claps and then suddenly everybody's clapping, and Clyde is laughing as if he's a Bundaberg night-club owner and then Sunningberg shouts:

'All I need is six kind men to hold me down!'

And there's absolute *screams* of laughter, as if this was the funniest thing in the world, and then that idiot pilot grabs Sunningstein by his arm, and then somebody else joins the so-called fun and grabs his other arm, and then suddenly half a dozen other of the men join in – *including* Clyde – and they sort of *grab* him all over, and the next thing Sonningberg is up there shoulder-high pretending to kick and scream and yelling:

'I've changed my mind! I've changed my mind! I don't want to be a Christian anymore . . . !' and everybody *screams* with laughter as if this was really funny, and they carry him off the verandah all laughing and staggering, and they *kick* open the living-room door where the doc's still setting up his gear, and they *slam* it behind them, and then there's a sort of moment's silence before more shrieks of laughter and then all kinds of *theatrical* bangs and shouts, Mavis says, and then more screams and then shouts of *'Police!'* and *'Red Cross!'* and *'Amnesty International!'* and then more bangs and screams – and then finally the living-room door *bursts* open and out staggers the Jew in his *underpants*, and his cheeks are all puffed up with cotton wool and he's got black paper over his

front teeth and he's got tomato sauce all over his nose and he lurches on to the verandah and cries:

'Anybody got a Band Aid?'

And, my dear, everybody ... simply collapses in laughter ...

That much, more or less, most witnesses agree on, give or take some percentage in the degree of humour. There are those who thought it was all bonzer, and there are some who had to force a laugh. But the over-all consensus is that, after a tricky start, that much turned out beaut. Or at least okay. And there was huge relief – even the unamused agree on that. It's what happened thereafter that is clouded. There are those who say that although the jeweller was really damn funny, Clyde – despite the fact that he was definitely seen to dash out of the clinic to the kitchen and come back with the tomato ketchup – was not really so amused by all the jokes Ben proceeded to tell, that his laughter was kind of forced and he was seen to be sort of uncomfortable and wishing the Flying Doctor would for Christ's sake hurry up with his patients. And all the time there was Helen, darting round with the teapot and lammingtons and laughing gaily every time everybody else did, while Sunningbloom stood up there at the tea-table in a sort of mixture of smugness and embarrassment whilst Clyde and half a dozen of the blokes led by that idiot pilot sort of hung on his words between guffaws.

On the other hand, there are a substantial number who don't think that the jeweller was funny. Oh, certainly he looked funny, with that nose and those stick-out ears and Rasputin grin, and even though he did often try to stop being the centre of attention he couldn't resist rising to the occasion with another wisecrack as soon as somebody said anything, and then everybody forced a laugh again. He wasn't at all funny, according to this school of thought. And all the time there was Clyde sort of wandering here and there, disappearing to the kitchen and coming back with more sandwiches, pretending to laugh while Helen dashed in and out with even more lammingtons like a lady with a load on her mind, while all the time the doctor's nurse was sticking her head out and shouting for the next patient. What this school of thought contends is that the whole jolly atmosphere of the Flying Doctor day was fraught, that there's no smoke without fire, et cetera, and that despite what an unlikely candidate for funny business the visitor looked, and despite Helen McKenzie being a lady, something very fishy indeed was going on.

Those are the two schools of thought. What both agree on is that when the Flying Doctor finally dealt with his last patient – Joe Branson and his piles – swallowed a cup of tea and asked to be driven straight back to his aeroplane, everybody suppressed a sigh of relief and sort of began to shuffle to their feet, and what is absolutely agreed upon is that Clyde and Helen *visibly* sighed with relief. It took less than twenty minutes for all those cars and aeroplanes to be reloaded with empty cake-tins and crockery and depart, which is doubtless a world record for a Flying Doctor day. What nobody really knows – though there are many theories – is what happened after everybody had left with such uncharacteristic rapidity and good taste.

Clyde walked slowly through to the kitchen, got a beer from the refrigerator and sat down heavily at the table. Helen appeared in the doorway with a tray. She looked at him wanly.

'Phew . . .' she said.

'Yeah.'

'Well done, darling.'

Clyde took a swig of beer. 'It's the little prick who did well.'

'Oh, Clyde . . .'

Clyde closed his eyes. 'Oh, he's all right, for Christ's sake.'

'Of *course* he is.' She came into the kitchen and set down the tray. 'I'm going to have one of those,' she decided limply. She fetched a beer and joined him at the table. 'I'm exhausted.'

Clyde stared across the kitchen at nothing. 'Was he really that funny?'

'Everybody was laughing, weren't they?'

'Not everybody. It was that pilot who started things off – thank God for that pilot. Some of the blokes weren't laughing too convincingly. And some of the women.'

'Then they haven't got a sense of humour. He was damn funny.'

Clyde snorted. 'No, they weren't laughing because they felt sorry for me.'

Helen groaned. 'Oh Clyde . . .' She looked at him. 'How can anyone feel sorry for *you*? You're a great big man who nobody would dare mess around with. Everybody *respects* you.'

Clyde snorted again. Then: 'And my wife loves me?'

She looked at him, and her eyes moistened. 'And your wife *loves* you! Oh, how can anybody feel sorry for you over funny little Ben Sunninghill? Do you feel sorry for yourself? There's only one thing to do – ignore them! He's going today anyway, he doesn't feel welcome. Ignore the incident, make as if nothing's happened – which it hasn't.'

'But I won't be here to ignore them,' he pointed out grimly.

'But *I'll* be here, they'll see me and *I'll* ignore it! And you'll be back at Christmas.' She shook her head. 'Just forget it, Clyde.'

Clyde sat in silence a moment. Then he said:

'You'd really like him to stay, wouldn't you?' He added reluctantly: 'I'm not criticizing you, girl. I'm just asking.'

Helen looked at him. She said quietly: 'You know I would, Clyde. It's damn lonely here without you. And it's nice to know that we're ... helping him, I mean to write his poetry or whatever – it's nice to know that some life's going on, that that empty cottage is being put to some use.'

Clyde massaged his forehead slowly. 'You'd feel the same if it was some hippy girl who'd shown up on her motorbike?'

'Of course I would,' she said earnestly. 'And I'd have more in common with a girl, wouldn't I?'

There was a silence. They could hear Ben on the verandah, loading crockery on to a tray. Clyde rubbed his eyelids, then sighed and said:

'Well, I don't want him to stay, girl. Not because I think anything's going on, but just because of ... appearances.'

Helen sighed and sat up straight. She had expected this. 'Okay,' she said. 'So be it.'

'I'm not saying he *can't* – I'm saying what I *want*. What I prefer.'

Prefer? She looked at him. 'So we'll do what you want, Clyde. He'll leave this afternoon, without being told, I'm sure.'

Clyde sighed grimly. 'But?'

'No buts.'

'You were about to say "But in that case I want..."' He raised his eyebrows.

'No, I wasn't,' Helen said firmly. 'I'm seeking no deals over Ben Sunninghill, Clyde.' She hesitated, then she decided to go on. 'But, yes, there is something that I want, Clyde, though it's got nothing to do with Ben staying or not. I've been thinking about this for a long time. And especially now I'm all alone.' She looked at him squarely. 'Clyde, next year I'd like to go back to Uni and finish my degree. I can work in the evenings to help pay for it.'

Clyde was taken aback. He studied her for a moment, digesting this. And feeling very, very sorry for her.

'Oh, girl,' he sighed, 'how can we afford that? Now of all times, with all the kids at boarding-school?'

She said earnestly: 'I can work as a waitress in the evenings – or as a barmaid, even a baby-sitter. And I can work every weekend and I'll find the cheapest digs in Brisbane.'

Clyde closed his eyes. He sat there a long moment, then shook his head. 'Oh, girl, I don't want my poor old wife working her guts out as a *bar*maid—'

'Less of the old, please. It'll only be for a year.'

'Or two?' He pursed his lips. 'Girl,' he said sadly, 'you'll never make enough as a barmaid to lodge and feed yourself, let alone pay tuition fees. Next year Tim's got to go to Uni. We just can't *afford* your fees, girl, not next year, not for God knows how many years unless Tim gets a scholarship. *He'll* have to work nights as a waiter, but that's okay, he's young.' He frowned at her. 'And you don't want to go back to living amongst all those kids, girl, you deserve a bit of comfort—'

'I *do* want to – not live with kids, but I want the *stimulus*, Clyde, and the . . . *achievement* of my degree.'

Clyde took a deep, regretful breath. He shook his head.

'I'm truly sorry, girl, but not next year, please.' He half-smiled at her. 'Maybe we can work something out for the year after next, if Tim gets that scholarship – maybe I'll get a promotion, and maybe I can do more overtime—'

She interrupted emphatically: 'I don't want you doing any more overtime, Clyde.'

He sighed. 'Well, there's nothing much to do with your free time at the mine, anyway. Maybe I could give up my share of the cleaning maid—'

'Oh, I'm not having you give up the cleaning lady – you work hard enough and I won't have you making any more sacrifices and living like a pig – you've already given up smoking.'

'Well, that was good for me – though it feels like I haven't had a nice day since.' He smirked. 'They say you don't live any longer, it just *seems* longer. But, anyway, it saves fifty bucks a month and that goes towards my beer. I could give *that* up, I suppose . . .'

'Oh no you're not!'

Clyde spread his hands, palms up. 'Then where else would the money for your Uni fees come from, girl? Every penny I make goes to the kids' school and the mortgage on this place.'

She sighed, and said guiltily: 'And on me . . .'

He smiled. 'You don't cost much, girl. And you're my *wife*. I can't remember when you last bought yourself a dress – and you don't eat much either.'

'More than I should, look how fat I am.'

Clyde smiled again. 'I think you're beautiful.'

She returned his smile. 'Thank you, darling.'

'And you're be-yoo-tiful in bed . . .'

She grinned at him, moist-eyed. 'You're pretty hot stuff yourself.'

'When I get going? Maybe this separation's good for us?'

She shook her head sadly. 'Oh Clyde, how long's this going to go on?'

He shifted on his chair wearily.

'Well, Wendy doesn't think she wants to go to Uni, thank God – though she'll have to go to Tech or something, to be trained as a secretary at least. Jackie and Cathy?' He shrugged. 'Tim will have to help, I guess, once he's qualified.' He thought for a moment. 'Maybe we should sell that plane before it gets too old; though it's not worth much now.'

'No,' Helen said emphatically. 'When you come back we're going to *use* it, we've got to have *some* social life – and you *love* that plane.' She sighed in resignation. 'No, forget it. Forget my degree.'

'I didn't say forget it, girl,' Clyde said gently, 'I just said not next year.'

She wanted to say 'Nor for the foreseeable future,' but didn't.

They sat in silence for a minute. Helen studied her fingernails glumly. Then she said firmly:

'Well, there's one other thing I want to do, and this won't cost much, only the diesel.' She turned to him. 'In May I want to go and see Mum and Dad and the kids, for their school holidays.'

Clyde smiled at her, relieved. 'Sure, why not, *that* we can afford. Lovely for you to see June and Harry and the kids . . .' He added: 'Though I don't like you driving all that way alone.'

'Oh, heavens, I'll be all right. Maybe somebody from Burraville or Charleville will want a ride and share expenses.'

'A thousand miles? That's two full days in that old Land Rover – three, more like. Maybe you can get a ride with Bill Simpson, he sometimes flies down to Bundaberg.'

'He always comes back the next day. No, I'll be fine driving.'

Clyde was relieved to give her something to look forward to. 'Okay,' he said. 'You better radio June soon, and book it up with the kids before they get any fancy ideas about going to stay with their pals for their holidays.'

'Yes . . .' She sighed, and looked again at her fingernails. They were short and unvarnished, and her hands were rough.

'No, not rough. Just *tough*,' she murmured.

'What?'

'My hands.' She gave him a little smile.

Clyde sighed. 'You're a good wife, girl.' His voice was gentle.

She looked up at him. 'And you're a good husband, Clyde. Working so hard for us.'

He smiled self-consciously. 'That's my duty, isn't it, to look after you all as best I can.' He sat quiet a moment, then took a breath and said: 'I'm glad you're writing a book, girl. Gives you something to do.'

Helen groaned softly, embarrassed.

'Oh, I'll never write a book. It's just a . . . rush of enthusiasm.' She smiled wanly. 'A rush of blood to the head. And I've got plenty to do, really. Paint the house, for example. Make some dresses, maybe. Make us some money doing things like that.'

'I don't want my wife taking in dressmaking, girl.'

'Why not? Help towards Uni. And I could breed some decent poultry – turkeys, maybe, and do the vegetable garden scientifically – make it at least pay for the diesel into town.'

Clyde looked at her and said quietly: 'It's Ben who gave you the rush of blood, I mean the enthusiasm to do your book, isn't it?'

Helen answered frankly: 'Yes. I told you.'

They heard Ben walking through the house, and stopped talking. He entered the kitchen carrying a laden tray.

'Thanks, Ben,' Helen said.

'Not at all.' He set the tray down and turned to go back to the verandah for more.

'Have a beer, Ben,' Helen said. 'You deserve it.'

Ben smiled. 'I'd better not—'

'Have a beer, for God's sake,' Clyde said. He heaved himself up and went to the pantry to get it. Then to Helen's astonishment he said: 'You can't leave now, the day's half gone, so sit down.' He returned with the beer and added wryly: 'Unless you're busting a gut to stay at Radio-Jack's in Burraville?'

Ben was as surprised as Helen. 'Oh, sure . . .'

He took a seat unwillingly; Clyde passed him a beer and opened a new can for himself. He sat down heavily. Then he said, as if rehearsed:

'You did good today, Ben.'

Helen was further surprised. 'Yes,' she murmured.

Clyde continued: 'And I dunno if I already done so, but I want to thank you for fixin' the washing-machine. And putting that generator switch in the bedroom for Helen – should've done that myself.'

'A great pleasure,' Ben said. 'Yes, you did thank me.'

Clyde smiled thinly. 'If grudgingly?' Ben smiled too, embarrassed, and Clyde went on: 'Guess I was a bit hard on you.'

Ben was blushing now. 'Please think nothing of it. It was very understandable.'

Clyde persisted: 'We Aussies are usually pretty hospitable types.' 'I know.'

'But we call a spade a bloody shovel.'

Ben grinned, despite himself. 'I know that, too.'

Helen was on tenter-hooks, not knowing what to expect. Clyde rubbed his chin self-consciously, then pressed on:

'And I want you to know that I respect Helen's judgement. She's the boss of this station while I'm away, and if she thinks something's okay I'm very likely to think so too.' He paused, then added: 'We have a very good relationship.'

Ben nodded. 'Yes, I know.'

Helen wondered where the hell this conversation was going. Clyde sat back uncomfortably. He said:

'And Helen and I have been talking. And . . . well, there's no rush for you to leave, Ben.'

Helen was astonished. And she had to conceal her happiness. *Oh, she loved Clyde . . .* Ben was equally taken aback. He started to say something but Clyde went on resolutely:

'We decided it's nice for that cottage to be put to some use for a change. With you a writer and all. Don't want to be a dog-in-the-manger. And it's nice for Helen to have some company, it's bloody lonely out here.' He shifted uneasily. 'And, well, if any little jobs come up, it would be nice if you could do them for her.'

Helen had to suppress her joy. Ben was bemused. He began: 'But I don't want to impose—'

'You ain't listening, Ben,' Clyde said. He scratched a rib that didn't need scratching. 'And,' he ended, 'it's nice that Helen's writing a book, and that you can give her some advice. 'Cos I sure can't.' Helen opened her mouth to gush her appreciation but Clyde continued: 'I have to leave tomorrow. So, stay a bit longer. A couple of weeks even.' He ended flatly: 'I'm sorry to have to leave Helen alone so much, but it's got to be done . . .'

4

21

And so it was that Ben Sunninghill came to stay on at Whoop-Whoop. But he did not stay for a couple of weeks only. At the end of the first fortnight Helen radioed Clyde and asked if Ben could stay a while longer because he was such a great help. Yes, with her book too, but *generally*: he was doing a great job on the vegetable garden and he had built a run for the turkeys she intended to get. He had also planted a big patch of maize to feed them, and every day he rode his bike to the Abbo's hut to check on him. Across two thousand miles of crackling airwaves Clyde reluctantly said it was okay for him to stay a bit longer. 'But not much longer, girl. I don't like him thinking he's . . . like a fixture, know what I mean? Over.'

'Oh, darling, he *doesn't* . . . Over.'

A pause, then: 'And there's no money in chooks and turkeys, girl, or veggies, unless you do it on a big scale and can get 'em to a decent market economically. I don't mean to be discouraging but any fool will tell you that, so don't get your hopes up. Over.'

'Yes, but I've put in iceberg lettuces and they're moneymakers, and if it just pays for the diesel we're ahead, aren't we? Over.'

'Sure. Okay, so try it. How's the book going? Over.'

'Oh, the book . . . it's *awful*. It's such hard work, and I'm no writer. Over.'

Another pause, more crackling over the airwaves: 'Well, girl, maybe you'll take us to Hawaii yet. Maybe we'll *both* go to Uni, huh? What should I take – literature or whatever it's called? Anyway, can you tell me what the book's about yet, over?'

Helen closed her eyes. 'Oh, darling, not on the air, I'm so embarrassed about it . . .'

'Well, maybe you can tell us at Christmas, hey? Anyway, have you told Mum and the kids you're coming for May? Over.'

'Yes – Mum's thrilled!' She added more soberly: 'But she's warned me the kids are all fired up about going to their friends for the holidays, so I've written them a circular letter. Over.'

'Well, if they've got any fancy ideas,' Clyde growled, '*I'll* write them a goddam circular letter – their mother comes first.'

It wasn't the best of blessings, and Helen reported none of Clyde's reluctance to Ben. 'He said it's fine, Ben – and I know he's very grateful that I've got your company, and for the jobs you're doing.' Ben wasn't sure whether he believed all that, but he had permission to stay on and that was good enough for him; for Ben Sunninghill was falling in love, albeit much against his better judgement.

He examined his feelings thoroughly before coming to this conclusion. His better judgement told him that it was doomed to be unrequited love, given his poor track record with women, his unprepossessing appearance and Helen's moral disposition. His better judgement cautioned him that although she did not have much of a life at Whoop-Whoop, it might be better for her than the life he could offer her; he must be very careful, for her sake, about destabilizing her. And common sense told him that any ill-considered move on his part would probably shock Helen and precipitate his departure. His conscience reminded him that he was in a position of trust; though he suspected Clyde didn't have complete faith in him, Clyde trusted Helen and Helen trusted Ben: he would be in breach of all that confidence, and he hesitated deeply, for Ben Sunninghill was a decent sort of fellow. He would rather love her in silence than be denounced by Helen as dishonourable and asked to leave. But a man is a man; Helen needed only to crook her finger at him and all his honourable qualms would have gone straight out the window. Ben did a lot of soul-searching about all this, whether he really was in love and what, if anything, he was going to do about it, and the best policy he could arrive at was: Wait and see.

So Ben Sunninghill stayed on, doing odd jobs, tending the new vegetable garden, nursing his passion for Helen McKenzie, and waiting. It was about two weeks after Clyde had left that he found the courage to make his first pass at Helen. It happened the day they took their first load of vegetables to town.

Any fool will tell you there's no money in veggies, but Ben showed a profit by cheating: when he found out at the Farmers' Co-op how optimistic his arithmetic had been he did a little creative accountancy on the invoice, increasing the weight of the produce to Helen's benefit, and made up the extra with his own money.

'There you are, we've paid for the diesel; you had to come to town anyway. And there's enough left over for lunch. When the iceberg lettuces are ready you're going to make a killing.'

Helen was delighted. But she didn't want to go to lunch.

'You know why,' she hedged. 'And it's afternoon anyway . . .'

Ben frowned. 'To hell with 'em, Helen. We've already been seen in town. How about a nice hamburger and a bottle of wine or two to celebrate our triumph in the vegetable market?' He sighed. 'You can't live like this, Helen. Either I should leave, or we should have the courage to go to lunch.'

'Oh, Ben, don't threaten me.'

'Threaten you?' It seemed the biggest compliment of his life. 'Helen, it's just that you've got to have the courage of your convictions. Is it Clyde you're worried about?'

'*No.* Clyde knows we have supper together every night.'

So they went to the Niagara Milk Bar & Grill. It was mid-afternoon on a Monday, Burraville was even emptier than usual and they had the café to themselves. Stavros Popodopolous had gone off duty and they were served by his plump wife. Ben had bought a supply of booze for Whoop-Whoop. It had not been his intention to get even mildly drunk, for they had a long drive home; even less had it crossed his mind to get Helen drunk – had he wished to seduce her with drink, Whoop-Whoop would have been the place to attempt it. But get tipsy they did, as they talked and talked, and Helen began to enjoy herself thoroughly.

'Oh, it's so good,' she said, 'to feel you're waffling intelligently about everything under the sun, isn't it?'

'You *are* very intelligent, Helen.'

'Damn right I am! And I'm feeling more intelligent every minute.'

'And very beautiful.' He smiled, and had to resist stroking her hand with his fingertip.

'I wish that were true. But what is true is that *you* are beautiful, Ben.'

He couldn't believe his ears, and it was with a huge effort that he stopped himself from grabbing her hand ardently – for he knew she did not mean physically beautiful. The third bottle of wine was followed by several Irish coffees made from Whoop-Whoop's supply of brandy and it was sunset when they set off carefully for home. At nine o'clock, when they were eight miles from Whoop-Whoop, the Land Rover broke down.

Ben knew from the sudden juddering what was wrong – either air was getting into the fuel line or the fuel pump was dirty. With a flashlight he could probably have fixed the problem in twenty minutes, but they hadn't one.

'What are we going to do, pardner?' Helen asked cheerfully. She peered around at the dark, featureless bush. 'How far to home?'

It would have taken Ben less than three hours to walk to Whoop-Whoop and return on his motor cycle with a flashlight, leaving Helen safely locked in the Land Rover. They would have been home by midnight. For an instant Ben wrestled with his conscience. 'Twenty miles,' he heard himself lie. 'Nothing for it but to wait for daylight, I'm afraid.'

'Oh well, let's have a party!'

He drove the shuddering vehicle thirty yards off the road, into the bush.

It seemed to Ben the happiest, the most exciting night of his life. He was tingling with alcoholic anticipation, hoping that this wonderful opportunity would bring fulfilment of his feelings for Helen McKenzie. His passion, his love. His lust. Here they were, legitimately marooned in the middle of nowhere, outside Clyde McKenzie's territory, beyond all the inhibitions that the confines of the homestead evoked in Helen – almost as if on a desert island, just the two of them. Ben built a fire and they sat grilling sausages from the Whoop-Whoop supplies, swigging wine, laughing and talking and getting happier and tipsier. He glanced furtively at the lines of her body, her strong legs pressing against her skirt, her slim ankles, the curve of her neck, the thrust of heavy breasts against her blouse, the tendrils of hair hanging over her happy face. Sometimes, as she recrossed her legs, he glimpsed a flash of thighs, all the way up to the sweet secret place of her panties. And with all his hungry heart he longed to take her in his arms, tumble her on to her back, look down into her sweet face and cover her sensuous mouth with kisses; to tell her he was wildly, madly, head over heels in love with her, that he wanted to take her with him to the ends of the earth. But no, not yet – later, when it was time to sleep ... They had no crockery or cutlery, only a tin mug which they passed back and forth. They ate sausages on sticks, the juice running down their chins, and the taste of her lipstick on the mug seemed the most intoxicating thing he had ever known. Then they started on the brandy, taking it with milk, smooth as silk: the bottle was half empty when Helen dropped her head on her knees and sighed happily.

'Ben, I'd better curl up in the Land Rover before I topple over.'

The moment had arrived. Ben said: 'We'll never get any sleep sitting up, Helen.' He got to his feet and made his way to the vehicle. In the back were four sacks and one small tarpaulin with which they had covered the vegetables. He spread the sacks on the ground beside Helen, held up the tarpaulin like a blanket and said huskily: 'Lie down.'

Helen raised her forehead from her knees, turned and focused on the bed he had made for her. Then she looked up at him questioningly. For a moment she seemed to hesitate, then she heaved herself over, and crawled on to the sacks. She rolled over on to her back. She lay there grinning up at him, her golden hair spread out untidily in the moonlight.

'Looking after me again, Ben? But where're you going to sleep?'

Ben looked down at her. Still holding the tarpaulin. And even with all the drink in him he nearly lost his nerve, or his better nature almost prevailed: he almost said 'Sitting up in the Land Rover' then he screwed up his courage. 'Right here on those sacks, Helen. There's only one tarpaulin.'

For a moment Helen's eyes seemed to steady; then she smiled widely and said: 'Sure. Clyde will never know. I can handle it.'

For a heartpounding moment Ben wondered what that meant. Yes, she would make love to him because Clyde would never know? Or yes, he could sleep beside her because she could handle that without making love? Then she made his confusion more confounded by murmuring: 'Take my shoes off, Ben, I'm too spaced-out to sit up.'

Ben dropped to his knees beside her. His hands felt shaky. He knelt over her feet, and began to untie the knots on her espadrilles. The touch of her bare skin was bliss. Helen lay supine, eyes closed. He lingered over the knots, then gently slipped one shoe off; then the other. He crouched over her, his breath trembly – it was now or never – and his heart seemed to lurch, and he lowered his head and kissed her bare feet. And the feel of her skin on his lips was wonderful, and with all his heart he just wanted to clutch her womanness and mount her. Ben kissed her bare feet ardently. Helen stirred and opened her eyes, and he threw himself down beside her. He clutched her in his arms and he thrust his mouth on hers.

For an instant the world seemed to stand still; for a long instant Helen seemed to hesitate, perhaps to yield, and Ben's hand went to her breast. The soft fullness of it was wonderful, and there was nothing more urgent in the whole wide world than to possess her. His hand slid down over her belly, and for a glorious instant his fingers touched the warmth of her soft thighs, then Helen twisted in his embrace and tried to sit up. Ben released her. She sat up straight and looked down at him, her hair awry, shock on her lovely face.

'No, Ben.'

Ben was propped on his elbow, breathing hard, looking up at her against the moon, his face and loins smouldering. He wanted desperately to plead, *I love you, Helen.*

'I'm sorry,' he said.

She stared down at him, and for a wild moment Ben thought that she was about to relent; for an instant he felt that if he reached out she would let him take her in his arms again. But she was silhouetted against the moon and he was not sure of her expression.

'Goodnight, dear Ben,' she said quietly.

She lay down on the sacks again, turned on her side, her back to him, and pulled her knees up. She tucked her skirt around them, put both her hands under her cheek as a pillow and closed her eyes.

'Sleep tight, Ben,' she whispered.

Ben stared at her back, eating her up with his eyes, his breathing still uneven. He knew he could not lie beside her again without touching her.

He got to his feet shakily, picked up the tarpaulin, and gently spread it over her. She seemed fast asleep already.

'Goodnight, Helen,' he whispered.

He walked to the Land Rover, feeling suddenly completely sober. And heart-broken. He got in, rolled up the windows.

He sat there. It was completely silent. He stared through the windscreen, turbulent with desire. Then he whispered: 'Serves you right, you stupid bastard. For breaking trust . . .'

He closed his eyes tightly and tried to force the image of her out of his mind, but he could not: oh, the wonderful feel of her in his hands, her soft full breast, the fleeting warm fullness of her thighs, the lingering ecstasy of her mouth on his . . . And, had there not been a moment when she almost yielded . . . ?

It took him a long time to go to sleep.

22

Ben was awake before dawn; stiff, cold and hungover. He got out of the Land Rover and looked at Helen. She did not appear to have moved all night. He walked stiffly to the embers of the fire. He poked some sticks into them, and blew. Small flames began to flicker up. Helen still had not stirred. In the east the first pale light was coming into the sky. Just then he heard a distant vehicle approaching. It was coming from the direction of Burraville. Its drone grew louder. Then Ben saw the lights flickering through the scrub.

He remained crouched by the small fire: there was no point in stopping the vehicle to borrow a flashlight to fix the Land Rover, because soon it would be light. The vehicle was almost abreast of their campsite, about to flash past, when the driver slammed on the brakes. The vehicle skidded to a halt thirty yards on; then it came grinding backwards. It swung across the road and turned its headlights on them.

Ben stood up creakily. Helen woke and sat up, her hair tousled.

Ben started walking towards the lights. The doors opened and two men climbed out. 'Hey,' the driver called, 'you okay?'

Ben shielded his eyes. 'Fine, thanks. We broke down last night but it'll be light soon and I can fix it.'

The two men came towards him, long-legged silhouettes against the headlights. The driver said: 'Hey, ain't this Clyde McKenzie's Land Rover?'

'Right— ' Ben began.

'An' you're the Jew,' the other man said. He turned to his friend. 'The guy you've heard about. Where's Helen McKenzie?'

'Here I am, Fred Morecomb!' Helen heaved herself up and clutched the tarpaulin about her. She squinted into the lights, then started towards them. 'And he's a *person*, a guest in our country—'

'You all right, Helen?' the driver called, walking towards her. The other man followed and Ben thought he recognized him from that first disastrous day in the Burraville Hotel bar.

'Quite all right, Bill—'

'Course she's all right!' The second man stopped and put his hands on his hips. 'Sure,' he gestured at the fire and the sacks, 'they've had a nice cosy little all-night session in the moonlight!'

There was a moment's silence; then Helen snapped: 'You watch your tongue, Fred!'

Fred whirled around and rammed Ben in the chest with the flat of his hand. *Didn't yer?*

Ben was taken completely off-guard. He lurched backwards, then sprawled with a thud. He shoved himself up on to his elbows, shocked; Helen gasped and Bill bounded at Fred and threw his arm across his chest to restrain him. Fred was glowering down at Ben, his face contorted. Helen had both hands to her mouth, the tarpaulin at her feet. *Now cut that out!* Bill rasped.

For a shocked moment they were still as a tableau; Helen horrified, Fred menacing with Bill's arm across his chest, Ben staring up at all of them, his hungover mind racing. Clyde, Helen, the makeshift bed flashed through his mind; and his better judgement prevailed.

'You're quite wrong about all this, Fred,' he said quietly.

'Oh, quite wrong, am I, Jew-boy?'

It was the 'Jew-boy' that did it. Afterwards Ben did not know why: certainly his blood was up, but he had weathered worse insults than that. Maybe it was because he was hungover, maybe it was because he had made a fool of himself last night by breaking trust with Helen, and certainly it was to avenge her honour, and even – he reasoned later – to avenge Clyde McKenzie's honour. But, however it was, it was the 'Jew-boy' that did it: Ben clambered slowly back to his feet, a small man covered in dust. Lanky Fred Morecomb grinned at him maliciously. Bill lowered his arm and said: 'Now take it easy, you guys.' And Ben said: 'Sure,' and began to dust off his pants, then he swung on Fred and hit him in the guts with all his might. There was another gasp from Helen, and a much bigger gasp from Fred; he staggered backwards, doubled-up, then collapsed on to his buttocks, into the fire.

Fortunately it was only a very small fire, little more than embers. For two seconds Fred sat there, winded, astonished at being hit, and Ben and Bill started towards him to pull him up; then Fred gave a howl, scrambled madly to his feet, and began to flail at his buttocks. He staggered about wildly, still bent over from the blow, beating his

166

smoking backside with both hands. Ben and Bill and Helen all scrambled after him to help put the fire out; Bill caught hold of him, shouting, 'It's okay, Fred, it's out!' and Fred swung on Ben again. Ben jumped backwards and Bill grabbed both Fred's elbows and bellowed: *'Cut it out, Fred!'*

Fred crouched there, pinioned, gasping, the seat of his jeans charred. He began to snarl something, and Bill wrenched him around and started marching him back to the car. 'You better get home, Helen!' Bill snapped.

He shoved Fred back to the road, into the vehicle, and slammed the door. As they pulled away Fred shouted out the window:

'I'll get you, you Jew-boy!'

The light was strengthening now. Helen stood at the fire grimly, the tarpaulin clutched about her shoulders again.

Ben said from behind her: 'I'm sorry. Guess I shouldn't have hit him.'

She glared at the fire. 'Guess you shouldn't. But I'm not sorry you did. And he hit you first. The racist shit.' She turned to him. 'I promise you these anti-Semitic jibes are not typical of Australians. You've just had a bad run of it from a few louts because Clyde's so popular.'

Ben sighed. He was still a bit shaky. 'And what'll Clyde think about this when he hears?'

Helen breathed deeply and glared at the fire again. '*If* he hears. He'll be mad – with me, for getting myself in the Outback news again.' She snorted, then added, to reassure herself: 'But he'll see reason – if we were up to monkey-business we'd be much better doing it in the privacy of Whoop-Whoop, wouldn't we? But that Fred Morecomb will probably keep his stupid mouth shut.' She was unable to suppress a wry smile. 'Not a very dignified story is it, his arse catching fire?' She added: 'And he's scared of Clyde. He knows I could tell Clyde a thing or two about *him*.'

Ben frowned. 'Like what?'

Helen shook her head angrily. 'Oh, he's a slimy bastard. He's made a few indecent suggestions to me over the years. *And* he claims to be Clyde's friend.'

'Suggestions? Like what?'

'Oh,' she sighed scornfully, 'the usual thing: "How about it, baby?" "You and I could make beautiful music together, baby." "Clyde'll never know, baby." Oh, he's just a sex-starved bore; he's been after me ever since Clyde went away.' She waved a hand. 'He lives on the next station to ours, in fact Clyde sold him some of our land, across the river. Used to drop around to try his luck.' She added: 'That last trip to town, when I said I could lick any man in the bar? It was that jerk Fred Morecomb who shouted "Yes, please."'

'But have you told Clyde about the indecent suggestions?'

Helen sighed. 'No . . . What's the point? Just cause unpleasantness. Ignore the bastard. Mind you, I did warn him the last time that I'd tell Clyde if he touched me again.'

'*Touched* you? How?'

'Oh, just a grab at my bottom. "Ha-ha, you could get me, baby, if you played your cards right."' She snorted. 'He's kept quiet, since I warned him.'

'Until this morning.'

'Well, he's just jealous, isn't he, seeing us in,' she waved her hand, 'this situation. And he's drunk.'

Ben sighed angrily. 'And I was stupid enough to hit him. I'm sorry, Helen. I won't do anything silly like that again.'

'Oh, forget the jerk.' She was silent a long moment; then she said quietly to the fire: 'But there *is* something that must never happen again, Ben.' She turned to him, her eyes steady. 'Namely, what happened when I got into that bed last night.'

The rim of the sun was just coming up, flushing her face with colour, glinting in her untidy tendrils of hair. Ben felt his heart sink and turn over at once. He held her eye.

'Okay, Helen. I hear you. And I'm sorry about that, too.'

She looked at him steadily. 'I hope it's not the case that you didn't think I'd remember, Ben.'

Ben frowned at her, his anger rising. 'Are you implying that I'd take advantage of you when you're drunk?'

She looked at him, then closed her eyes and shook her head.

'No, I'm not, thank God. I think far too much of you for that. Anyway, yes I was drunk. Or very tipsy – and so, no doubt, were you. But I remember everything clearly, Ben.'

Ben wondered if she also remembered that heart-stopping moment when it seemed she might have yielded. 'Then you'll also recall that as soon as you resisted I stopped.'

'I do. And thank you for that.'

For a wild moment he wondered if she was thanking him for saving her from temptation. He said quietly: 'What exactly do you remember, Helen?'

168

Helen took a breath. 'I must have fallen asleep. I woke up, and you were ... kissing my feet.' She turned to him. 'Is that why you did it, Ben? Because you were drunk as well?' She said it as if she wanted him to say Yes.

With all his heart he wanted to say, No, I did it because I love you.

'Because I wanted to ...' He hesitated; then decided to say half of it, to test her: '... to worship at your feet.'

Helen stared at him, the sunrise gilding her face; she closed her eyes and turned back to the fire for a moment. Then she looked again at Ben.

'Oh please, Ben, don't use words like that!' She shook her head at him. 'Please don't ruin everything with words like that. If you say that – and if it's true – it means ... oh God, it means that I'm being deceitful to Clyde because I'm living with – I don't mean *living* with, I mean I'm ... harbouring' – she closed her eyes in exasperation – 'oh God, there must be a better word than that, sounds like "harbouring a criminal" – but I'm *permitting* a man to stay on Clyde's property who is in ...' She took a deep, anguished breath: 'Who thinks he's in love with me.' She looked at him. 'And that would be deceitful, Ben, it would be betraying Clyde's trust in me. And in *you* ...' She paused, then waved her hand and appealed to him. 'Say you did it because you wanted to "fuck" me! I can handle that – any woman can, we're told that often enough in our short unhappy lives by any Tom, Dick and Harry we're mugs enough to get near to – but *"worship"* ...?' She frowned at him and whispered: 'Please, Ben – I want you to stay, but with a clear conscience ...'

Ben didn't know whether to be hurt by all this, stung by her tone, her rejection, her putting him in his place – or grateful that she wanted him to stay. And, oh God, God, was there not a confession implicit in this appeal? He looked at her in the sunrise, and suddenly he had had enough of all this: enough of weeks of hesitation, of silent prayer. So, he was a funny-looking little man and he was grateful, *grateful* for what had befallen him, he had met the most wonderful woman of his life and she was pleading with him to admit that he was talking nonsense, and he had just been thrown to the ground. Ben Sunninghill had been shoved around just once too often and suddenly he no longer cared if he had to leave, if he had to ride away into the sunset today, and he said:

'Because I wanted to worship at your feet, Helen.'

She stared at him as if he had just played a dirty trick on her; she turned away to the fire in dismay. Ben's determination weakened, and he added: 'Which means: Because I wanted to make love to you, Helen.'

Her back was to him; she slowly turned half around.

'And that's all?'

Ben wanted to clench his teeth in anger for being a coward, for losing the courage of his convictions, for inviting rejection again. He said grimly: 'That's all.' Then to brutalize himself, and the moment, he added: 'Because, as you put it, I wanted to fuck you.'

Helen looked shocked by the word she herself had used. She seemed to force herself to weigh it; then she moaned: 'Oh, that's almost as bad! Ben, we can't *live* like this.'

And again Ben had had enough of all this, of Clyde, of living on another man's territory, of being a supplicant – it wasn't worth it anymore. He took a deep breath and said:

'Then I must go, Helen – I've caused nothing but trouble, anyway. And now this morning.'

Helen froze, as if she had sucked in her breath and held it. Then she clenched her fists and cried:

'No! I don't *want* you to leave! I want you to *stay* . . .'

Ben's voice came out as a whisper: 'Because you also wanted to make love last night? Because you almost yielded?'

Helen froze again, her eyes wide.

'No, Ben. No, no, no, I don't. Because you're my *friend*!'

It felt as if he'd been punched on the heart. He believed her. He blinked, then forced a wounded smile.

'I must leave, Helen.' He added: 'It's light enough for me to fix the Land Rover now.' He turned and started walking towards it.

Helen stared at his back, anguished, her lips parted; then she flung off the tarpaulin and ran after him.

Ben!' She grabbed his sleeve and pulled him round to face her. 'Oh Ben, please don't leave now! I want you to stay! You're my friend . . .' Her eyes implored, she groped for words, then blurted: 'I love you, Ben – as my *friend* . . .'

23

So Ben Sunninghill, against his better judgement, stayed on at Whoop-Whoop.

As a friend? Yes. For perhaps there are such things as platonic friendships – Lord knows he had enough sad experience of women almost to believe that. Anyway, he believed *her*, that she wanted him as a friend. And that hurt – male pride, lurking even in a body as unprepossessing as his, was wounded: rejection, never mentioned again, but clearly understood each day, is anguish to the love-lorn. *Love-lorn?* How fucking pathetic, Sunninghill – if that's how you are you should definitely leave! Or harden your heart, and just enjoy what you started out to do, have an adventure in the Aussie Outback for a while with your very, *very* nice friend, and put all that other nonsense out of your mind . . .

So Ben Sunninghill hardened his heart. Which is crap, of course, because though he believed Helen McKenzie, he didn't entirely believe her. Because, had there not been that moment when he held her breast and kissed her, that heart-stopping moment when she had almost yielded? Had she not said, when he challenged her about that the next morning, 'No, no, because you're my friend?' – wasn't that saying that she hadn't wanted to spoil their friendship by yielding? And he didn't entirely believe her because of her anguish when he had announced that he was going to leave – as if alarmed that she had gone too far in throwing their friendship at him. So, the truth of the matter is that in Ben's heart hope still festered. Which he denied to himself, most of the time. And which he certainly did not show to Helen. To her he only exhibited his usual cheerful, laid-back self. Indeed, most of the time that's how he managed to feel. He was *enjoying* it here at Whoop-Whoop playing farmers.

And Helen loved having him there and she was very grateful for all his work, even if his laid-back confidence in his own abilities scared the hell out of her sometimes. One evening Ben asked her why she never watched television, and she explained that though the set had been repaired a few months ago it still wasn't receiving properly.

'I'll have a look at it in the morning,' he said.

'No, the repair's still under guarantee, I'll take it in to Charleville sometime.'

The next morning she found Ben seated on the living-room carpet, the television spread around him in pieces.

'Ben!' She was aghast.

'I think I've found the problem, should be fine now.' He held up a component.

'*Ben* . . . That's a very expensive telly, and the guarantee's invalid if you tinker with it.'

'No problem,' Ben said airily, 'silly to take it to Charleville – fixed my own tellies before, used to build crystal sets when I was a kid—'

'That is *not* a crystal set, Ben: it should only be touched by experts!'

'See that?' He pointed at a wire. 'It's just got to be soldered on again, that's all. There's a soldering iron in the barn. It'll work fine, Helen.'

It did, just fine. Helen was immensely relieved – she had not relished explaining another repair bill to Clyde. A few days later she was working on her book when she heard a distant engine. At first she thought Ben was revving his motor cycle up to maximum on the airstrip: then she realized that she was hearing the aeroplane's engine. She stared across the kitchen, horrified; then she scrambled up and ran out into the yard. Yes – it was definitely the plane! She turned for the Land Rover – but it was not where she normally parked it. She ran around to the other side of the house – and it wasn't there either. Then it dawned on her that he'd used it to tow the aircraft. *Hey!*' she hollered furiously. She ran back to the kitchen, put on her shoes and started running up the track towards the airstrip.

She arrived five minutes later, out of breath, just as Ben finished his check-list and was about to release the handbrake. She ran across the strip, yelling, but Ben did not hear her; he let go the brake and the aircraft rumbled forward. It went roaring down the rough strip, faster and faster, dust and grass flying behind it and blasting over Helen. She clutched her head with one hand, eyes wild, and impotently watched him go hurtling down the strip. Ben eased back the yoke; the flaps came down, the nose lifted and the machine raced along on its tail wheel. Then it left the ground and went droning up into the clear blue sky, getting smaller and smaller.

Helen stood rigid, fists clenched, her mouth open. The aeroplane rose and rose, then it banked and disappeared behind the treetops. She banged her forehead and ran to the Land Rover parked at the treeline. She jumped in, started it and roared out on to the airstrip, so he would see her. She peered up through the windscreen for him.

There he was, the aircraft's nose up, climbing steeply. Helen slammed on her brakes and scrambled out. *'My God, he's going to stall it!'* Higher and higher and steeper the aircraft climbed, almost vertical now, then it stalled.

For a moment the machine seemed to stand in the air, on its tail, its propellers still vainly turning; then its nose turned downwards, and it dived. It went screaming down towards the earth, faster and faster. Ben pulled out of the dive, and Helen slumped against the Land Rover in relief. He levelled off and banked towards the airstrip, then he saw Helen down there, and he grinned and began to clown.

He waggled his wings at her in greeting and zoomed towards her at an altitude of five hundred feet, then he went into another climb. He climbed and climbed, higher and higher, and Helen's hands shot back to her mouth as she thought he was going to stall again; then he flipped the plane over into a rate 3 turn, sweeping steeply, his wheels almost to the sky; then he shoved the nose earthwards and went into a dive again. The aircraft hurtled towards the ground, and down on the strip Helen shrieked. Ben drove the screaming plane straight at the hard earth, then he pulled out of the dive. He banked gently towards the airstrip and prepared to bring her in to land. Helen jumped into the Land Rover, roared it off into the trees, stopped and scrambled out.

Ben lined the plane up with the airstrip and Helen held her breath, wide-eyed. He brought the plane down steeply and her eyes widened further and she cried helplessly: 'Too *steep*, for God's sake!' Lower and lower the plane came down and, as Helen was about to screech again, Ben levelled off. The plane touched down with a spurt of dust from the wheels.

He came spluttering and roaring down the strip, slowed and turned around. Helen began striding towards him. Ben pulled on the handbrake and cut the engine. The propellers feathered. He climbed out and jumped to the ground.

'Hi!' he called. 'Nothing much wrong with her at all.' He was very pleased with himself.

Helen came to a halt in front of him, her hands on her hips, and glared at him, her breathing shaky. She had such a hell of a lot to say that her mind fumbled. She glared at him some more, then she suddenly dropped her hands to her knees and whispered: 'Ben, what the hell are you doing?'

Ben frowned at her. He had been expecting squeals of gratitude for fixing the plane. 'Doing?' he echoed. 'I fixed your airplane, that's what I'm doing.'

'Oh Ben . . .' she said to her knees. 'I've never been so scared in my life.'

'Scared? But I told you I've got a licence!'

'And you also told me you could ride a horse.'

'Yeah, but that was a joke – it's no joke that I can fly. You saw me.'

'Yes, Ben, yes, you can certainly fly.' She straightened and looked at him grimly. 'But, Ben, you had no right to take the plane without my permission.'

Ben was astounded.

'No *right?*' He frowned at her, amazed. '*Right* – to do what? To take it for a joy-ride? To take it to visit my pals in Burraville? To take my girlfriend to the movies?' He stared at her. 'Good God, Helen, I've fixed your plane and I was test-flying the thing!' He shook his head. 'I've just saved you thousands! There was nothing wrong with it but some loose wires and dirty plugs, but you'd have paid thousands for a mechanic to come up from Charleville to tell you that! But it's no good thinking I've fixed it if I haven't *tested* it, is it? Like I'd test the tractor or Land Rover if I'd just repaired them – it's not a question of having a *right* . . .'

Helen had her eyes closed. 'Yes, Ben . . . And I'm very grateful for saving us thousands of dollars.' She opened her eyes. 'But the plane's a dangerous thing—'

'Not if you know what you're doing. And I do.' He glared at her. 'Don't I?'

She sighed. 'Yes, Ben, indeed you do. In fact, I'm amazed. But Clyde—'

'Oh *Clyde!*' He jabbed his finger at the plane. 'Clyde should be bloody grateful! Was the plane grounded for a year or was it not? Was Clyde facing thousands of dollars for nothing to fix it or was he not? Was it doing the engine any good to be sitting unused on the ground for the next three years while he scraped up the money? Engines have to be *used*, Helen . . .' He turned away in exasperation. 'So I'll put the bloody thing back in the barn.'

Helen stood there.

'Ben, I'm sorry . . .' He perked up immediately, and turned back to her. Helen explained: 'It's just that I had no warning, I was taken completely by surprise. Of course I was frightened, knowing what a dare-devil you are. And when I saw you *stunting* . . .' She closed her eyes, then gave a weak smile. 'You should have discussed it with me first, Ben.'

Ben smiled at her. 'Okay, guess I just thought I'd give you a nice surprise. However, now she's warmed up, let's go for a ride – and really show me this ranch of yours?'

Helen looked at him. 'But Ben—'

'Helen,' he interrupted. He slumped his shoulders in exasperation. 'I'm a good pilot. And that's a perfectly good little airplane. But it's been languishing in that barn for a year and in the few minutes I was up there I only blew the cobwebs out of it.'

The aircraft rose; the treetops dropped away below and the Outback opened up before them, low rolling downs of scrub going on and on in every direction, all the way to the horizon.

'Do you want to take over?' Ben said over the intercom.

'No,' Helen said, 'I'll be the guide; turn north.'

'You're the boss.' He banked the little plane and turned. Helen's house was down on the left, the ducks and chickens in the yard, the reservoir behind the eucalyptus trees sparkling blue. Ben's little cottage was half a mile away beyond the dry stream-bed. Five miles to the left was the big dark green square of the lucern field near Green's hut and Fury's paddock. A mile away to the right, beyond the causeway and the ridge of low hills, was the farm gate and the road to Burraville. Ben flew the aircraft parallel to the road, heading north. He had not been in this direction before. He peered down at the ground.

'Man, it's hard country.'

'Uh-huh,' Helen said. 'The northern section is our poorest.'

Only hard brown earth down there, sprinkled with scrub and sparse tufts of yellow grass; no sign of life. 'Does it ever get green – can you ever run cattle on this chunk?'

'Yeah, after the rains.'

'Is there ever water in that riverbed?'

'Only immediately after the rains.'

They droned on northwards. Ben could feel the oppression of this hard, brown loneliness. After about ten minutes he saw a fence in the distance, running westwards from the road.

'That's our northern boundary,' Helen said. 'Beyond is Fred More-comb's station.'

'Where's his entrance road?'

'Miles on, you can't see it. Turn left now.'

Ben banked, and they flew westwards above the fence. Gradually the terrain seemed to improve and the grass grew less sparsely. They flew over the fence of the mid-northern enclosure, where Whoop-Whoop's cattle presently were. They could see some of them scattered about. There was their feed-rack, near the drinking trough. They flew on. Then, far away to the north, on Morecomb's land, Ben saw a house midst eucalyptus trees. 'That his house?'

'Yes. And it's a pig-sty. Clyde and I were last over there when we did the land deal – his wife had left him a few months before – and we were shocked at the filth.' She snorted. 'Unflushed loos, unwashed crockery, the whole place reeking of unwashed bodies. *Yuk.*'

'Does he live alone now?'

'The word is sometimes he gets some sheila from Charleville or somewhere, but she soon quits. And he occasionally has some dead-beat white jackaroos when he's mustering his cattle.' She added: 'He hates Abbos, none of them will stay for long.'

'Has he got a lot of cattle?'

'Oh, he's got a good station, three times the size of ours. And a lot more wells.'

'And how much of yours did you sell him?'

'Oh, only ten thousand acres, to the west beyond the river. I'll show you. It was some of our best land, unfortunately, good wells, but we had to do something drastic about the mortgage with the kids going off to school. And the drought.'

Ben thought, *only* ten thousand acres? Lord, what a country! 'And does Clyde share your opinion of Morecomb?'

Helen sighed. 'Oh, Clyde tolerates just about everybody, except Bob Hawke and Keating. Live-and-let-live's his motto.'

Yes, Ben could believe that of Clyde, under his dour exterior, after the way the man had handled him. Indeed, he liked Clyde.

Some minutes later Helen pointed. Ben could see a long, grey, winding line of a riverbed ahead. She said: 'Our western boundary. It's a tributary to the Charle River system. Beyond that is the land we sold to the dreaded Fred.'

Ben peered down. From here it didn't look different to the hard, dry land they'd been flying over, but then he spotted a windmill, then another, then another, and in the distance, a huge tract of green. 'Lucern?'

'Yes. And corn, and grass. Oh, the jerk's a good farmer. When we get to the river, turn south-east. We'll do a figure-of-eight over the property, huh?'

Ben looked down at the riverbed as they banked – wide, winding, hard-arsed dry, dry, dry. *God, what a country!* And he felt for Helen and Clyde McKenzie – maybe it was okay country if you were not in debt, you could survive. But if you couldn't roll with the punches because of mortgages and school fees, oh boy! No cushion, no leniency down there. You sell ten thousand acres, sell the stock, count yourself lucky and go back to the mines.

They droned diagonally back across Whoop-Whoop. They flew over the mid-northern enclosure again, over the cattle, the lucern, the main house over to the left. Then the Burraville road came into sight again. 'Turn south,' Helen said. They flew on, over the low-lying southern enclosure, the hard brown earth dotted here and there with sheep. Helen pointed, and ahead Ben saw a wide sandy riverbed winding through the low hillocks.

'That's another tributary to the Charle River system; it runs under the causeway past our farm gate.'

Ben was getting the overall picture of the property now. He had not visited this area yet. He peered down. The scrub was sprinkled across the vast expanse, patches of skeletal shade on the hard earth, yellow grass scattered between the occasional sheep. Way over there was a concrete trough which he knew was fed by a pipe from the reservoir at Green's hut. The earth glared up at them, yellow-grey and flinty brown.

'Man, it's hard country,' Ben said again.

'Not when it rains. When it rains it's perfectly good country, all this would be green.'

'But it hasn't rained for three years?'

'We had a bit year before last, but not nearly enough. That stream-bed,' she pointed again, 'when it really rains, that causeway near our gate gets flooded. *Feet* under water. And all around here the river breaks its banks and floods for miles and miles; and all those little hillocks become islands, and all that over there looks like an inland sea.'

It was unimaginable, looking down on that hard dry expanse under that bell-jar sky. 'How often does that happen?'

'Only once in the twenty years I've been here. But it's a hell of a mess when it happens: it floods from way up north, through here, all the way down to Adelaide and Melbourne. Inundates millions of square kilometres.'

'Lord.' It seemed incredible.

'Yeah.' She pointed ahead again. 'See that hill – it's got a beacon on it? That's our southern boundary, it runs in a straight line from the Burraville road over to the right,' she swept her finger across the horizon, 'across to the riverbed we turned at.'

Ben knew properties were vast in this country, but Whoop-Whoop was a *small* station? They droned along the southern border, following the hill-tops.

'I'd like to fly a bit lower and see more, okay?' Ben said.

'It's just more of the same. Turn for home, please.'

'Hell,' he said, 'we've only been up a short while – you take over for a bit.'

She turned to him with a sigh. 'Let's go back now?'

Ben wanted to say, Oh fuck Clyde! 'Stop worrying about Clyde – it's good for the plane! Now take over for a bit. I'm here to catch you.'

For a moment anger flashed across her face, but she took the yoke. 'Okay, Mr Sunninghill!'

She pushed the yoke forward and the nose came down. Ben's stomach lurched, and the plane began to zoom down towards the scrub. The force of the descent pressed his back against his seat and he had to restrain himself from grabbing the controls. He stared through the perspex at the earth looming up at him, closer, closer, closer, and he was about to shout 'That's enough!' when Helen grimly pulled back the yoke. She levelled off a couple of hundred feet above the scrub and turned to him.

'Close enough?'

Ben was grinning. 'Fine.'

'Great country, huh?'

They zoomed above the scrub-tops, and the country got harder the further west they flew, the trees even further apart; many of them were dead, just skeletons, and the earth changed colour from brown to grey.

'Seen enough?' Helen asked.

'Okay.'

She pulled back the yoke and the plane began to climb. Then Ben saw the kangaroos in the distance and pointed excitedly. 'Are those roos?'

Helen peered. 'Damn.' She banked the plane towards them, flying at about four hundred feet.

They were almost the colour of the dry earth, a dozen or so of them standing up on their haunches, peering uncertainly at the machine droning towards them. When they were about a thousand yards off the kangaroos turned and fled. They went leaping away towards the dry riverbed, the western boundary, forepaws up, long tails streaming, ears back, bounding away for dear life.

'We'll chase 'em back to Fred's land,' Helen said grimly. She zoomed up from behind and flashed over them, then banked sharply to the right. She took the plane around in a circle and came up on the fleeing kangaroos from behind again. She roared over them again and banked around for another run.

'Come down lower,' Ben said.

'You do it, then.'

'There's nothing dangerous, Helen.'

'*You* do it.'

Ben took the yoke. He brought the plane around. 'How far to your boundary?'

She pointed. 'That's it ahead, the riverbed, about a mile.'

Ben eased the yoke forward and the earth loomed up. He levelled off at fifty feet and began to close in, the plane's shadow racing ahead. They buzzed the fleeing creatures again. Ben banked the plane and looked down. 'They're beautiful.'

'Oh, they're dear animals, but my sheep have a tough enough time without competing with them.'

'Do you get a lot of them?'

'No, we're so dry – the surrounding stations get more. Clyde shoots 'em. It breaks my heart, but it's got to be done.'

Ben began to bring the plane around again. 'The fences don't keep 'em out?'

'They can usually jump over ordinary cattle fences like ours, and the joeys creep through underneath.'

It broke Ben's heart too, to think of shooting them. He roared up on the tails of the frantically bounding animals. The riverbed was only a hundred yards ahead now, and as he zoomed over their heads the leading ones were leaping at the fence along the bank. Ben turned for one last run, climbing over Fred Morecomb's side of the river and swinging back east towards Whoop-Whoop. Most of the kangaroos were over the fence now, the joeys wriggling under the lowest strand. Ben banked around. By the time he roared up on the last two they were springing across the riverbed and up into Fred Morecomb's territory. Ben zoomed after them for one last buzz to impress them that Helen's side of the river was a no-no. The kangaroos were two hundred yards inside Morecomb's land, the plane roaring towards the river for one last pass, when Helen saw the vehicle racing along the track towards them. 'Uh-oh,' she said. 'Turn right!'

'Fred Morecomb?'

As Ben turned the plane to fly up the riverbed, the truck slammed to a stop and Fred Morecomb leapt out. He waved both arms and hollered up to the sky. Ben flew past him, then began to bank over Helen's land to go round in a circle to fly past Fred again.

'Keep going!' Helen snapped. 'Leave him alone! Turn for home, please.'

'But you're entitled by law to chase wild animals off your land, aren't you? *Ferae naturae*, that's ancient Roman law!'

'But Fred Morecomb wouldn't care about any law, would he?' She sighed tensely. 'So I can expect a nice raspberry on the radio from him.'

Ben grinned. 'Invite him over for a cup of tea and explain about *ferae naturae*.'

Helen snorted. 'That's probably *exactly* what the bastard will do — this is *just* the excuse he needs to come over.' She slumped, and seethed: '*Oh*, what bad *luck* he was there...'

'Well, I'll be there when he calls. Relax, Helen.'

Helen snorted again. 'Oh, I just knew we shouldn't have done this.'

Ben groaned. 'Now you're worried about Clyde again? For God's sake, Helen, you're perfectly entitled to fly the family plane! Please relax...'

24

But Helen could not relax. That night she managed to get through to Clyde on the radio, ostensibly to tell him the good news that the aeroplane was now functional again, but really, Ben knew, to confess she had flown it before he heard about it from somebody else on the Outback telegraph.

'Jesus Christ!' Clyde said. '*Fixed* it? Over!'

'Well it flew, didn't it? Over.'

'Maybe, but he's not an aircraft mechanic, the bloody thing could have conked out in mid-air! Over!'

'It flew perfectly, darling! Ben says there was nothing wrong with it but some loose connections somewhere. Darling, I thought you'd be delighted, all that money a mechanic would have cost us. Over.'

'I wouldn't have been delighted if you'd crashed, would I?' He sighed; then went on grudgingly: 'All right, of course I'm pleased there ain't much wrong with it, but I don't want you to do that again, girl, until a qualified mechanic's had a look at it. And as we can't afford that, it means you can't fly it, period. Anyway, it's due for its hundred-hour inspection soon, and until we've done that it's *illegal* to fly it. Got that? So just you tell Ben I'm very grateful and all that, but will he please now tow it back to the barn. No, okay, leave it up on the strip and start it once a week for a few minutes, on the chocks. But no *flying*. Okay? Over.'

'Okay, over.'

'Anyway, we can't afford the bloody fuel . . .' He sighed. 'And Ben? How much longer's he staying? Over.'

Helen hesitated before pressing the transmission button.

'Oh, I think he'll be on his way soon. I think he's getting restless. He's a Peter Pan type, here today, gone tomorrow . . . Over.'

A brief silence. 'Hmm . . . Tomorrow, huh? And how's the station, girl? Over.'

'Oh, it's so dry. It looks terrible from the air. Over.'

'Hmm . . . Well, maybe we'll get some rain this year, huh? Over.'

'And,' Helen said, 'we saw some roos in the south-west enclosure. Over.'

Damn . . .

Helen was relieved at how well that conversation went off. And to her further relief, Fred Morecomb did not radio, nor did he take the excuse to come over. Helen relaxed. She reported Clyde's instruction concerning the aeroplane, and Ben henceforth refrained from tackling jobs without discussing it with her first.

Before dawn Ben got up, showered and went to work at his kitchen table on his journal. At about eight o'clock he started on the vegetable garden, whilst it was still cool. When he'd finished that, he went to ask Helen if she had any maintenance chores for him; then he rode his motor cycle up to Green's hut to check on him and the cattle and sheep, and to ride the horse. In the late afternoon he returned, had a swim in the reservoir, then he went back to his cottage to work some more on his journal while he drank a good deal of beer. He found his mind worked best in the late afternoons: his perceptions clearer, his imagery more vivid, his language richer, his inspirations quicker, his feelings deeper when the hard physical day was almost over and softening, the shadows lengthening and one's feelings mellow and there is the legitimate pleasure of booze to supe one up. ('It's a pity to experience that precious hour and not try to write it down, Helen – the wisdom that may be thus alcoholically unlocked.') When the sun had gone down he walked over to the main house. Each evening he had to re-armour his heart as he walked in the kitchen door and saw her poring like a fevered schoolgirl over her own book, wisps of hair hanging, ink smudges on her brow and fingers. Sometimes she wanted him to read it, but more often ('No, it's terrible, Ben . . .') she just wanted to talk, talk, talk. Sometimes she accompanied him on his chores, as if she had to squeeze as much as possible out of him while she had the chance.

'I wish you'd let me read what *you*'re writing, Ben.'

She had come to help him weed the vegetable garden: they were each astride a row of lettuces, hoeing.

'I'm not writing anything very constructive, I'm afraid. Mostly I just sit and think.' He elaborated: 'And sometimes I just sit.'

She dug in her hoe aggressively. 'But is it a story or just a kind of diary? I mean, what are you trying to *achieve*?'

'Ah,' Ben said. 'The embarrassing bit. The criminal waste of cerebral effort. Oh, if only I had an economic *purpose*.' He moved backwards a pace and worked his hoe again. He could see the line of her panties as she bent over in the next row. 'But, alas, I have no commercial instinct at all anymore. My only ambition with my book is to become wise. And meanwhile to live my life to the full.'

She moved a step backwards. 'But for that you need money. If it was published you'd have it.'

Oh, to carry her off on the pillion of his motorbike, the wind blowing through her hair, free as the air and free of money. 'Not much. And I've got enough, for my simple needs. The only material thing I want is a boat one day, and I've got enough for that even now.'

She said, her rounded backside to him: 'But what about love, Ben? A wife costs money.'

For a moment it crossed his mind that maybe she was trying to find out something. 'Indeed. But in my case that's academic.'

She straightened and looked back at him. 'Oh *Ben* . . . Do you really think you'll never find somebody who loves you?'

Oh, Jesus . . . Was this not living verbal proof that her feelings for him, her 'love' for him, really *was* purely platonic? He forced a cavalier grin and hoed on. 'I wouldn't want to have anything to do with the kind of girl who'd marry me, Helen – she'd be a real desperado.'

She groaned. 'Be *serious*, Ben, you're not Quasimodo!' She bent and started working again. 'Would you even *like* to be married, with your footloose life?'

Oh dear . . . Not Quasimodo, huh? He *felt* like the fucking Hunchback of Notre Dame now! He forced a smirk and tried to find an honest answer to her frank question.

'Sure. Provided she wanted to be footloose with me. It's a wonderful life really, being footloose. And of course I want somebody to share things with – I'm lonely too.' (Maybe rousing her sympathy was the way?) He straightened and said to her buttocks: 'Whenever I see a nice-looking girl – I mean a girl who looks a nice person as well as being physically attractive – I wish I could find somebody like her. And then I feel sorry for myself. Oh . . .' (He closed his eyes. Oh fuck her sympathy!) He bent to his work again. 'Not sorry for myself – I mean, I'm just an incurable romantic, Helen.' He snorted: 'So, when I see a happy-looking couple, having a nice time together, just sitting on a beach or in a restaurant, I think how great it would be to be like them. And for a while I feel as lonely as hell.' He added (and this was more to the point): 'And, of course, I'd like to be married for the sex.'

Helen looked back at him. 'Oh, Ben . . .' she said sympathetically.

Oh Jesus, Jesus – her sympathy he definitely did not need. He jabbed with the hoe. 'Don't feel sorry for me, Helen – I do okay. I jump on my motorbike and go on to something new – another museum, another art gallery, another bar. Another town. And remind myself how lucky I am to be alive and *free*.'

She said earnestly: 'Have you ever thought of trying a marriage bureau?'

Ben stopped in mid-stroke. Oh dear, *dear* . . . Not Quasimodo, but how about a marriage bureau? Out, out, damned spot of love-lorn foolishness! Oh, heart, where is thy metal?! Here it is, Sire! Well, re-gird thy ventricles, Fool, and realize the lady doth not protest too much, she's fucking genuine . . . He took a deep breath, stooped and worked on.

'Sure. And I used to be a prolific advertiser in the Lonely Hearts columns. The *Village Voice* in New York, *Time Out* in London.' He sighed and almost saw the funny side of it. What the hell, Sunninghill, you arse: just enjoy. Enjoy, and no more nonsense over this lovely lady. 'I tried a marriage bureau once in New York, years ago.' (On the other hand, maybe self-effacement was the trick?) 'But when I fronted up to get myself computerized my statistics sounded so bloody discouraging I walked out. "You are a rather *specialized* case, Mr Sunninghill," the computer-lady said when I told her I liked my ladies highly intelligent, very articulate, great sense of humour, tall, blonde, beautiful, with magnificent tits.'

Helen was giggling. She half straightened and leant on her hoe. 'Ben, you're not a specialized *case*!' She giggled again. 'And how did you get on with the Lonely Hearts columns?'

Ben smiled ruefully. 'Oh, I met some nice people, even made some friends. But didn't get laid, I'm afraid.'

Helen laughed. 'Oh, you're *funny*, Ben . . .' She dabbed her eyes and resumed work. 'And? What did you say in your advertisements?'

Okay, give her a laugh. 'Ah, that's the tricky part. You see, your advertisement must be clever, an eye-catcher, amusing but dripping with sincerity, to sell yourself. So I spent hours – *days* – composing my first one. It was splendid stuff. Could have got myself a job on Madison Avenue with it. Trouble was I didn't mention the bad news – you know, the bit about being five-foot in my socks, my dandruff, buckteeth—'

Helen guffawed down at the lettuces. 'You haven't got buckteeth! Or dandruff!'

Ben was grinning. 'Anyway, I only told them the good news in my advert. So when the first respondent turned up for the romantic meeting, agog with anticipation – *tingling* with excitement and *burning* with desire – she got the anti-climax of her life. You should have seen her face when I identified myself. She fled. Clutching her anguished brow.'

Helen was still laughing. 'Oh, Ben, I don't believe she *fled* . . . What was she like?'

Ben came to the end of his row, the last for the day. He turned and sat down in a heap on the edge of the garden. He looked at Helen's buttocks with longing and said: 'Great, just how I like 'em, a real diesel-driven blonde.' Helen giggled. 'No, she didn't exactly flee, but she did promptly happen to remember a dental appointment. At seven o'clock at night? And she did tarry long enough to give me a brief but succinct admonishment about how it's "much better to be *honest* in this life". Then she fled.'

Helen straightened. Her eyes were moist. (Maybe self-effacement was working?) 'Oh, how *awful* . . . Did you say anything?'

He smirked bravely. 'I hardly had time. Just said I was sorry. Proceeded to get quietly drunk. Later I saw the funny side of it.'

'Oh, Ben, you didn't have anything to *apologize* for! She was a *beast.*' Helen took a last few jabs at her row of lettuces, then turned out of the furrow, dabbing her eyes. She came and slumped down near him, flushed. (Are we getting somewhere, Sunninghill?) 'And,' she grinned at him, 'what did the other girls do?'

(No, we're not.) 'Well, I never met that batch of respondents, because I wrote back to them first, giving them the bad news, to spare further embarrassment. And I went to one of those automatic photo kiosks and had pictures of myself taken, beaming my most charming smile, and included one in each letter. And, would you believe, none of them replied?'

'Oh, Ben. *So?*'

What the hell. 'So in my next advertisement – and all my many subsequent ones – I was more "honest". I socked it to 'em, warts and all. And I still got replies, so that blonde was right.'

Helen was shaking with giggles. 'What did you say in that next advert?'

Oh, to reach out and take her earthy, sweaty body in his sweaty arms. 'Something like "Brace yourselves, ladies, 'cos I'm no oil-painting – despite what my Jewish mama says – and I'm unquestionably only five-foot-six in my custom-made built-up blue suede shoes. Indeed, I'm the Before guy in the Before-and-After Charles

Atlas ads, so you're going to have to have a terrific sense of humour, but I *have* got this razor-brain and golden heart and I'm a humdinger in bed – as far as I remember. PS. Don't stampede."' He smiled wanly at her. 'Something like that.'

She was convulsed with laughter, the corks on her hat dancing about her flushed face. 'Oh Ben, you're not the Before-guy!' She wiped the corners of her wet eyes with the back of her wrist. 'I think I'd have fallen for an ad like that – if I'd had the courage.'

Oh, if she had the courage . . . but it probably wouldn't have worked then, either. Because he *was* the Before-guy. So put it out of your mind, chum . . .

'Even got replies to that ad. And not all of them were desperadoes – it's amazing how many lonely people there are in the world . . .' He paused (significantly enough?). 'In fact, I think marriage bureaus and Lonely Hearts columns are excellent institutions. We spend our lives looking for mates – that's why we join clubs, go to parties, et cetera, but it's all so hit-or-miss, a matter of luck, and at least fifty per cent of us make a mess of it and team up with the wrong person. So, surely it's only sensible to go to the experts, as you would if you were investing money. In the matter of love you're investing your whole *life*, your heart. So surely it's sensible to go to a marriage bureau and tell 'em what you want, and let them do the difficult leg-work for you and match you up? Or at least to advertise . . .' He ended on an upbeat note: 'Anyway, I made some really nice friendships that have endured – and I've met *their* friends, who I wouldn't otherwise have met.' Then he smiled bravely. 'But no romance, I'm afraid.'

Helen had her head on one side. Oh God, he could have groaned when she said:

'Ben, I so admire you – the experiences you've had. Your courage, to stick your neck out . . .' She smiled, and added: 'I hope you're writing about all this?' Then she appealed to him: 'I *wish* you'd let me read what you're writing.'

Oh, it was a hopeless case of unrequited love. Yes, she admired him – she really *liked* him, he knew that. Even, maybe, loved him – but only for his friendship. So gird thy loins, Heart . . .

But there are more ways of killing a cat than stuffing its throat with butter, more ways of winning a fair lady than wearing your faint heart on your sleeve, than smothering her feet with kisses.

Sometimes he wrote poetry, but mostly it was an erratic flow of observations, some of it profound, some ironic, sometimes tender, sometimes vitriolic, often funny as hell. He wrote a good deal about the environment: whales, the fur industry ('of soft and furry things that upon our shoulders lie/ Of little things, of timid things that took so long to die'), the greenhouse effect, the ruthless rapacity of man. 'That's the kind of crap I'm writing, Helen,' he said, adding, 'but one day I'll go and do something about it.'

Helen had thrown down her pen in frustration and come with him to feed the sheep; they were grinding through the low-lying enclosure in the utility truck with a load of lucern.

'Oh it doesn't sound like crap to me, Ben, it sounds wonderful. But what will you do about it?'

Wonderful Ben Sunninghill and his brilliant mind?

He stopped the truck near the drinking trough.

'There's so much that can be done, Helen, even if it's just stuffing leaflets through letterboxes for Save-the-Whale, or working for Greenpeace as a clerk, or making a fuss to get zoos improved. Rescuing animals from vivisectionist laboratories, or helping catch ivory poachers in Africa. And shooting drug-dealers.' He got out, climbed on to the back of the truck and picked up a pitchfork. Sheep were converging from all directions.

Helen climbed out. '*Shooting* drug dealers? I don't believe you're capable of hurting anything.'

From up here Ben could see down her shirtfront, the lovely full cleavage of her breasts, and his hands ached to touch them. '*Drug* dealers? People who destroy others for gain? I'd do it without the slightest compunction if I knew I could get away with it. It wouldn't be murder, it would be a service to mankind. Like President Bush invading Panama to get rid of that arch-criminal Noriega. I take my hat off to President Bush.'

He jabbed his pitchfork into the lucern and tossed a load down to the sheep. Helen said: 'But America had no right to invade.'

'She had a *moral* right!' He tossed down more feed. 'The right conferred by Natural Justice.' He leant on his pitchfork and said down to her: 'Good God, Noriega was one of the biggest tyrants and purveyors of human misery in the world; he had to be got rid of, and Bush had the guts to do it, despite what international law said!' He frowned at her. 'I don't understand you bleeding hearts, Helen – you're all in favour of the underdog, but you protest in favour of the *unjust* "legal rights" of the tyrant.'

She glared up at him. 'I'm *not* a bleeding heart, Ben. I'm simply

saying the answer is to improve society so that drug-dealers are driven
out of business!'

Oh, he longed to scoop her breasts in both hands. He dug his
pitchfork into the lucern instead. 'Sure. And while we're tackling that
nigh-impossible task, let's shoot the bastards to hurry things up. *And*
the ivory poachers, before the elephants are all gone!'

Yet she found him surprisingly cynical when the conversation
turned to the suffering caused by natural disaster. Did he enjoy shocking her – impressing her with No-nonsense Sunninghill? Oh, bullshit
again.

'Of course I feel sorry for the people of Bangladesh when a typhoon
strikes, and for the starving of Ethiopia, and for the Aids sufferers in
Africa. But there are enough incompetent politicians and churchmen
and United Nations officials blabbering about that without me adding
my two-bits' worth. Keep your finger on that inlet and pass me the
wrench.'

They were repairing the ball-cock valve at the drinking trough.
Helen passed him the wrench with her free hand. Ben continued as
he unscrewed the nut: 'And remember that the typhoon and the famine
and the Aids epidemic are all part of Nature, they've only come about
because there're too many people using and abusing the environment
– the typhoon would not cause such human havoc if there weren't too
many goddam humans living there, and there *are* too many because
we're over-breeding. Same with the famine. Same with Aids – it's only
reaching epidemic proportions because human beings screw so much
because Nature's evolved us to be horny as hell. So, Aids is Nature's
response, like typhoid will correct the problem of the over-crowding
which caused it, if given the chance.'

'"If given the chance"? That's *very* cynical, Mr Sunninghill.'

Ben grinned. He loved working with her – and he loved working
her up. He peered into the ball-cock's union intently and said: 'There's
your problem.' He pointed at a piece of twig clogging the valve, then
scraped it out with a screwdriver.

'I said you're being *very* cynical, Ben.'

'Oh?' Ben blew the union clean, then started screwing the nut back
on. 'Helen, of course we should do our best to curb epidemics and
alleviate human suffering. But if we fail we should not be too despon-
dent, because we're only trying to combat Nature's efforts to enable
the environment to survive – upon which our very lives depend.'

'That's *very* philosophical. Wow! Yippee for good old Mother
Nature and her environmentally-rehabilitative nasty diseases. Indeed,

do you not discern the Divine Will in all this suffering – can't we give *that* a bit of credit?'

Ben smiled. Oh, he loved her ... He surprised himself by saying: 'Helen, you've got the most beautiful eyes.'

Helen blinked, and suddenly she was blushing. 'Oh, be serious, Ben!'

'I *am*.'

'Ben,' she sighed flusteredly, 'I said do you think it's the Divine Will that there should be suffering?'

Ben smiled wanly. She didn't want any nonsense, did she?

'I don't know enough about The Divinity to venture an opinion, Helen. But – since you ask me – I do suspect He knows what's going on, yes.'

'And approves? You think it's all part of His grand plan for us unworthy mortals?' Her blush was subsiding.

'I don't know what to think. But if scorned for that reply I'd venture what a Churchman would say: "His ways are higher than our ways".'

'Oh you're a clever bugger, Ben Sunninghill, turning the Testament against us poor Christians. And how do you feel about the victims of war?'

Clever, huh? *Good.* 'Well, war is part of Nature too. Political ambitions, territorial expansion, the AK47, they're as much part of Nature as the plague and the boomerang. Okay, you can take your finger away now.' She did so and water flowed into the trough. Ben shoved the ball-cock's union to the pipe, and screwed it into place. He put the wrench to the nut. 'Of course I feel sorry for the victims of war, Helen, particularly because most wars are conducted by politicians. Left to themselves the ordinary people wouldn't do it – they'd just resort to some ineffective bitching and football hooliganism. But, alas, the human propensity for accepting leadership is part of Nature too, ever since we dropped out of the trees and decided we had to band together in order to catch our prey in competition with more efficient lions and tigers.' He gave the nut a last twist, and sat back on his haunches. 'However, people have a voice, in their own political machinery and in the United Nations. The ones I feel truly sorry for are the *voiceless*, the ones who have no power to help themselves, namely the animals we brutally slaughter for ornamentation and pet-food, and the animals we coop in tiny cages pending slaughter for our dinner-tables. And the pathetic animals we keep in zoos.'

She sat down on the rim of the trough; oh, she was enjoying this. 'And where does God fit into this?'

'He doesn't. It's pure *Godlessness*.' Ben stood up and started putting tools into the box.

'But why doesn't He put a stop to it?' She hadn't had so much fun in years – since Uni. She never talked to Clyde about *anything* except school-fees and drought. 'Do you believe in the Devil? Or an evil power?'

Ben smiled. Your *mind*, Sunninghill, that's what you've got instead of muscles. 'There is a spiritual life in addition to this terrestrial one we're presently undergoing, Helen. That seems clear, from the learned men of all religions and from countless reports over the centuries of paranormal experiences – ghosts, the supernatural, et cetera. All those people, all those theologians, they can't all be wrong. So it seems safe to say there is also a spiritual side to this physical world we know – to Nature, in other words. And there is also an *evil* side to Nature, if only in the evil men do. It seems entirely possible, therefore, that the evil of some men survives death into the spiritual hereafter. Be that as it may, in my view – for what it's worth' – (hopefully your heart) – 'the evil we see on this earth is Man's – Man's fault, not the Almighty's. Because Good *can*, with effort, be made to triumph over Evil, as is proved every time we impose a just solution on a problem of injustice. So, to take this to its logical conclusion, surely we can eradicate most Evil by rounding up all the evil buggers. Namely the drug-barons, the warmongers, the ivory poachers, the fur-traders, the vivisectionists, the battery-farmers, the zoo-keepers – and shooting 'em.'

Helen giggled, delighted with this! Even Helen Dumbo McKenzie could shoot peas through this one. *'Zoo-keepers too?'*

'Well, maybe a lengthy term of imprisonment will be enough to rehabilitate zoo-keepers and battery-farmers. Provided their cells are very, *very* small.'

Helen laughed. *'Oh Ben, I love your bullshit!'*

'*Bull*shit?' He picked up the toolbox and turned towards the Land Rover, grinning. Bullshit baffles hearts?

He would not let her read what he was writing. But then, one hot Monday morning, in the fifth week after Clyde's departure, she had the chance to do so.

She usually did the washing on Monday afternoons, but because she was tearing her hair out over her book she threw down her pen and decided to start it early. Ben had not yet delivered his laundry so she stomped over to his cottage to collect it. She expected to find him there, for normally he went up to Green's hut later in the day, but the place was empty and his motorbike was gone. She stripped the linen off his bed, then went to the bathroom to look for his dirty clothes. On her way through the kitchen she saw all his notebooks on the table. She stopped, wrestling with her conscience – but only for a moment.

She stuck her head out of the kitchen door furtively. He was nowhere in sight and she would hear his motorbike when he returned. She trampled her conscience underfoot, sat down and grabbed the nearest books.

None of them was numbered or labelled. She opened two and glanced at both, trying to determine a sequence. But the entries were not dated. And it appeared that Ben's mind jumped around all over the place: one entry seemed to have been written in Africa, the next in Europe, the next in Africa again, the next in America. She read:

'A commendable step. I have today solemnly taken the hip-flask from my pocket and stuck it in the bottom of my saddle-bags. This means I have to get up, climb down the ladder, creep through the bush to my bike, unpack, top up, re-pack, creep back through the bush, climb up the ladder to my platform without spilling too much, every time I want a drink. Is this, or is it not, a step in the right direction?'

She smiled. But *ladder? Platform?* Was this an observation platform he had built in the African bush? Oh, how wonderful . . . She flicked over half a dozen pages and began reading again:

'Who says "Candy's dandy but liquor's quicker"? She guzzled my chocolates, swigged all my booze, kissed me goodnight on my fevered forehead and fled into the subway.'

Oh, poor Ben . . . But which subway did she flee into: New York? London? Paris? Do they have subways in Africa? The next entry read:

'I awoke in my sleeping bag to the sound of crashing branches. There, in the moonlight, were five elephants, feeding, not ten yards from me. I lay still, petrified of moving lest they charge. They came closer, and closer, and my fear was exquisite, until their great bodies blocked out the moon. Then, one by one, they carefully, politely, stepped over me, and slowly continued on their unhurried way. And my breathless happiness was complete.'

Helen closed her eyes. Oh, how marvellous! The things he had done. . . . She sighed and turned over a few more pages.

'The colonial powers were unfair to the Africans, and to the world, when they granted their colonies independence. Because they did it as self-centredly, as cold-bloodedly as a businessman cutting his losses. Surely it was their natural duty to stay long enough to ensure that their offspring had the economic and political infrastructure to survive? Surely education and employment is every

child's right? But we heartlessly denied it to them when we folded our economic tents overnight and went off about our adult worldly business.'

Helen pulled a face. Child? Adult? The next page read:

'Never disagree with a woman: it may not be true that the hand that rocks the cradle rules the world, but they've got an absolute one hundred per cent Lloyd's A1 guaranteed monopoly on pussy.'

Oh *Ben*! . . . And she was surprised that her reproof included a stab of possessiveness. *Pussy . . . ?* She reached for another book, feeling like a Peeping Tom, and opened it at the first page.

'At last the Second Wind of Change is blowing in Africa and, ironically, it is coming from the same quarter as the First: the Kremlin. Mr Gorbachev has put fear and fury into the hearts of Africa's one-party politicians. In South Africa we now have Pretoriastroika, we have pro-democracy riots in Zambia, Kenya, Gabon, Ivory Coast – and many others will follow. Even the Organiz-ation of African Unity is uncomfortably talking about democracy now that the Berlin Wall's come down, and seems to realize it can no longer blame their disasters on colonialism. At last it looks as if true freedom will come to Africa, thirty years after the first Wind of Change, after thirty years of black tyranny. But it will all come to naught when the tyrants are overthrown, unless the white man comes back – not as colonialists, of course, but as no-nonsense trustees of insolvent estates. Because, as the World Bank has just announced, a quarter of black Africans live in a state of "chronic food shortage", which means starvation and absolute poverty; infant mortality is soaring, school enrolment is plummeting, the population growth is 3.1% and will double in the next twenty-two years, agriculture has failed hopelessly to keep up for the thirty years since the white man left, so food imports have doubled in the last fifteen years, while the per capita income to pay for it has fallen 20% below what it was ten years ago, while the environmental degradation has been horrific: tropical deforestation has been proceeding at the rate of 11,000,000 hectares every year (22,000,000 in 1988), which has resulted in much lower rainfall and droughts, as well as driving Africa's wildlife towards extinction.

Those are the World Bank's figures, folks, not mine. Where will it all end? Do we want to save Africa – its starving people, its forests, its wildlife? Do we want to give them real freedom, Freedom From Want? If so, the white man must go back, before it's too late – not even Russia can save itself without our help. The time for slogans, rhetoric and pride is past – this is an international emergency. So, onward Christian soldiers!'

Helen gave a sigh, and stared across the kitchen.

Oh . . . Oh, yes, she would love to be a Christian foot-soldier . . . To go out there and really do something to *help*. She didn't accept at face value his criticism of African leaders as one-party tyrants – she *did* largely blame the colonial period for most of Africa's ills – but by God those World Bank statistics spoke for themselves and cried out for the Western world's help. Wouldn't it be wonderful, worthwhile, *exciting*, to join something like the Peace Corps for a few years instead of languishing here on Whoop-Whoop, empty-handed, waiting for Clyde to have earned enough money to come home – wouldn't it be wonderful to do something worthwhile with that time? Oh, how she envied Ben for having the freedom to do just that, even if it was only for the animals – and they were just as deserving! She would love to join him in that. And she admired him – thoroughly *liked* him – for having these feelings . . .

She glanced guiltily at her watch, then reached out and hastily searched for his current notebook – she wanted to see what he had written about Australia, about the Outback, about Whoop-Whoop. About *her*? Had he written anything profound about Helen McKenzie? She found the current book and flipped it open near the end.

She did not hear Ben approach: he had left his motor cycle at the barn in order to service it there later and he had walked to the cottage. Through the open door he saw her sitting at the kitchen table, her back to him, poring intently over his notebooks, and he froze.

He stood stock-still: and seeing her prying so avidly into his secret thoughts seemed almost as significant as hearing her whisper his name in her sleep. For a breathless moment it stumbled across his mind that this was his chance, his opportunity to tiptoe in behind her and catch her at a disadvantage, to slip his arms around her . . . crush her to his chest and throw his heart down on the table. For a moment he stood there, devouring her with his eyes; then his nerve failed him, and he backed off out of sight.

He went shakily around the side of the cottage, then walked towards the front door, whistling loudly.

Helen burst out on to the porch, clutching his laundry, flustered.

'Hi! Just this minute popped over to fetch your things for the washing-machine – doing it early today!'

Ben felt flustered too. 'Thank you, I should have brought them over this morning.' He mounted the steps. 'Come in for a beer?'

'No, I'll wander on back, the machine's waiting—'

'Relax and have a beer, Helen.' It was a plea.

He went into the kitchen, to the refrigerator, still shaken by what he had almost done. His notebooks appeared to be as he left them – he could not tell whether she'd seen the current one or not.

Helen stayed for one beer, but she could not relax. She could not tear her mind off that last notebook, off the paragraph she had read just before she'd heard him whistling:

'Indeed it is better to have loved and lost than to have never loved at all. But to have loved without hope, to love and lose without even a contest, without even the telling of it, to love and ride away manlessly, is not better than never having loved at all – it's fucking pathetic. So put it out of your mind, chum.'

25

But Helen McKenzie could not put it out of *her* mind.

She had thought, she had believed – anyway, God *knew* she had worked at it to put that drunken episode round the campfire out of her mind. No, there *hadn't* really been that moment of hesitation after she'd realized he was kissing her feet, she hadn't almost surrendered to the voluptuousness of it! Had she? Nor when he'd then taken her completely by surprise by collapsing on to the sacks beside her, and seized her breast and kissed her and then thrust his hand on her thighs. *Had* there? No, she'd just been astonished, completely taken off guard by all this unheralded passion from her friend Ben Sunninghill, that's why he'd thought there'd been that moment of 'hesitation' which he'd confronted her with the next morning. Complete astonishment, that was clearly the reason. And she'd certainly made it clear to Ben, hadn't she, that he was mistaken if he'd thought she'd hesitated, that such nonsense must never happen again, that she couldn't live with the fact of him nursing a secret passion for her because that would be deceitful to Clyde – Clyde trusted her, Ben was Clyde's guest and it would be tremendously deceitful to let Ben stay under such circumstances. And when Ben had then announced that he should leave, and she had begged him to stay, she'd made it perfectly clear that she wanted him to do so only as a *friend*. He had accepted that, hadn't he? He had not done or said a thing since that night to suggest otherwise, to indicate that his grab at her had been anything more than drunken opportunism, the sort of thing just about any man would have tried under the circumstances. So surely that paragraph in his notebook wasn't about her? Please God, couldn't she put it out of her mind with a clear conscience? She was being entirely honest with herself, wasn't she?

Helen McKenzie took a deep, troubled breath. Because no, it was not quite so, and her conscience was not quite clear. Because, to be brutally honest with herself, she had to admit that she had not been quite asleep when Ben had untied her espadrilles and slowly slipped them off: to be brutally honest she had been almost overwhelmed by the tenderness of that moment, indeed by the sensuousness of it, when he had suddenly, ardently kissed her feet. Yes, fleetingly, through the surprise, it was a wonderful feeling, of ... astonishing voluptuousness, yes for a moment she had been transfixed by the feeling, and wanted it to go on ... Then he had come collapsing down beside her and plunged his mouth on to hers, and seized her breast and thighs. And, oh God, now she was being honest, yes, of course there had been a moment of hesitation, even of sexual excitement, maybe she *had* almost surrendered ... But wouldn't *anybody* feel something like that, isn't that human nature? And she had stamped on it, hadn't she? And the next morning she'd made her attitude one hundred per cent clear, so she wasn't being disloyal to Clyde because she *had* put that flash, that whole episode out of her mind, hadn't she? Good God, anybody only had to look at Ben Sunninghill and know she was speaking the truth, right?

But Helen had to sigh again. Because it was also a sneaky little fact that she *had* had another look at him and that although, yes, he was a little fellow, with sticking-out ears, and unquestionably was three inches shorter than her, wasn't it also the honest truth, Helen McKenzie, that you've thought what lovely crinkly eyes he had, what a lovely sexy smile. Haven't you felt absolutely charmed by him, and isn't it true you absolutely love his *mind*, and, well, haven't you kind of forgotten about his size and all that? So wasn't that being kind of deceitful to Clyde? In fact wasn't it true that, though he hadn't *done* anything since that night by the campfire, she had sometimes been aware – when she was working with him, for example – of a kind of ... flirtatiousness in the air, and isn't it true that she had even enjoyed it? He had told her once that she had beautiful eyes, and she remembered blushing furiously. What's a blush if it's not a physical reaction? And isn't it a psychological truism that when two people work together a kind of intimacy develops that, in Freudian terms at least – was it Freud? – has a physical element? – that's why the boss of a business often has a big pull with his secretary because he's in command, and that has – or can have – a latent sexuality about it. Ben wasn't exactly the boss, but he certainly was the male in command around here. In fact, why had she gone out to work with him? Was it only because her book was driving her mad, or to keep an eye on the station? No, she had complete confidence in him. But was not that confidence a manifestation of her female dependency, and is not dependency partly physical in that she regarded him as her protector? Oh come, come, Helen, we're being rather ruthlessly analytical, aren't we, rather dramatic? Maybe, but didn't all this add up to something more than a platonic relationship?

And now that paragraph in his notebook . . .

Oh God, if that paragraph was about her, if Ben Sunninghill was secretly, passionately in love with her, he would have to go. She would owe it to Clyde. And to herself – she did not want to live a lie, have a guilty conscience. Oh, she could handle her side of it easily: dammit, it *was* platonic from her side, she had been unfair to herself – but she simply could not bear the *tension* of knowing he was in love with her, of waiting for him to do something, of being on guard. It was unnatural. But how was she going to discover the truth? Ask him? Confess she had read his notebook and confront him with it? No, that was ridiculous, and would make *her* look ridiculous, especially if the paragraph *wasn't* about her . . . In fact the only detail connecting her with the lament was that it was written in his current notebook, but his entries in all of them jumped all over the place. He could be referring to somebody he'd met in Timbuktu, or Buenos Aires. Like the girl who ate his chocolates, drank his booze and fled into the subway, the heartless bitch! So how the hell was she going to find out?

Wait and see if he made a move, gave any indication at all – that was surely the only way. (Did she *want* to find out? The thought of Ben leaving was awful . . .) So, wait and see. And meanwhile put it all out of her mind.

But it always came creeping back, for two reasons. One: whoever the girl was, it *was* pathetic, as he said, to love without hope, to lose without a contest, to ride away wordlessly – 'manlessly'. That brought a burn to her eye. Oh, Ben . . . She didn't want him to be man*less*, she wanted him to be man*ful*, happy . . . And two: if that lament wasn't for her, who the hell *was* it about? In her sound and sober senses she managed to convince herself that she did not care, because her feelings were platonic, that it was none of her business; but at the end of a long day's frustrating work on her book, when shadows lengthened and the Four-X came out, she was nagged with curiosity about the woman. Who was this female? *Oh, no, no, she was not jealous!* She only wanted him to be happy, only protecting his well-being. If that paragraph *was* about her she wanted to do absolutely nothing to complicate the situation, nothing to hurt him . . . Yes, Helen put it out of her sober mind as none of her business – but, yes, she also wanted to know. And then, the following Monday, it seemed the question was answered.

Again she was having a terrible day struggling with her book. Once more she said to hell with it, decided to do her laundry early, and walked over to the cottage to collect his clothes and bed-linen. Again she expected him to be in, for it was still early, but again his motor cycle was gone. And there, on the kitchen table, was his current notebook.

Helen stared at it. Then she walked guiltily to the back door, and peeped out. She returned to the table.

The book was open at the latest page. Many entries had been added since last time she had seen it. She flicked the pages back until she found the lament. She hastily read it again, to see if there was possibly anything she'd forgotten that connected her to it. No, there wasn't . . . Then she came to the last line.

It had been *changed*! She was absolutely sure the original ending had been: *'So put it out of your mind, chum.'* But words had been carefully rubbed out and replaced, and now it read: *'So I'll put it out of my mind, Jane.'*

Helen stared at it.

Jane? Who the hell was Jane . . . ?

Her mind fumbled with this. Okay, thank God it wasn't written about her, but why had he taken the trouble to change the sentence at all? Why had he changed it from a subjective note to himself to a direct speech addressed to this Jane?

She felt her nerves tighten – she thought she knew why.

He had made the change because he guessed she had read the notebook last Monday, and he did not want her to think that the lament was about her. He knew that today she would come over to collect his laundry again if he did not bring it himself, so he had made the alteration, deliberately left the notebook out and done a disappearing trick. He had reasoned that she was likely to read it and thus realize that she was not the object of his desire, not the cause of his pain. He wanted to exculpate her, to spare her any unease. To rid their friendship of complication, and save himself the embarrassment of appearing pathetic over her . . .

Helen took a deep, tense breath. Oh, if it were true, if that paragraph was about this Jane woman, then thank God. He did not have to leave Whoop-Whoop. And she was grateful to him for taking the trouble to reassure her. Touched by his concern. Even if she was now consumed by a new curiosity and for a ridiculous moment even felt almost cheated, as if he had no right to be mooning about this Jane if he was living with her on Whoop-Whoop. But – *was* this Jane business true?

Was Jane for real? Or did he invent her, write the name into the paragraph simply to exculpate Helen McKenzie?

She sat, staring out the kitchen door.

Oh God ... Not only was it a possibility, it even seemed likely. If there really *was* a Jane, if he had been thinking about Jane all along, why hadn't he used her name in the first version? Why go back and change it? Jane could just be a red herring.

'Oh God, please not ...'

But the more she thought about it, the more distinct appeared the possibility, and her relief of a moment ago was evaporating. Was she back to square one?

She took a deep breath and rearranged the book as she had found it. She went into his bedroom. She stripped his bed and collected up his laundry. She walked slowly back to the house, carrying the bundle.

And there was something else about this Jane that was remarkable, almost eerie. *Only yesterday* Helen had decided that the heroine of her book was to be called Jane. She had tried using several other names until then, but none of them had sounded quite right and finally she had settled on Jane. It was a nice, straightforward name, a wholesome name, a girl-next-door name. Jane was Helen McKenzie in the book, but she could be any ordinary woman found the world over. Could Ben know that she had chosen the name? She had not told him and he had not read her manuscript for several days – she only allowed him to see it when she was feeling brave. But he could have gone into the house and glanced over her work when her back was turned. By using the same name was he trying to tell her something ... ?

Oh, but surely he wouldn't be as devious as that. He couldn't even be sure she'd read his notebook again. If he wanted to tell her he loved her there were easier ways than that! No, surely it was just a coincidence, and not such a big coincidence, at that – Jane is a common name. Of *course* his Jane existed. Her anxiety of a moment ago was groundless ...

Helen entered her kitchen, threw Ben's laundry on the floor beside the machine and stood looking down at it.

So, she could forget about it – let sleeping dogs lie? She did not have to wait and see anymore – she could put that paragraph right out of her mind: she was not deceiving Clyde and she did not have to come on all moral and make dear Ben leave. Jane existed (probably svelte and long-legged), and Helen McKenzie did not have to feel responsible for Ben Sunninghill's 'pathetic' heart.

No. So everything was absolutely A-okay again, wasn't it?

Blame it on Jane.

But who the hell was this Jane? What kind of a person was she? Was she one of those Christian foot-soldiers . . . ?

26

But although she could, with a clear conscience (more or less), as regards Clyde, let sleeping dogs lie – Ben hadn't done a damn thing since that night, had he? – she could not put Jane out of her mind. Here she was, trying every day to write about *her* Jane, who was unquestionably Helen McKenzie, and it was pure *hell* trying to reveal Jane's thoughts and feelings. What an arse her Jane was turning out to be in black and white – 'tongue-tied and made of goddam cardboard' – oh what a zero! But what was *his* Jane like? What would *she* say and do under such-and-such a circumstance – and what did she look like? Was she a tall and sophisticated New Yorker, or a Southern belle with golden ringlets and heaving breasts, or an Israeli kibbutz kid with a machine gun, or what? Of course, none of this mattered to your actual Helen McKenzie with her cellulite-dimpled thighs (But otherwise not bad, huh – I mean not bad?) and indeed it should not matter to *her* Jane, Jane McDonald of New Orleans, Louisiana, who was wrestling with her pathetic problems. But was *his* Jane beautiful? Did *she* finish her goddam degree? Oh, Helen certainly did not care (Jane sounded a beast, like that girl who drank his booze and pigged-out on his chocolates and then hot-footed it into the subway) but, on the other hand, it *was* her business: because whoever Jane was, Ben was in love with her, and if Jane was Helen McKenzie she not only had a right to know, she had a *duty* to know, for Clyde's sake, so that she could . . . control the situation and avoid doing anything to aggravate it. (And if Jane really existed, she also had the right to know, so she could put the whole silly business out of her tiny mind.)

Anyway, it bugged her. For several days she womanfully resisted the temptation to try to steer the conversation around to his Jane. Then one afternoon, after a particularly bad day's writing, it happened. Ben came back early from his cattle and sheep rounds, and when he went over to the main house in mid-afternoon he found Helen drinking already, to try to help herself write. Ben was in a drinking mood too, and together they progressed from beer to wine. He started talking about Africa, about the foot-soldiers he was going to join to help save the animals; about the horrors of poaching and the fur trade, the long, thirst-crazed agonies of the snare; then, suddenly, he began to recite a poem.

'The steel jaws clamped and held him fast,
None marked his fright, none heard his cries,
His struggles ceased; he lay at last
With wide, uncomprehending eyes;
And saw the sky grow dark above,
And quailed in anguish while he strove
To gnaw his prisoned leg away.
Then at last day came from the east.
But still the steel jaws kept their hold,
And no one watched the prisoned beast
But Fear, and Hunger, Thirst and Cold . . .
Then through the gloom that night came One
Who set the timid spirit free;
I know thine anguish, little son;
So once men held and tortured Me . . .'

The tears were rolling down Helen's cheeks when he finished. He looked at her with big soulful eyes, and with all her crumpling heart she too wanted to *do* something about the terribleness of it, the horror, the agony, and she whispered: 'Oh, I'd love to join your foot-soldiers . . .' And maybe it was the pathos of the poem, or maybe it was her envy, or maybe it was the weeks of frustration of trying to write about her Jane with nothing worthwhile to say; possibly it was all the booze she had drunk, and more than likely it was a combination of all these things, but she heard herself blurt:

'Oh Ben, who is Jane? Is she for real? Is she one of the foot-soldiers . . . ?'

There was a short silence.

She stared at him, her tears glistening on her cheeks, aghast at her stupidity of blurting the game away. Ben looked at her, taken aback by the suddenness of her question, the emotion in it – and by the success of his ploy. Because, yes, he *had* seen her manuscript, and yes, he had altered his notebook in the hopes of thereby telling her he loved her. He *had* deliberately left it out the following laundry day.

Later he had regretted his decision, even derided himself for doing it that way, for lacking the courage to tell her man to woman and fuck the consequences – it was pathetic to leave coded notes around on matters as momentous as Love, and he had been immensely relieved when she had made no reference to it. Until this afternoon. Ben looked at Helen, the love of his life, and for a moment he was not sure what was happening, whether she was just moved by the poem and the drink, or whether she was actually jealous. That she might be jealous seemed too good to be true and for a confused moment he tried to slap his hope back into its place, to spare them both if he was wrong: he temporized:

'I see ... So you've read my diaries ...'

'Oh, Ben, forgive me,' Helen implored him tearfully.

Ben's knocking heart sank. 'Forgive me?' Those words did not spell jealousy ... And suddenly he did not care anymore whether he made a mistake, he did not care whether he blundered in now and he fucked up everything and had to leave. *Now* was the time to say it, to tell her how he felt and spare himself from manlessness, from living this pretence of being good ole Ben Sunninghill who knew his place – he did not *care* if she told him to leave this very night! He said:

'Yes. Jane is for real ... but she is ...' And he saw the look in her eyes and his nerve momentarily failed him. Then he recovered himself and got to his feet. He didn't give a *shit* anymore. He stood, looking down at her frightened face, then took three heart-knocking steps around the table towards her. Helen sat there, watching him, her tearful eyes wide. With all her heart she wanted to blurt out *Please no Buts*, with all her heart she wanted him to stop this. Ben stood at her knees, and, he saw his hairy arm reach out and his hand touch her cheek. And oh, that contact was *bliss*, pure desire. He bent slowly towards her upturned face to kiss her parted lips: Helen sat still, her heart pounding, watching his mouth coming down towards hers, and she wanted to cry out *Please don't do this, Ben* – then the kitchen door burst open and a drunken voice rasped:

'Gotcha!'

Helen gasped and Ben straightened and spun around. Fred Morecomb sauntered lankily into the kitchen.

'Gotcha in the act!'

It was like a bad dream: the generator thudding away like a heartbeat, the afternoon sun glaring down outside, Fred Morecomb dominating the half-gloom with another man she had never seen, both leering and sweating. Helen and Ben stared at them, astonished; Fred put his big fists on his hips.

'Caught in the act, Helen McKenzie!' He jerked a thumb at the window. 'Had a front-row view, you'd have seen us comin' if you hadn't only had eyes for each other.' He grinned maliciously at her. 'What's Big Clyde going to say about *this*?'

Ben got a grip on himself. He barked: 'Get out!'

Fred pondered this, then turned to the other man. 'Mr Sonning-bloom wants us to get out of his house, Jim.'

Helen got to her feet and yelled: *'Get out of my house!'*

Fred turned back to her, with a leer. 'Oh, *your* house, is it? Last I knew it was Clyde McKenzie's, bought with the sweat of his brow. But now you've got yourself a boyfriend it's *yours*.'

'I'm not her boyfriend,' Ben rasped, 'I'm her *friend*! Which obviously you are *not*!'

Helen hissed softly: 'Clyde's going to make mincemeat of you, Fred Morecomb, when I tell him all about you—'

'I think' – Fred held up a gnarled finger – 'he's going to make mincemeat of *you*, Helen – and of Mr Bloomingstein, here, if he's so stupid as to stick around any longer after I've finished with him ... In fact I think Big Clyde's going to thank me, Helen, for telling him the truth about you and Mr Ginsberg, and for showing you what a little runt he really *is*. Because Jim and I didn't come here to make *trouble*, Helen, oh no, we just came to help you with your kangaroo problem, seeing you've got so many you've got to chase them on to my land. We just came to take you on a little kangaroo hunt, it's not our fault we catch you in the act—'

In two bounds Ben crossed the kitchen and swung at him. But Fred was ready for him this time, and it was as if Ben had hurled himself face-first into a fist. His head seemed to explode, and he sprawled backwards on to the table, stunned, crashing over wine glasses. Fred came after him, grabbed his shirt-front, wrenched him up and slugged him again. Ben reeled across the room and crashed on the floor. Fred leapt after him, grabbed him by the scruff of his neck, wrenched him up and slung a hand under his armpit, over his shoulder and heaved down on his neck. Ben crouched, immobilized, gasping, shocked, blood running from his face.

'Lesson number one, Mr Finkelstein – this is how real Aussies kill kangaroos. It's called a half-Nelson. One shove of my hand and the roo's neck is broken. Get my message?'

'Let him go!' Helen shrieked.

Fred rasped to Jim: 'Now you take Mrs McKenzie politely to the car, Jim—'

'Let him go!' Helen screamed, and she flew at Fred, her fingers like talons, her eyes wild. Fred shoved Ben aside and grabbed Helen's wrists. He swung her around and wrenched both her arms up behind her back. Ben crashed against the wall, and Jim bounded at him and seized him in a half-Nelson.

Helen was writhing furiously. *'Let go, you bastard!'*

Fred panted: 'I'm not going to let you go when you're trying to tear my eyes out, am I? Now, no harm is going to come to you, Helen, we're just going to help you with your kangaroo problem, and we'll see what a big strong man your Mr Lover-boy is . . .'

27

The whole thing was mad, like a nightmare: the battered Ford roaring flat-out through the hot dry Outback in the late afternoon, swinging around stumps and fallen trees, churning up clouds of dust, the kangaroos fleeing panic-stricken ahead in great bounds, tails flying, fleeing for their lives from the yelling, yahooing drunken wildmen in the roaring, skidding, swerving vehicle. Jim was driving, bawling and spinning the wheel crazily; Ben sat in front wedged between him and Fred, the blood congealed on his face, his head splitting. Helen sat in the back between a barking dog and two drunken reeking men she'd never seen before, jolted from side to side, her eyes screwed up in terror of each looming tree, her heart sickened for the terrified kangaroos, outraged at what was being done to her and Ben. Then the dog was being thrown out to run down a young kangaroo, the car careening, crashing, racing behind, the men screaming encouragement. The dog pulled down the flying roo in a fury of bloody kicking and snarling, tearing its throat out to bellowing applause and screaming laughter. Then the crazy vehicle was gaining on a terrified kangaroo, the battered car roaring closer and closer, the men mad with excitement. There was a sickening thud and the animal flew upwards in mid-bound, landed on the bonnet in a shattered heap, hit the windscreen and flew off to the side. It hit the earth and rolled, then scrambled up and tried to run, but its hind leg was shattered, and it collapsed. The vehicle swung around to a halt, the doors burst open and the men tumbled out, cheering and laughing. The crippled kangaroo tried to leap away, but it crashed over on to its side again. The men roared with laughter and Fred yelled: 'Now let's see how big and strong your boyfriend is – tell him to kill it, Helen!'

'*Shoot the poor thing, you beast!*'

'Let's see your boyfriend put the poor thing out of its misery, Helen!'

'Shoot it!' Ben roared. He grabbed at Fred's rifle but Fred pranced aside and held the weapon above his head gleefully. Ben whirled on the others: 'Give me a fucking gun!'

'Bare hands, Mr Finkelstein – be sporting!'

'You beasts!' Helen screamed.

Ben whirled on Fred again and swung his fist at his guts. Fred leapt backwards and swiped the rifle-butt down on Ben's temple. Ben sprawled against the car, stunned. He shook his head and looked at Fred murderously. Fred had the gun pointing at him, from his hip.

'Now,' he leered, 'are you going to show Helen what a big brave man you are, or do we leave this poor animal here to suffer because you're too chicken?'

'Don't try it, Ben,' Helen cried, 'it'll slash your stomach open!'

Ben leaned against the car, gasping, bloody. The animal crouched ten paces away, its left leg buckled, blood oozing from its head and shattered hip, ears back, staring at them, terrified. Ben wanted to vomit.

'Of course I'm chicken! Please shoot the pathetic thing.'

'Rather let it suffer, huh? Or maybe I should show you how it's done so you can show Mrs McKenzie how brave you can be with the next one?'

Helen shrieked: 'Shoot it, you bastard!'

Fred gleefully tossed the gun to Jim. He shrugged his big shoulders and hitched up his pants and held up a finger at Helen. 'Now watch how a *man* does it, Helen . . .'

'You're a beast!'

Fred hitched up his trousers again, and took off his hat. 'Get him, Fred!' Jim shouted. Fred grinned and dropped into a boxer's stance, his hat in one hand. Then he advanced on the kangaroo, leering, prancing; the terrified animal watched him come, ears back, nose twitching. Then it tried to whirl around and leap away, and it crashed over on to its side. A roar of laughter went up and Fred lunged at its tail, but the kangaroo scrambled up again in the nick of time and turned on him. Fred danced in front of it, feinting with his hands, grinning, and the kangaroo jerked up on to its hindleg, its short forepaws up like a boxer's, and as Fred feinted the kangaroo swiped back and the boys roared with laughter and encouragement – 'Get him, Fred!' Fred pranced sideways to get around to the animal's back, feinting and swiping, and the kangaroo swivelled jerkily, trying to keep its front to the enemy; then Fred lashed out with his hat and the kangaroo crashed over on its broken hindleg, scrambled up again panic-stricken, turned to try to flee, and Fred got him. With a drunken lunge he seized the crippled animal's long tail, and as the kangaroo sprawled, clawing the air, he leapt on to its back and seized it by the neck.

Fred bounded astride the kangaroo's back, one hand clasped around its gullet, shaking and strangling it, his other fist pounding its head. The boys yahooed and the kangaroo twisted desperately, clawing the air as the blows pounded down. Again and again Fred punched it whilst he throttled it, grunting and snorting. Then the animal was stunned senseless, and its struggles ceased. Fred grabbed its neck in both hands and heaved downwards. There was a snap of cartilage and the kangaroo collapsed, dead in his arms. He let it fall dramatically, then stood up, chest heaving, grinning triumphantly at Helen. The boys were staggering about with laughter and cheering.

Fred came lankily back towards the car, shakily triumphant, his knuckles covered in the animal's blood. Helen was leaning against the car, eyes closed, her stomach heaving. Fred panted at her:

'Now we'll see if Mr Finkelstein can do that, Mrs McKenzie...'

The nightmare got worse. The battered car grinding through the Outback in the dark, the big spotlight swinging slowly over the scrub, lighting up the twisted trees, searching for the telltale glow of kangaroo eyes. Helen sat, eyes closed, her tears dried, the taste of vomit in her mouth, hating, hating. Ben hunched grimly in the front, his aching brain trying to think. On, and on, the mad juggernaut ground through bush; then suddenly there was a sprinkling of startled eyes, the animals on their hindlegs peering blinded at the light, big ones and small ones; in the middle was a big male, and Fred rasped gleefully: 'There's your boomer, Mr Finkelstein.' The car stopped and the men scrambled silently out. Their rifles clicked as they leant on the car and took aim at the mesmerized kangaroos; then *crack! crack! crack!* The kangaroos leapt into the air and collapsed, but the big male struggled up again, full of blinded, frightened fight, and Fred shouted: *'I just hit him in the hindleg for you, Mr Finkelstein!'*

He grabbed Ben by the collar and hauled him out of the car, and slung him. Ben sprawled in the dust, shocked; then he heaved himself up on to his elbow, full of fury. Fred leered down at him malevolently.

'Now, go'n show Helen McKenzie what a big brave boy you are; go'n finish off that roo like a *sportsman*, Mr Finkelstein.'

Ben looked at the bloodied, crouched kangaroo, then he turned to Fred:

'Sure. Easy,' he said.

There was a moment's astonishment, then the men roared with laughter again.

'Don't do it, Ben!' Helen cried.

Ben clambered to his feet. He dusted off his hands and walked to the front of the car. He peered intently at the kangaroo in the headlights. The frightened animal stared at him; blood flooded through the dense fur on its haunch and its forepaws were held up aggressively.

'Don't do it, Ben . . .' Helen sobbed.

Ben took two steps towards the animal, then stopped. He turned and said: 'Is a man entitled to a drink first?'

There was a ribald burst of laughter, and Fred held out the bottle. 'Sure, Mr Finkelstein!'

Ben walked back towards him, his hand up to shield his eyes against the lights; and he reached out and grasped the neck of the bottle, snatched it away from Fred, and lashed out blindly with it.

It caught Fred across the forehead and he reeled away and sprawled. Ben blundered after him, snatched up the rifle, turned and ran. He ran doubled up into the dark bush, then he dropped to his knee and swung on the kangaroo, the rifle up to his shoulder, aimed and pulled the trigger. *Crack! Crack!* The kangaroo sprang into the air and then crashed down motionless. Then Ben swung the rifle wildly around on to the car, and he saw silhouettes scattering, diving to the ground. He aimed at the spotlight on the roof and pulled the trigger again. There was a shattering crash as it went out. He crouched there, heart pounding, eyes wide, panting, then he threw down the gun and shouted. *'All right, you bastards, I'm unarmed! Throw down your guns too if you're sportsmen!'*

He got shakily to his feet. His head splitting. He turned to look at the kangaroo: it lay still. He looked back towards the car, his chest heaving, and he saw Fred Morecomb clamber up. Then Jim, then the two other men. They stood there, big black silhouettes against the diffused glare of the headlights; then Fred Morecomb started towards him, his arms out at his sides like a gunslinger. Then, one by one, the others followed him, and Helen shrieked.

Ben did not hear what Helen was shouting as they advanced on him. All he knew was that he did not care what these bastards did to him as long as he did his best. He bunched his fists and crouched and began to prance from side to side on his toes, rasping: *'All right you bastards . . .'* Then the big shape of Fred Morecomb blocked out the light, and Ben charged and swung his fist at it with all his might. He felt Fred lurch, and he swung wildly at another dark figure – and then came a blow like a sledgehammer, and Ben saw stars and sprawled. Then they were all on to him – boots and fists, and there was nothing in the world but the blows and the gasping and the shouts and red-black stars, and somewhere in the middle of this was Helen McKenzie, shrieking like a banshee and clawing like a cat and kicking like a kangaroo. Then there was an explosion in his head and the world went black.

It took Ben and Helen two hours to walk back to the homestead through the starlit bush. Ben was hurting all over, his head throbbing, but he was going to be all right.

'It takes more than that to kill a Jewish jeweller, Helen.'

'Oh God, Ben, I'm so sorry . . . And you were so courageous.'

Ben snorted. Courageous, was he? He'd been shit-scared until the end, but he could do with all the praise he could get.

It was eleven o'clock when they limped into the kitchen of the main house, to Dundee's slobbering welcome. Ben went to the sink and gingerly washed his battered face while Helen fetched the first-aid kit. Ben dabbed his face dry, then shuffled to the refrigerator, got out a beer, up-ended it to his mouth and glugged it down. It felt like the best medicine in the world. He finished the can, hung his sore head in appreciation, then reached for the brandy bottle. He sloshed a big shot into a glass and tossed it back in one go and stood, eyes closed, savouring the fortifying burn. Helen came back anxiously, clutching the medicine box.

Ben sat on the edge of the table, his head back, while Helen cleaned up his face with cotton wool and disinfectant. As she dabbed and wiped and tutted, Ben watched her through half-closed eyes, his heart aching at the proximity of her: the warmth of her just inches from him, the woman smell of her, her beautiful eyes so close to his, her full lips, her skin, her tousled golden hair, her breath brushing his face as she spoke – and as she finished and began to step back, he slipped his arms around her and clutched her. For a glorious moment he had her warmth in his arms at last, her body in his hands, her thighs between his legs, her loins against his; for a long heart-stopping moment he held her, looking into her eyes, the most wonderful feeling he had known; then he began to slide off the table, to get to his feet and take her into his arms properly, fiercely, and he felt her go rigid. And Helen backed off, out of his embrace.

Helen moved backwards across the kitchen, and banged against the sink. She stood there, her eyes smouldering, her face flushed. Ben stared at her tumultuously, then took a step towards her, to possess her come what might, but she gasped: *'No, Ben!'* and he stopped. He stood there, staring into her anguished eyes, his heart and loins in riot. With all his pounding heart he loved her; no longer could he hold back. He raised a shaky finger at her and said softly:

'This afternoon, just before those kangaroo cowboys arrived, you were going to kiss me, remember?'

Helen stared at him, her eyes nervously bright, her lips parted; then she gave a tiny nod.

'And then you would have made love to me, Helen . . .'

Helen looked at him imploringly; then she whispered: 'I don't think I would have, Ben.'

'What d'you mean you don't *think*, Helen?'

'I mean I would have . . . stopped.'

Ben looked at her grimly; then he nodded. He took a deep breath and said: 'We can't go on like this, Helen.'

Helen's eyes were glistening. She whispered: 'It won't happen again, Ben.'

Ben wanted to bellow with rage at that answer. He said: 'Then I must leave, Helen.'

She drew in her breath. Ben went on: 'And apart from . . . *this* . . .' he waved his hand to include the two of them, 'I seemed to have caused nothing but trouble. And now today these guys . . .' He shook his bruised head at her. 'I'm giving you a bad name, Helen. And if I don't leave they'll be back.'

'You *haven't* given me a bad name, Ben! Clyde gave you permission to stay, you're here perfectly legitimately, for all the world to see! We've got nothing to hide! And there *won't* be any more nonsense from Fred Morecomb because when they sober up they'll be terrified of Clyde! *And* of the police!'

'Tonight's story is going to be all over the Outback, Helen. Those guys ganged up on us because they think I'm screwing you. And what's Clyde going to think about that?'

'It *won't* be all over the Outback! Those guys will keep their mouths shut when they sober up and realize what they did, they'll be terrified I'll blow the whistle on them! And I'm not going to tell Clyde and open a can of worms! It's just not worth it to put a brainless jerk like Fred Morecomb in his stupid place! So you can forget about giving me a bad name!'

He took a tense breath. 'But that still leaves the problem of us.'

Helen blurted: 'Oh Ben, there isn't any problem of us! Why can't we just be friends, just *friends* who laugh and talk about everything under the sun – *why must there be this problem of*—'

She stared at him, her eyes wide, aghast at the confession contained in that, and Ben's heart turned over.

'The problem is this, Helen,' he said. 'I want you . . .' He was going to say 'love you' but he changed it at the last instant lest the solemnity of it frightened her. 'I want you more than I've wanted any woman in my life, Helen. More than I can ever want any woman again.'

Helen stared at him, then she dropped her head and held her face. She held her breath, to get back under control. Then she tossed back her head, the tears running down her cheeks, and spoke softly.

'Thank you, Ben. I mean that, with all my heart. And I mean it with all my heart when I say I don't want you to leave.' She swallowed. 'The world would never be the same without you.' She took a resolute breath. 'I love you, Ben. I love your company, your mind, your wit, your sense of humour, your wisdom, your help – and just having you as a neighbour. You're a lovely person, Ben . . .' She swallowed, then continued: 'But I . . . do not want you physically. I love Clyde, Ben.' She looked at him, her face tilted back a little, the tears running down her cheeks. 'And what happened this afternoon, before the kangaroo hunt, was only . . . tenderness.'

The word was a blow. *Tenderness*. For a moment he did not believe her. He had *seen* her . . . Then he did believe. The story of his life again.

'I understand,' he said. 'Perfectly. And that is why I have to go, dearest Helen. Tonight.'

Tonight . . . Helen stared at him, shocked by the brutality of it.

Ben wanted more than anything to walk the one, two, three paces across the kitchen and put his lips to hers. But he really was leaving tonight. Not tomorrow. *Now* was the time to leave. He forced his charming smile on to his battered face and said: 'It'll take me half an hour to pack and tidy up the cottage. Then I'll be back to say goodbye.' He turned for the door.

She stared at him, aghast. *'Ben!'*

He stopped. Helen stood with her back to the sink, her hands gripping it, her face anguished. 'Please let's talk this over in the morning.'

He looked at her. 'We've said it all, Helen. So I must go.'

She looked at him tremulously, then closed her eyes. 'Please sit down for a moment, Ben,' she whispered.

He looked at her; then turned.

'Okay.'

He walked back to the table and sat. Helen slowly sat down across the table from him. Her face was suffused, her cheeks wet.

'You're right, Ben,' she admitted, 'I was going to kiss you this afternoon. And then, yes, I probably would have made love to you. Because of . . . Because of the moment. Adults don't usually kiss and not make love, do they?'

Ben's heart was knocking again, in renewed hope. The 'moment', huh? He waited. Helen looked him in the eye, then went on: 'But, oh God, I'm glad that we didn't, Ben.' She looked at him imploringly. 'The *guilt* I'd be feeling now. And that *you*'d be feeling – because you're an honourable man. It just wouldn't be worth it – I don't want to spoil our relationship with guilt . . .'

Ben looked at her. Guilt? To hell with guilt! He said softly:

'Not worth what? The bliss? The relief? The wanting? The *joy*?'

Helen shook her head and whispered fiercely: 'No, I don't *want* to want you like that, Ben!'

Ben's heart was singing. 'But you do . . .' he said ardently.

'It was only the moment, Ben!' she cried. 'But really and truly I don't want to know – I'm like the husband in that example of yours who doesn't want to sleep with his neighbour's wife because he absolutely refuses to entertain the guilty conscience!'

'But the man in my example *does* want his neighbour's wife,' Ben said huskily.

'Oh, this is semantics, Ben! The fact is yes, I *did* want you for that moment – but I *refuse* to think about it and I'm glad we passed through that momentary crisis unscathed!' She glared at him tearfully, then she reached out and grabbed both his hands. 'That's as straight-talking as my tiny mind can be right now, Ben.' She squeezed his hands. 'But please don't leave . . . I *need* you . . .'

Ben looked at her. What she had said was both a kick in the balls and a half-kiss of promise. He heard himself say: 'You need Clyde home again, Helen, not me.'

She closed her eyes in exasperation and said fiercely: 'Oh, of *course* I need Clyde home again! Clyde's been in my life since for ever, Clyde's the father of my children – Clyde is part of me, I'm part of him.' Ben wanted to say *'And I'm part of you now and you of me!'* but he held his tongue. Helen stared at him, then she declared fiercely: 'I love Clyde, Ben, like I love my children. I need them all like I need . . . my own body, my parents, like I need food and water – and God. I

213

need to know they're there, alive, well, happy.' Her eyes were glistening. 'And if we'd made love this afternoon, all that would never have been the same. All those feelings would become . . . almost *fraudulent*! Because we'd have become lovers, Ben – two furtive people with a secret life! I would have pretended to be one thing, a wife and a mother, while in reality I was a woman who had another man in her life – who hungered for another man . . . took off her clothes and . . . *clutched* another man to her body. Oh God, Ben, I don't want to lead a double life like that – to be a fraud to my family – and just as much I don't want to be a fraud to myself! I want to be able to look myself in the eye and say Hi, Helen McKenzie, warts and all, overweight and bushwhacked but doing her best . . .' She stared at him bright-eyed. 'I want to stay as I am, Ben – good old Helen McKenzie, married to good old Clyde, salt of the earth, for better or worse – and mostly for better, by the way – and mother of those four great kids who're doing so well at that expensive school. Oh God, Ben, I don't *want* to be anyone else.'

Ben held her eye. 'You *do*,' he whispered.

She squeezed his hands again. 'Of course I do! I want to be smart Helen McKenzie, who's written a good book, who's used her brain, who's travelled and seen it all, who's got her degree and knows how to use it. Helen McKenzie who goes off to Africa with the Peace Corps and teaches black kids to read and write or joins the foot-soldiers and fights poachers – of course I want to be all those things, Ben! But I'm *not*! I'm your original, good ole Helen McKenzie's who's born to moulder in the grave – I'm simply not *strong* enough to become that other person!'

'You are,' Ben said softly.

She leant towards him. 'I'm not *emotionally* strong enough, Ben – not emotionally tough enough to defraud those people.'

Ben still held her eyes. And come hell or high water he was going to get to the truth of this. He said quietly:

'How's your sex life with Clyde?'

Helen stared at him, shocked by the bluntness of the question. She let go of his hands and sat back. She said:

'That's got nothing to do with it, Ben.'

'Oh, it's got a great deal to do with it, Helen! And you asked me to sit down and talk this through.'

She looked at him, still shocked. 'Very well. If you must know, our sex life is pretty normal.'

Ben snorted. 'What does that mean? And I don't mean during the

214

first week he comes home for his annual holiday, Helen. I mean like before he went away? Once a week? The national average?'

She looked at him. 'That's the national average, is it? That cheers me up. Yes, about that, Ben. Anything else?'

'Sure, you bet. Like: Or once a month? And, do you have an orgasm every time?'

Helen bridled. 'Is this necessary, Ben?'

'Oh yes, orgasms are very necessary, Helen . . . Come on, tell me, since you wanted me to sit down! Most of the time? *Half* the time? Now and again?' He added: 'Be honest, Helen. That's what you're trying to be, isn't it?'

She hesitated grimly. Then she said slowly: 'About half the time, I suppose. How does that stack up against the national average?'

'And the other half? Or the other two-thirds? What do you do? Bite the bullet and put up with it? Put it down to life's rich tapestry, to the lot of wifehood? Or do you jerk off? Or what?' Helen was glaring at him, half outraged. Ben continued relentlessly: 'And how does he make it up to you when he doesn't give you an orgasm, Helen – does he give you lots of love? Does he tell you he loves you, does he touch you in passing, does he make you know that you're his love, his most special person?' He felt the tears begin to burn his eyes because with all his heart that's how he wanted her to be for himself. '*Does* he, Helen?' She looked at him angrily, but made no answer. 'Yes? Or does he take you for granted, Helen?' Before she could muster a reply, he bulldozed on: 'And when he gets into bed with you at the end of the long day, how is it? Just another case of two people who've been married for twenty years going to sleep in the same old bed, two old friends, who six nights out of seven – or twenty-nine out of thirty – just switch out the light?'

'Yes Ben!' she cried. 'Two *dear* old friends, who trust each other! And that's called *marriage*, Ben! It's called *security* – just to know he's there—'

'And on the night when he decides to make love to you, how is it, Helen?' Ben wanted to drop his head and sob. 'Does he take you in his arms and worship you, does he cover your body in reverential kisses? Or does he say "Brace yourself, Helen . . ."' He held his face in his hands for a moment, took a deep breath, then looked at her. He said wearily:

'Okay, Helen. You're right. It's called marriage and security, and that's what you need.'

'Ben, it's not so much what I *need* – it's just the way it *is*.'

'Yeah?' Ben took another deep breath and heaved himself to his feet.

'That's what marriage is all about!' Helen cried up at him. 'Oh Ben, you've never been married – you're such a romantic, you imagine it's all roses and kisses – it's not!'

'No?' Ben sighed.

'No! It's *survival*, Ben. It's ... Us against Them! It's ... overdrafts and drought and putting up with ...' She waved her hand.

'Farting in bed?' Ben said quietly.

Helen blinked. Wondering if she'd heard that right.

Ben looked down at her and said quietly: 'Yes, I'm a romantic, Helen. I don't believe marriage need be like that. I'd rather bust a gut than fart in bed. But, as you say, you know all about it and it's what you need and I have no business interfering with ... that equilibrium of yours. And that's why it's time I left, dearest Helen. Tonight.'

Helen stared up at him, her mind fumbling. 'Please sit down, Ben, you can't leave tonight. Where'll you sleep?'

'Where I usually sleep – beside the road.'

'*Please* sit down! We haven't finished talking this through!'

'We've said it all, Helen. I couldn't bear to go through it again.'

'We *haven't*, Ben!' she cried. 'I haven't finished telling you how I need you! I've only told you why I need Clyde.' She stared up at him with bright pleading eyes. 'I need you in an entirely different way, Ben! I need you for your soul, Ben!' She shook her tearful head at him. 'For your mind, your worldliness, your ... *guts*. Oh God, I admire you, Ben, and what you're doing.' She waved a hand impatiently. 'I don't mean for riding round the world on a motorbike, I mean for your *values*, for the adventures you want in preference to money! To the value you place upon *life* because, as you say, we pass this way but once. And ...' she shook her head again, 'how you feel about animals, and the environment, and what you're going to do about it. The rest of us just *talk*, Ben, but you actually get up and *do* ...'

Ben's armoured heart was beating faster. He said: 'I haven't done it yet – how d'you know I will?'

'Because I believe in you, Ben! Don't you see? I *believe* in Ben Sunninghill who's chucked up the jeweller's trade and gone out into the big wide world to live his life to the full, a man who says sticks and stones may break my bones but words cannot hurt me – a man who can stand up to the kind of crap you had to on Flying Doctor day, and in Burraville. A man who stands up on a goddam horse and says he can ride when he hasn't got a clue! Who thinks he can fix anything and then *does* it!' She waved a hand. 'And then how you took those bastards on tonight...' She looked up at him with tear-filled eyes. 'You're a real *man*, Ben.'

Ben's heart seemed to swell. A real man... Nobody had ever told him that. He had never thought of it that way before. All his life he hadn't given a damn what people thought about him – except certain women – he'd only known that he was what he was, warts and all, that he wanted what he wanted and did what he had to do about it – but a *real man?* He looked down at Helen, the woman above all others he wanted to be a man for, but before he could speak she blurted on:

'And, oh God, Ben, I need you to help me with my book, with all this wisdom of yours...' She paused, groping for more reasons why he should stay. 'And, Ben, I just love you being here, and I love the way you make me laugh. Oh, Ben, I love your *bullshit*...'

Ben felt the tears burn his eyes. A smile twitched the corners of his mouth. '*What* bullshit?'

Helen laughed, tearfully. 'See what I mean?' She grinned at him with shining eyes. 'Oh, if you want to go away for a bit, I'll understand. Why don't you just go to Brisbane and the Gold Coast for a couple of weeks? But *please* come back. I really *need* you, Ben.'

He sat there. Yes, she needed him, he believed that. And oh God, he did not want to go, and oh God he could not refuse her that... He heard himself say:

'All right, Helen, all right. I won't leave yet.'

A smile broke across her tearful face, and she seized his hands again across the table, and cried: 'Thank you! Thank you, dearest Ben.'

Ben lowered his eyes. And he had to say it, to rearmour himself, to restore something of his pride, to save face. He said:

'And what happened tonight won't happen again.' Helen opened her mouth to agree but he went on grimly: 'And one other thing, Helen.' He looked at her, his eyes bright. 'Yes, Jane does exist. But that's all I want to tell you about her. And now I think I'd like to take my battered body to bed.'

5

28

It was much against his better judgement that Ben Sunninghill stayed on a while longer at Whoop-Whoop – for God's sake, was it not time to accept her rejection gracefully, and take a powder into the wide blue yonder while his heart was still more or less intact, time to acknowledge that whatever inroads he'd made into Helen McKenzie's heart, however close she'd come to kissing him, for all she'd admitted that if she had done so she would have made love to him, for all that she'd begged him to stay and told him that he was a real man, for all that heady, heart-disarming stuff, it was also a heartbreaking fact that, at the very end, she'd made it clear that it was only for his soul and wit and friendship she wanted him. So, why did he stay on at Whoop-Whoop when many another man would have folded his tent?

Out of friendship and compassion, certainly, for friendship meant a great deal to Ben. But, above all, he stayed because he could not bear to tear himself away from Helen McKenzie.

But he was a wiser Ben Sunninghill now, who shook his finger warningly and reminded himself of all his other unhappy experiences with women. It had been painful, that 'wait-and-see' stage, desperately hoping for the moment when Helen would succumb to myopia, when Nature would suddenly give her a romantic seizure and she would throw herself into his arms. When he first agreed to stay on he had resolved to give it just another two weeks to see if she came around – but in the cold light of dawn he decided that that was wrong and undignified. And it was dishonourable, a shit thing to do. To Clyde, whose guest he was – though fuck Clyde when the chips were down, if we're being brutally honest, Sunninghill – but much, much more so to Helen who was vulnerable. Ben Sunninghill had been a veritable snake-in-the-grass, hadn't he, and now he had managed to persuade himself that he actually was glad that they had been interrupted that afternoon by Fred Morecomb, that they had not made love. Because she had not been in her sound and sober senses – she had been destabilized by drink, and afterwards she would have been torn apart by what she had done. Oh, he would give his right arm to make love to her, but Ben Sunninghill did not want that kind of responsibility. It would not have been a happy business afterwards, it would have been a breast-beating business. Helen McKenzie was a woman for whom adultery would have very serious consequences. He would either have had to leave alone, immediately, or she would have had to leave with him, which would probably have been wrong, for her, and thereby wrong for him. Yes, Fred Morecomb barging in was probably the best thing that could have happened. And, now because he had got all that in perspective, he could just love Helen from afar. 'Love her', note, not '*be* in love with her'. Whatever the hell that meant. But, whatever it meant, Ben Sunninghill felt much, much better, and stronger, being dignified.

So did Helen McKenzie. She was glad with all her heart that the crisis seemed to have been overcome, and very grateful to Ben for how he had taken it. For the truth was that she *had* been thinking more and more about him as something other than a platonic friend, hadn't she? She had not only become consumed with curiosity about his foot-soldier Jane, she'd even become not a little jealous about the woman. She had chosen from time to time to go out with him on his chores just to *be* with him. Isn't it true that there had been moments of intimacy, a glance down her cleavage, a touch of fingers when she'd passed him a spanner? And wasn't it true that a man who makes you laugh has a kind of sexual charm? Yes, all in all, for a while Ben had become something more than just a friend in her mind – thank God for Fred Morecomb. And thank God they had talked it out and cleared the air. For true friendship it was, now, wasn't it? She had been uneasy the next few days, waiting to see how Ben behaved, but he had made no reference to it, been nothing but his usual sunny, helpful self. And anyway he had never said he was in love with her, he had only said that he 'wanted' her, meaning the way that most men seem to 'want' just about any woman they see. She could put that paragraph in his notebook out of her mind too; it was *not* about her: Jane *did* exist, because he had told her so. She could love Ben Sunninghill as a friend, without either of them being on probation. With almost a clear conscience she could say to Clyde on the radio:

'Darling, he's being such a help. The vegetable garden is looking a treat, and the iceberg lettuces are going to make a bomb. And, remember that old deep-freeze that's sitting in the barn? Well, Ben's fixed the motor and he says he can build a cool-room for the veggies so we can cut them the day before they go to market. Isn't that a great idea? He's already started on it. Over.'

'A cool-room, huh? What materials is he using?'

'Just those old bricks, and some planks and that polystyrene stuff for insulation. Over.'

Clyde snorted. 'Okay, no harm in trying I suppose, but don't be surprised if your veggies go bad. Over.'

'And he's offered to paint the house. It sure needs it. Is that okay? Over.'

There was a brief silence, then: 'How long is he figuring on staying, Helen? Over.'

'Oh darling, he'll go as soon as we ask him to, of course. But can't he at least stay until I go to the kids in May – and he can paint the house? Over.'

There was another pause. Then Clyde said: 'Have you heard from those damn kids yet about May? Because I haven't. Over.'

'Yes! Or I've heard from Mum and she's spoken to them and it's all stations go! Oh, I'm so excited, I'm expecting a letter from them next time I go to town.' She sighed. 'Oh darling, this is a hell of a way to live, isn't it, us all separated?' She added: 'Apparently Tim's even giving up a sailing trip to see me – he was invited by the Giles boy to go with his father up to the Whitsunday Islands. Over.'

Clyde grunted. 'Yeah, well he's a good lad, Tim, and he knows I'd kick his arse if he didn't. But how long does it take to paint the house, for God's sake? A fortnight? The May holidays are still weeks away. Over.'

'Well, I suppose he'll only do a bit each day because he does at least an hour in the veggie garden and then at least two hours, maybe three – sometimes four – up at the Abbo's. And of course he's got his own writing to do. Over.'

Pause. 'Sounds real busy, huh? And how's your writing coming along? Over.'

Helen sighed. 'Oh darling, it's so awful, I know it is. But I'm hanging in there. I have to finish it, over.'

'Is he still helping you on that? Over.'

Helen closed her eyes. 'Yes. When I let him read it – usually I'm too embarrassed. Over.'

'What you writing about to make you embarrassed, girl? Sexy stuff and all that? Over.'

'Oh *Clyde*. I'm only embarrassed because it's so awful. But he gives me advice. *You* know ... Over.'

'No, I don't know, girl, what I know is that I made my living the hard way.' There was a pause and Helen took a tense breath. Then Clyde said gruffly: 'Sorry, I shouldn't have said that. Didn't mean it like that ... Did you hear that? Over.'

'Then how did you mean it? Over.'

Clyde sighed. 'I said I'm sorry. And I'm glad you're writing your story-book, girl. Gives you ... an interest. I didn't mean anything against him, really. It's just that – well, I don't want him thinking that he's a fixture, know what I mean? I mean, him so busy running the station, and all that ...' He ended: 'Over.'

'He's not running the station, Clyde. I am. Over.'

'Sure, girlie,' Clyde said wearily, 'and I'm very grateful to you. Over.'

Helen breathed deeply. 'Okay, darling, so just tell me, do you want him to paint the house or not? You know how you hate painting. So do I, and so do the kids – forget about them doing it at Christmas time. Over.'

Clyde hesitated, then said: 'Sure, girl. The house painted would be good.' He added: 'Thank him for me, will you? Over.'

'Okay.' Helen smiled, and decided to use her advantage. 'And is it okay for him to stay until I go to Mum's in May? If he wants to. I mean, it'll probably take him several weeks, doing a bit each day, if he does the job properly, two coats. Over.'

Clyde sighed. 'Yeah, what the hell – we can hardly say you can paint the house but then you must piss off, can we? Over.'

'Exactly. And he's more than paying his way financially, I mean for groceries and that, I'm actually saving on housekeeping, it'll pay for my trip to Mum's easily! He's really such good value, over.'

'Good value, huh? Yeah, well, he's getting accommodation for free, isn't he? Not that I begrudge it,' he added. 'Well, you save your housekeeping, girl, and buy yourself a nice dress in Bundaberg, it's about time you had a nice new one. Over.'

Helen's eyes moistened. She sighed. 'Oh darling, it's such a long time till I see you at Christmas ...'

It was such a good feeling to have a clear conscience with Clyde, such a relief that there was going to be no more romantic nonsense from Ben, such a relief that his Jane was real.

And indeed Ben made himself good value, and enjoyed doing so.

In the early part of the mornings he worked in the big vegetable garden he had extended, weeding, hoeing, irrigating – he was proud of his vegetables and very pleased at the prospect of making money for Helen, and it was satisfying to make the earth bring forth food. When he finished he went to work on the cool-room, which he was building in the corner of the barn. This was taking longer than anticipated because Ben was no bricklayer, and he had to smash the walls down twice and rebuild them. The carpentry was much easier, but the door was a bugger: he ended up using the one off the old deep-freeze, which meant he had to build an airtight frame for it. The one he tried to build of steel wasn't good enough because he was not an experienced welder, so he built it of wood, and that took several attempts. Then came the problem of gas to drive the refrigerator's motor. He started brewing up chicken droppings, cowdung and grass in a drum and piped the resultant methane gas into an old tractor-tube for storage. But it was going to take a long time to fill it. While he waited for that to happen – if it ever did – more chicken-shit? More grass? Less water? How about some sugar? – he started painting the house.

That was a bugger too. Ben had personally redecorated all the apartments he had lived in, and he had always done a good, tasteful job – all his female friends in New York had raved about his artistic sense – but he had always hated the physical labour of painting. The mess, the fiddly bits, paint running down into your armpits, in your goddam hair and eyes. God knows why he had offered to do this job – only because Helen McKenzie was a lovely person who was hard-up and it was a repayment of hospitality, whereas the vegetables and the livestock were fun. Even the cool-room was almost enjoyable by comparison. The outside of the house wasn't too bad, just a dogged slapping of white paint, though he hated that fucking rickety ladder – he fell twice – but the interior of the house was a real pain in the ass. Not only was there the problem of the ladder, the bother of covering furniture, his aching arm, there was also the problem of Clyde. And Helen.

'Helen,' Ben said in the store in Burraville, 'believe me, as your ally, that living-room should not be repainted pink.'

'It's not pink. It's a kind of . . . *pastel* shade of pink. And it goes with that rosebud carpet.'

'Helen,' Ben said, 'Helen, my dear. I want to talk to you about that carpet.'

'Are you telling me it should go? Well forget it. Clyde likes that carpet and so do I.'

'Helen, as a rosebud carpet it's not bad. It could have a future – or an old age – in some English vicar's low-beamed study. But Helen, you've got an old colonial-style house and those floorboards under that riotously rosebud carpet are lovely old pine. They cry out to be *seen*. Nice cheap woollen rugs, just the odd one or two here and there. And you should re-cover that zebra-striped lounge suite in a neutral corduroy—'

'Clyde likes the zebra effect, Ben.'

'Ah . . . And the daisies on the curtains as well?' He cut out 'And the ducks on the wall?' in the nick of time.

'Okay, there're better flowers in the world than daisies, but we can't afford to refurnish the whole house, Ben – even this paint is costing a bomb.'

'Then maybe we could dye the curtains a sort of biscuit-colour? That'll cost nothing.'

'Ben, I dare say you know better than me, but, believe me, Clyde chose those daisies. He's very touchy, Clyde is, about his personal things. So – pink, please.'

'And your bedroom?' Ben ventured. 'Please consider a sort of creamy off-white?'

'Lime, please,' Helen said firmly. 'Same as it is now. It goes with the red bedspread and the checkered rugs . . .'

It was certainly a labour of love painting the McKenzie house, and the infuriating part was that there *were* some nice old pieces of furniture; a lovely sideboard, some superb wardrobes and a splendid dining-table. It would really have taken so little to do the whole place up tastefully – but forget it, chum. You can lead a horse to water but you can't make it drink. Helen McKenzie was the nicest person he knew, but she had no fucking idea. It was with enormous relief that he staggered back down the ladder each day at noon (so she wouldn't feel obliged to invite him to stay for lunch), cleaned the paint out of his armpits, got on his motorbike and set off to the hut to check on Green. This was the best part of Ben's day, because after supervising the delivery of the lucern to the livestock and servicing windmills when they needed it, he rode the horse, Fury.

He was a competent rider now, if lacking in style, and he loved every minute of it. Theoretically he inspected the livestock and fencing while he rode, even if Green solemnly said he had just finished doing so, which he did say even if he hadn't. Ben knew when he was lying by the condition of the horse.

'Green, this horse is fresh today.'

'Yes, boss.'

'Yesterday it was sweating and tired.'

'Yes, boss.'

'How come, Green?'

'Yes, boss.'

'Let me guess, Green. Today it was the horse's turn to ride you?'

'Yes, boss.'

He loved riding through the bush, singing, feeling like a cowboy. If Green was impudently using the horse, Ben did the inspection on his motor cycle. (He tried to teach Green to ride it so that he could always have the horse, but he drove straight into a tree.) Yes, he was enjoying Whoop-Whoop, enjoying being useful to Helen McKenzie, and although it was unquestionably true that embers of hope still smouldered, for the time being he could handle things: he was satisfied (not 'content' – *satisfied*) just to be her friend; to love her and not show it. The wait-and-see game again? Well, maybe that was how it felt when he lay in his lonely bed at night with half a dozen beers awash inside him, thinking of the Helen he'd just chastely bade goodnight, or when he lay wallowing naked in the windmill reservoir at the end of the day wishing she would come and swim too – yes, at times like these the old Wait-and-See Sunninghill came skulking back. But mostly it was for the pleasure of her friendship that he stayed on and worked. It was the first time in his life he had had the attention of a woman who wanted his company so much. He was accustomed to being popular with most women because he was entertaining, and regarded as a social asset at their dinner parties, but in Helen he had a woman friend whose interest in him was almost complete, who needed him all the time. And what a woman she was! Ben considered her the nicest person he had ever met: delightfully natural, sometimes to the point of naïveté, a romantic bruised into being a realist, an innocent with a maturity acquired the hard way. And very, very sexy, in her compelling, wholesome, Earthmother way. She was highly intelligent. And, in general, very articulate. But – she was no writer.

Almost every evening now he was allowed to read parts of her manuscript. Helen hovered nervously while he did so, on tenterhooks for his judgement, watching him for the slightest sign of approval. 'I know it's awful,' she would say.

'It's not.'

It was. But he did not tell her so, for three reasons. First, although he considered himself well-read and a sound judge, he was not sure that her work had no value: an awful lot of crap found its way into print these days and he did not feel qualified to predict what those unpredictable publishers would think, let alone the unpredictable public. Secondly, though he tried to be objective, he was emotionally involved with the work, and perhaps he so wanted it to be good that his judgement was clouded: and when, trying to avoid this, he read passages a second time, he found himself wondering if it didn't indeed have a certain tortured charm, an innocence, perhaps something like those primitive paintings from Haiti – like a Marc Chagall. And, thirdly, he did not want to discourage her: above all he wanted her to finish the daunting task she had undertaken, for her self-esteem and for what he hoped she would learn along the way, both about the craft of writing and, possibly, about herself.

'Why "tortured" charm?' she demanded.

He sighed. 'Because you're trying too hard to write perfect, correct sentences describing intense, *imperfect* human feelings, Helen. You're torturing the details, the constructions, the grammar out of yourself as if you're writing an essay, as if this were going to the printer tomorrow, instead of letting it come tumbling out the way people really feel and think. The way *you* feel and think. There are some good thoughts and feelings in this,' he tapped her pages, '*interesting* thoughts, but in your determination to write perfect English you stylized it, as if you want to put things in pigeonholes. As a further consequence you tell the reader too much, rub his nose in facts, instead of letting him see for himself from action and dialogue what's going on in the heroine's breast. You must *reveal*, not instruct.'

Helen looked hurt, annoyed and humble, all at once. 'And "innocence"?' she demanded in an injured tone.

'There is a directness in places which is innocent and therefore charming,' Ben told her. '"This is how she was feeling, reader – get that into your fat head and take it or leave it." Sometimes it works, but usually it doesn't. Usually it irritates.'

' *"Irritates"*?' All humility and embarrassment now. 'Oh, Ben, what am I going to *do*? With my fat head?'

He smiled. 'Loosen up. Let your interesting female thoughts and soul be laid bare, layer by layer. That's what the reader wants to see, for himself. Let it all hang out.'

But Helen could not let it all hang out. She was too shy, she lacked the self-confidence. Day after day she toiled at her table, chewing her ballpoint pen, scratching out and trying again, but she could not reveal herself layer by layer, she simply had to dress it up as if formulating definitions.

'You're hiding things from the reader behind the prose, Helen, as if you're worried about what your mother will think. Or Clyde.'

She confessed lamely: 'I *am* worried what Clyde will think.'

'To hell with Clyde! Write it as if you have no relatives, as if nobody is ever going to read it but you. Let it all hang out in action and dialogue. Something must always be happening, developing, relevant to the story.'

'But what *is* the story?'

Ben waited. 'Well, what is it?'

She felt hopeless. 'I don't know . . . I'm aimless. So *I'm* not much of a story.'

'Ah, but you are,' he said quietly, 'and you're like millions of other women in that respect: you're aimless until something happens, until something comes along to change you and your aimlessness.' He felt his heart squeeze.

'Like what?'

'What, indeed?'

Actually, he decided, the parts of the book that described her aimlessness were quite well done, and improving, day after painful day. 'It's getting better, Helen.'

She wanted to jump up and hug him in gratitude. 'But?' she said guardedly.

'But you're still being cramped, inhibited.'

'It's got nothing to do with sex, you know,' she said, sullenly.

Ben sighed. 'Well,' he murmured, 'it should have.'

'Why?' she demanded indignantly. 'I'm not writing that kind of book!'

He sighed again. 'Because,' he said, 'sex is a major part of our thoughts. It influences most of our actions. You're not writing a biography of a cherished public figure, Helen. You're writing a *story*, about a woman like you, called Jane, based upon your own experiences and knowledge of life. We, the reader, want to know about this Jane, about women like you. See what makes her tick.'

'So Jane has all kinds of sexy thoughts, does she?'

'Doesn't she?' Oh, Lord . . .

Sullen pause. 'No.'

'Then she should. At least *some*.'

'To make it commercial?' she said disparagingly. 'So readers get a turn-on?'

'To make her human. And there's nothing wrong with giving your reader a turn-on now and again.'

'To make it *commercial*,' she insisted, aggrieved.

'Let's worry about the commerciality of it after it's finished. Right now the problem is to write it *truly*, as Hemingway said.'

'Well, it wouldn't be truly in my case.'

Oh, that was a smack in the chops to Hope. 'Wouldn't it?' Then he felt as if he didn't care; what the hell. 'Don't you miss sex? A healthy woman like you?' He added: 'And Jane.'

'But that doesn't mean Jane totters around thinking about it all day.'

He noted her evasion of the question. 'No,' he said regretfully, 'Jane evidently is not the sexually frenzied type. Nor are most women. But isn't she at least the type of woman, like most of us, who would have to masturbate occasionally?'

'Ben!'

He enjoyed shocking her with that. She needed to be shocked. 'Don't you?' Their agreement about him staying on allowed him to ask that, surely?

'*Ben!*'

He smiled. 'Does your indignation flare because I have the audacity to ask the question, or because I think you might do such a thing?'

'Both!'

He sighed. 'Well, I have the audacity to ask because I'm trying to make you think – about Jane.' He smiled again. 'Maybe you are the exception that proves the rule, but Jane isn't. Jane's human. Jane's interesting.'

She glared at him. 'And I'm not?'

Oh, was she not? For a moment he was almost optimistic again, because he had obviously stung her female pride.

'You are. One of the most interesting women I've met. But you don't write about it very well, yet, Helen, because you're uptight about yourself, about your ... image.' He added thoughtfully: 'So would Jane be, I guess.'

'But,' she demanded archly, 'Jane does, however, masturbate like hell?'

He grinned. 'Now you're talking. Jane's getting *very* interesting.'

'Be serious!'

For the next two evenings she would not let him read what she had written. Both evenings, when he arrived, she was a little tipsy.

'Been hitting the bottle, Ben. To get it all hanging out.'

'And is it?' he grinned.

'Like a Fourth of July parade. Isn't that a big day in America? Well, that's going to be nothing compared to Burraville when *A Woman Called Jane* hits the one and only street. Radio-Jack's going to be hoarse. Mavis Johnson's going to be temporarily speechless before unleashing multi-syllabled abstract nouns which will hopefully terminate in a heart-attack. Edna and the girls are going to turn into closet nymphomaniacs.'

Hope stirred again. 'Can I read it?' Ben grinned.

'Only if I can go and hide.'

She really did disappear while he read it. He began with anticipation, and ended with sad amusement. Helen came tiptoeing back into the kitchen.

'Well? No, don't tell me!'

Ben smiled. 'Helen, parts of it are really quite good.'

'Parts, huh? Jane's private parts?'

He grinned widely. 'Well, that really was quite a turn-on when she's examining herself in the hall mirror, lamenting her fading youth. Though I would try to find a better simile for her buttocks than "like two ostrich eggs".'

Helen bridled. 'I have seen ladies' buttocks thus described by a certain best-selling international author – in *all* his books.'

'Well, maybe he's got a thing about ostrich eggs, but most of us can take 'em or leave 'em. It doesn't quite go with her "silken thighs". However, that's a small point, easily corrected. The big problem is that here we have Jane, in this big empty house, standing naked in the hall, critically examining her pretty-good body, her hips still rounded and her breasts still self-supporting thanks to her Jane Fonda exercises, and it's a hot afternoon, and we think something really sexy is about to happen, when suddenly, for no rhyme or reason, her nipples harden and she dashes into the bedroom and – *boom* – she masturbates. In one line. End of scene.'

Helen glared, blushing furiously.

'We need to know why, Helen.'

'She's feeling horny, that's why!'

'Well, we can guess she didn't do it to distract herself from acute appendicitis. She wasn't thinking about her next root-canal when the Flying Dentist comes. So, what *was* she thinking about, Helen?'

'Can't you guess? Oh, Ben, if you knew how difficult it was for me even to let her nipples harden!'

Ben sighed. 'Okay, but the reader paid money for this book.' He waved his hand airily. 'Maybe she's just spied a tall handsome motorcyclist swimming naked in her windmill reservoir.' (Helen blinked.)

'But whatever it is we want to see into her pretty head at a time like this. Why *did* her nipples harden, Helen?'

'Oh, Ben . . .'

'Did she even lie down to do it?'

'Oh *Ben* . . . So, you want to see each glistening pore?'

'Hell, no, for that we can buy any number of girlie magazines. I'm only looking for some realism that doesn't cheat the reader. So? What *are* Jane's thoughts? What are her fantasies? And why *those* fantasies?'

'Oh, I don't *know* . . .'

Ben sighed inwardly, and hope withered. 'Then invent some,' he said sadly. 'Start by asking yourself what your sexual fantasies are – or might be, even if you do refrain from masturbation.'

'Ben . . .' she warned.

He sighed hopelessly. 'Don't tell me, tell the reader – but they must be relevant to your story, to your character-building of Jane.'

'Oh, *what* story?'

Ben leant forward, a touch exasperated. 'Helen, what does Jane want? And why? Ask yourself what *you* want to happen? To *you*.' He waved a hand impatiently. 'Then, when you've decided, it's your job as story-teller to make it happen. Credibly . . .'

That night he went to bed knowing that his was a hopeless case of unrequited love. But the next night Helen announced:

'Okay. Jane wants love.'

Ben's heart missed a beat. 'Okay. And? Doesn't she get that from her husband?'

'Yes, but he's never there, is he? He's off being a big wheeler-dealer in New Orleans.'

'Has he got a girlfriend on the side?'

'No. He's not that type.'

'Okay. Boring?'

'No. Well, maybe a bit boring.'

His hopes flickered. 'Do we meet him? To see how boring he can be? Or have we only got Jane's word for it?'

'Yes – that's enough, isn't it? Don't we believe her?'

Ben sighed. He ached to see, in black and white, Jane's version of how boring Clyde could be. 'Possibly. Depends who she says it to. To the Flying Psychiatrist? Or the dog? We'll believe it more readily if she says it to the dog, by the way; that shows she's really lonely.'

'Ben, are you taking the mickey out of us Aussies? "Flying Psy-chiatrist"!'

Ben sighed again. 'And, what does Jane do about it, the love she wants?'

Helen took a deep, sullen breath. 'Nothing,' she said.

Ben looked at her, hope shrivelling in embarrassed despair. 'Nothing?'

'Nothing.'

'Hmm . . .' he said. 'So nothing happens, huh?'

'Of course something happens, but finally she does nothing.'

He frowned at her. 'What happens to make her do nothing? Or despite which she does nothing?'

'Despite which,' she said firmly.

'Well, what?'

'I'm not sure yet.'

Ben sat back, almost annoyed, though he didn't show it. 'Well, is it the bank manager who tells her she can't possibly afford the ticket to go off and seek love because of the mortgage on the plantation and her boring husband's gambling debts?' He waved a hand. 'The Flying Priest who catches her masturbating when he sneaks up on her by parachute? The tall handsome motor-cyclist who spurns her frenzied advances in the windmill reservoir?'

She appeared not to notice the bit about the tall handsome motor-cyclist. She said with a thin smile: 'I don't know yet.'

Ben persisted: 'But you *do* know that, despite whatever it is, she does nothing?'

'She de*cides* to do nothing, Ben. She makes a conscious decision to accept her lot.' She glared. 'And to advance, inexorably, towards the involuntary, disgusting process of putrefaction in the grave!'

Ben sat back. 'Ah,' he made himself say evenly. 'Now we're getting somewhere. Her hormones shrivelling on the vine. That's the pathos.'

'*That*,' Helen said, 'is exactly it. And now I don't want to discuss it further, because you're making fun of me.'

Ben took a sad breath, sat forward and said: 'Yes I am, Helen. Because Jane doesn't just want love, Helen. That's all a shop-girl wants. And Jane doesn't live on a steamy sugar plantation outside New Orleans, surrounded by rich enviable friends.' He pointed at the floor emphatically. 'She lives right here in the Outback, on a station called Whoop-Whoop. And her husband may well be boring, but he's a hell of a nice guy, who's loyal and hard-working, called Clyde. And her child hasn't died, she's got four strapping Aussie kids who have gone off to boarding-school and don't need her anymore . . .' He shook his head at her, and had to work on it to keep the plea out of his voice. 'Jane doesn't just want love, Helen, she wants to be a fully liberated woman. Not a women's libber, leave that to *Cosmo* – Jane wants to *live* the rest of her life, experience, widen herself, enjoy, become wise. Before she *does* shrivel on the vine . . .'

29

When he went to bed that night, Ben Sunninghill could convince himself that he'd said all that to Helen with a clear conscience because it was the honest-to-God truth, because she should write about what she knew, namely herself; and that truth was good for her, because she should wise up to the woman who lurked in her breast instead of thrashing around in a mass of tongue-tied inhibitions. But it was also true that he had said it with the distant, wan hope that if she did ever become the liberated woman Jane should want to be, she just might come to see him in a different light, as more than just her friend; then he would be the happiest man in the world. But in the cold morning light that hope was so far away that it dwelt in the realm of dreams, and it was a far greater truth that he henceforth gave advice for the good of her book, because he genuinely wanted her to have the fulfilment of doing a proper job on that. He could almost truthfully tell himself that Ben Sunninghill was back to his razor-brain self and not about to fuck up this relationship with a lovely lady. He had as clear a conscience as just about any man could have, in the circumstances. But then, three evenings later, something happened which, had he known of it, would have destroyed his dubious fortitude and filled him with rampant hope.

That afternoon he had returned later than usual from Green's hut. Again it was Monday, laundry day. Helen had started her housework late – she had hit a winning streak with her book – and the generator was thumping so she did not hear his motor cycle. Ben walked from his cottage to the windmill, and plunged into the reservoir naked. He was quietly wallowing in the sensuous caress of the water when Helen approached, wearing her swimsuit. The sun was low; she supposed that Ben would have had his swim long ago, and his motorbike was not in evidence. Soundlessly, on bare feet, she began to mount the concrete steps. Then the exotic notion occurred to her to swim naked.

It was a lovely evening, and she was alone. (And, in her book, Jane was swimming naked every night, now.) Acting on this impulse, she peeled off her swimsuit. Then she ran up the steps, came breast-bouncing to the top – and stopped. In the middle of the reservoir lay Ben Sunninghill, with a hard-on.

Or half an erection. Helen stared, recovering her balance, astonished. Ben had not seen her; he was floating, his toes pointing the other way, and there, in the middle of his scrawny, hairy body lolled, awash, this surprisingly lengthy, remarkably substantial, wicked-looking penis. And Ben was evidently humming to it.

Helen teetered on the brink of the reservoir, her face shocked; then she recovered her senses and she shuffled back from the brink. And she was about to turn and run back down the steps; then she stopped, and looked again.

Afterwards she tried to convince herself that she did not stop out of sexual response – that it was involuntary, just astonishment, almost wonder at the size of it (*far* bigger than any she'd ever seen – not that she'd seen many), that it was only . . . *curiosity*, the sort of thing most women would have done, just having a natural second look – while Ben, still humming amiably at his disconsolate manhood, was oblivious. But, later, when she was being brutally honest with herself, she admitted it was more than that. It was the animalism of the moment that made her stop, not lust – for women are different to men – but it *was* a sexual response. And for that moment Ben Sunninghill was more than just her friend; he was – and much more vividly so – the real *man* she had put out of her mind after that kangaroo hunt. For fully five confused seconds Helen McKenzie stood naked at the lip of the reservoir, unable to tear herself away; then she became aware of the blood flooding to her face, and she recovered her senses, and she turned and fled. Like the girl who ate his chocolates and drank his booze, she raced down the concrete steps, snatched up her swimsuit and ran through the blue-gum trees, back towards the house.

Ben heard something, turned, grabbed the rim of the reservoir and peered over the top. He saw Helen running naked through the trees. He stared at her in astonishment. Then she was gone into the hot dusk, and he groaned, and he closed his eyes.

He hung off the rim of the reservoir, his head down. He knew what had happened – or he thought he did, and her running away like that was very dramatic evidence indeed of her rejection of him. Hurtful evidence, possibly the worst, most distressing evidence he could have – like overhearing those you love tell others how they like you but can't stand you near them . . . Ben gave a big, tense, bitter sigh.

It was a hopeless, pathetic case of unrequited love. And he knew he could not bear to stay much longer at Whoop-Whoop.

Helen ran to the back door, through the kitchen and down the passage to her bedroom. She slammed the door and slumped down at her dressing-table. She held her head, then she whispered aloud: 'Oh please, we've been doing so well . . .'

For a minute she sat there, eyes closed, trying not to re-live those vivid moments, trying to force it all out of her mind. And failing to do so. For another minute she sat there, not trying anymore. Then, finally, she could bear it no longer; she got up, walked to the door and locked it.

She turned and walked slowly to the bed and lay down.

She lay still for another minute, eyes closed, dealing with her conscience. Then she took a big tense breath, and reached out and opened the door of her bedside table. There stood the bottle of Johnson's Baby Oil. She had not touched it since Clyde's last visit.

She looked at it, trying to reconsider what she was about to do. Slowly, she picked it up and unscrewed the top. Then she realized she surely didn't need it. She replaced the cap and returned the bottle to its place. Then she lay back again and parted her thighs; she slid her hand down to her pubic triangle, closed her eyes and thought of what she had just seen.

But Ben Sunninghill knew nothing about that, and more is the pity. Perhaps, if he had happened to turn his head in the reservoir that afternoon and seen Helen's face, seen the confused smoulder that crossed it for a few seconds, and if he had known what she did thereafter, this story would have turned out differently.

Perhaps. But Ben did not turn his head in time, and instead he knew he just had to leave, before he broke his heart or ruined their friendship, or just became a pitiful supplicant, or all of those things. He could not bear to sustain a platonic pretence any longer, and he resolved to leave as soon as he had finished painting the house, got that cool-room working and sold the iceberg lettuces. But he said nothing of this to Helen, to whom he seemed his usual self. Two days later, determined to get his show on the road, he cut the first of the lettuces, sooner than he should have done, and they took them to Burraville.

They didn't make the bomb Helen had hoped for, but that day she received a letter from her children confirming that they were all going to Granny's for the holidays, and she was delighted with life. Overjoyed! Only three weeks to go! She was so looking forward to seeing them – two glorious weeks with all the kids together! *We'll go to the beach . . .'* And she was dying to be with her mother, and to see Bundaberg again. *A bit of civilization, real shops . . .* She couldn't give a damn about the lettuces, and not even the fact that those approaching holidays also heralded Ben's departure – or that's what Clyde had indicated he wanted – dampened her enthusiasm. Because wouldn't it be only sensible for Ben to stay on at Whoop-Whoop while she was away, to look after the place? Surely Clyde would agree to that? And, then, well, when she came back it would only be fair, only hospitable, for Ben to stay a bit longer if he wanted to – God knows there were plenty of things for him to do if he felt like it. The bathroom plumbing, for example – it was a disgrace and Ben had once said he could fix it. He had mentioned he could build her a solar panel to provide free hot water instead of having to rely on gas bottles – that would be a big saving. The electric wiring really should be overhauled: some of those lights were so damn unreliable. And, anyway, it was doubtful whether he'd finish painting the whole house – two coats, of course, you've got to have *two* coats – in three weeks at the rate he was going, and she could hardly ask him to hurry up. Oh, there was no reason for Ben to leave – though she hadn't discussed any of this with him yet. But she'd fix it with Clyde when the time came . . .

The next batch of iceberg lettuces was a disaster, and all because of that damn cool-room. 'It's working!' he had yelled, racing down from the barn. 'The fucking thing's working, I pulled apart the motor again, come and feel the temperature!' And yes, lo and behold, it was cooling, and Helen was vastly impressed; they had immediately set about cutting and storing a large quantity of lettuces to take to town in two days' time. But the next afternoon the goddam cool-room was reminiscent of a Malayan jungle, the motor truculently silent again, the jam-packed lettuces perspiring in sullen steaminess. It had been too late to rush them to town that day, the next morning they were dead on arrival at the Farmers' Co-op, and not even Ben's creative accountancy could improve the dark invoice he received for selling them as poultry-feed. But that day Helen received another letter from the kids – usually she considered herself lucky to get *one* a term – *and* there was a letter from Clyde! 'Clyde *never* writes!'

And Clyde had written to say again that he was sorry for being a bit cranky about Ben on the radio, that he really was glad that she had some company, girlie, and how it was beaut that she had something to do; no harm in writing a story-book, and please to thank Ben for painting the house. 'I'm sorry to leave you alone so much, girl, but maybe it'll be over year after next if Tim gets his scholarship, meanwhile what about Christmas, hey?' Helen sighed and folded the pages.

'Nice letter?' Ben said with a brightness he did not feel.

Helen nodded at him – yes, it was a lovely letter, despite 'there's no harm in writing a story-book'. Oh, dear Clyde, he meant it well ... Ben wanted to take her to lunch, 'to celebrate'.

'To celebrate what? The bloody lettuces?'

'No, the *letters*.' And he almost meant it, despite his stupid jealousy; he was glad to see her happy, and pleased he had got this unrequited-love business in perspective. The house-painting was nearly finished, he thought he knew where that bug was in the refrigeration motor, and the last of those bloody iceberg lettuces were almost ready. But, as usual since their first disaster at the Niagara Milk Bar & Grill, Helen did not want to stay in town for lunch.

'I'd love to, Ben ... but I'd rather keep a low profile, okay?'

Ben felt badly about spoiling her few human contacts, especially as he was leaving soon; and it was because of his determination to make her resume her normal social life that, on their next trip to town to sell the last of the lettuces (prudently unreliant on the cooler-room, which was looking good but still under close observation after major surgery) he resolved that they attend the horse races being held in Burraville the following week. He had almost finished painting the house and the races would be the grand finale of his stay in the Outback – and he would ride Fury in them! He came back from the Farmers' Co-op brimming with enthusiasm. 'Hey, they're having horse races on Saturday week! We've got to go to that, huh?'

Helen climbed into the Land Rover. 'Oh, the Picnic Races. Hmm. They're fun.'

'A big social event? I overheard two guys talking at the Co-op.'

'Yes. They're a big deal in the Outback.'

'You enjoy them?'

'Oh yes. See the people you haven't seen for ages, everybody comes in from miles around.'

'With their horses? I mean ordinary horses, but they race them and have bookies and they're properly organized, with a steward and all?'

'Yes. But it's rather rough and ready.'

'How long does it go on for?'

'Usually from Friday till Monday.'

'Wow. How many people come?'

'Maybe five hundred, counting kids and all.'

'Where do they all sleep?'

'Some at the hotel. Most of them camp round the track.'

'Is there a bar and all?'

'In Australia? Course there's a bar. In a tent.'

'And is there dancing and all that?'

'Yes.'

Ben started the Land Rover, and for a moment he didn't care that it would be his swan-song. 'Helen, I'd love to ride Fury in a race.'

Helen looked guiltily through the windscreen, and sighed. 'Oh, Ben . . .'

He knew she was thinking about that low profile. 'Maybe I'd win! Is there a purse for each race? A prize?'

'Yes,' she admitted.

'Well! Imagine the excitement. And do the riders wear any livery – colours and all that?'

'Some of them. But most just wear working gear.'

'I'll ride in my motorbike gear. Enter me as The Black Jew!'

She gave him a wan smile. She really did not want to expose herself and Ben to Outback scrutiny and gossip again, but she could not throw cold water on his excitement.

Although Ben was determined that the Picnic Races would mark the end of his stay, for all that the thought of leaving Whoop-Whoop crunched his armoured heart, he prepared for them with enthusiasm.

Every day for the next week he was up at Green's hut early, exercising Fury. He made his livestock inspections by motor cycle, to spare the horse for his training. He made a special trip into Burraville to buy oats and corn to beef him up. Three hours a day the horse was galloped up and down a measured mile, with appropriate rests in between, being clocked on Ben's wrist-watch.

'He's improving!' he exulted to Helen.

'Remember he *is* fourteen years old.'

'He's as strong as a horse!' Ben grinned. 'He's knocked twenty-seven seconds off his time so far!'

'Yes, he's fast,' Helen admitted. 'Clyde often won on him.'

(Oh, fuck Clyde.) 'Why don't you ride him in a Ladies Race?'

Helen smiled. 'It's your day, Ben. You've got him in two races already, he'll need the rest between.'

'It's your day too, Helen.'

He was determined to make it a good day for her amongst her old friends, a day that would launch her back into Outback society so that she had that to fall back on when he was gone.

When he was gone . . . Oh God, that was a terrible thought. All in all he had loved it here, notwithstanding the Burraville Hotel, that awful Flying Doctor day, Clyde McKenzie, Fred Morecomb and his kangaroo hunt – indeed, he even valued all that crap, with hindsight. God, he didn't really regret a moment of it, and the Outback would live in his memory for ever. And Helen – he would never forget her; and hopefully she would live in his dreams – for lovely things can happen in dreams – for ever and ever. And, as he washed down Fury each evening, and fondly watched him chomping through his wheaties, he did not want to leave the smells and sounds and feelings of Whoop-Whoop. Most of all, he did not want to leave Helen McKenzie, the loveliest woman he had ever met.

But he had to. Didn't he?

30

The Picnic Races are a big deal in Burraville. People came from hundreds of miles, by private aeroplane, by car, by truck, trailing their caravans and horse-boxes, loaded with tents, bedding, barbecues and booze. Radio-Jack did a roaring trade for three days, Stavros Popodopolous of Niagara Milk Bar & Grill fame equally so. Everybody was very jolly. Sergeant Vince Keenan occasionally had a punch-up to settle, but the circuit magistrate never got to hear about it and only once in the last ten years had anybody had to cool off in the cell for the night – Vince's police work consisted of banging their heads together, then taking them both for a beer. Ben was delighted by the festivity as they drove into town towing Fury's horse-box: bunting bearing Four-X emblems hung from the hotel's eaves, Stavros had decided to put up his Christmas decorations, Aborigines were overflowing from the Paradise Bar and there were at least fifty cars parked in Main Road. A mile on, around the cricket and football fields, there were over a hundred vehicles, horse-boxes, caravans, tents, and a crowd of people milling. Ben drove the Land Rover towards the paddock, Helen waving through the window to her friends. *'Hi ... Hi ...'*

'It's *great*,' Ben said. He tried to shut his mind to the fact that this was going to be his second-last day in the Outback. They offloaded Fury into the paddock.

'I'll go'n find the steward and report,' Helen said. 'You have something to eat.'

Ben understood. 'Where'll I meet you?'

'Well, I'll go'n talk to some of the girls.' She waved her hand restively. 'Haven't seen them for yonks. And maybe I'll go'n check the post office. Meet you back here before the first race? Say a quarter to two?'

He was going to be glad when his heartache was over, but he was pleased she was going to meet the girls. 'I'll drive up to the post office,' he said.

'No, I feel like a walk. And there won't be anything, anyway.'

'But how about a drink before the first race, huh?'

'Should you have a drink before the race, Ben?'

'Sure! I'm going to have a drink right now, at the Niagara with my hamburger. Two drinks. This is supposed to be *fun*, Helen ... How about meeting in the bar here, at about one?'

Helen smiled gamely. 'Okay. Saddle-up is half-past, though.'

'Great ...'

Oh, he was glad he was going to leave soon, that this low-profile business was going to end.

But it wasn't great. He bought some wine at the bottle store, then drove on to the Niagara Milk Bar. He went in and stopped at the beaded curtain. The place was jumping, full of people, smoke and chatter. There were empty chairs here and there, but no unoccupied tables. Stavros was sweatily threading his way through the tables with a tray, beaming professionally, but when he saw Ben his smile froze. Ben caught Edna Parker's eye, and he saw her smile freeze too; then she twiddled her fingers at him self-consciously. At that moment a couple at a table for two got up to leave; Stavros was smilelessly indicating it to Ben, when suddenly the grill-room went quiet as people realized who was standing in the doorway. For a moment Ben Sunninghill stood centre-stage at the beaded curtain in silence; then he nodded to Stavros, gave Edna an embarrassed wave, and turned away.

He walked back to the Land Rover and got in.

Boy ...

The only other place for lunch was the Burraville Hotel, and no way was he going to stick his long nose in there after Stavros' frosty welcome. He drove slowly back, but when he reached the race-track he drove past it. He turned on to the road towards Charleville, pulled off on to the verge and stopped.

There were a couple of sandwiches left over from the breakfast Helen had prepared for the road. He unwrapped them, pulled out the corkscrew on his penknife and opened the bottle of wine. He picked up a sandwich and lifted the bottle to his mouth. He had over an hour to kill.

When he got back to the race-track, Helen was waiting for him at the paddock, her face suffused with anger. As Ben walked up to her, his heart sinking, she blurted:

'Those bloody kids of mine don't want to spend the holidays with me after all!'

Ben stopped, amazed. Helen glowered at him, her chin trembling, then her eyes filled with tears as she went on angrily: 'Got another lovely letter! The little bastards have put up a united front! Tim can't bear to miss his golden opportunity of cruising in the Whitsunday Islands, and Wendy's going too because she's got a goddam crush on the Giles boy now! And lady Jacqueline wants to play tennis and Mum hasn't got a tennis court, has she, oh no! And that little witch Cathy doesn't want to spend *her* precious holidays on a *"farm"*...'

Again Burraville history is divided on what happened that afternoon.

There are some who say it was shitty, what happened to Sunningstein, absolutely *shitty*, and that it was *not* an accident; but there are just as many who insist it *was* an accident, because Australians are *sportsmen* and simply wouldn't do such a thing deliberately. And there are those who opine that, accident or not, it was beaut anyway, because the jeweller had it coming to him, and they were glad for *Clyde's* sake. What everybody agrees is that Helen McKenzie made an absolute arse of herself. And they also grudgingly agree that her boyfriend would have won the race.

Not that anybody had bet on him. And what an arse *he* looked, in his black leather motorbike gear, like one of those Hell's Angels, sitting up there on Clyde's horse – even Helen looked embarrassed. How she went through all that parading they have to do with everybody watching her every move – really, how had she the nerve to show up at a Picnic Race, flaunting the guy like some kind of a toy-boy? I mean has she completely lost her marbles, can't she see what a tart she's making of herself? And I mean I *like* Helen, and Clyde's beaut. Anyway, even if the boyfriend is a nasty piece of work – and I don't say he is, and I mean Clyde's putting up with him, isn't he? – but you know what an old softie Clyde is – but anyway, I could have died when it happened, accident or no accident! It *looked* so terrible, right there in front of the grandstand, and it *did* look deliberate, even though Mike Parker swears it was an accident, and the steward's satisfied it was – or so he *says* – and we know how Mike Parker *loves* that little Jew, after him getting Edna so pissed that day Helen slapped his face in front of everybody in the pub. Anyway, there they were, thundering down the straight towards the finishing post, and everybody's shouting and yelling, and Sunningbloom and Mike Parker are right in front with everybody else bunched behind them, and there's

Sunningbloom, his legs and arms flapping like a duck and a wild *Machiavellian* grin all over his face (Mavis Johnson says), and he's thrashing his horse, and there's Mike Parker right beside him thrashing *his* horse, almost neck and neck they were with Sunningstein just a nose in front – no, the *horse's* nose, you fool! – then they're into the last fifty yards, and everybody's cheering for Mike Parker – except Guess Who? *She's* jumping up and down yelling her head off! And then they're just coming up to the grandstand . . . galloping, *galloping* . . . and there's only another twenty yards to go . . . and then *wham* – Mike Parker's whip hits Sunningstein right in the face . . .

And a roar went up, and all Ben knew through the wild thrill of the race was the sudden blinding blow, a stunning whiplash across his nose; he saw a bright flash and jerked his head aside, his arm flailing, stunned . . . and then he was falling. Ben was struck sideways out of the saddle, his arms and legs wild, and all he knew as he felt himself go was stunned terror of the horses behind him. Then he hit the ground with a bone-jarring crash. And there was nothing in the world but the thundering of killer hooves, the shaking of the earth, killer hooves crashing and flying all about him, and he rolled himself up into a shocked ball and clutched his head as horses went leaping over him and swerving around him; for an eternity the hooves pounded and thundered about him, then they were gone.

Ben scrambled up blindly, shocked, staggering, still clutching his head; and he tried to run, to get the hell out of the way, and he crashed. He crashed on to his face, and he scrambled up wildly again, and staggered across the track, blinded, reeling, terrified, trying to run. Then people were running across the track to him.

Helen was the first to reach him. Wild-eyed, gasping, horrified, she flung her arm around his shoulders, crying, *'Ben, Ben, darling Ben . . .'*

An hour later they were on their way back to Whoop-Whoop.

Ben was not seriously injured; he was going to have a couple of bad black eyes for a week and his nose was very swollen – 'unrecognizable, even in Burraville' – but it was not broken. Most of the pain had subsided and the cold beer wasn't doing him any harm.

'Oh God, I'm so sorry,' Helen lamented again.

'That's life,' Ben said. It was her he felt sorry for, he had so wanted her to have a good day with her friends, to get back into the swing of Outback life. And on top of everything along had come that awful letter from the kids.

'It *was* an accident,' Helen tried to persuade herself.

'Sure,' Ben said. But he did not believe it, not for a moment. That swipe with the whip was an elaboration on the Burraville Hotel Bar fiasco, the campfire scene with Fred Morecomb, the kangaroo hunt, the Niagara Milk Bar today. And that hurt him and angered him like hell, but he could live with that – what he couldn't live with was what this was doing to Helen and her life in the Outback community, to her reputation. It really was time for him to go; all his second thoughts and misgivings and heartache had to be ruthlessly pushed aside, for *her* sake. *But now there was that letter from those damn selfish kids.* He had intended telling Helen today that he was leaving, but now he couldn't until she'd got over that letter, for Christ's sake. She had had a miserable day, a shitty day – he was going to write to those kids himself about letting their mother down, about breaking her heart . . .

3 1

But Helen forbade him to do that. Nor would she permit Clyde to order the children to change their plans. 'Darling, I don't *want* them to come if *they* don't want to. I don't want them to do their "duty" with long-suffering faces; the little swines have made it perfectly clear where their preferences lie and anyway I'll have them for six whole weeks at Christmas. I'll be fine, I'll get over it. Over.'

She did get over it – she even managed to rationalize away their selfishness. As she said to Ben: 'Oh, I understand kids, they want fun and it's their holiday too, they're all working hard at school and I suppose it *is* a bit dull at Mum's, and it is a wonderful opportunity for Tim and Wendy to go sailing in those Whitsunday Islands, seeing something of the world. I wish *I* could go. And after all, that's what a good school's all about, isn't it, meeting other kids from nice families who do things and give your kids opportunities like that. And Jacqueline really is mad about her tennis, she really is terribly good and two weeks' concerted practice at her friend's place could do wonders – you see, that's another benefit of a good school, your children's friends have nice rich parents with tennis courts. That's what Clyde's working for, isn't it, to give the kids opportunities? And as for little Cathy, well, she's such a scatterbrain you can't hold anything against *her* . . .'

Ben looked at her through black, swollen eyelids and kept his opinion to himself.

And there was a bright side to it: after her bitter disappointment, Clyde had not hesitated in agreeing that Ben could stay a little longer. 'Yeah, course, girlie. And it would be beaut if he built you a solar panel, nothing to it really, and that plumbing does need fixing, should have done it myself last Christmas. Just you keep punching, girl, but I'm sorry to hear about the lettuces: is he re-building that cool-room, over?'

Helen did not report the whole conversation to Ben, she simply announced brightly: 'Clyde says he'll be delighted if you stay longer, Ben – I knew he would be!' as if there were no question about Ben's wanting to stay. Ben looked at her lovely face and simply did not have the heart to say that he intended leaving now. Give it another week, he thought. There were a number of jobs to do, and, to tell the truth, he was relieved to have the pressure taken off his decision: it was going to be tough enough on himself to go, without adding to her disappointment over the children. And, who knows, it might just come to pass in an extra week that something wonderful just might happen to make her see him in a different light . . . Oh, no, that was too much to hope for; put that right out of your mind, chum, and do the right thing and wrap up those jobs and then tell her gently you must be on your bicycle and go, go, *go*, without breaking your heart.

That week went quickly for Ben, because he wanted it to go slowly. But Helen knew nothing about all this, and for her the week went slowly, because of her bloody book. (She would probably never have persevered with the book if the holiday with the kids had come off and Ben had left – that was part of the bright side, wasn't it? And she had put that nonsense at the reservoir and the unnecessary Johnson's Baby Oil right out of her mind, honest she had.) Every day she toiled over her manuscript at the kitchen table, clutching her chewed ballpoint like a hated weapon, desperately trying to let it all hang out, unaware of Ben's planned departure. She would not let him read any more of her work, although she tried to pick his brains about what one would say or think or do under this circumstance or that. But Ben could not piece these random pieces of consultation together sufficiently to figure out whether she was making the changes he hoped she would. He told himself he did not mind, that he just wanted her to get on with the task she had set herself, and be happy. But he did mind. Each night he looked at her earnest face as she hung on his words, and he yearned to reach out and touch her, and tell her he loved her, but as he couldn't do that he badly wanted to be taken into her confidence about the book. He wanted to help her as much as he could, and above all he wanted her to be confident, before he left.

He worked hard, determined to leave on schedule, and that week another thing happened to spur his haste: a big trough of low pressure developed over the Pacific, and the radio warned of heavy rains to come, and possibly floods. Helen was overjoyed at the news – 'perhaps this is the end of the drought, Ben!' – but he didn't want to be caught in the Outback by heavy rains. He did not like riding in rain and he wanted to be on the coast when it came. He worked from sunrise until after dark to try to finish the jobs he had undertaken before the weather closed in. Each night the radio warned that the low pressure was coming closer to Australia, but it had a long way to go across the Great Dividing Range before it reached Whoop-Whoop. ('If it ever does,' Helen said.) He made a trip to Burraville to buy the materials for the solar panel and the plumbing. ('No, my shout, Helen – to thank you for all your hospitality . . .') In town he got the news that it was raining heavily in Sydney and in central and coastal Queensland; but over Burraville the sky was bright blue.

It stayed cloudless all the rest of that week whilst he built the solar panel. He erected it on the kitchen roof and connected it to the insulated tank: all that remained now was to link it to the hot-water pipes after he had repaired the bathroom plumbing. That night the radio reported minor floods in Sydney and storm-water pollution of the beaches, and flood warnings were issued for the Nepean-Hawkesbury river systems in New South Wales, and some flooding was reported in central Queensland. But there were starry skies over Whoop-Whoop. The next day Ben drove to town to buy the final bits and pieces for the plumbing, and to sell the very last of the vegetables. He resolved to break the news to Helen that night that he was leaving as soon as he had finished connecting the solar panel. These threatening rains and the last of these goddam lettuces marked a natural end to his responsibilities towards Whoop-Whoop. The beginning of the end of his self-inflicted heartache.

He was at work at dawn, cutting the vegetables; and that sunrise was different to all his days in Australia: there were riotously pink thunderclouds in the east. The morning was pregnant with something new, the earth and bush seemed altered, the air smelt different, change was imminent. There was a rich and important feeling to that morning, and it squeezed Ben Sunninghill's heart. That dark sky, that air, that bush, that feeling, and Helen McKenzie were all one, part of each other, and sky and clouds and earth and woman would never be the same as this again – Helen McKenzie *was* this sky, this bush, this air. And even Burraville's deserted main road, Radio-Jack's hotel, the Niagara Milk Bar & Grill he did not want to leave. When he walked into the Farmers' Co-op, where he had had so little success, and smelt the dry earth's fruits, and once again had to do his creative accountancy on the invoice to show a small fictitious profit for Helen's benefit, he wanted to come back again and again and for ever with his offerings, even though the Co-op clerk was, as usual, cold towards him. 'D'you think it's going to rain?' Ben asked, and the man just grunted: 'Dunno,' and shoved him his invoice. Ben didn't care; this unyielding Outback seemed his home now, even if the clerk was how almost everything was. He drove home – *home?* – under a leaden sky, and made himself rehearse his lines to enable him to break it to her gently that he was leaving in two days.

He was a few miles from the Whoop-Whoop gate when the first drops of rain appeared on the windscreen. And a smile spread across his face, a welcome to the skies coming to talk at last, and what he had to say tonight crunched his heart. He turned into Whoop-Whoop and drove over the ridge of hills, and as he was approaching the causeway across the dry riverbed there was a flash of lightning, followed by a rumble of thunder. Then the rain came down. First in a flurry of fat drops, landing in splats; then in a rush, then teeming down, drumming on the Land Rover, and within moments he could hardly see the bush beside the road. By the time he approached the main house the track was already running with water.

Helen stood in front of the house, her arms wide to the sky, the rain beating down on her, her hair plastered to her head and sticking to her neck, a laugh all over her upturned face. Ben pressed the horn, and Helen turned and came running down the track towards him, her arms wide, grinning, plastered wet. He stopped the vehicle and got out. Helen came sloshing up to him, laughing, and flung her arms around him, and his heart seemed to turn over. She hugged him and cried: *'It's raining, it's raining . . .'* Then she grabbed his hands and danced him around and around in a circle, the rain beating down on them, her blonde hair sodden and her shirt clinging to her. Ben laughed with her and let her swing him around, and he thought his heart would break with his wanting of her and the pain of what he had to say.

Helen ran joyfully back through the rain to the house, and Ben drove the Land Rover to the backyard. It was a quagmire already. When he entered the kitchen Helen was vigorously drying her hair with a towel in front of the sink, and she had two cans of beer ready. *'Oh, Ben, isn't it wonderful, this rain?'* She threw down the towel, snapped the lid off a can and thrust it at him. 'Please God it keeps up!' She opened the other can and shot it aloft. *'Here's to the rain!'*

'To the rain,' Ben said with a smile he did not feel.

'Oh Ben, this is real *rain* – not the piss-willy stuff we've had for years!'

'It's wonderful, Helen . . . Shouldn't you change out of those wet clothes?'

'In a minute. I'm just revelling in the feel of that rain. Oh Ben, this is such good news!'

Ben asked: 'If it does keep up, and really breaks the drought, will Clyde come home?'

'Not yet, but at least we can get a loan to buy some more stock. Oh *Ben* . . .' She came and flung her arms around him again, then she let him go and asked happily: 'How did the icebergs go today?'

Ben smiled, pulled the invoice and money out of his pocket and put them on the table. 'Not too bad. But I wouldn't rely on veggies after I've gone; evidently Australia is a nation of goddam carnivores.'

'Oh stop talking about "after you've *gone*",' she cried, 'you're not going anywhere for ages and today is a day to celebrate!'

Ben felt his heart squeeze. Oh no. He hadn't meant it to come about like this. But it was out now, and he made himself say the rest of it:

'Well, I've really got to get going in the next couple of days.' He added: 'I can't stay for ever, Helen . . .'

She blinked at him. Her wet hair hung in tresses, raindrops trickling down her neck, her sodden shirt clinging to her bosom, water dripping from her jeans on to the floor.

'In the next couple of days?'

She stared, and she wanted to tell him, *Yes, you can stay forever* – but, of course, that wasn't true. And the awful reality of life on Whoop-Whoop without him dawned upon her again, and she blurted out in panic: 'Oh, Ben, you can't leave *yet!*' She groped for reasons. 'I haven't finished learning from you yet!' She stared, her mind fumbling, then appealed: 'Oh Ben, you can't leave till I've finished with *Jane!*'

Ben had never wanted to stay more than he did now but, dear God, now was the moment to be firm with her, to put an end to procrastination, and he forced a gentle smile.

'Well, Jane may take quite some time, Helen, and I really feel I must get going.' He soldiered on before she could interrupt: 'Tomorrow I'll connect the solar panel and I should leave the next day.'

'Why must you leave the next day?' Helen cried. Her heart seemed to well over and she banged down her beer. *'Why?'* She stared at him, eyes bright, then she blundered across the kitchen and flung her arms around him, her smooth wet cheek pressed against his rough wet face. She clutched him tight and cried: 'Oh, please don't leave me, Ben, until I've got rid of Jane!'

Oh God, here was Helen McKenzie pressed against him, and with all his heart he wanted to clutch her close, clutch her and tell her he loved her, that he would never desert her. His heart swelled, and his armour cracked and he took a handful of her sodden hair, pulled back her head, and he plunged his mouth on to hers.

And, oh, the bliss of her tight against him, her wide mouth pressed against his, the sweet woman smell of her, her breasts and belly and thighs crushed against him as he kissed her and kissed her, writhing against her. For several, gasping, blissful moments Ben Sunninghill held Helen in his arms at last, devouring her with kisses, then through his passion he realized that she was struggling. She frantically broke the kiss and he released her. She backed off, her face suffused, her eyes wide and her hair awry; she leant against the table. Ben said ardently:

'I love you, Helen . . .'

There was a short silence; then Helen took a deep, trembling breath and whispered:

'I love you too, Ben. But not in that way . . .'

Ben looked at her shakily. And whereas most other men would have refused to accept that, he did. Most other men would have refused to accept that, would have crossed the space between them and tried again after the brief ardour of those kisses. But Ben believed her because this was the story of his life; and he had not turned his head and seen her face that afternoon at the reservoir, he had only seen her running away naked through the trees, and he did not know what she had done thereafter. Ben stood there, feeling that he might burst with love and pain: then he forced a weak smile.

'I'm sorry,' he said. Helen stood holding the table, her breast heaving, confusion in her bright eyes. 'And that's why I've got to go away,' he added huskily. 'Tomorrow . . .'

Helen bit her lip.

'Tomorrow, Helen. I have to. You understand that, don't you? Do you understand?'

Helen looked at him and her eyes filled with new tears. She breathed deeply to try to control herself, and nodded her head. *Yes . . .*

'And I must never come back, Helen. I can't go away for a while and come back, because I simply could not bear it. Do you understand that?'

Helen tilted back her head, the tears running down her cheeks, and she closed her eyes and nodded again.

'But do you believe me, Helen?'

She shook her head and sobbed: 'No . . .'

Ben's eyes filled with tears too. He whispered: 'You must believe me, Helen.' Then he turned and walked out, into the rain.

Helen stared after him. She could not believe this was happening, that it was all coming to an end. Then the reality struck home, and she threw herself down at the table. She lifted her head and cried to the skies: *'Oh why can't we just be friends?'*

Ben heard her, and his heart seemed to break; but he kept on walking through the rain, back towards his cottage, to pack.

There was a flash of lightning that lit up the world, then a crack of thunder right above his head, and the rain came crashing down even more furiously.

32

It rained all that night, drumming on the tin roofs, teeming down on the bush and turning the earth to mud, running off the hillsides in streams which came together to make rivulets, the rivulets joining to form swirling ponds. And all the time the thunder, and the lightning. By the time Ben had finished packing and cleaning up the cottage he knew it would be crazy to leave in the morning. The rain would make for dangerous visibility even on a tarred road – muddy, slippery roads would be treacherous. But he was nevertheless grimly determined to go; he could not bear another day at Whoop-Whoop in the physical presence of Helen McKenzie.

He was awake long before dawn, the rain still beating down. He had a shower and dressed in his leather gear. He shone his flashlight out into the darkness, but all he could see was thick silver rain. He shone it on the ground; it was under an inch of jumping water. When the very first light came into the sky he descended the porch steps.

His motor cycle gleamed silvery black in his flashlight. His boots sank into the mud and the rain hammered on his crash-helmet. He gripped the handlebars and kicked the machine into life, then turned and took one last look at the cottage that had been his home for over two months. His eyes were glistening. He took a deep breath, then put the bike into gear and began to ride towards the main house to say goodbye to Helen.

He rode in lowest gear, his rear wheel spinning and skewing, and he needed all his strength to control the machine. The water became deeper and the mud beneath it more treacherous; but it would not be as bad on the open road. Ben went grinding down the track, throwing up stuttering plumes of muddy water, the rain blurring his visor, and only his determination to ease his aching heart kept him going. Even if he only got as far as Burraville tonight. The water got deeper still, and he knew that when he came to the gulley between the two dwellings it would be up to his axles. When he was halfway to the house he saw the Land Rover's headlights.

Helen had not slept all night and she had been up for hours listening to the two-way radio. She came grinding along in four-wheel-drive, peering with puffy eyes through the swishing windscreen wipers. When she saw Ben's headlight looming ahead through the sheets of rain she gave a blast on her horn. She revved the engine, the wheels spun and she went surging and churning towards him. Ben's light swerved to one side of the submerged track, and she came to a sloshing halt alongside him. She pushed back her window, her eyes brimming, and she looked at the rain teeming down on him, bouncing off like pellets.

'You can't leave, Ben! Burraville's flooded. The rivers've come down, the whole town's surrounded by water and all the roads are cut – there's no way you can get out in any direction, a dozen towns are going to be cut off for weeks.' She grinned at him through her tears. 'Don't you see, Ben? You weren't *meant* to leave yet...!'

Ben Sunninghill stayed only because he had no choice – not only were the roads flooded but, by God, this time Helen McKenzie really needed a friend; but a *friend*, pure and simple. She had made it very clear last night that it had to be thus, and Ben was not going to lose the remnants of his dignity by trying again.

First they went to check on the causeway. The windscreen wipers going slosh slosh, the bush on both sides standing in quagmires. Suddenly the track disappeared into a sheet of water; they slithered to a halt and peered. All they could see was a swirling lake, fading away into greyness: no causeway, no ridge of hills beyond – they could not even make out where the black sky ended and the dark earth began. Ben got out and trudged in, feeling with his feet. He waded in up to his knees, and felt the water tugging at him. His feet found the beginning of the causeway and he moved cautiously on to it. In the middle he saw dark mounds of sodden wool showing above the water. He plodded back to the Land Rover and got in.

'There's some drowned sheep blocking the culvert. If we come back with a chain and drag them out of the way the water may subside.'

'My *sheep*!' Helen moaned. She rammed into reverse, turned and roared up the track to rescue her sheep.

They ground the five slippery miles to Green's hut, wheels spinning, mud flying, crawling across rushing rivulets. The lucern field was flattened by the rain, a soggy mass, and the windmill's reservoir was overflowing. Fury stood in his paddock, head down, up to his hocks in mud, the rain beating down on his back. Green and his family had dug a ditch across the door of their hut to deflect the water. They were sitting on their bunks, looking thoroughly miserable.

'Green!' Helen cried. 'What about the sheep?'

She bundled him into the Land Rover whilst Ben saddled Fury. They went down to the south-west enclosure, mud flying from Fury's hooves. Ben reined in at the gate and Helen came grinding up beside him. Through the teeming rain they could count twenty sheep along the fence, huddled together, up to their knees in a sheet of water that stretched away into the mistiness.

Ben shouted to Helen: 'Where're the rest likely to be?'

'Oh God . . . Caught on the other side of the riverbed.'

They plodded into the enclosure, rounded up the sheep, and herded them through the gate on to the higher ground beyond.

'You can't take the Land Rover much further – you ride, and Green and I will go in on foot. How far to the riverbed – half a mile?'

'More like a mile,' Helen said.

Ben thought he knew this terrain like the back of his hand but the water disoriented him. 'And how much lower is it than here?'

'A couple of metres? But it may be twice that in places.'

'Can't take Fury either, then. Come on!'

They set off into the water, peering ahead for sheep. Within twenty paces they were in up to their shins. On they plodded, strung out abreast, unable to see more than ten yards ahead. Now the water was up to their knees and they could feel it tugging. They waded on, peering through the half-submerged scrub, stumbling over stones, their feet sinking deep into mud. When they had covered fifteen hundred yards the water was up to their thighs. Then the bush gave way to a naked swirling expanse and they were near the bank of the river. Green pointed and they saw the first sheep.

It was coming downstream towards them, a waterlogged mass of curly wool, its hooves weakly churning the water. It was closest to Ben, trying desperately to cut across towards him. He felt his way forward, then sank up to his waist and grabbed the frantic sheep by its neck. Helen and Green both had their hands outstretched for his. He reached out for Helen's, slipped and crashed over, and let go of the sheep. He felt the current take him, but he scrambled to his feet and plunged after the bleating animal. He seized it by the neck again and hauled it around towards the bank and grabbed Green's hand. He clambered up. The sheep was astonishingly heavy. On the bank the water still reached above its back and its legs still paddled frantically.

'You drag him back to the gate, Helen, and Green and I will cross and look for the others. You come back and make your way upstream and find the high ground on this side.'

Helen grabbed the bleating sheep and started off into the curtains of rain. Ben beckoned to Green and began to wade across the current.

The hummocks of high ground were tiny islands in a muddy lake that meandered off in all directions over scores of square miles. Ben and Green waded, passing one drowned lamb after another, their pathetic bodies drifting by or tangled in bushes. Then ahead loomed some higher ground the size of half a tennis court, twelve inches above the water, and on it clustered three ewes with lambs. Ben waded up on to the hummock and the sheep shuffled down to the end, the lambs toiling after their mothers, complaining. Ben grabbed the nearest ewe. The sodden wool was crawling with caterpillars and spiders taking refuge from the floods.

'No, boss,' Green said, 'mothers follow lambs.'

Ben let go of the ewe, grabbed her lamb and shoved it under his arm. The ewe stamped her forefeet in the mud aggressively, bleating. Green had snatched up the other two lambs; he tucked them both under the same arm, leaving one hand free, and plodded back into the water. Two ewes hurried after him anxiously. Ben followed, and his ewe followed him.

They waded through the water. Soon the ewes were struggling, the water up to their backs, their wool dragging them down. Green seized one by her neck and dragged her alongside him to give her a rest. Then he let her go and dragged the other. Ben did the same with his single charge. All the time the bleating and the splashing and the rain teeming down. They passed three more dead lambs on the way back. When they came to the flowing river, Green said: 'Wait here, boss.' He thrust one of his lambs under Ben's free arm, held the other out and demanded of the ewes: 'Who b'long this one?' One of the ewes tried to jump at the lamb and Green grabbed her by her neck. Ben grabbed Green's other ewe and pulled her between his legs, then grabbed his own again. Green waded into the current.

The water rose up to his waist. He went ploughing across, dragging his ewe, her lamb under his other arm. Ben waited, trying to control two frightened ewes at once while holding their lambs. Green toiled across the current, then up the other bank, and plodded off into the dimness.

Ben waited, clutching his armful of lambs and his handful of ewe, his knees gripping the other one. Then one of the lambs pawed at his face; he jerked his head back and it wriggled out of his grip and fell into the water. Ben let go of one ewe and lunged after it, and he sprawled over the ewe between his legs. He hit the water with a crash, still clutching one lamb. He struggled frantically to his feet and saw the other lamb three yards away in the current, its little head up, its mother plunging after it. Ben went after them, and the other ewe followed him. He lunged into the current, trying to run, rasping, splashing, staggering. He blundered ten lurching paces and he lunged for the ewe, and he crashed face-first into the water, lamb and all. He thrashed frenziedly, coughing, gasping, and plunged after the ewe again. His hand clawed into her wool, he heaved her backwards with all his might, then let go of her again and went on after her lamb.

It was five yards ahead, down-current, its head thrown back, its hooves flailing. Ben lurched after it, the mud sucking at his feet, and as he grasped its back he sprawled again. He crashed underwater, clutching two terrified lambs, and gasped in muddy water. He snorted and gagged and thrashed to regain his feet, and he crashed over again. He kicked furiously and gushed upright, retching and staggering, clutching two half-drowned lambs. He looked wildly upstream for the ewes and the foremost was almost on top of him. He desperately thrust both lambs under one arm and grabbed at the ewe as it swirled past him. His fingers hooked into its wool and he reeled and looked wildly upstream for the other.

It was swimming frantically towards him. He staggered across the current towards the far bank to draw her that way, dragging the other sheep; the swimming ewe tried to veer towards him. 'Come on!' Ben rasped. The ewe was only a yard upstream of him now, bleating loudly, and he stooped down with his armful of lambs, grabbed the top of her head and hauled her towards the bank with all his strength. Now he was dragging two sodden ewes and two lambs across the current and they were impossibly heavy. He heaved again, his feet deep in mud, and *again*, his teeth clenched. *'Green!'* he bellowed. He heaved again, his head down. The far bank was only one pace away now. *'Green!'* he bellowed frantically into the rain, and a lamb struggled out of his grip again.

It crashed under and Ben bellowed in rage. It bobbed up again a yard downstream, and Ben struggled after it, hauling the two ewes and the other lamb with him, yelling *'Come back!'* He plunged two four six eight rasping gasping paces after it, then he stopped, chest heaving, furious. It was hopeless. The lamb was five yards downstream of him, then ten, churning the muddy water, and its mother wrenched and strained in Ben's grip, bleating at it frantically. The lamb went swirling away into the rain, further and further, then it was gone, into gloom.

Ben took an anguished breath, turned for the bank again, and heaved the struggling sheep up it, cursing and gasping, teeth clenched, his legs shaky and his heart pounding. He got them up into the shallower water, but still the two struggling ewes could barely stand. He crouched half a minute, head down, getting his breath back, letting the knocking in his chest subside; then he started towards the gate, towing the two bleating sheep.

That was the start of the first day.

33

They worked until darkness stopped them, toiling from island to island, lugging, dragging sheep to the high ground beyond the gate. By nightfall they had saved seventy-eight animals and counted twenty-nine dead. That left about two hundred unaccounted for. They left the sheep around Fury's paddock and drove back to the main house exhausted, ravenous, cold to the bone. Helen wanted them to come into the kitchen to dry out and eat but Ben said: 'Cook us up a storm, Helen, while Green and I start on that raft.'

He had been working it out all day as he toiled. There were half a dozen empty diesel drums in the barn, and the two old tractor-tubes he was using as the gas reservoir for the cool-room. A raft made of drums would be heavy to drag through the water laden with sodden sheep, but a raft made of tractor-tubes would be light by comparison. There were all kinds of timber stacked in the barn. He measured likely pieces with his eye. Then he trudged over to the cool-room he had so painstakingly built. He examined the motor. It was humming away like a bird. He sighed and opened the door, and the chill air he had worked so hard for wafted out at him. *God, the thing really was working at last* . . . He sighed, turned the valve off, disconnected the tubes, and dragged them across the barn and out into the rain, one at a time. He found a floating twig, pressed it to the first valve's teat, and precious methane gas began to hiss out.

He crouched, holding the valve open; God, he was exhausted. But it was better to be here in the freezing rain, doing something that had to be done, than sitting in that warm house watching the unattainable Helen McKenzie cooking.

Green came back from the kitchen, where he had been cutting up drowned sheep for the deep-freeze, and helped him build the raft. At ten o'clock Helen came driving through the rain to tell them dinner was ready. The three of them ate ravenously in a weary silence, then

Ben and Green returned to the barn to continue work. It was past midnight when they finished.

It was a good raft. 'It's great, Ben,' Helen said. 'Now come for a coffee and brandy.'

Ben would have loved a coffee and brandy – half a dozen brandies. But he was in no mood for unrequited love tonight.

'No, thanks, Helen, I'm going to bed. We start again at dawn.'

It was raining even harder in the morning, and in the gulley between the cottage and the main house the water was almost knee-deep.

In the dawn they loaded the raft on to the tractor's trailer and set off, Ben driving. Helen and Green followed in the Land Rover as far as the gate. There the water had risen several inches. They got out and climbed on to the trailer. Ben drove on into the water, chugging between the half-submerged scrub.

They stopped about twenty yards short of the stream-bed, when the water was touching the sump of the tractor. They could have gone in deeper, because the exhaust was above the driver's head, but Ben was keeping that trick until it was absolutely necessary. They offloaded the raft. While Green held it, Ben tied a long length of rope to it, then waded across the stream with the other end. In the middle the water was well above his waist. He tied the rope to a tree on the far side.

'Let her go!'

Green clambered aboard and Helen shoved the raft out into the stream. It moved sluggishly out into the current until the rope restrained it, then swung slowly across, and Ben hauled it in. It was heavy, the water curling around the tubes, but not as heavy as dragging sodden sheep.

Helen climbed up on to the tractor and drove off, towing the trailer, to look for islands on that side. Ben rearranged the rope into a harness and they set off into the rain dragging the raft, looking for sheep.

It rained without ceasing. Darkness was falling when Ben and Green towed their fifteenth raftload of trussed, bleating sheep back to the notional bank of the river. They were several miles downstream from the point where they had crossed in the morning. Ben waded out into the current, taking the end of the rope with him, struggled up the opposite bank to the nearest tree and lashed the rope around it, then shouted:

'Let her come, Green!'

Green shoved the laden raft out into the stream, hanging on to the end to keep it steady. The raft was halfway across when Green tripped over a rock and lurched on to the corner of the raft. There was frantic bleating as trussed sheep slid across the tilted deck and into the water. Ben gave a bellow of rage, and came blundering furiously down the bank and launched himself into the midst of the chaos.

He felt the bite of cold water in his nostrils, then the sheep were all about him, twisting and thrashing their bound legs, trying frantically to swim. Ben seized two, heaved them and bellowed: *'Green!'* And there was Green, blood flooding from his brow, wildly seizing a sheep. Ben looked around for the raft: it was five yards away; he heaved again, then let go of one sheep, sank both hands into the wool of the other, staggered forward and lifted it up on to the raft. It landed with a thud. He turned to grab the other again, and forty pounds of sodden lamb hurled by Green smacked him in the face and he crashed backwards underwater. 'Sorry, boss!' Ben broke surface gasping, snorting, coughing, he grabbed the lamb and heaved it up with all his might and slung it on to the raft. He turned and plunged off downstream again; Green was ahead of him, flailing the water with his hands. Ben thrashed on past him, hurled himself at another sheep. He lugged it around and went struggling back upstream to the raft, gasping. He heaved it up on to the raft and plunged around feverishly for more.

But there were none in sight. Green was thrashing off downstream. Ben scrambled up into shallower water and ran splashing along the bank. He overtook Green and went blundering on. He saw a sheep and plunged off the bank and grabbed it, but when he heaved it up its head hung lifeless. He dropped it with a cry of fury and plunged on downstream towards another, but when he reached it, it too was dead.

All except four of the sheep on that last raftload drowned, their legs tied together.

By late afternoon of that second day they had rescued a total of a hundred and ninety-seven sheep and lambs and they had counted fifty-one dead. Perhaps another forty or so were still out there marooned on patches of high ground, but they were too tired to look for them that day. They drove the survivors up to the high ground, to join the cattle, then they set to cutting lucern. It was flattened by the rain and it was exasperating getting the sickles underneath it. They carried it in sodden armfuls and threw it down in the mud for the livestock. Then the Land Rover wouldn't start – it had air in the fuel line again, but Ben was too exhausted to fix it.

It was dark when they got back to the main house on the tractor, soaked, cold, exhausted, hungry. They let Green off at the barn to skin and cut up more drowned sheep for freezing. Ben stopped the tractor outside the kitchen door and unhitched the trailer, then climbed back up into the saddle.

'Where're you going?' Helen demanded.

'Home, for a hot bath and bed,' Ben shouted above the engine.

'But you're coming back for some hot supper after your bath?'

'Not tonight, Helen, thanks.'

Helen was astonished. 'But *Ben* . . . ?'

But Ben smiled down at her sadly through the rain. 'Friends, Helen, remember? And friends are allowed to say that they want to be alone.'

He gave a small wave and went rumbling off, leaving Helen staring after him.

34

Those were the circumstances under which Ben Sunninghill stayed on at Whoop-Whoop.

The next day they rescued another thirty-seven sheep but when they got them to the high ground around Green's hut they found that thirteen of the lambs rescued the previous day had died of exposure. They spent the rest of that day cutting more lucern and ferrying ewes with lambs down to the barn on the trailer; everything that could be removed from the barn, except the aeroplane, had been taken out to make space for the sheep. They spread lucern wherever they could to get air to it: on the plane's wings, on top of the cool-room, hanging in big bundles from the rafters, even along the verandahs of the main house and Ben's cottage.

It was dark when they finished. The sheep milled in the big barn, dripping, bleating, the place reeking of wet wool and droppings and dank feed. Helen drove Green back to his hut while Ben finished securing the sheep. When she returned, she walked into the barn, hair plastered to her head. She said, as if rehearsed:

'Ben, I think you should move out of the cottage over to the main house, to Tim's room. That gulley is full and it's crazy to trudge all that way in weather like this. We can light a fire in the kitchen and get your working clothes dry for tomorrow.'

Ben's hair was matted, he had mud up to his elbows and his body ached; he looked at her, water trickling down her muddied face, her sodden jeans clinging, and to him she was the most beautiful, admirable woman in the world. He would have loved to move over to the main house, to be warm and cosy and homey with her, the fire crackling up while the rain drummed down, like a couple; but no way could he bear to sleep under the same roof and not possess her.

'No, I'm fine in the cottage, Helen, I don't mind wading across that gulley, it's not dangerous.'

She said with exasperation: 'But it's damn uncomfortable!'

He thought, Not as uncomfortable as knowing you're asleep in the next room, baby. 'I don't mind.' He changed the subject. 'Helen, we've got the situation under control now, Green and I can finish cutting the lucern tomorrow and the next day, so why don't you take this opportunity to get on with your book?'

Helen looked at him.

'Take this opportunity, huh? To get me and my book off your back so you can push off?'

Ben sighed. He hadn't meant his suggestion to sound like that. But before he could explain, Helen went on: 'Why have you treated me so distantly for the last two days, Ben? Why didn't you come to have supper with me last night, after we'd worked so hard? Why the "Friends are allowed to say they want to be alone" routine?' She glared at him, exhausted. 'What are you trying to do to me?'

It was his instinct to be evasive, but before he could answer she demanded: 'We're friends, right?'

'Of course, Helen.' He wanted to add: *Just* friends', but didn't.

'Well,' Helen said softly, 'will my friend come and have some hot supper with me tonight?' Then she changed it impatiently: 'Or let me put it this way, Ben: I'm going to heat up some very nice, very nourishing lamb stew. It'll be ready in about half an hour. I would love you to join me, Ben. But if you don't want to I'll quite understand. And you can go to hell!'

She turned on her muddy heel and walked resolutely out of the barn, tears in her eyes, leaving Ben staring after her. He hesitated, then followed her outside.

'Helen?' he called.

She stopped ten yards away. They looked at each other, the rain teeming down on them, running down their weary faces, dripping from their noses and chins. Ben forced a grin and said: 'I don't want to go to hell, Helen. I want to come for some hot, nourishing lamb stew . . .'

Helen's eyes burned. She wanted to splash across the mud that separated them and fling her arms around him; but she just grinned.

'Great. *Pardner* . . .'

She turned and strode off jauntily.

Pardner? Yes, most of the time, Ben could handle his feelings for Helen like that because he had to, with the rain drumming down, spluttering upon the rivulets that ran past the houses and barn; he was capable of biting the bullet for one more day, and then another, just taking one day at a time, because Helen McKenzie was the most worthwhile woman in the world to make that effort for. He was prepared to roll with the punches, and there was nothing else he could do about it anyway, until the rain stopped.

But the rain did not stop. Sometimes it eased off for a while, the curtains turning to drizzle, sometimes the dark sky grew a little lighter; then *down* it came again, and you could not see ten paces. Every night they listened to the radio and watched the television, and the news was astonishing. One third of Queensland was affected by flooding, ten towns were isolated, roads and railway lines washed away, and the State Emergency Services had evacuated thirty thousand people. The floods stretched from Muttaburra in western Queensland to Nyngan in New South Wales, an area of one million square kilometres, and the floodwaters from here in the north had yet to reach the south. The Barcoo River was nine metres higher than normal, the small towns in the Channel Country were inundated, and the Royal Australian Air Force was ferrying in tons of food to isolated towns like Longreach and Jundah. Charleville, just a hundred and fifty miles from Burraville, was like a war zone: the water had risen two metres in three hours and swept through the entire town. All four thousand residents had been evacuated to a tent-city set up on the high ground of the aerodrome, and eight RAAF Hercules aircraft and ten helicopters were busy airlifting food in and the sick and aged out to Brisbane. The stock and crop losses were high; twenty-five thousand sheep drowned so far, another hundred thousand at risk, all of them carrying a year's growth of wool. Near Dubbo, farmers were working flat out to save sixty thousand sheep with the help of two Caribou aircraft. In towns like Nyngan, Boyle, Wanaaring, Enngonia, Cunnamulla, bulldozers were building levees and the whole populace was frantically filling sandbags against the floodwaters about to descend from the north. The Army and police were rescuing hundreds of people out of trees and off rooftops, the Air Force had dropped four thousand bales of fodder to sixty thousand stranded sheep on forty properties on the Barwon River, and in New South Wales the State Emergency Service had airlifted thousands of animals, but they'd had to shoot many more to spare them the misery of starvation. Around Nyngan they were unable to drop fodder at all to fifty thousand animals because there was insufficient high ground, and thousands were dying. Now Charleville was a stinking disaster area of polluted water and rotting food, whole houses swept off their foundations, twisted railway trucks strewn across tracks, furniture floating down streets, cars upended on hedges. Medical teams had been flown in to cope with a gastro-enteritis epidemic, and sandflies added to the nightmare. Further downstream in the sandbagged town of Cunnamulla, where the floodwaters from Charleville were expected to arrive soon, the plague of sandflies and mosquitoes was so bad that kangaroos were trying to enter the houses and a mob of them had taken up residence on the hospital verandah. It was the worst flood in white man's history in Australia.

Ben and Helen watched the astonishing, heartbreaking scenes on television. They saw the town of Nyngan lose its battle of the sandbags against the Bogan River. Nyngan means 'dry pond' in Aboriginal and that is what the Bogan River usually is, but it had flooded twice in living memory. Years back the Shire Council had built a permanent levee around the town. Now the Bogan was rushing and rising as never before, and for days the townsfolk had been feverishly engaged in the backbreaking job of filling and stacking two hundred thousand sandbags on top of the levee. But to no avail. The ramparts broke and within thirty minutes the town was waist-deep, the rushing water swirling down the streets, over doorsteps, smashing down shopfronts, carrying away cars, furniture, houses. The whole area was polluted with petrol, garbage and sewage, and people were clinging to rooftops and marooned up trees and perched on top of wardrobes. People were rescuing each other by boats, and helicopters were crisscrossing the leaden sky airlifting two thousand people to the high ground around the railway station; families were separated, pets lost and possessions swept away. Ben and Helen stared horrified at the screen, and they felt the heartache of ruin. Insurance would not cover floods like this. This was an Act of God.

That's how Ben regarded the enforced prolongation of his stay at Whoop-Whoop – as an Act of God. And, by God, he was determined to keep his heart under control. But there was not much for him to do now the sheep were safe: there was enough lucern for two weeks and surely the floods would subside in that time? If not, they could call for a fodder-drop from the State Emergency Service. And so, while Helen 'took this opportunity' to write her book, Ben looked for work. After ploughing a water-channel around the main house and barn, then hacking it deeper with a hoe, he got stuck into the bathroom walls with a chisel and replaced the plumbing; but he could not connect the new solar panel to it until the sun returned to the skies. He decided to have a look at Helen's old VW van. He cleaned up the engine, tightened things up and recharged the battery. It worked. Then he set to work on the wiring of the main house and patched up several circuits. Every afternoon he drove up to Green's hut to check on the livestock and the water levels. At night he cooked the evening meal, to give Helen more time to write.

'You're being a great help, Ben.'

'That's what pardners are for, Helen.' And, yes, he meant it. But that night they had a good deal to drink and they talked until the small hours; again he felt that yearning to reach out and touch her, and after he had trudged back to his cottage he poured all his passion into his notebook; but the next morning his head was back in command and he rubbed it all out.

But that night he found he had to move over to the main house: Helen drove him to the edge of the gulley, and as he waded across in the Land Rover's headlights he slipped and fell full-length, and Helen cried: 'For God's sake, Ben, stop this nonsense and come back to the house!'

So, with misgiving, Ben moved into Tim's room, next to Helen's. And, oh, it was so much nicer; it was heart-achingly lovely to sit around the kitchen hearth at the end of a cold wet muddy day, the fire crackling up and the rain drumming down, his clothes drying in front of the fire, drinking wine and talking, knowing that when bedtime came he did not have to set out into that rain and mud.

'It's cosy, isn't it?' Helen said to the fire. 'I mean, it's tragic what's happening all over the country, but isn't it kind of snug, just the two of us, the fire blazing and the waters lapping all around – it reminds me of Winnie-the-Pooh and Owl and Eeyore, and Christopher Robin floating in his upside-down umbrella in the Hundred Acre Wood . . .'

Just the two of us . . . Like a couple. With all his heart Ben wanted it to be just the two of them for ever; *with all his heart* he yearned to reach out his hand and touch her and make his soulmate his glorious sexual mate. Each night, when bedtime finally came and they walked down the passage, it would have been the most natural, wonderful thing in the world to walk into that double room together, get undressed, go to bed and make wonderful, gentle, passionate love. But each night they just bade each other goodnight outside Helen's door. It was very hard for Ben to lie quiet and hear through the wall the soft sounds of Helen preparing for bed; it took him a long time to go to sleep.

But in the morning he had it more or less straightened out in his mind again.

35

And Helen had it straightened out in her mind, too, for she truly believed in platonic friendship and she had rationalized that that is what she had with Ben. Not without difficulty, since Ben had told her very ardently that he loved her. But that declaration she also had been able to discount, as arising from momentary passion, or frustration, just a kind of fleeting infatuation. She had felt it herself a few times when she was a student – and she had seen plenty of her friends go through it at Uni. The passion he had shown when he kissed her was simply the reaction of any sex-starved man who finds a woman in his arms – and poor Ben was sex-starved, he made no bones about that. And the same sort of explanation applied to her – because, since we're being honest, she *had* reacted to those kisses, she *had* felt arousal, passion in fact, a feeling very like love – but it was all explicable in terms of the sheer physical impact of the moment. Let's face it, wasn't she sex-starved too? She was familiar with the argument that there is no such thing as platonic friendship, even when corporealized in a body as unprepossessing as Ben Sunninghill's and – since we're being intellectual about this – didn't it follow from her judgement that it *was* unprepossessing that she was reacting at his masculinity, didn't her very dismissal of his body as a sexual entity mean that the possibility of making love to it *had* occurred to her? And, because it occurred to her, did it not follow that she found it attractive enough to consider it? Did she not always think that he had such charm? Is charm only incorporeal, or does it invest the incumbent with something approaching physical beauty? Yes, Helen had taken all those tortuous arguments into account in reaching her conclusion that her friendship with Ben Sunninghill really was nonetheless platonic now.

Day after day she laboured at her book as the rain teemed down, and in her story Jane wrestled with metaphysical enquiries very similar to these, for she was also bent on platonic friendship. Helen sat, twisting her hair around her finger and gnawing her pen as Jane had long, intense conversations with her tall dark stranger, Trevor, who had a hell of a lot more going for him than Ben Sunninghill, being very handsome. But oh, Jane's conversations with Trevor were not nearly as good as Helen's with Ben, no matter how hard she tried to remember each day all they had talked about the night before – 'about anything and everything' as Jane repeatedly explained herself to her drunken husband, Howard, when he reappeared from time to time from his gambling sprees in New Orleans. (Finally he got so pissed off that he kicked in the sides of Trevor's black Ford Thunderbird convertible.) Jane's 'spirit soared' during these conversations, like Helen's did with Ben, though for much less reason, Trevor coming off the page as dull as ditchwater and terribly fond of the sound of his own voice. But Jane evidently didn't notice these shortcomings, being, obviously, a perfect listener (indeed, it was these conversations alone which, from time to time, made her nipples harden), whereas Helen worried thoughts through.

'Helen,' Ben smiled, 'if you write as well as you talk, your book will be very good.'

'If *only*.' Helen closed her eyes and clenched her fist in frustration. 'If only I could write as *you* talk, if only I'd *lived* as much as you've lived.'

Oh, if only ... That ember of hope glowed up a little. 'Then why is Jane going to do nothing, Helen?' The rain beating down. 'You can make Jane do anything you like.'

'Oh, don't talk to me about that piss-poor, pusillanimous woman! Jane makes me *sick* ...'

Ben threw back his head and laughed, despite himself. She laughed wanly with him; then she said in a serious voice:

'Ben, please don't leave until I've got rid of Jane.'

Ben's heart squeezed. 'Let me read about her now, so I can help you get rid of her.'

'No ...'

No, she would not. Because she did not want him to hurry Jane along, and because she was so *embarrassed* about Jane. Ben had to close his mind to wanting her, and, dear God, he wished the floods would subside. He could not bear to wait for Jane. But, on the other hand, he was almost sure that Jane almost was Helen McKenzie, in artless disguise: alternatively, Jane almost existed as a separate person now: and might not Helen become that Jane? And, would that not be absolutely wonderful, worth waiting for? He did not know for sure what

Jane wanted because he had not been allowed to read the manuscript for so long, but certainly she really existed now, living in this very house, trying to demand to live her own life – and might she not come to persuade her creator to do the same? It was a fanciful thought, but stranger things had happened, and sometimes, with the rain teeming down and the kitchen fire crackling, the whole world out there a little mad, it did not seem so fanciful to Ben. On the other hand, in his sound and sober senses, he doubted Jane would ever change anything, and she would take a lot of getting rid of, and, oh, he felt responsible for that, in encouraging Helen to create her. And he did not think he could bear this much longer.

And then, that very night, the rain stopped.

Ben woke suddenly, and after a moment he realized why: the silence. He swung out of bed naked, and went out on to the verandah and shone his flashlight: the silver curtains had gone. And his heart sank – but it would still take some time for the floods to recede, surely? The road out of Burraville would be cut for days still? It took him a long time to go back to sleep. In the small hours of that morning a strong wind sprang up, lashing the dripping trees, roaring across the black Outback. With the dawn the sun appeared. And it seemed to Ben that the rains had been the best time of his life. He drove the Land Rover down to the causeway. The water had dropped enough for him to get a rope around the heads of the dead sheep blocking the culvert and drag the bloated animals out of the way. The sheet of muddy water began to ease away.

That night they got the overall picture on the television: flood levels were dropping in Queensland and New South Wales; although the floodwaters from those parts had still to move into the Darling River system, ten metres higher than normal, and reach the south, at least it had stopped raining in the north. For the first time there were brief pictures of Burraville: the town was soggy and slushy; Radio-Jack was mopping mud out of his hotel, Shanty-town was like a paddy-field, and the Farmers' Co-op and railway station were still under inches of water. But the rest of the town on the high side of Main Road was only muddy: there was Stavros outside the Niagara, mop in hand, beaming at the camera, for all the good publicity would do him; and then there was Sergeant Vince Keenan saying to the camera:

'Well, it's been a tough ten days, and as you can see there's quite a lot of damage, mainly to business premises on the low side of town. But it's nothing like in the rest of the region, and we've had no loss of life, thank God, not even any Aborigines over in Shanty-town, which was hardest hit because it's lowest lying of all, though many of them have lost most of their possessions, poor devils. But in the surrounding districts there's been a tremendous loss of livestock, of course, tens of thousands of cattle and sheep, and reports of more coming in all the time. However, the good news is that in a day or two both the road south to Charleville and the railway line should be open again. Though Charleville itself is still a disaster area, the railroad from there to the east will be open tomorrow and we'll be able to get much-needed supplies through. Meanwhile, we're launching an appeal for clothing, blankets and cooking utensils to help our Abbos . . .'

Ben sat in the repainted living-room on the zebra-striped sofa and he thought his heart would break. If he was going to be true to himself, he would have to leave very soon. Helen turned her head to him, her eyes moist, her lips about to speak. For a moment they stared at each other; then she got up and walked out wordlessly. She hurried down the passage to her bedroom, closed the door and slumped down at her dressing-table.

Ben remained on the sofa, his heart cracking; then he got to his feet and walked slowly down the passage. He knocked lightly on her door. 'Helen . . . ?'

Helen said into her hands: 'Please, Ben, I want to be alone – like *friends* are allowed to be. Please make yourself some supper and leave me be.'

Later that evening Ben sat in the kitchen with Dundee, trying to wrestle his fantasies about Jane out of his mind, hoping for Helen to appear. It was after midnight when he finally walked down the passage and past her hallowed door to his room. He stripped off his clothes, toppled himself into bed, and stifled a groan.

It was in the small hours of the morning that there was a creak of floorboards in the passage, and his door opened. Ben woke up, and he could not believe his eyes: there stood Helen McKenzie, in his bedroom. She wore a plain cotton nightdress: it reached to her feet and there was nothing seductive about it, but the moonlight streaming through the window showed up the outline of her womanness, the curves of her breasts and thighs, even the shadow of her pubic triangle. Ben stared at her, and she whispered:

'I can't sleep, thinking of you leaving.'

Ben's heart was hammering. He shoved himself up on to his elbow. Helen whispered down at him:

'Please don't leave yet, Ben. The roads aren't safe. And you've got to help me edit the book now, it'll be finished tomorrow or the next day – you've got to go through it with me page by page so it's got a chance of being published. Please don't desert me now, Ben.'

Ben stared up at her in the moonlight, and he wanted to sweep back his blankets and get to his feet in all his naked manhood and take her in his arms and possess her possess her possess her and tell her that he would never desert her. His hand went to the cover to whip it back, and Helen impulsively sat down on the bed beside him and scooped him into her arms. She clutched him tight and cried: 'Please tell me you won't leave yet!'

Ben half lay in her embrace, her breast pressed against his arm, her soft cheek and neck crushed against his bristly chin; and oh God the sweet female scent and feel of her. He clutched her tight and whispered hoarsely:

'All right, darling . . .'

Helen gave a sob of gratitude and she hugged him and rocked him and squeezed him, like a child. And his hand began to slide around to her breast, and he tried to sit up so he could topple her over on to the bed and roll himself on top of her, the love of his life, and she released him and sat up straight again. She took both his hands tightly in hers. 'Thank you, Ben,' she whispered.

Helen had not noticed his hand moving towards her breast – that was not why she had taken his hands. She did so because she was grateful the crisis was over: now she could go back to bed and sleep at last. 'Thank you,' she whispered again, and she plunged her lips to his fingers and kissed them hard; then she let go and stood up. She smiled down at him, then turned and padded out of the room before Ben could summon any words.

He heard her bedroom door close; and he ripped back his covers and swung out of bed. He strode naked out of the room and down the passage. He stopped outside her door, reached for the handle and twisted it. But the door was locked.

Ben Sunninghill stood stark naked outside her door with the hardest erection he had ever known, and he raised his hand to knock – then his knuckles stopped an inch from the wood as the question flashed through his mind: Why was the door locked? He knew she used to lock herself into her bedroom at night but that was when she was alone and afraid of spooks – she was not alone now, she had just torn herself out of his arms, had just bestowed the huge compliment of begging him to stay. She had walked into his bedroom in the middle of the night and that implied trust from a woman as principled as

Helen McKenzie – and here he was, seconds later, recklessly naked outside her door with his cock in his hand trying to breach that trust. How did this look . . . ?

For a long moment Ben stood outside Helen's door, knuckles poised. Then the recklessness passed, and common sense and decency returned, and Helen called: 'Ben, is that you?'

Ben swallowed. 'Yes,' he said hoarsely.

'Is anything the matter?'

Ben screwed up his eyes. He croaked: 'I just wondered if you were okay.'

'I'm fine now, Ben, thank you.'

Ben took a deep, shaky breath.

'Okay,' he heard himself say. 'Goodnight.' He added: 'I'll move back to the cottage tomorrow.'

He turned and walked back to his bedroom. He threw himself down on the bed and stared at the beam of moonlight. And he knew he could not bear to sit beside her for another fortnight, another month, to edit her book, feeling her physical presence radiating like warmth, looking at her soft golden hair while she agonized over changing words, the tiny soft hairs on her cheek, the fullness of her chewed lip, her big harassed eyes, and not take her in his arms and possess her. He simply could not bear the rejection any longer, no matter how high her affection and esteem for him, no matter how much she wanted his help.

And, oh God, he wanted never to leave.

36

But the next day he learned that he had to leave immediately: and this was for her sake, too.

Early that morning he found Helen in the kitchen packing a pile of her children's old clothing and an assortment of foodstuffs, including two whole sheep from the deep-freeze, into big plastic bags. 'Hi,' she greeted him, 'I'm taking this into Burraville for the Abbo relief fund – the poor devils have lost everything, Vince said on telly last night.'

'Do you want me to come with you?'

'If you want to.' She packed busily.

'How long will you stay in town?'

'Well, I have to be neighbourly after floods like this, see if anybody else needs help. But I'll try to be back by mid-afternoon. I want to finish my book tonight.'

Ben knew she would rather go alone, after the Picnic Races, and he had no desire to expose himself or her to comment again, or to hang about unobtrusively while she did her neighbourly duty. So he was left alone that day. He connected the solar panel to the new plumbing; then, having wrestled briefly with his conscience, he went to look for her manuscript.

He had to search high and low for it. He finally found it in a suitcase, deep under her bed. He took it to the living-room. From there he would be able to see the Land Rover returning.

And within an hour he knew that tomorrow he had to leave Whoop-Whoop, either alone or with her.

The book had hardly improved: it was still written in a cramped style, bristling with clichés squeezed amongst ardent research through Roget's Thesaurus, but Helen McKenzie *was* trying to let it all hang out. And though she was not succeeding as a story-teller it was clear to Ben, reading between the lines, how Helen's mind was working. Here was Jane McDonald, of Ruttsville, Louisiana, a lovely woman who has recently lost her child, gradually being besieged against her WASP will by her lust for this tall, black, handsome stranger from Africa, Trevor, in his old black Ford Thunderbird convertible in which he's touring the world in order to savour life, become wise and, apparently, to spread the socialist gospel, of which he has an imperfect grasp rendered more confused by the collapse of the Berlin Wall. After many slings and arrows of outrageous fortune, abuse from white gas-pump jockeys, being refused many a fifty-cent beer in white-trash bars, he rocks up at the imposing gates of this sugar-plantation, about a hundred and five miles from New Orleans, to borrow a spanner to fix his ailing Thunderbird. 'Wearing his poverty with dignity', he approaches the back door and is surprised to find the mistress of the house cornered on the kitchen table by her enormous Rottweiler dog, which has inexplicably turned rabid. Trevor has a way with animals and he charms the beast into tail-wagging submission by sheer force of personality. As a result (after he's also fixed her washing-machine) Jane employs him to stay on the plantation, with his own cottage, as foreman over her labour-force of sweated blacks, now much reduced because her spendthrift husband, Howard, is always off squandering the family fortune in the gaming halls and whorehouses of New Orleans, *despite* (underlined) the Aids scare.

Jane's upmarket plantation neighbours become *absolutely* unjustifiably suspicious of Jane's growing friendship with Trevor and her reliance upon him as general factotum, and they freeze her out of their swish cocktail parties, barbecues, and fancy-dress balls. Jane is deeply wounded by this, wonders why, masturbates a bit erratically (oh *why?*) before she chances to spy Trevor swimming naked one moonlit midnight in the huge swimming pool – which is another of Howard's follies and partly accounts for the goddam overdraft. Jane, being *genuinely* (underlined) hot and sweaty herself, plucks up all her courage to put on her swimsuit, and *saunters* out, *pretending* she too has taken it into her pretty head to have a moonlit dip before proceeding to her chaste double-bed with its silk sheets, which she can also ill afford. And what happens when she thus provocatively plunges into the crystal clear, sensuously cool water? Does this black Greek God come thrashing across to enfold her in his muscular, ebony arms?

Does he hell. What does this paragon of virtue do?

He talks.

But *talks* ... The hindleg off a donkey. Night after naked moonlit night. This guy Trevor is inexhaustible when it comes to communication. And not only is Roget's Thesaurus clearly his favourite reading

– he never uses the same adjective twice in any given moonlight swim
– he never pauses for breath or moves a muscle in a dozen pages of
monologue, he never uses slang, his grammar is perfect and he never
ends a sentence with a preposition. And, throughout these mighty
monologues, Jane never interrupts and never moves a muscle either,
evidently transfixed in the water for yet another night, though her
spirits do soar and her nipples do harden. And what does Trevor talk
about to induce this sexual frenzy? Exactly what Ben Sunninghill talked
about. Not word for word, for nobody could talk so monotonously as
Trevor, but subject for subject, fact for fact, proposition for proposition, principle for principle, dragged into the manuscript by the
scruff of their necks. All you had to do was study Trevor and you had
all the wisdom of Ben Sunninghill, writ large. And what was the
upshot of all this erudition?

Ben's heart almost broke: because Jane was in love.

But incognizantly so, for Jane does not admit this to herself. Jane is
a loyal, old-fashioned woman who also still loves her worthless husband. Jane resolutely denies her emotions, calling her relationship with
Trevor a platonic friendship, and she spends pages rationalizing away
her hardened nipples; but it seemed clear that the reader was meant
to read between the lines and know that Jane was beside herself with
love even if she doesn't . . .

Ben stared at the pages, his excitement mounting. He wanted to
jump up and shout 'Hallelujah!' and waltz around the room. Oh God,
his patience and swallowed pride and persistence were vindicated! He
could see Helen McKenzie sitting on his pillion, the wind in her hair
as they set off into the wide blue yonder, to laugh, to love, to explore,
to become wise . . .

But Ben did not jump up. He made himself sit and think this through.
Was it that clear . . . ?

Was the reader meant to read between the lines and gainsay Jane's
rationalization of the state of her heart?

Ben feverishly re-read the relevant pages several times; and each
time, with a sinking heart, he was less sure of his first impression of
the author's intention. What *was* Helen saying about Jane? Was she
being artless, expecting us to believe Jane's protestations of platonic
love? Or was she being artful, inviting us to conclude that Jane doth
protest too much?

Ben sat there, staring at the pages. He was not sure now. He
read on earnestly, looking for more evidence, and what followed was
equally confusing. For Trevor's attitude was quite clear.

Trevor ardently urges Jane to run away with him, to turn her back on her dull, residual wifely functions which are not appreciated by the prodigal Howard, to turn her back on her sadness for her lost child, on her isolation on the plantation with its fading colonial grandeur, and to fly, *fly* (the only time Trevor repeats himself) away with him in his Ford Thunderbird convertible, the wind blowing through her hair, the sun sparkling on his smile and the new paint-job he had to give the vehicle after that shit Howard kicked the sides in. Together they will be free spirits, go where they like (Trevor evidently has a buck or two saved up despite the poverty he wore with dignity), *do* what they like, learning, experiencing, *living* ... Around the world they would go, across both Americas, then they'll buy a yacht and sail the enchanted islands of the Pacific to the mysterious excitement of the Orient, then they'd sell the yacht and buy a 1000cc Harley-Davidson motorbike (Ben's eyes really burnt) and together they'll cross the mountain passes of India and Afghanistan into the dangerous fastness of the Middle East. From the raptures of the Holy Land they would turn south for the majesties of ancient Egypt, the pyramids, the sphinxes, the Nile carved out of the mighty glaring desert, on a steamer they would chug up into the very heart of Africa, to the dense verdant forests and vast plains and valleys of Kenya, teeming with all manner of wonderful game, great lumbering elephants and graceful gazelles and happy snorting hippo. ('But only three rhino left in the whole of Kenya, do you know that, Jane, *that*'s what Man's done.') Down the mighty Zambesi river they would drift on a raft, into Zimbabwe, the Land of Monomotapa, whence Trevor comes. And if you think Jane would have had a great time hitherto, you ain't seen nothin'. Because in Trevor's charming mud-and-thatch village the tribe would give them a tumultuous welcome and there would be feasting and singing late into the night and Jane would dance with the hot dust of Africa between her toes. (The dust would be hot late at night?) And after this most *real*, most satisfying, most *basic* period of her life, during which Trevor intends to give his people a crash course in Enlightenment, they would tackle the real nasty business, those bloody wildlife poachers. Setting up camps all over the place, they would knock the living shit out of the bastards before handing them over to the authorities for rehabilitation into well-fed, contented conservationists, because all the guys really need is a little understanding. Then, having straightened out that problem, they would take their farewells of the grateful tribes and remount their motorbike and ride up the rest of Africa (Trevor got a bit vague on his geography here) until they found themselves crossing the mighty Sahara, churning through the sand-dune lands of the Arab nomads with their camels and tents and gorgeous belly-dancers (and amongst these friendly tribes Jane would learn to belly-dance too, complete with a ruby in her navel). (This was the first time in the manuscript where Jane interrupted Trevor's monologues to make a jolly suggestion. Trevor, in his sweet reasonableness, responds 'Indeed,' before continuing. And oh God, Ben thought his heart would break at this image of a joyful, sensuous Helen.) Then, before them, as they crested the last sand-dune, would lie the sparkling Mediterranean, its shores groaning under sundrenched vineyards, the whole of Europe beyond, from dazzling fashion shows to the delights of ancient museums and art galleries, from bodegas with sawdust on the floor to towering castles along the Rhine, 'the veritable movable cultural *feast* of Europe . . .'

That was Trevor's proposition to Jane. And what did Jane reply?

Ben closed his eyes and put both hands to his face.

With 'glistening eyes' Jane says she'll think about it. She says she'll give him his answer tomorrow . . .

The manuscript stopped at this point. Helen was going to give Jane's reply when she came back from Burraville.

Ben put his hands to his face. Because he just knew what Jane's answer would be. No way was Jane going to run away with her beautiful Trevor to live and love the big wide world together, become wise: because, when all was said and done, although Jane McDonald was Helen McKenzie, no matter what Jane really wanted to do, Helen would be strong and break her heart tomorrow . . . And that broke Ben's.

And, oh, he felt sorry for Helen, and guilty for what he had done to her: he had made her write this book, and now she would want it to be published, her creation to be recognized and rewarded, and she was in for repeated bitter disappointment. For months to come, maybe for years, she would post this book off to publishers, full of hope; for months and years, all alone at Whoop-Whoop, she would count the days between trips into Burraville to check the post, cautioning herself not to expect anything yet, but each time desperately hoping that there would be a letter of acceptance today. Time after time her trip was going to be wasted and, when a letter finally did arrive, she was going to be crushed again, until she was finally numbed into believing it was hopeless, and that she was useless. Oh Christ, Ben didn't want her to feel that – and indeed, he was not even sure that her book deserved that: because, although it was unpublishable, it wasn't as bad as he had just made it out to himself to be – in fact, was not his disparagement at least partly born of his jealousy over this fictional Trevor? With the towering superiority of his degree in English Literature he could honestly say it was corny as hell, but did it not also have a certain refreshing charm in its corniness? He was not sure. Was there not a romantic naïveté which made one smile in sympathy, which made Jane an endearing woman, a woman one could love? Indeed was not the simple romanticism almost irresistible? Did you not want to turn the page to find out what romantic inanities would next happen to our Jane, and was it not therefore exciting? Didn't you *worry* about her? Indeed, given some strenuous editing wasn't this passable soap opera stuff? Wasn't it the sort of crap people want to read these days? Didn't you *want* Jane to throw caution to the winds instead of getting skin-wrinkles in that folly of a pool all night, didn't you yearn for her to do something about those hardened nipples? *Wasn't* Howard a real first-class shit – especially for kicking the sides of poor Trevor's Thunderbird in? *Didn't* you want her to jump into that repainted T-bird and ride off into the sunset with her black knight, even if he was a pain in the arse? Jane obviously didn't think he was and it was *her* you wanted to be happy, wasn't it? *Did* you really want her to shed her rose-coloured spectacles and see Trevor for the boring, sanctimonious Zimbabwean he was? No. And if she decided not to go tomorrow, would you not blink back some tears as Trevor drives off alone into the sunset – not tears for that jerk, but for Jane? And if she *did* decide to go off with him, would you not worry about her decision? And if all this was so – and Ben didn't know what to think anymore – wasn't it his human duty to stay and help Helen McKenzie edit Jane into shape, into a person who was not going to be a crushing, bitter disappointment for years to come?

And, furthermore, Ben felt guilt because, by urging her to write, he had opened doors to her, tempted her to abandon her duties, to spread her wings, to have all the adventures she had always wanted, and to become wise. He had shown her temptations, and they would be the more painful to her because she would resist them. It was just possible that tomorrow Jane might find the courage to go and have her wonderful life; but Helen McKenzie herself would not have such courage, and Jane's decision would be the more painful because of that. Jane may go, but Helen would stay . . .

Finally, Ben Sunninghill ached for himself: the feverish hope that had flickered up when he first read about Jane being in love was

281

pathetic. Indeed, *was* Jane in love with her Trevor – should we not believe her protestations? And, when all was said and done, if Helen was in love at all, was it not with the man she had created? And that sad possibility was the more painful because in that case had not Helen, albeit unwittingly, written down in black and white that black man equals Jew and had more chance than your unprepossessing Ben Sunninghill? But the most painful part of all this was that Helen had given him her own glimpse of what might have been, if only he had been physically different; together they might have taken off on his 1000cc Harley-Davidson, for the first time in his life Ben Sunninghill might have had a woman to call his own, to share his life. And *what* a woman! A woman who, given the chance and his better looks, would have loved every minute of her life with him. It broke his heart to think about it.

But he made himself sit there and think about it, about what he had done to this woman he loved, how pathetically restrained and indecisive he had been, about the pain he had thereby caused her. Wouldn't Jane's decisions fester in her heart? And, just as bad, was the pain he had caused to himself by not grasping the nettle of rejection.

Well, Ben Sunninghill was through with being fucking pathetic: he refused to ride away from Whoop-Whoop manlessly. This afternoon, when Helen came home, he was going to tell her how he felt, man to woman, and ask her to run away with him. And doubtless she would say no: but at least he would have tried. So he would leave – tomorrow. Yes, tomorrow – he had done enough damage to Helen, and to himself, and he refused to be responsible for any more. He did not even want to find out what Jane McDonald decided to do. He would torture himself no longer.

6

37

That afternoon he moved his bedding back to the cottage: he could not sleep under the same roof as her another night.

It was dark when Helen came back from Burraville: a ghostly moon was just rising. Ben had begun to worry in case she had skidded off the muddy road after a boozy lunch with Edna and the girls at the Niagara. He was on his way to his motorbike to go to look for her when he saw her headlights flashing up the slippery track.

He walked back towards the main house, his heart tense. He had had a few drinks to fortify himself, but he was completely sober. Helen parked at the back of the house, climbed out without seeing him and strode purposefully for the back door, her handbag tucked under one arm.

'Hi,' Ben said.

'Oh, hi!' She flashed him a smile and strode on. 'Come in! But do you mind if we don't work up our usual cerebral storm tonight? I've had a big day with the girls.'

Ben closed his eyes. Evidently it was not going to happen tonight: he required an attentive Helen for the solemn things he had to say.

'Sure, but you should have something to eat, I've defrosted some lamb chops.'

She turned to him and said pleasantly: 'Oh Ben, I know this sounds ungracious, but do you mind leaving mine in the oven? I'm desperate to work because I've finally figured out driving back what Jane's going to *do* . . .'

Ben looked at her in the moonlight outside the kitchen door, and he didn't know whether his heart quickened or sank at that news. But would it make any difference? He smiled sadly.

'Sure, I'm not hungry either, go for it, baby. I'll still be here in the morning.'

Helen did not seem to catch that last bit. She smiled gratefully and kissed him on the cheek.

The brief smell of her, the touch of her! He turned and walked away into the night, his heart weeping for what was going to happen tomorrow.

The first light was showing in the east when Helen drove over to his cottage. Ben was already long awake, staring at the dark ceiling. He had cleaned the cottage before going to bed, packed up his things and loaded his saddle-bags. Helen skidded the Land Rover to a stop at the porch.

'*Ben,*' she shouted, '*I've finished!*' She clambered out of the vehicle and slammed the door. '*Ben . . . !*'

Ben had swung out of bed when he heard the vehicle approach. He was coming out on to the porch, pulling on a shirt, as Helen came up the steps. 'Ben, I've finished my book!' she shouted.

Ben smiled. 'Congratulations . . .'

Helen slumped down in a heap on the steps and held her ink-smudged face. Ben stood over her. She said into her hands:

'Oh, forgive me for waking you but I just had to tell you! I've *finished*, Ben.'

He said: 'That's wonderful, Helen. I wasn't asleep.' He sat down slowly beside her. Helen still held her face, and it was wet with tears. His eyes were moist as he smiled: 'Do you want a drink, to celebrate?'

Helen shook her head in her hands and took a deep, quivery breath. 'Not yet. I'm absolutely sober, I'm just . . . *moved.*'

'Of course,' Ben said softly. 'Congratulations again.'

She breathed into her hands. 'Oh Ben, it's so *good*. The ending, I mean.'

Ben felt numb, and he didn't know what to expect.

'That's wonderful, Helen.'

Helen sat there, holding her face. Ben waited; then he asked gently: 'And? What does Jane decide to do?'

Helen took a quivering breath, then lowered her hands. She did not turn to him. She said tremulously to the dawn:

'She decides to go, Ben . . .'

Ben's heart seemed to miss a beat. Then it began to soar.

'Oh, that's the right decision, Helen,' he whispered.

There was a silence. Then she said to the dawn, tears running down her cheeks:

'At first, when Trevor asks her to go with him, she decides she can't do it. She agonizes such a long time, but she finally says No. And so Trevor packs up to leave, by himself, to ... carry on exploring the world. To ... take *on* the world. And Jane is heartbroken, watching him get ready. But she knows she is doing the right thing. The *right* thing, Ben ... And ...' Helen sniffed and wiped her knuckle under each eye. 'And, they say goodbye. Trevor doesn't say he'll write, he doesn't say he'll always be waiting for her because he knows ... he knows this must be goodbye for ever ... And so he just kisses her, on the cheek, the first time he's ever touched her. He just climbs into his car. Jane stands on the verandah, and she watches him drive away. The tears running down her face ...' Helen closed her wet eyes and clenched her fist, and then whispered: 'And *then* – in a *flash* ...'

She stopped, and dropped her face into her hands again. For half a minute she sat like that, reliving it, and Ben waited, not daring to speak. Then she took a big breath and went on resolutely:

'In a *flash*, she sees the rest of her life stretching before her. The emptiness of it, the uselessness of it now, the sheer *waste* of it ... Advancing inexorably towards her involuntary and disgusting putre-faction in the grave. And she asks herself, Is this what God made a beautiful world for? Such a fascinating, interesting world – to *waste* it? And ... suddenly her heart fills with joy, and she *knows* what she must do!'

Ben's heart sang; Helen sat up straight and took a deep, tearful breath, to control herself. She said tremulously:

'And she *shouts* to Trevor, and waves from the verandah! But he doesn't hear her! So she goes *running* down the steps after him! She runs desperately down the drive, as fast as her legs can carry her, Ben. But she isn't catching up, Trevor is accelerating, driving out of her life for ever, and she is desperate, *crying* ... But there's a short-cut through the plantation and maybe she can get to the main road ahead of him! She runs for her life through the cane fields, down the paths, heart pounding, gasping, sobbing, she *runs*, and *runs*, and then there ahead is the main road, beyond the fence! She *throws* herself at the fence and scrambles through it, and she *bursts* on to the grassy verge beyond. And, *yes*, she can see Trevor's car just a hundred yards away, driving towards her! And she dashes out into the road, her hair awry and a laugh all over her face, and she waves her arms joyfully ...'

Helen paused, and stared at the dawn tearfully; then she closed her eyes and slumped her shoulders. Ben's heart was knocking. Then Helen dropped her face in her hands again, and sobbed.

Ben waited. 'And?' he asked.

Helen swallowed and sniffed, then whispered: 'And she is so full of joy, Ben ... And then, *simultaneously*, there is a screaming *hiss* behind her, and a shattering blast of horn, and a screech of brakes. And she whirls around! And all she sees is this dreadful great truck hurtling down on her ... And she *screams*, and throws up her hands across her horrified face. And...' Helen closed her eyes and burst into sobs. 'And it hits her ... And kills her ...'

The tears were running down her face. She turned to him, eyes glistening. 'Do you see?' she whispered.

Ben's eyes were brimming too. Of course he saw.

'Yes.'

Helen said tremulously: 'Jane finally has the courage to do the right thing, I mean to do what she really wants to do ... And then, just as she's about to do it, a senseless accident robs her of everything.' She looked at him. 'And that could happen to any one of us *today*, Ben. That's how precarious life is. And short.'

Ben swallowed, his heart trying to sing. He said:

'So the moral of her story is: Go for it while you can.'

'Yes,' Helen sniffed.

Ben felt as if he were holding his breath. Helen looked at him tearfully. She said:

'Is it good, Ben?'

He wanted to both shout and sob.

'It is, Helen.' And, oh God, he meant it.

She whispered: 'Do you care about Jane?'

Oh, he wanted to shout it. 'Yes.' Jane broke his heart. Jane also filled his broken heart with joy. And *now* was the time to say it, now was the moment to use Jane. He said huskily:

'And I care about you, Helen.' He looked at her, and took a deep breath and said: 'I'm leaving today, too, Helen.'

Helen drew in her breath and stared at the dawn; then slowly she turned her head to him. She looked at Ben for a long, tearfilled moment. Ben knew what was coming and he could not bear to hear it.

'It's time, Helen! The *right* time. For me, and for you. It's been lovely. But it must end now, before it spoils. You don't need me any more. You've got rid of Jane.'

Helen started to speak, her heart crying out to say she knew not what, and Ben could not bear to argue, to explain the obvious – there was only one thing more to be said; what he had resolved yesterday, the most important of all, and the most heartbreaking, for he was almost sure what Helen would say, no matter what Jane had decided; but it simply just had to be said.

'I love you. Come with me, Helen...'

There was a silence.

Helen stared at him in the grey dawn, her face anguished, a sob welling up, and she began the tiniest shaking of her head, and Ben said urgently:

'*Come with me, Jane...*'

Her face began to dissolve, and she clenched her fists, and she swallowed and cried: 'Jane is dead. She doesn't exist anymore!'

Ben held her tearful eye and shook his head urgently.

'You can make her come alive again! You can save her from the grave! It is within your power to bring her back, Helen. Your *creative* power – and your *real* power. You can do *any*thing, Helen!' His eyes were burning, and he repeated, for the last time: 'I love you, Helen. Come with me.'

And Helen's tears flowed over, her face crumpled, and again she dropped her head into her hands. She sobbed and sobbed, her shoulders jerking; then she clapped her hands to her cheeks and squeezed them tight. Her breathing trembled, then she raised her tear-smeared face and straightened to give the moment the dignity it deserved. She looked at him with anguish, and whispered:

'Thank you. With all my heart. But, I cannot, dearest, darling Ben.'

No... He had known it. But he was glad with all his breaking heart that he had asked, because otherwise he would die one day not knowing for absolute sure. No way was he going to urge her further, and if the truth were known, deep down inside he was relieved that he would not have to fail her. Because although he could have given her the whole wonderful world, Ben Sunninghill, the physical man, would not have satisfied her for ever, and she would not have had the courage, the brutality, to leave him, and it would all have been spoilt. Ben did not want it to be spoilt. It was best left the way it was, almost perfect in the unknown, the unrealized. His eyes brimmed for what might have been; he stretched out his hand and squeezed her wrist, then stood up.

'I'll go and pack my toothbrush.' She started to protest, and he leant down and placed his finger on her upturned lips. 'No, dearest Helen. Not tomorrow. *Now* is the right time.'

He smiled down into her eyes, then turned and walked into the cottage. Inside, he held his face. He sobbed once, and his heart finally broke.

He emerged five minutes later. The rim of the sun was coming up, blazing the eastern sky in red and pink, casting long shadows through the damp, golden-grey trees. He was dressed entirely in black, as the day she had first seen him, black leather breeches and lumber-jacket, boots, big gauntlets in one hand, his black crash-helmet in the other. He was three inches taller in his boots. She looked up at him, tears flooding, and he smiled, stretched out his hand and took hers. She dropped her head and burst into racking sobs. She sobbed and sobbed, then she flung back her head, to master herself, and she climbed to her feet.

She was one step lower than him, and for the first time he seemed taller than her, and for a moment he glimpsed how good that felt, how different life could be. He said huskily: 'Goodbye, dearest Helen. And thank you.'

Her chin was trembling and her throat was tight. She began: 'Ben . . . ?'

Ben shook his head slowly, his eyes wet. 'Yes, dearest, Helen, I must.' She began to protest but he put his finger to her soft lips. 'Yes, dearest Helen . . .'

She looked at him, weeping, then she whispered:

'Will you write?'

He knew he would not write, could not bear to write, but he made it easier for her. 'Yes.'

She whispered: 'I wish I had the courage, Ben.'

He closed his eyes. Oh God, *God.* He shook his head and said: 'You have the courage not to.'

But that wasn't true either, and they both knew it. Her lips began to tremble, and he leant forward and kissed them lingeringly, tremblingly.

'Goodbye, Helen.'

He turned and descended the steps quickly, his steel-tipped boots loud on the wood. Helen watched him, as if she couldn't believe this. He put on his helmet and raised the visor, pulled on his gauntlets, gripped the handlebars and slung his leg over. He sat on the saddle and put his foot on the kick-starter. Then he hesitated, and turned to her.

'One last thing about Jane.' He paused, his throat thick. 'For your book, I mean. And it's this, Helen: it was a man who finally made her find the courage . . .' He looked at her and shook his head. 'She shouldn't have needed a man to do that.'

Helen wasn't sure what he meant, but before she could ask he raised himself and kicked down on the starter.

The motor cycle roared into life, and the noise seemed to fill the Outback. Ben raised a hand in a wave, and smiled, and for a moment the whole world seemed to stand still. Then he lowered the visor, gripped the handlebars, let out the clutch, and the cycle rumbled forward.

Helen stood on the verandah steps and watched him ride off into the sunrise, a small black figure on a big black machine. Her hands were clenched to her chin and her face was full of anguish, the tears running. He got smaller and smaller down the soggy tree-lined track, the sound of the motor cycle diminishing, diminishing.

Then he ground across the muddy gulley, and up the other side, and he was gone into the trees.

Helen felt the pain welling up her breast, bigger and bigger, and then out it burst in a gasping cry. She slumped down on the steps of his cottage, dropped her head into her hands, and she wept, and wept.

38

The sun was well up when Helen drove back to the main house. For two hours she had been unable to make herself leave the cottage, the last place she had seen him. Dundee emerged, wagging his tail amiably. She walked slowly into the dim kitchen. Her eyelids were swollen but she had wept herself out now and her streaked face was dry. She felt numb: she had been up all night and yet she felt wide awake. There, on the kitchen table, was her manuscript.

She turned away from it. She could not bear to think of Jane any more. Ben had said it was within her power to bring Jane back to life. It was true. She had the power of life and death. But Jane was dead. She wanted her dead. Over. Finished.

Helen stood in the middle of the kitchen, her arms limp. And now? What? What, and for how long? And she heard the deafening silence of the Outback.

She took a deep, anguished breath, then walked slowly down the passage to her bedroom. She went into the bathroom and opened the taps into the tub. The sound of the water seemed the loneliest, emptiest sound in the world. She undressed numbly and got into the bath. She stared up at the ceiling; and then she realized that the hot water she was lying in came from Ben Sunninghill's solar panel, and she put her hand to her eyes and began crying again.

The bath water was turning cold when she heard the sound of a vehicle. For a wild moment her heart leapt. *Ben . . . ?* Then she identified the noise as that of a motor car.

She got out of the bath, pulled on fresh underwear and her bath robe without drying herself, then walked to the front door. She opened it.

She saw Clyde's car disappearing around the side of the house towards the backyard.

Helen stood in the front doorway, staring along the verandah.

Clyde . . . ? What was he doing here? She was numbly surprised to find that she didn't want him here. Not today. Today she wanted to be alone with her sadness, today she wanted to be private, to grieve, to remember. And, oh God, she knew that was a terrible admission, a terrible way to feel when your husband's come home unexpectedly; it was . . . unwifely, unnatural – disloyal even, but that's the way she felt, she just wanted to be alone. But she had to make him feel welcome.

She turned and walked down the passage, trying to compose herself, to hide her feelings. She entered the kitchen at the same moment Clyde walked in the back door.

'Clyde! What a surprise!' She went to him and put her arms around his waist and kissed him.

Clyde said: 'What's so surprising? You must have known I'd be worried about the floods. Been trying for two weeks to get through to you on the radio, so finally I just came.'

Helen let go of him. 'Oh, yes, the atmospherics were terrible, I tried to call you but finally gave up—'

'And gave up listening, too? The atmospherics weren't that bad all the time, girl, you'd have heard me some time if you'd listened!'

Helen looked at him. Yes, maybe she had been remiss – maybe she had been less than thoughtful about Clyde during the floods.

'You're right,' she agreed, 'I should have listened in more, but I really was terribly busy, Clyde.'

'Doing what?'

'We had to rescue all the sheep from the south-western enclosure and cut all the lucern—'

'Why didn't you move the sheep earlier? You know the south-western's low-lying.'

Helen blinked, and felt anger rising. 'Because we didn't know it was going to storm so badly, Clyde.'

'You'd have known if you'd listened to the weather reports on the radio, girl!'

'But they were indecisive—'

'Not the ones I heard – and anyway you take precautions in case floods come, not wait and see *if* they come! I left you in charge of this station.'

'And we did a bloody good job!' Helen cried.

'We, huh?' Clyde said. 'And how many sheep did *we* lose?'

Helen said slowly: 'Fifty-odd. And yes, *we* did a good job. *And* we brought the lambs to the barn, and we cut the lucern in the pouring rain *and* stacked it everywhere we could—'

'You should have cut the alfalfa before the storms started, you know that, and you *would've* if you'd done your job and listened to the radio properly instead of . . .' He glared, then turned away in disgust.

'Instead of *what*, Clyde?'

He snorted, then muttered: 'Instead of writing your damn stupid book.' He turned back to her. 'How many days did it take to rescue the sheep and cut the lucern, girl? Three? Four? Five at the outside. And the rest of the time, what did you and Mr Wonderberg do, while the rain was pouring down?'

Helen looked at him, and suddenly she wasn't hurt and angry anymore, just sad.

'His name's Sunninghill, Clyde,' she said quietly. 'But for the rest of the time while the rain poured down he replaced the bathroom plumbing, and installed a solar panel, and fixed the wiring, and got that cool-room working at last. But me? Yes, I took the opportunity to write my book.'

Clyde snorted softly. He jerked his head at the manuscript on the table. 'And is that it?'

'Yes, darling, that's it. And you'll be pleased to hear it's finished at last. I finished it last night – or rather at five o'clock this morning.'

'About time,' Clyde said. 'And when's Mr Sunninghill leaving?'

She said quietly: 'He's already left, Clyde. He left three or four hours ago.'

'For good?' Clyde asked grimly.

'Yes, Clyde, for good.'

'Good.' Clyde said. Then added: 'Yeah, thought I passed him on the road, a little guy in all that black leather gear. Thought maybe he was just goin' to town to buy some more paper for your book. Or maybe ribbons for your hair.'

Helen blinked. Ribbons for her hair? She was about to rise to that when Clyde said: 'Is that why your eyes are red, girl? Because he's gone? You been crying?'

Helen looked at her husband, and she understood: and, yes, she did love him. And oh dear, yes, other things too.

'Are they red still? Yes, Clyde, I have been crying because he's gone.'

Clyde studied her. 'You fancy him?' he demanded.

Helen closed her eyes. 'No, Clyde, I didn't fancy him. I just loved having him here, and I'm very, very sad he's gone.'

Clyde stared at her, then he snorted and turned away. 'Well – a fine welcome-home this is!'

'I'm sorry, Clyde,' Helen said quietly. 'Can I get you a sandwich and a beer?'

'No – I'm not going to sit here with a wife crying over her ... *friend*! I'm going to check on some of those wonderful things he's done!' He turned and began to walk outside, then he stopped at the door and glared back at her. 'And I want a decent lunch ready when I come back, not a goddam sandwich – I want steak, eggs and chips.' He jabbed a finger at her. 'Not *rare* – just *usual*!'

He stalked off, out into the yard. He got into the Land Rover, slammed the door, started the engine and roared off.

Helen stood quite still, eyes closed, listening to the sound of the engine dying away. For a moment it could have been the sound of Ben driving away up there, to check on Green and ride the horse. 'Not rare, just usual.' Then the silence of the Outback returned, and with it reality, and Helen felt her heart would break.

She stood there enduring the sound of emptiness, trying to master it; then she turned and walked slowly down the passage, back to her bedroom, and into the bathroom again. She had not yet washed her hair: mechanically she undressed again, turned on the shower, and stepped under it. She let it soak her head, feeling Ben's hot water. Then she reached for the bottle of shampoo.

She was dressed again, drying her hair, when she heard the sound of another vehicle. At first she thought it was Clyde returning from the Abbo's hut. But Clyde could not be returning yet, surely. Then she identified the direction of the sound: it was coming from the gate. Still holding her towel, she walked up the passage to the front door.

She saw a Land Rover coming up the soggy track. She recognized it as a police vehicle.

It came grinding up the drive towards the verandah, and stopped. There was one man inside. It was Sergeant Vincent Keenan from the Burraville police station. Helen stood at the front door, in numb surprise. Vince climbed out, and took off his cap.

'Good morning, Helen.'

'Good morning, Vincent.'

Vince walked slowly to the verandah steps. He stopped at the bottom, and looked up at her apologetically. He said:

'I've got bad news, Helen. Your friend ...' He paused, then shook his head: 'I'm sorry, I can never remember his name. But your friend from New York – I'm afraid he's dead.'

Helen stared down at Vince Keenan, her face blank. She tried to smile, as if at some kind of bad joke, but her mouth refused. Of course Ben Sunninghill wasn't dead, Ben was alive and well, riding his Harley-Davidson into the big wide world. She opened her mouth, but no words came.

'He had an accident,' Vince said. 'About twenty miles outside Burra-ville. He got into a skid and hit an oncoming truck. He was thrown a hell of a long way. The doc hasn't seen him yet, but I reckon death must have been . . . instantaneous, Helen.'

Helen stared at him. None of this was true . . .

'I see,' she whispered.

She didn't. This was somebody else the policeman was talking about. Vince said uncomfortably:

'It was very unwise of him to ride on that road so soon after the floods – a car, okay, but a motorbike? Anyway, I thought I'd better let you know. You're the only person around these parts who . . . knew him.'

A distant ringing was coming into Helen's ears. But it didn't matter because it wasn't true. 'I see,' she whispered. 'Yes. Thank you . . .'

'And,' Vince said uncomfortably, 'maybe you know about his family, and so forth? We've got to notify them. I've searched through all his things and there's only his passport. Lots of notebooks but no address book, letters, nothing. There's a space in his passport for details of his next of kin, but he never filled it in. Do you know his address back home? Or where his parents are, for example?'

Helen wanted to smile at this silly question but couldn't. She shook her head. 'Just that he was a jeweller from New York.'

'Yes, well,' Vince said, 'we'll notify the New York police. And the American Embassy, of course.'

'Yes,' she said faintly. 'Of course . . .'

Vincent Keenan shifted uneasily. 'It seems from his saddle-bags that he was all packed up to go?'

It was a distant, academic question to Helen. The American Embassy would clear this up . . . 'That's true.'

'He didn't leave any forwarding address? For you to write to, perhaps?'

Helen shook her head. 'No. He didn't . . . But the Embassy will tell you.'

Vince glanced at her, ill-at-ease, but persevered. 'Do you know where he was heading?'

'Yes. To Africa.' That was proof he wasn't dead.

'I mean his next stop. Friends in Australia, for example?'

Helen shook her head. 'No. He had no friends in Australia. Except me.'

'And no address in Africa, friends he gave you the address of?'

Helen shook her head again. 'No . . . Just that he's going to be a foot-soldier.'

Vince frowned at her. Then decided to let that one go. 'Okay,' he said. 'One last thing, Helen. Sorry to ask you this, but would you please come into the station? Tomorrow. To formally identify him?' He added: 'For the post mortem, when the doc arrives from Charleville.'

Post mortem? But it didn't matter because it wasn't true. Ben Sunninghill was alive and well, as free as the air.

'Yes. Of course. Tomorrow.'

Vince Keenan looked at her uncertainly. 'Would you like to go inside, Helen? Get you a drink, or something?'

It was another academic question, not a real question.

'No, thanks, Vince. I'm fine.' She added: 'Clyde's here. He's up checking the cattle.'

'Oh, is he?' Vince looked relieved. 'Okay,' he said, 'okay, I'll leave now.' He added: 'I'm sorry, Helen.'

'Thank you, Vincent.'

Vincent wondered whether to mount the steps and shake her hand, and decided against it. It didn't seem appropriate, somehow. He put on his cap and gave a small salute.

'Well, thank you, Helen. G'bye.'

'G'bye, Vince.'

He turned, walked back to his Land Rover and climbed in.

Helen watched him. And then suddenly she had a question. It didn't seem important, in principle – but perhaps one should know these things.

'Vincent?'

'Yes, Helen?'

She said: 'Where is he? The Jew?' Why did she say that? She didn't think of him as a Jew or as anything else, just a person, alive and well and beautiful.

'In the clinic,' Vincent told her. 'Refrigerated,' he added.

'Oh. Of course.' Then she said: 'I didn't know we had a refrigerator big enough there.'

'Yes. Special mortuary job. But we only crank it up when we need it, of course.'

'Of course,' Helen said. And the cool-room Ben had tried so hard to build flitted across her mind. Ben was really pretty good at refrigeration.

'Well, g'day, Helen.'

'Goodbye, Vince.'

He twisted the ignition, and the engine rumbled. He gave half a salute again, then he let out the clutch and drove off down the track towards the distant road.

Helen numbly watched the police vehicle go. It was all unreal: the vehicle was unreal, Vince Keenan was unreal. None of what he had said was real, it had all happened to somebody else, not to Ben Sunninghill. She watched the Land Rover disappear with a numb detachment, then she turned and walked slowly back into the house, down the long passage to the kitchen.

There was her manuscript, sitting on the table. The manuscript was real, Jane was real. Any time now Ben Sunninghill was going to show up to ask if she had any jobs for him to do before he went up to check on Green and ride the horse. Then, of course, she realized that Ben would not show up, today or any more, because Ben had left . . . There was a terrible wrench in that, but even that was tolerable because Ben was somewhere way out there riding his motorbike, going on to live his wonderful life. Of course it wasn't true, what Vince Keenan had told her.

And then, suddenly, like a distant sound that slowly gets louder, and louder, and then mounts, and redoubles, until it becomes a scream, and then explodes – suddenly, it was all real and true, what Vince had said. All true, *true*, and Ben Sunninghill was not riding his motorbike way out there, he was lying in a mortuary refrigerator specially cranked up for him in Burraville, it was suddenly all true, *true, true and real, Ben lying there was real* . . . And oh God God God she just wanted to go and break into that clinic and rip open that refrigerator and grab Ben and shake him and hug him and hug him and shake him alive and tell him he couldn't do this to her, he wasn't dead so get up you stupid bastard, and she felt it all well up in her breast in a long slow agonizing cry. She stood, fists clenched, feeling it come, the terrible realization of Ben in that terrible refrigerator, dead, dead, smashed up and bloody. And she threw herself down at the table, and clutched her head fiercely. She banged it on the wood, and then out it came erupting from her heaving breast, her cry of grief, grief, grief.

Helen wept for a long time, uncontrollably. Finally, jerkily, she began to pull herself back together. She sat in silence, the tears streaking her suffused face, staring across the kitchen where it all began. And slowly, with a faltering but mounting certainty, she knew what she had to do.

She reached out for the manuscript. It was neatly stacked, but she pushed the pile so it collapsed across the table. She pulled out the last page. She reached for her chewed pen.

She looked at the second-last paragraph. Where Jane bursts out on to the road and joyously sees Trevor's car coming towards her. Then, in the last paragraph, the deafening hiss of brakes and the blast of the horn . . .

Helen took her pen and ran it across the last paragraph. Expunging it, eradicating it. So that it had never happened . . .

And there was Jane, her hair awry, her bosom heaving and her heart soaring, full of joy as Trevor's car slowed, coming towards her to pick her up, about to go off and live her wonderful life.

There . . . Helen McKenzie had the power of life and death . . .

Then she slowly reached for a fresh sheet of paper. She did not have to think what to write. She began:

'My darling husband and children, Mum and Dad . . .'

It took only ten minutes to write the letter; it was simple, straightforward. One day she would write them a better one.

Helen McKenzie got up and walked down the passage to her bedroom. Dundee followed her. She went to the wardrobe, stretched up, pulled one suitcase down off the top and placed it on the bed.

Dundee watched her. She packed only essentials. She found her post office savings book. Then she went back to the kitchen and stacked up her manuscript neatly again. She carried it back to the bedroom and placed it in the suitcase. It took up the remainder of the space.

She closed the lid, slid the case off the bed and picked it up, testing it for weight. It was heavy, because of the manuscript. She considered for half a minute, then she swung the suitcase back on to the bed, and re-opened it. She took out the manuscript. She turned and slowly carried it back to the kitchen.

She went to the wood-burning stove. She opened it. She stuffed the pages inside. She stood back. She watched as they began to burn.

There ... She had finally got rid of Jane. Jane was no more a separate person, to be envied for her courage.

She turned and went back to the bedroom. She stripped one blanket off the bed, bundled it under her arm and picked up the suitcase. She carried them through to the kitchen. For a moment she stopped and looked at the letter on the table, considering. Should she not wait for Clyde to come back, to explain it to him personally? Didn't she owe him that?

Yes, she did ... But, no, she would not wait. She *could* not wait, could not bear it. Nor could she bear to explain herself, it was all too complicated and private, and Clyde would not understand, and she did not want to have to listen to what he would say. No, it was better this way. Cleaner. Simpler. She did not want to hurt him more than she had to. One day, perhaps, she would have the chance to explain.

She turned out the back door. Dundee followed her. She walked across the muddy yard, up to the barn. She went to her old van, opened the back door and put the suitcase and blanket inside. She closed the door, then turned to Dundee.

'Goodbye, Dundee. Be a good boy with Clyde ...'

She wanted to fondle him in farewell, but she could not. She turned and got into the driver's seat, and started the van. She drove out of the barn, and turned down towards the house. She could not bear to look back at Dundee in the mirror. The tears were running silently down her face.

Nor could she look at the nice old house. She drove around the back of it, and on down the wet drive, heading for the gate and the big, wide world beyond.